Year of the Demon

UNHALLOWED
LOVE SERIES
BOOK 2

TARA FOX HALL

PROLOGUE

"I'm sure we have an Incubus down here."

Debbie followed the demon Rack down the wooden stairs into the heavy gloom, feeling with her feet for the stairs and hanging onto the curved rail. "You may be able to see in the dark, but you're going to have to flip the light switch for me."

She heard the smile in his reply. "You've got some dark sight from Shaker, Debbie. You should use it, since you're paying for it."

"Don't be so dour, Rack dear," Mrs. Triss called down the stairs after them. "You can't live in the 1800s." Light abruptly flooded the basement, making Debbie stop mid-stair and blink.

The wine cellar held very modern wooden stands of bottled wine, and also large unusually shaped old bottles, earthen jugs of various colors, and monstrous wooden casks in large sturdy supports. "You must entertain a fair amount, Mrs. Triss," Debbie quipped, as she walked down the stairs to join Rack.

"Just Triss, dear," the young woman said as she came down the stairs, her expression that of a much older woman. She smiled. "We provide the vintages for the various demon gatherings throughout the year. These are safer here under our close supervision."

Safer from whom? "Thank you again for agreeing to provide the alcoholic refreshments for our office party last night," Debbie replied. "The New Year celebration was a great success."

"Yes, it was," Rack said, turning to Debbie with a dusty bottle. "Demonkind thanks you, Debbie Deal. Here you go, one bottle of Incubus. Congratulations."

The lights abruptly went out, making Debbie take a quick breath. Various candelabras around the basement sputtered into life, the warm glow transforming the room into something out of a gothic romance story.

"I prefer candlelight," Shaker intoned, appearing behind Debbie. He kissed her hand, his vivid blue eyes flashing his true red briefly.

You look good, Debbie thought to him, her eyes lingering on his chiseled features and wide muscular chest. "How was Jett's interview?"

"My interview was very good PR," Shaker corrected gently, flipping his black hair out of his eyes. "I'm not sure if I'll make the cover, but they did take a few pictures of me in my costume for *Smoke and Ashes II.*"

"That's fabulous!" Debbie said excitedly, giving him a hug. "This will be great press for Pandora Productions. Were you able to talk much about the sequel?"

"Yes. Plus I mentioned I got engaged last night," Shaker said with a shark's smile, displaying several rows of serrated teeth. "But I waited until the end as you coached, so they weren't able to make the entire interview about that. But they had a lot of questions."

"We have a lot of questions," Triss broke in, her smile no longer so wide. "So will the others."

She means demonkind, in reference to me and what's next for Pandora Productions, Shaker said in Debbie's mind. *Let me answer this and go along with what I say.*

"I'm not sure why," Shaker drawled in response, his expression

2

deliberately casual. "You can see I'm Jett now. Debbie's shooting star actor was falling fast from drugs and disease. He'd likely have died of an overdose or heart attack if I hadn't stepped in, so to speak. Possessing him was the only way, especially after he betrayed Pandora and sold us out to our competitor, Titan Pictures. Now that Jett's clean—and he's got a brain to direct his brawn—we won't have any more problems with him."

"You know we mean about you two getting engaged, Shaker," Rack said pointedly. "You getting attention as Jett for the company's good is one thing. You marrying your boss is another."

"Shaker's my lover and my demon, like Rack is yours, Triss," Debbie said evenly. "He can't put on Jett like a suit of clothes every other week. So Jett's become my lover. But I'm not a fan of scandal, and you're right, the CEO dating their lead rates headlines. That's why the engagement. We're getting married for the same reason you two did. It solves several problems while displacing interest."

"Told you," Rack said triumphantly to Triss.

"You have our support," Triss said, ignoring him. She laid her hand on Debbie's arm. "That is unchanged. We just want to make sure what we're building isn't going to collapse."

"How can you say that?" Debbie's throat was suddenly so dry all she could manage was an offended whisper. "You know what I went through last year to save Pandora from being taken over by Titan Pictures? My best friend Sheila nearly died from that Hellfire meant for me. That renegade priest nearly killed me. Shaker was badly wounded multiple times." Her tone could have etched steel. "I have killed for Pandora."

"All of us here have," Shaker rumbled, glaring at Triss. "Except you."

"Because call it what you will, catastrophe often follows demonworkings," Triss went on, ignoring Debbie and Shaker. "Karma, fate, divine intervention…they mean the same thing for us: failure and a lot of wasted time. Rack and I have worked hard at making Triss Vineyards into a global name. We've had more than our share of hardships." She paused. "You know what I'm saying, Debbie. You remember last year. It was a good year, yes, but you had major struggles every single month. You're a smart woman. Don't take risks this year like you did then. None of us can afford it. There's been enough death linked to Pandora…and you."

"I am a smart woman," Debbie said slowly. "And you're right that there's been enough death. Which is why I'll ask you right here and now: are you the same Mrs. Triss that I had lunch with the day you told me about demons and what they were capable of with their mortal cohorts? And later, the true story of how you met Rack? You are, aren't you? You pretended to be that woman's daughter yesterday at the New Year's party when you appeared, suddenly fifty years younger, telling me that your mother died. But when you said you were going to marry Rack in the same conversation, there was no grief, just eagerness."

Triss smiled.

"When I met you, you were old, close to death," Debbie challenged. "Now you are young enough to be my own daughter, Triss. Don't talk to me about risks while you're trying to pass off a lie as big as that one, especially to me."

"If you're saying I told you something, I would guess I was there and that same person," Triss said with a cold smile.

"Enough," Rack said quietly, his expression somber. "Triss and I did what we had to in order to be together, now and always. No one was hurt to make that happen, though you likely suspect otherwise to say what you just did."

"I'm not judging you," Debbie said bluntly. "I'm telling you that if you want to be in the inner circle with us, then stop playing games. I have no intention of Pandora going down in flames. Or this year being anything but better than the last year. I'm not going to take risks. Shaker's been around for a thousand years and he and I have made a good team."

"Yes, you do," Triss said approvingly, her smile for the first time genuine. "I agree, no more secrets from now on." She took the Incubus from Shaker. "Now that we have that out of the way, let's get back to celebrating. I'll be upstairs." She turned and left.

What a bizarre woman, Debbie thought.

Not one to tangle with, Shaker replied in her mind.

"Come and let me show you my wine cave," Rack said proudly, gesturing to the stacks of bottles. "Most wine anymore comes in bottles, but there are larger sizes. A methuselah is a container equivalent to eight regular bottles. A balthazar is twelve liters or about sixteen bottles. A nebuchanezzer is about twenty. A cask is equivalent to a barrel and is about two-hundred and twenty-five liters or twenty-four cases of twelve bottles each."

"Rack is a Master of Wine, also known as a sommelier," Shaker said.

"Triss Vineyards will provide you a cask of the Incubus for all your upcoming parties at Pandora this year, provided you like what you taste," Rack went on. "It's hedonistic, decadent and velvety, with a long finish or aftertaste. Alternately, we could provide you with Incubus for some months, and alternate with some others of our cult wines."

"Cult wines?" Debbie echoed.

"Wines that demand a high price because of rarity or desirability," Shaker said. "I would rather the latter, Rack. I like the Incubus myself, but let's alternate full with light bodied, and vary ages. But shades of red only."

"That sounds good to me," Debbie agreed. "As of right now, I know we have planned several launch parties after first screenings of the newer bigger movies, like *Smoke and Ashes II*. Also a spring picnic, a Halloween party, a Christmas party, and a New Year's Eve Party. If possible, make the bottles look as different as you can, to showcase your versatility. Even differentiate the openings, like screw tops and corks."

"We should nix the planned Christmas party," Shaker said. "Someone is sure to bring some kind of religion into it. You know that it doesn't matter what faith believers are: what matters is their belief."

"All right," Debbie said with a shrug. "I'm not sure anyone will care, with the New Year's Eve party the week after."

"Not as long as they get their Christmas bonuses," Shaker laughed.

"We do have a lot of different newer wines," Rack interrupted, beckoning them to the more modern section of the cellar. "These are blendings, where we take a mix of two or more wines to make a consistent singular wine. The AOC—or DOC if we were in Italy—states the origin of the grapes, where they are from. If the grapes are young, they have an aroma. If they are old, it's referred to as a bouquet. How long the wine is in the cask determines the body, if it's light or full. A charcoal burned into the inside of the wine barrel gives wine what is referred to a its "toast." Above all, though, wine should have balance. Acid should be checked by sweetness, fruit flavors should be checked by tannins, and alcohol should be checked by acidity or flavor." He nodded. "If you will provide me with some keywords for different months, I'll make sure we have the perfect wine to represent Pandora."

He clearly is a master of wine. We should definitely use that expertise. "Wonderful, Rack," Debbie complimented. "But you really don't need me to provide you with keywords, when you're involved enough with Pandora's upcoming movies to know what the focus of each is. You have approval to make choices in wines and bring them to me right before the scheduled celebrations, just so I have advance notice of what they look like."

"Then I thank you for your confidence," Rack said, giving her a small bow. "Let us go upstairs. Triss is asking me what's taking so long."

The three walked back upstairs, where Triss was waiting with the Incubus wine. She handed glasses to Shaker and Debbie. "To our partnership, and a fabulous year!"

"To the year of the demon," Shaker said, grinning and raising his glass.

The others raised their glasses, clinking them together. "To the year of the demon!"

CHAPTER ONE

"No calls this morning, Kaitlyn. Thank you."

"No problem, Ms. Deal." Her secretary laughed. "And let me offer congratulations on your engagement."

"Thank you." Debbie breathed deeply, the soothing aroma of fresh coffee at odds with her churning thoughts. She shut the door of her office, strode over and plunked down her Starbucks cup on her messy desk, then sat in her chair and began making a list of the week's priorities.

Remember the gun, Mistress, Shaker said in her mind. *Secure it in your drawer, before you forget.*

Yes. Debbie reached into her handbag and drew out the handgun, slipping it into the drawer. *The one that killed Cahill.*

Technically no. This is new, with no police history. It's better to have a clean gun, Mistress. I have contacts that can supply more as needed.

Let's hope they aren't needed. I've got to go. I'll talk to you later.

Shaker severed the mental link with a kiss. *There's a magical ward on your office now. Nothing will be breaking it, Titus made it himself, at my request.*

Debbie thanked him, but his mind was silent. Turning her

attention back to her list, she looked over the meetings already on her schedule, then focused on the first one of the morning.

The first week of a new year is always exciting, but daunting, too. She sighed aloud, then began jotting down notes as fast as she could. Her first meeting of the year with Sheila was in an hour, and there was no time to waste. Pandora's upward momentum couldn't lapse, not even for a second.

~

"I hope you had a great holiday," Debbie said earnestly to her assembled team. "I won't give a speech this morning, other than to thank you all once more for all of your hard work to make Pandora the leader in independent films last year. As you heard Sheila say at the New Year's party last Friday, we had a record year of profits. This morning, I want to go over both your current project plans for your individual departments, and what you hope to achieve this month, after we introduce the newest members of our team and my VP and I do a little recap." She turned to Sheila, who was bringing up a presentation on the large wall monitor screen. "The floor is yours, Sheila."

As Debbie sat down, Sheila began speaking. "As you all know, *Smoke and Ashes* was our big hit of the past year. The story of a murdered man partnering with a demon to get revenge on those that killed him, and his family released close to Christmas, and pulled in four million gross for that weekend. Early speculation estimates that gross take for the following weekend will be at least two million. We have some hope that the movie may be considered for an Oscar for best supporting actor, but it's too soon to be sure. Yes?"

"Likely, Cahill, the actor who played the hero priest character who dies onscreen at the end of the movie, will be considered for the award," Giorgio, head of Pandora's legal department said. "As you new people may or may not know, he died from a freak accident during filming caused by malfunctioning blanks."

He died because I shot him in self-defense in my office, Debbie thought. *He was a real priest turned demon hunter who came to kill me and was going to kill Shaker.* Harp, Sheila's demon, had possessed Cahill's body afterward, and covered up the murder by staging the actor's death on film.

I should have been considered for best actor, Shaker chuckled in Debbie's mind. *But then I only got possession of Jett's body after he'd finished filming.*

Didn't I tell you to stop referring to Jett as another person? Debbie thought back to him, irritated. *It makes me feel like I'm living with a zombie.*

You do it all the time, Shaker grumbled back. *Fair's fair.*

"I'm mentioning the accidental death as I think we need to improve our safety precautions," Giorgio continued. "We don't want people regularly dying onset."

"Very true," Sheila replied a little too brightly. "Which is why we have retained a safety consultant, Mr. Minor. All guns and other weapons will now be doubled checked for possible malfunction."

Mr. Catarella has also been retained as permanent legal counsel for you and me, Shaker added mentally to Debbie. *Just in case.*

"Jeremy and his team will be handling distribution and marketing, and Carolina and her Art Department will continue to dazzle us with scenery and costuming."

"I'll be adding in an assistant for help with costuming, specifically for this new historical film *Immortal Confessions,*" Carolina added demurely. "All the films we have done until now were contemporary, and didn't require much research or anything elaborate, but this year that will change."

Debbie jotted down *talk to Sheila to make sure Devlin's added that to his investor offering.*

"I'm Mark, and I handle the bones of the shoot, like lighting, grips, and camera work," a man in jeans and a flannel shirt said.

"I'm off to reshoot a couple scenes this morning, which is why I'm dressed down."

"You always dress that way," the man next to him said dourly, then chuckled. "I'm Nelson, Post Production et al. You likely won't see much of us the rest of the year unless you see us on set. Sheila just asked us here for this meeting, so we could meet everyone."

"We do have an intern, Joshua," Mark added. "He's not here but will be meeting with Sheila and I later on. He's going to take over Location."

Joshua's a vampire, on loan from Devlin to help find locales for his movie, Shaker said mentally to Debbie. *If we like him, we can offer him a position. Devlin says he has experience in film.*

"We have a few new directions we are going in this year, which require more personnel," Sheila added. "I will also continue with Acquisitions, and I'm very pleased to tell you we have some great new projects lined up. I'll be going over them next, after introductions are made for our new hires and Debbie goes over a few things."

Sheila's whole-hearted enthusiasm rang though every word, yet Debbie's stomach twisted nervously as she stood. "Thanks, Sheila."

"The stock sale went through in early winter," Debbie continued. "As you know, Pandora Productions is now a public company. We have high growth prospects for the coming five years, but in order to remain competitive in our industry and also retain our innovation, not to mention turn a good profit, we have added more than a few new faces." She smiled. "Please tell a little about yourselves as I introduce you. You go first, Mr. Triss."

The demon Rack Triss smiled, his usual row of shark's teeth hidden behind closed lips. "Hello, I'm Mr. Triss, but you can call me Richard. I'm going to be helping Sheila with Acquisitions, and also looking for additional investors, so we can continue to increase the number of movies Pandora produces and releases per year."

Hopefully not all demon-related ones, Debbie mused.

Now don't be prejudiced, Shaker said with a mental chuckle.

"I'll also be coordinating Pandora's celebrations this year, to encourage team building now that we're growing," Rack continued. "A spring festival, a Halloween party, and a New Year's Eve party are planned, as well as release parties for *Smoke and Ashes II*, and *Immortal Confessions*. Others may be added, if management decrees. Thank you."

"Hi, I'm Adeline Lake," a thin tall brunette said coolly. "Interactive Media Department, and new director of Pandora Promotions. I'll be focusing on Pandora's website, to start. Pandora had a simple portal to accept applications/inquiries, and a page telling a little about the company's origin above a backlist of movies already released. That is being redone to include buy and stream links to all those movies on popular sites like Amazon, trailers, ratings, plus graphics of the promotional materials originally used in the film's release. There will be a page for news, where we can post any mentions of our movies in press and TV, or any other big news we have to announce."

"That revamped online presence will help tie us into the streaming market, which is where a lot of the money is to be made," added Debbie, turning to the next person, a woman in very short blond hair and overly loose clothes.

"Hello, my name is Stacy and I'm going to be working on managing and coordinating production of the films this year," she squeaked out. "I'm very excited to get started on *Absolution*, which will finish shooting this spring."

She sounds like a mouse. I hope she's got the soul of a tiger. Debbie nodded. "Good to meet you."

"I'm Nicole, otherwise known as Continuity," the next woman said cheerfully. "I will be checking over scripts and assisting directors on set."

"Director," the man next to her corrected. "Single, not plural. We only shoot one movie at a time. For you new people, my name is Bart Farrow, but you can call me Master Chief."

No one thinks you're funny except you, Bart. "Thanks, Bart,"

Debbie said quickly. "That is everyone here, except our new intern Joshua. But there will be one person more coming, we just haven't filled the position of Compliance."

I can help fill your position, Shaker leered mentally. *I'm always compliant...*

"Compliance is directly related to our stock going public," Debbie said, ignoring him. *And will hopefully be short term, only.* "Which is slated to happen in another week. Does anyone have any questions?"

There were several smiles, Mark whispering something to Nelson, and the both of them smiled wider. But no one spoke.

They're talking about my engagement to Jett. "Go ahead, Sheila," Debbie said, taking her seat.

Sheila brought up a movie poster on the screen of a leering demon behind an angry man, with the silhouette of a couple in the foreground embracing. "As we mentioned before, *Absolution* is finishing shooting this spring and should be released this fall. A man's journey to forgiveness for his wife for having an affair with his brother, with a demon who appears now and again to try to push him to murdering her instead."

"It's a version of Othello, with a happy ending," Bart commented. "Almost a romance. The brother is more evil than the demon, really."

Man after my own heart, Shaker laughed.

Sheila brought up another poster, this one of Jett Black and his sixguns standing in fire and wreathed in smoke, a transparent priest at his shoulder. A little girl of about five years stood resolute beside him, a bloody stake in her hand. "This is the promo poster for *Smoke and Ashes II: Out of the Ashes.* Shooting is almost complete, and this is in post-production now, and Jeremy's working out distribution and coordinating with Adeline on marketing. We hope to release right before Christmas."

"We want twice as many theaters opening day," Jeremy chimed in. "This is a franchise in the making. This is a good year for it, with no action-hero movies due for release in late December."

Sheila brought up one more poster, that of a man's face, his golden eyes resolute and fearless, a faint arrogant smile on his lips. "This is *Immortal Confessions*, our first picture done with investor funds. We have a larger budget for this film, but the investor is controlling a lot of the details, so this picture may not release this year. We will be handling the distribution and marketing for this one, also. We are aiming for a fall release, though."

"Is this another demon horror picture?" Nelson asked. "This is the first I'm hearing of this."

"You haven't seen anything come through to you because the score is still being written, and although we have the actors lined up, we haven't begun filming," Sheila explained. "As Carolina said, she's still working on costumes. But this romantic thriller should begin filming in February, and we hope to wrap up all cold weather scenes by spring. Then *Absolution* will be shot, then we will go back to *Immortal Confessions* to finish out the hot weather scenes. If all goes well, this will be finished by end of August."

"But is it horror romance?" Nelson pressed. "Immortal means another demon, right?"

"No," Sheila said reluctantly. "It means vampire."

"You've got to be kidding me!" Nelson said in disbelief. "No one's making vampire films now unless they're horror or really weird. The *Twilight* years are over."

"Our investor wants this movie, and it's going to be our first really big budget movie, an epic, if you will," Sheila said defensively. "Pandora has made more than a few movies over the years than transcend genre, and we want to do that with *Immortal Confessions*. It's a historical romantic saga that just happens to have a cast of paranormals, including demons."

Nelson looked about to reply with another snarky remark, so Debbie cut in. "That is all for today, thanks everyone. We will have a meeting the first day of every month now to make sure we are on schedule and under budget, as well to introduce new projects as they are acquired. If you can't make it, send your report to me directly in advance, either in person or via email, the latter only if you have no issues to report."

The team got up, some of them talking to one another. Everyone left but Rack, who shut the conference room door, and then turned to them. "We should meet now for a few moments, ladies."

I hope he's not going to be this bossy all the time. Debbie sat down reluctantly with Sheila. "What's on your mind, Rack?"

"I don't have any parameters for what you are looking for in terms of future acquisitions, other than of course demon-related scripts," he replied. "But after hearing your schedule, I wanted to caution you about working with Devlin. I know he's musically inclined, and I'll guess he's the one writing the score?"

Sheila nodded. "It was one of his investment conditions."

"I'd push for *Absolution* to be finished before starting *Immortal Confessions.* Devlin is a perfectionist, especially telling some of his own history, which I'm guessing this is. He will want each detail to be perfect…and expect that since he's paying for the movie, that you'll comply with his wishes."

Sheila and Debbie looked at one another. "We are planning to do that secretly," Debbie admitted. "But not because of time constraints solely, though that is a factor. The main reason is because of the stock going public. We're—"

"And that is the other concern of mine," Rack said darkly. "That you shouldn't go forward with the stock deal."

Debbie blinked. "Why?" Sheila asked, eyes narrowing. "We screwed around with that fucking deal all last year. Everything went wrong with Dante and Titan Pictures trying to take control of Pandora away from us, not to mention that asshole Titan Pictures lawyer Henry making moves on Debbie. Debbie finally has the majority of shares though, and we're ready at last to—"

"The real advantages of going public are to strengthen your base capital, thereby making future acquisitions easier. Yes, the prestige of being publicly traded helps a great deal with this. But there are a lot of disadvantages, like increased pressure on Pandora to steadily produce coupled with rising costs. You'd be forced to disclose Triss Vinyards and Devlin as investors publicly. But the main issue is that you're going to lose control of the major decisions made about the studio. Triss and I stated that you shouldn't take risks. This is a risk that can be avoided, now that Dante is out of the picture and you retain the majority of shares."

He's a demon of many talents. I should have hired him sooner. "You make good points, Rack, but I'm not sure that we can back out of the stock deal now."

"You might not be able to. What I suggest is a take-private transaction immediately after the stock deal. Right now, your debt load is minimal, and you've got fair cash flow. Doing this will free you up from having to do compliance, and a need to micromanage profits so you show steady growth all quarters. You'll retain control. When good projects appear, Sheila and I can snap them up, instead of waiting to get approval from a board."

"That sounds great," Debbie said. "Sheila?" *Shaker?*

"I agree, as do Harp and Song."

Rack knows his stuff, Shaker said in Debbie's mind. *Have him type up his proposal and send it to you, then send it to Catarella to look over. But I believe it's the best way forward.*

"Type me up a proposal for this, then send it to Catarella and copy me," Debbie said. "If it's legal, let's do it." She moved to stand.

"One last thing," Rack said quickly, as Debbie put her hand on the door. "I wouldn't depend on your sequel to win at the Oscars, even if Cahill does win posthumously for his performance in the original."

"Why is that?" Sheila asked, affronted.

"The release date of a film closely aligns with a film's chances of winning the Oscar for Best Picture. The later in the year a film is released—the closer the film's release corresponds to the start of

Oscar voting—the better the film's chances of winning the Oscar. *Smoke and Ashes II* is set to come out in late spring or early summer."

"Historically, movies with multi-genres, like a historical romance that also doubles as an action adventure movie, do okay at the Oscars," Sheila said.

"But only if the there is a heaviness to the movie, like a death of meaning, or it's a period piece with a lot of historical backstory around a famous event," Rack replied. "Straight action adventure doesn't even have its own category at the Oscars. We can hope *Smoke and Ashes II* will be a contender in the Critic's Choice Awards. I think it has a good shot."

"A death of meaning?" Sheila said skeptically.

"In the struggle or conflict, someone dies either close to the end, or near the end that the audience mourns or keenly feels, even if the character wasn't exactly good," Rack replied. "Ned Stark's was a death of meaning in *Game of Thrones*. So was Claudia's in *Interview with the Vampire*, and Melanie Wilkes in *Gone with the Wind*. Their loss adds a seriousness to the film that elevates it from its genre."

"Rack, do you think any other of the films slated for release this year have a chance for critical acclaim, outside of independent film awards?" Debbie asked.

Rack shook his head. "Most of what we have slated for release so far are horror films or thrillers, aside from Devlin's vampire romance film, *Immortal Confessions*. That should actually do well with its heady mix of history, action, and romance, if critics look beyond the vampire label."

"Which they likely will not," Sheila said grumpily. "Not when they have Titan Picture's glossy war-romance *Escalation* coming out this fall."

"Remember, we are new to even having more than two pictures released a year," Debbie reminded her. "Pandora was never into making either pure cash movies or heavy epics weighted specifically to garner awards. We want to make quality movies that are original and tell stories no one else dares to tell. We can just afford to make maybe one other movie this year, other than the three Sheila introduced at the meeting. That's only because *Smoke and Ashes II* is almost complete, and *Absolution* is not only very low on actors, but also half shot."

"Hmm, a good title," Sheila said thoughtfully. "Rack, make it one of your priorities this year to find us a good movie with a story people will want to rally behind. We'll call it *Dare to Tell*. If you can get script approval from Nicole by the end of summer, we can start shooting that as soon as we wrap *Immortal Confessions*."

"There's also Lash's story," Debbie reminded her. "While the title *Dare to Tell* is not going to fit his movie, his proposed weresnake movie does have to go onto the list of upcoming films. Did you have a chance to look at the pages I left for you?"

"Yes, and honestly, it's not a bad beginning," Sheila said grudgingly. "If even half of it's true, Lash had a horrific childhood, and his teens weren't much better. Yes, he needs a lot of work elaborating on scenes and dialogue, but the sheer brutality of what he endured is riveting, especially in regards to his family. You may have a good epic there, too. But it's going to need a ghostwriter to help him finish the story."

"See that vampire Josh, the intern that Devlin sent. Have him work with Lash to get some kind of workable script…and to keep the budget inside the low hundred thousands."

"There is an additional investor that I have to offer," Rack inserted. "John and Madeline Centaurian."

The way he said it told Debbie all she needed to know. *Demon and human couple?* "They're like us, aren't they?"

"Very similar," Rack said with a nod. "They are also looking to invest, but only John will meet with us. Madeline never leaves her home."

"Why not?" Sheila asked.

"The Chalet is a great old mansion deep in a forest, and she prefers to stay there an make a home for John, much as her great grandmother Victoria made a home for her husband Donald close to a century before," Rack mentioned. "They are from old money, but John wants to diversify his investments. He will not be asking to make a screenplay of his life story. He may choose to invest without any face-to-face time."

Pandora has gotten attention for its willingness to feature demons, Shaker said in Debbie's mind. *There weren't many demons on hand at the New Year's Party, because I wanted that night to be ours. But several have contacted me and Rack, after hearing we were part of Pandora, including John. He's a loyal and ancient being and will be an asset.*

"Good," Debbie said, nodding. "Please arrange a meeting with him, if he wants one."

Additionally, I have two brothers: Titus, whom you met, and Rip, who's in trouble constantly but good muscle. Both have offered to help out as needed. Titus of course will be the better help, if we need a spell I can't provide. He has a much more extensive magic skill set than I do.

Good, Debbie thought back. *We can use all the help we can get.*

~

"Hey, you're watching Pandora's Box: Unleashing Evil," Shaker said with glee, as he came into their bedroom later that night. "Who's the subject? I always like to guess whose handiwork it is by the nature of the crimes."

"Please, Shaker, it's been a long day," Debbie said with a groan. "No more evil jokes today."

"There's always room for a little evil." Shaker laughed. "Why do you think that they have channels devoted to this type of true crime? Because evil fascinates humans as much as it always has."

"But these are real people suffering," Debbie protested, her tone hardening to steel. "Women raped and killed for kicks, or money, or just because they wanted to get away from someone who was hurting them."

"Are you saying this for a reason?" Shaker said, suddenly attentive.

"I've thought about what Triss said, about how we need to be ready for more than our fair share of struggles," Debbie said carefully. "I know what you are, Shaker, and most of the time, I accept that. I really enjoy our time together, but—"

"But you're having second thoughts?" Shaker said, stripping his shirt off. He stalked toward her in only his jeans, his muscles moving like a great cat.

Trying to distract me with your killer abs won't work. "Stop," Debbie said softly, putting her hands out before he could touch her. "I'm being serious."

"I see that," Shaker said, disgruntled. He sat on the bed, keeping his distance. *What is it? Speak to me mentally, so we can't be overheard.*

Debbie shivered, knowing that the reason he was asking was because he worried his hellish master might be listening. *Is there anything we can do, so we don't have to struggle as hard as last year?*

"We've got a good team, and we're doing everything we can to forge a path of least resistance," Shaker soothed, sliding closer. He put his arms around her shoulders loosely. *No. You can't buy off the Heavenly Host. Even if Pandora donated ten percent of its earnings to churches, it would buy us no favors. We can't stop whatever's going to come, for good or evil.*

"Thank you for what you've done. Rack is a great asset." *Can you look ahead then, see what's coming? The future's not set, right?*

"I'm a greater asset," Shaker teased, but his eyes were serious. *Yes, but sometimes that's a can of worms, getting glimpses of the future. I may see just enough to decide to change plans only to give us a worse result than if we stayed with the original plans.*

"You're a greater ass, anyway." *Please do it. What we don't know might hurt us.*

"You come over here!" Shaker growled, reaching for her. Debbie shrieked and tried to get out of bed, but he grabbed her to him, molding his body to hers. She felt the press of his erection as his lips sought hers, his soft mental *I'll do it* almost lost in the sensations.

Debbie's hands clawed at his jeans, then pulled his erection free, the organ throbbing in her hands as Shaker went rigid with a groan. She straddled him, then began to ease down.

CHAPTER TWO

"WAIT," SHAKER RUMBLED. "DON'T YOU WISH PROTECTION, Mistress?"

Debbie stopped, then gave a loud annoyed sigh. "Why do you always have to say "mistress" in the crucial moment?"

"The crucial moment is the climax, not the foreplay," Shaker corrected teasingly. "I'm just being proper. We've never before had sex with no protection."

"Yes, we have," Debbie snapped. "Many times before."

"Not with me looking like this," Shaker reminded, pushing long black curls out of his suddenly vivid blue eyes. Then those eyes reddened again, as his full lips curved into a sexy grin. "You're asking me to expend a lot of energy as Jett, plus do a great deal of magic. I'll need you to make a choice soon for January."

He means choose a victim for him, our now monthly ritual. "Teleporting me to work isn't 'a great deal of magic'."

"You're asking me to teleport you now most places you go, scry the future for possible problems, plus possess someone twenty-four-seven who's a celebrity, which equals always being noticed and being filmed daily by strangers who would gladly sell any odd footage like dagger teeth or a flash of red eyes to the press. On top of already handling our daily crises and defending you."

"What daily crises? And no one's attacked us."

"There'll be another priest coming to avenge the one we killed," Shaker said with a grim smile. "But they won't try the obvious, to send in another as an undercover actor. I've been on watch for that, as have the other demons at Pandora."

Debbie repressed a shudder.

"Daily crises like how it feels to bang the CEO," Shaker went on, his narrowed eyes not in sync with his crude speech. "I got asked that by one of the gaffers today. I refrained from hitting him but threatened to. He immediately went sniveling to HR, and you're likely going to hear some crap tomorrow about my official write up."

"HR wrote you up?"

Shaker nodded. "Hostile work environment, worker harassment, and workplace violence, blah blah blah. But they wrote him up as well when I explained my provocation." He grimaced. "It's amazing what this world is coming to. Men can't even fight anymore with words, much less their fists."

"That's why people like movies like *Smoke and Ashes*," Debbie quipped, running her hands over Shaker's bulging chest muscles. "Watching you kick ass onscreen is gratifying because we aren't allowed to even give voice to our anger."

"I know you're a woman in a position of power, and that some men as a rule are chauvinists. I'm just not used to feeling like a boy toy, I guess."

"You're not a boy toy," Debbie said, stroking the six-pack of his abs, the warm thick ridges of muscle firm under her hands. "But you are mine." Her hands slid lower, gripping his semi-hard penis, running across his length. "Now give me what I want."

Shaker grunted, then pushed up with his hips beneath Debbie, as she sank down on his length. Gripping her hips, he began to move her on him, pushing her down to receive him every time he thrust home.

Debbie rubbed her breasts on Shaker's chest, then ground against him, her eyes closing as she focused solely on the sensations running through her nerve endings: the tug of his hands on her warm skin, the press of his hard shaft stroking her, and the climax that was slowly building between them.

~

Debbie sighed, then rolled over to find Shaker lying near her. But instead of Jett's body, his own half human-half beast body was present, his cloven hooves clicking as they hit a bedpost, his furred thighs warm against her human skin.

"What's going on?"

"I like sex with you in the flesh," Shaker murmured, pulling her atop him. "But it's limited, Mistress. It only made me want to feel your body more with my own, especially inside."

Debbie gave a low moan as she felt Shaker's extra large cock began easing into her slick channel, the touch of his hard hot flesh so pleasing. "But I just...came..."

"There's coming and then there's coming." Shaker laughed mercilessly then, the press of his cock unstoppable as he pushed deeper inside her. "It's been a few months on the demon celibacy wagon, but your body remembers mine...and welcomes it."

"You're...so big..."

"I'm much larger in my true form. I love the feel of your small body yielding to mine." He kissed her throat. "It's possession in the truest sense of the word." He rolled over on her and began stroking gently, slipping in and out. Debbie groaned, then grabbed his furry ass, making his thrusts in deeper as she began to cry out.

"You want deeper? I'll give you deeper." He rolled again, putting her atop him, then pulled her down for a kiss. "But I want to be deeper too, mistress."

Debbie only had a moment to wonder what he was talking about and then she felt a gentle caress of her ass. To her shock, Shaker was kneeling behind her, lubing up his erection with K-Y. "What the hell?"

"What in Hell, you mean," the Shaker beneath her quipped.

"I am easily able to manipulate form in dreams, Debbie," Shaker behind her said. He grasped her hips, then she felt the tip of his penis begin to ease into her ass.

"Wait! Wait! I don't think—"

"Do you trust me?" both Shaker's said at once.

"Yes."

"Then hold still."

Debbie felt the press of Shaker's body entering hers in a way she'd never allowed before, her heart beating wildly. But the feeling was again one of ultimate possession, no pain.

"Now enjoy yourself," Shaker rumbled, as both beings began to thrust. "Scream for me, Debbie."

Debbie moaned as the twin penises stroked her body, clawed hands squeezing her breasts, mouths enveloping her taut nipples, sucking and teasing. Her first climax was guttural; the one a few minutes later louder but longer. Shaker's roar when he came was also brutal in intensity, as if he'd cracked open the bowels of the earth by will of his lust alone.

"What in Hell…indeed," Debbie panted, rolling off Shaker onto her side.

"That was great." Shaker smiled, showing his many rows of shark's teeth. "Damn great, to be true."

"Why haven't you asked for this before?"

"You weren't ready," Shaker murmured, drawing her close, his clawed hands running down her hot bare arm. "You had trouble coming to terms with what I was. Giving you another sign of my inhumanity wasn't a good idea then."

"But it suddenly is now?"

"I have fantasies, just like you," Shaker said grudgingly. "I have not gotten to indulge them, Debbie. I want to now, if you'll agree." He paused. "I am not a sadist. Nothing I'll ask for will hurt you. In fact, some of my desires may surprise you."

His tone was very guarded, as if he wasn't sure she would agree. "Why wouldn't any partner want to indulge your fantasies?"

"Because I never shared them in the first place, usually," Shaker said grimly. "I'm very much an actor in my own perpetual play, Debbie. A puppet on strings, a script already written in front of me. Most other beings want demons to be what they think we are: hideous, evil, ancient, all-knowing, all cruel, sex-crazed fiends."

Debbie was tempted to quip and say that was what he was. But his tone was the one she 'd heard only in a handful of fleeting moments the preceding year: full of past disappointments and resignation about future ones. "And if you were to define yourself instead?"

"I'm a being that made a mistake once and is being punished for it forever," Shaker said bitterly. "I thought what I was doing was right at the time, fighting for freedom, and pointing out a pretty glaring mistake." He grated his teeth. "Why is it only humans get a million chances to be forgiven, when they only live a mortal lifetime? I will exist for eons, and never be offered even one chance at redemption."

"You eat people," Debbie said softly. "You steal souls."

"Barter for souls."

"Barter for souls. Murder people, entrap and corrupt people, do black magic. Want me to go on?"

"If I don't do those things, I get tortured. If I enjoy myself, I get tortured. I have had to live with that for centuries. Is that right?"

I'm sorry, Shaker. I don't want you to be hurt. "No, it's not," Debbie said, hugging him. "You're different from me, Shaker. I could not have done the things you've done and keep going."

Shaker didn't answer, but he turned away. Debbie let him, curling against his back, lost in her own troubled thoughts.

〜

The next few weeks were a whirlwind of work and late nights at the office, too many of them ending with Debbie driving home alone as Jett was on location shooting some of the last scenes for *Smoke and Ashes II*. When Shaker called mentally to tell Debbie that he wouldn't be home until the following morning, Debbie didn't bother trying to hide her anger. *Fine. Goodnight.*

She grabbed her coat and briefcase and stalked to the door. Sheila was on the other side, her expression hopeful. "Feel like inviting me for a sleepover?"

"Depends what you had in mind." Debbie grimaced.

"So you've been stood up by your demonic lover, too. I propose a bottle of wine and some talk to unwind, if you're game."

"I think it's just what I need," Debbie agreed, and the two began to walk to their cars. "I guess a night trip to the Black Rose is out?"

Sheila made a face. "Harp and Song would love for you to visit. In fact I think there's still some credit under your name."

Credit Dante paid for in a trap meant to kill me. Instead, it snared Sheila, burning her with Hellfire that required regrowing new layers of skin, and a hell of a magical price tag.

"But I'm not going back there, ever."

"I understand why you wouldn't want to," Debbie said carefully. "But the danger's gone. Harp and Song are more loyal to you than anyone else. They wouldn't hurt you."

"Consider it 'Spa PTSD'," Sheila said heavily. "I hope you have wine at your place."

"Wine or scotch," Debbie said, starting her car. "Get in."

A few hours later, both women sat on Debbie's large deck, polarfleece coats wrapped around them. The night air was cool, but not really cold.

"I've never got used to the warm winters," Sheila mused. "It should be snowing in January."

remembered Sheila's screams of pain. "I think we feel more anger when we are blindsided by an attack, even if we get hurt less. Something direct that you're ready for...you can prepare. You went to the Black Rose to relax and instead you nearly died. It was a betrayal. So you're probably feeling like you can't trust anything around you that's supposed to be comforting, because something else nasty might be hiding inside, waiting to strike."

"That's it exactly," Sheila whispered, sagging slightly against the railing. "I went to my doctor, and told her a whitewashed version of what happened, told her I've been having problems sleeping. She diagnosed me with "situational stress" and gave me some anti-anxiety drugs."

"Well for God-sake, take them. I need you, Sheila." Debbie paused, sipping wine as she tried to formulate her words. "I know it's none of my business, but what you said about Harp, well... could he and Song have had a fight?"

Sheila bit her lip. "I know what happened, really. It was my fault."

Debbie sipped her wine, waiting.

"She..." Sheila faltered, again hugging herself and looking away.

Debbie put her arm around Sheila. "Tell me."

"Demons have access to magic. They can change their form, how they appear to us. Some, like Shaker or Rack or Harp, always choose the same form. Others, like Song, sometimes choose to appear differently."

"Glamours," Debbie mused. "Shaker's told me about them."

"More than that. I mean actually having a different body, not just looking like they do. Song...Song is sometimes a male, sometimes a female. His full name is Bloodsong." Sheila cracked another smile, but it came out a horrible grimace. "Bloodsong and Boneharp. Great names, don't you think?"

Shaker arranged for Sheila to meet her demons. He passed on Sheila's bi-tendencies. That's why Song chose to be a female, and they appeared together, so she'd agree to bind to them. Debbie felt a chill but covered it quickly. "We knew they were demons going into it, Sheila. They wanted a human to bind to. It's not surprising that they tried to make the best possible…presentation to you. We would do the same, in their place."

Sheila didn't answer.

"It's also clear if Song—*don't say Bloodsong, ick*—is giving you space that she's okay with you having some time to deal with knowing this. Um, how did you find out, anyway?"

"I got home early one day and Harp's sitting in the living room with some guy I don't know, both of them in boxers. They weren't doing anything but talking, but it was obvious that they were too comfortable to be strangers. I started screaming and yelling accusations, and suddenly the guy's gone, and there's Song instead looking upset and trying to assure me that everything's okay, she just didn't know I'd be home early."

Debbie almost smiled, imagining the scene, and bit her lip. "I don't think you need to worry about liking men more than women, Sheila. Song's just obviously enjoys being a woman sometimes, and she obviously cares for you."

"If she does, why didn't she tell me the truth up front? And why is she back to being a guy when I'm not there, if she enjoys being a woman so much? I just…I'm not sure I can trust either of them now."

Debbie grabbed her phone, then tapped out the message *are they connected to you now hearing this* and showed it to Sheila.

Sheila shrugged. "I don't think so, I asked Harp for privacy tonight, and Song's been absent from my thoughts since it happened. But how can you tell?"

"Let's find out," Debbie said, steering Sheila inside.

~

"'Ten signs a demon is haunting your house'?" Sheila griped. "We already know they're inside: they live with us. How's that a help?"

Debbie skimmed through the article fast, scrolling madly. "I'm looking for some kind of test we could do on ourselves to tell if they're with us when they say they aren't listening in. Some aspect of them must be present when they see through our eyes, right? Now get over here and help me look through this article!"

Sheila grumbled, but pulled up a chair. "A demon is a fallen angel. A supernatural and malevolent entity that exists in many religions around the world, under different names. In the Bible, they're described as angels who were hurled down to Earth along with Satan, whose sole purpose now is to revolt against "God's plan' and his people'. But is that true?"

"Shaker said he used to be an angel, and has talked about falling from grace before, though he didn't elaborate."

"Mine never talk about that. But Shaker did mention that one time last month. He said that was the reason speaking of God or Christmas bothered them and not him, because he used to be an angel and they were born demons."

"According to this article, the process is Invitation, Obsession, Infestation, Oppression, and Possession, the last being the goal. But that doesn't seem right, either, Sheila. Shaker never wanted a body." *But he's wearing one right now, isn't he? Was that his goal all along?* Debbie pushed the thought away. "Did yours ever mention possession?"

Sheila shook her head. "Maybe there are different classes of demons? This article is about ones in houses that don't seem to be able to take physical shape and so need a body to inhabit. They are something like a ghost or spirit."

"You're right on that." Shaker chuckled, moving into view from the dining room. He was smiling, but Debbie could see it didn't reach his eyes, which were like hot coals in the dim light. "I thought this was girl's night out: some wine, chocolate, and rom-coms. Instead you're looking at online garbage."

Sheila had taken a step back behind Debbie. *She's afraid of him.*

"I can tell you now what the sites say about us: crap. Most say there's a foul odor associated with us. That's not true. But when demons are sent back to Hell, the doorway that opens usually lets some of the vapors escape from there. Hell literally stinks, not just figuratively."

"The sites say that someone with a demon hears voices: whispers either about them or in their mind. That's true: it's the preferred way we communicate with those we bind to, as you both know firsthand. Some people can't handle that step and lose it, especially in the past. People who renege on our deals usually get driven insane as there's no way for them to get the demon to stop talking to them. And we get desperate once out of Hell not to return there."

Driving people insane by whispering to them mentally is one of the things Shaker said he did those first months last year, on Pandora's behalf. Debbie kept her face neutral.

"The websites probably mentioned shadow figures seen from the corners of your eyes or the feeling of a heavy presence next to you? Nightmares? Depression? Confusing interpersonal relationships? Fear. Rejection of the Holy Spirit. Always feeling cold. Animals behaving strangely. Knocking or banging on walls. Electrical short circuiting. General feeling of chaos, bad luck, missing items, HIV, cancer, the common cold, psychosis, drought, earthquakes, volcanic eruptions….everything bad at some point has been attributed to demons throughout history. There are sites right now online that still say this." Shaker took off his jacket and hung it up. "The only one that's true is the animals behaving oddly. They know what we are."

Debbie began to speak, but Shaker talked over her. "I don't fault you for having questions. You're both intelligent women and you know you're in over your heads. What I take issue with is looking for answers in a nest of online lies."

"By your own admission, some of the things online you just

said are true, not lies," Debbie replied, not backing down. "We both are informed enough to know some of what we read which you have said is false is false. And we are also informed enough to know that there's a lot you aren't saying that we do need to know now, even if we didn't ask you before tonight."

"Such as?"

"Shaker," Song called, her sudden rapping on the deck sliding glass door startling both Debbie and Sheila. Harp stood beside her, glowering. "Let us in before you say anything else."

"Ladies, if you would come outside," Shaker said, leading Debbie and Sheila to the deck door.

Debbie thought to resist, then went with him. *I've already signed on with him, for worse or better.*

We aren't married just yet, Mistress, came his sardonic mental reply. "Let's all sit down, shall we?" He turned to Harp, as Debbie and Sheila sat in patio chairs. "You, please go get some flowers for Sheila. You are making enough profit at the Black Rose, so get something nice."

"I'm not your servant," Harp griped, but disappeared.

"Song," Shaker intoned formally. "Show us your true form."

Song gave a look as if he'd rip Shaker's human face off, then shrugged and began changing. The metamorphosis was quick, the slender female with cropped dyed black hair and red tips being replaced by a man of the same height. He looked at the ground, running his hands through his hair, the color turning from black and red to a dark red-brown curly mass.

"Sheila, this is Song's true form. Don't fault him for what he was born as, especially when he's only tried to please you. He is not very old, respectively, neither is Harp. That means that they don't have a lot of experience with women." Shaker turned to Song. "Chime in here anytime."

"It's true. We don't. This is the longest we have been out of Hell since we were born."

Why are you helping them? Debbie thought to Shaker.

Because we need them as a whole functioning unit, not in fragments. "Hell is not Paradise, but we are given the option of looking the way we want after we are born. Some choose to be monsters, others choose to be beautiful."

"Then why change back when I'm not around, Song, if you like being a woman?" Sheila challenged.

"Because it takes enormous energy to maintain my female body. Harp and I...we need to be fed. We're overdue actually. But we didn't want to ask. We failed you when we let you get injured."

"Tell her it all," Shaker rumbled.

"We don't just eat the flesh of people," Song grated out. "We need some of their soul to survive. It's what sorcerers call Life Force in their spells. It's a bit of soul."

"A bite of soul," Shaker corrected menacingly. "Go on."

"Yes, a bite of soul, that's what demons call it for slang," Song said hatefully, glaring at him. "It will regenerate, if you just take a very little. Vampires sometimes use it in place of blood, if they are adept enough at magic. They feed through a spell that lets them access it without touching the victim. But this is also where you hear about the illness being attributed to demons, because if the demon takes too much, or repeatedly, then the donor sickens and dies."

"And that's why we ask you to choose," Harp interrupted, laying down a dozen blood-red roses beside Sheila. "We have given you power and influence that you wouldn't have had without our help. Pretty it up any way you want to, but that's the truth." He lay down another dozen near Debbie. "We can survive on just flesh, yes. But we gain more power, reserve power if you will, when we get a bit of the soul."

"But you have killed people," Debbie said pragmatically. "I know of at least twenty, maybe forty between you three. You're getting more that a bite, if the person's dead you don't need to worry about overfeeding. So why can't you feed less?"

Song made a face. "Because most people at heart have enough

good points that we can't just snack on their souls. Hell, we aren't even permitted to lay a hand on the truly blessed ones, like that priest Cahill. Some others might be bad to the bone, but they know how to defend themselves."

Lash, the weresnake, he had a blessed knife, and those throwing stars when he fought that demon in my office, plus the holy water he admitted getting the night I saw him at the church. "So why haven't any of you come back telling us that we have to choose someone different?"

"I did when you asked me to pick Dante," Shaker replied. "Otherwise...we've just been lucky. You usually pick people that have been rude in public, Mistress. They all happened to be pretty nasty people so far overall, so I had no barrier to killing them or making it look like an accident." He paused. "But that doesn't mean we got their souls."

"Careful," Harp warned. "You're going to get us into trouble, telling them all this."

Shaker ignored him. "We don't get souls of the people we kill or possess. That's more of the crap you get told. Even Jett who gave up this lovely body, when he dies, I won't get his soul. I may get a bite then, but it's not guaranteed." He paused. "See, people are easily forgiven if they suffer on earth—their souls are safe from us. They get forgiven if they repent and ask forgiveness. Only we demons don't."

"Stop, you're going to make me cry," Harp said cuttingly. "I and Song are going to take Sheila home now, before you make things worse, Shaker."

"No," Sheila said, holding up her hand, her face resolute. "If souls are what you'd really like, why not go after them, if they really are so powerful?"

"Because everyone knows we like them best!" Song said in exasperation. She got up and began pacing, shifting again to a slender woman with black/red hair. "Because everyone freaks if you ask for that up front, unless they are unbelievably desperate.

37

Besides, what does the average demon have to offer that's equal to that? Nada. If you're powerful enough to command that price for your services, you usually aren't standing on a street corner trying to pick up a Master or Mistress."

Debbie stared at Shaker. *But you are, aren't you? You are powerful enough to command that price.*

Shaker met her eyes. *Yes.* He turned to Sheila. "This is the twenty-first century. I don't believe in asking for souls, or trading for them. I'm not trying to amass power in Hell, or really here in California, either. I want to remain out of Hell and have enough resources that I'm neither starving nor wanting for anything, and I'm willing to work hard for that. So I look for partners who can be trusted and have the will to do what needs to be done." He clasped Debbie's hand. "And I found one."

"Harp's right, save that emotion for the big screen," Sheila said sarcastically. "Why is Hell so bad?"

"It's not bad being there," Shaker said. "What's bad is if you're not already in a position of power, then you're a laborer. That means you have to make sure that things keep functioning, souls getting tortured, fires staying lit, etc. Before you say it," he hissed, shooting daggers at Debbie, as she was about to open her mouth. "I meant using magic to light them, not only having flames. Do you think there's endless stacks of wood in Hell? No! Fires have to burn with no fuel, or fuel like bodies. That makes for a lot of smoke—"

"This is gross, and I've heard enough," Debbie said dismissively. "Sheila, give me a call if you are free tomorrow, we can go over those new acquisitions. I wanted to talk to you about them, if you have time."

Sheila nodded, then offered each hand to a demon. Both Song and Harp took them, the former looking very relieved before they disappeared.

"So you were listening," Debbie offered up, plopping on the couch.

"You said my name aloud twice," Shaker said with a sheepish

grin. "I checked in to see if you were boasting about my prowess. Instead I find you looking at the wrong kind of smut."

"Why'd you say all that?"

"Because she was afraid of me. I need her to trust me, and if she can't do that, to at least conclude I'm not an overt threat." He got up, then headed into the other room.

Debbie followed him. "You said we needed them as a functioning unit. Did you foresee something coming?"

"Yes," Shaker said. His tone was odd. *Despondent?*

Resigned. He turned to her. "The future usually can't be changed. Yes, we're going to have bad things happen. But we're going to have good things, too."

"Why did you cut me off," Debbie said softly. "You knew what I was thinking didn't have to do with fuel for fires."

"What you'd have said would have added some here, though. You were thinking that Song admitted that we need a bite of soul to survive. You were going to ask where we get it, if we don't get that from our victims."

Yes.

"We get it from our bonded humans," Shaker whispered, caressing her arm gently. "Like Song said, there's a price to pay being bound to us, and that's the key piece."

"Are you taking my soul, bit by bit?"

Shaker laughed. "No. That wasn't part of our contract, though I know at the time you would have agreed. As I stated before, I didn't want a servant, or to be one. I wanted a partner." He kissed her hand.

"Why not go for the easy bite?" Debbie teased.

Because I wanted to build something, not just destroy. The mental words were fleeting but laced with real yearning. Shaker met her eyes for a fleeting second, then kissed her. "I didn't want a nibble, my Mistress. I wanted a feast."

~

"I do have one other question," Debbie said, as she got into bed beside Shaker.

"About the difference in demons," Shaker finished. "I know. I heard you thinking about it."

"Well, answer."

"There isn't a handbook that Hell gives out, you know," Shaker replied grumpily. "And mortal sources aren't much better."

"So tell me about the immortal ones, like yourself."

"The truth is, I don't know," Shaker said, leaning back in bed thoughtfully. "One aspect of both Heaven and Hell that no one ever gets right is that they are both always changing. And I don't mean scenery, or people, but those change, too. I mean its nature. So much of what we classify as bad or good has to do with respective culture or values. There is no one list of wrongs, not even the Ten Commandments. For example, are you supposed to honor your father and mother if one rapes or beats you, and the other pretends not to see it? Men kill in war all the time, is it not a sin if it's in defense of their loved ones, their gods, or their country?"

"Why is it you always talk a lot when you're supposed to answer something but never give me any more real information that I started with?"

"No need to be bitchy," Shaker said, holding up an index finger and wagging it. "What I'm saying is that there's no hard and fast rules. For example, you can't judge someone in Heaven for eating a cow if their culture teaches it's okay. But if they're Hindu, then it's a problem. I'm saying that there are different rules for different people."

"I think the cow would judge. Or don't animals go to Heaven?"

"Didn't I say to stop being a bitch? Damn. As I was saying, things are changing all the time. People are grouped together in both places by what they believe, because usually people get along better with those that have similar beliefs."

"So there's no diversity in Heaven, but a lot in Hell?"

"You're really on a roll tonight," Shaker complimented

sarcastically. "You should star in your own movie, it could be half comedy, half error."

Debbie ran her hand up his heavily muscled thigh to his groin. "What about the sex? All movies need good sex."

"They do. But not yours, you're too focused on endless dialogue."

"Ass. Go on."

"Heaven and Hell are places, but they aren't finite to souls that get sent there. I haven't seen all of Hell, only the places I was told to work in."

"But there must be a barracks, right?"

"You don't get to sleep in Hell, unless it's something you fear," Shaker said sadly. "Or unless part of your punishment is the waking up to realize you're still damned."

"You're saying psychological torture."

Shaker nodded. "A soul is energy, the remnants of a person that endures once they die. On earth it's what makes a ghost. There isn't any need to physically torture anyone there, because no one has their body anymore. It's more something like The Matrix, where demons of low standing patrol the soulbeds, making sure that punishment is uninterrupted."

"But if a soul is energy, does that energy ever become depleted?"

Shaker nodded. "Sometimes, but not often. See, fear gives the soul a charge, makes it pulse with electricity. That's one of the patrol's responsibilities, to make sure that the souls keep generating power." He paused. "That's what Hell runs on: soul power. That's another reason the devil doesn't like losing people destined for Hell to God's forgiveness."

Debbie went to laugh, then swallowed it. *He's not joking.* "So that's why the devil wants souls: power supply."

"Yes. You didn't think he was doing it for the high retail value, did you?"

Again Debbie began to laugh, then saw to her horror he was still serious. "People sell souls that aren't their own?"

41

"Sure. Even poor quality souls are very expensive. The more resilient ones that generate higher power are hard to come by. The strongest people are the least desperate ones; getting a soul like that's difficult." He hugged her close. "Yours is valuable, as I'm sure you've surmised."

"But it's compromised now, being linked to you."

That's not permanent, he whispered. Before she could answer, he said, "But we were talking about demons. You were right in that I'm a different class from Song and Harp. Those like us that are fallen are different than those born in Hell. You might say we're a more complex evil. Those like Song and Harp are more base, causing mayhem because they were created with it as their only purpose. There are far more of them than of those like me. There are even more of the very weak demons like the house haunters you were reading about online. They go around feeding off souls they scare for that purpose, hoping to become strong enough to form a body of their own. But they can't, they'd need to get a whole soul to do that, maybe several. That'd never happen. So they try for possession, because that's easier. But they're like children, they don't know how to tend to the body they've stolen, even sometimes hurt it intentionally. They always end up getting kicked out by a priest, or getting their flesh suit killed, so they get evicted that way. Because of that, true demons refer to them as Homeless or Takers. We don't associate with them, as a rule. They're scavengers. Evil with no intelligence or endgame."

"You know, you always manage to spin it so you come out looking like a good demon."

Shaker laughed heartily. "There's no such thing."

CHAPTER THREE

"WELL, ITS FEBRUARY FIRST," DEBBIE SAID BRIGHTLY TO HER assembled team. "What do you have for me?"

"I have a question," Adeline said loudly. "I heard that hiring a person to do Compliance isn't going to happen after all. Because a private deal was done right after the stock went public and now Pandora is a private company again."

"That's correct," Debbie replied. "It shouldn't affect any of this year's projects or any of you directly. In fact, we have secured additional funding from our investors to add on another movie this year. Acquisitions will meet with me directly after this to go over the list, and I'll announce the name of the movie and script idea mid-month, if we secure the rights and a script exists. Anything else?"

"I heard there was an accident on the set of *Smoke and Ashes II* on the last day," Jeremy said. "Something about Jett almost getting kicked to death."

Shaker wasn't kidding when he said that animals know demons. Jett always did his own stunts. "A horse was frightened by one of the snakes we were using in the scene, and it panicked."

Both animals knew what I was, Shaker said mentally. *They reacted.*

"No one was hurt, but we also can't jeopardize our lead again," Debbie went on. "So we asked the stunt double to do the last scenes. Once that's done later this week, that film is finished shooting and can move to the editing stage."

Adeline and others were supposed to get shares of stock as part of the plan, Shaker reminded. *If you pay those in cash instead, that should solve her issues. That's almost certainly why she asked.*

"I will add that for those of you who were supposed to get stock shares as part of the deal, comparable compensation will be provided. Now onto business. *Immortal Confessions* begins filming this month. Can all of you tell me your prognosis...sorry, progress, on getting ready for that. Richard Triss?"

Rack smiled without showing his teeth. "We are fully funded, as already stated in the previous meeting. I will add that for this and other big releases Pandora will host aforementioned launch parties, and they have partnered with Triss Vineyards to showcase special wines specifically chosen for the pictures."

"You're a man of many talents," Stacy flirted, smiling widely and leaning closer.

"Thank you for the compliment," Rack said with a formal incline of his head. "For this picture we wanted something well-aged, limited in release, with a long finish made from French-linage grapes. They call what gives wine its flavor and unique properties 'terroir'." He produced an old-fashioned bottle kept in a metal filigree holder. "This is Timeless. A red, of course."

The rest of the group tittered.

"Very good. Carolina?"

"We're doing fine with the costumes, but they're taking a bit longer than anticipated, because although the major scenes of the story take place in the early to mid-1800s, we have to have about half the costumes from other periods. For instance, the main character's flashback to getting made a vampire takes place in the early 1600s, and he's with a group plus this mad vampire monster. The monster's getting rags, but the rest have to have period clothes plus period weapons. Then there's also a few scenes in the late 1800s, and then one or two from the 1900s. For the 1900's we only need to have clothes for the main character, Devlin, as he's mourning the love of his life, Anna. But for the 1800's, we have to have clothes for Devlin's henchmen and his adversaries, plus his brother Daniel."

"That's Danial with an 'a' at the end," a man said at the end of the table with a faint smile. He offered his hand with a flourish. "I'm Joshua, good to meet you all."

"I thought you were location?" Stacy said, craning closer to the handsome stranger.

"I'm location and fact-checking," Joshua said with a reckless grin. "Or you might call it fiction-checking. To look for locales I had to read the script a few times to get a feel for what I'd be looking for. In doing so I became familiar with the names."

"Glad to have you on board, Joshua. Since you spoke up, how are we doing on locations for this?" Debbie asked.

"The investor initially wanted us to shoot the scenes as written, as in go to France and Spain, as well as to New York," Joshua said. "I convinced him we could do it all here in the United States, though we could go north to Washington to shoot the outdoor forest scenes that take place in New York and France, because of the vegetation. Most of the scenes in the script are interior though, so I think we could do those here, and just get a few shots of the exterior of a secluded mansion with the right northern vegetation."

"Did you find one?"

"Yes, there's a house in Minnesota called The Chalet," Josh said. "The exterior is wild enough that it fits the description of the house as written. I am in the process of securing rights to filming it from the outside."

Remember John and Madeline? That's their house, Shaker said mentally. *They've already agreed to the filming and also to invest in the picture but have stipulations. John will be here later this week to meet with you regarding investing in Pandora.*

"The other shots of the castle and home in Paris can be done with CGI, as there should only be an initial shot of each one in the film as the vampire moves his home base," Joshua concluded.

Thanks. Debbie nodded. "Very good. Adeline? How is the website coming?"

"Almost finished, we just have to update the release dates for both the home viewing of the first *Smoke and Ashes* and put in the proposed release date for the sequel. All links except for those are already active. Download sales of *Tinderbox* and *Hell's Gate* are low, but that's to be expected. I have samples of promotional items like pens and such done through Pandora Promotions. Debbie, you should have those for review later this week."

That woman rubs me the wrong way, but she's good. "Great Adeline. Home viewing date. Jeremy, do you have that?"

"We're aiming for May," Sheila said, hurrying in the room with some folders. "DVD's should be done by that time, and Amazon's all confirmed along with the other major streaming sites. Sorry I'm late."

"As for the proposed release date for the sequel, we are thinking November," Debbie said. There was a collective groan. She held up her hands. "I know, usually releases for sequels try to wait a full year until the new ones are released, otherwise oversaturation of the market can happen. But we're facing both a popular comic series installment and an action-bestseller-turned-movie in December. I know, I know, last meeting I said that there wouldn't be competition and we were releasing in December, but we didn't know about these two movies coming out then. We can't risk losing sales, so we need to release early. We can't chance that we won't get forgotten if we release at the same time. The press is already toting them as "must-see" and they have more commercials and ads out now this far ahead than we will the two weeks before our movie releases. Stacy, how is *Absolution* coming?"

"Sorry," Stacey said, her face reddening. "But I have been focusing on the vampire movie the entire last month. As Carolina said, we have multiple time periods and multiple settings. This calls for multiple teams, even if we do as Josh suggests and keep almost all the shooting here. I've gotten these assembled and we're ready to begin shooting. My only problem is that I also have read the script and I think if we don't shoot a few scenes off the lot, we're going to have to pull in someone to do CGI. There's a scene in Paris where Devlin, the main character, does an elaborate ruse while murdering someone that needs at least several streets: a flat, two separate pubs, and a nasty looking alleyway. Further, another scene earlier depicts events near a castle.

"Now we can do the same thing Josh suggests with having an outside picture from several angles and just having the scenes within it done on a set. There's a lot of different rooms, but it's doable. But there's also a scene in the forest where Anna and Dev cement their love after he kills a bear." She rifled pages. "And an earlier scene where he sneaks out to kill a deer. Trying to make a forest is one thing, and we could probably fake a deer carcass. But we can't fake the bear. I've talked to the local animal actors' guild and there's a guy we can get who has a grizzly that could do the scenes here. But we can't put him near water because that's not something the bear does. Apparently, it likes to swim, so if it sees water, it's done performing. So it's CGI, or we have to change the scene to take place near a glade instead of a riverbank."

I can already tell you, Devlin will not want to change the scene, Shaker said to Debbie mentally. *Shoot the scene with the bear here, then cut in to the scene shot offsite with the river and sex.*

"Shoot the scenes separately with the bear here and the couple off lot near a river, then splice them. Try to use a river in this country, ok? Anything else? Nicole isn't here today, she's meeting with Bart about *Absolution.* She's going to meet with me later in the week to go over its progress. Anything else?"

"Just that I and Richard have those other possibilities for scripts for you to look at, if you have time this morning," Sheila said.

"Yes, come in right now," Debbie said, heading to the door. "I have a meeting at noon, but nothing until then."

Don't forget, you promised to stop by the sound stage later this afternoon, Shaker said mentally. *I'm beginning to feel ignored, and a rumor's going around that we're on the outs, because you used to come watch filming at least once a week and haven't yet come once this year.*

I'll be there, Debbie thought to him, as she entered her office. To her surprise, she and Sheila had just sat down when there was a rap on the door. "Debbie?"

"Who is it?" Debbie said, immediately going for her gun in her desk. To her surprise, Sheila had pulled one from her briefcase, and already had it leveled at the door.

"Joshua. It's about the script you asked me to help write."

Debbie sighed inwardly, but also didn't move out of reach of her gun. "Come in."

Joshua came in, looking tired. He sat gracefully in the chair across from Sheila, then beckoned to the doorway where, to Debbie's chagrin, Lash stood.

"Hi Lash," Sheila said brightly, stowing her gun. "Sorry about that."

"No worries, you can't be too careful," the snakeman hissed nastily. "Especially you two." He sauntered in and leaned on the edge of her desk, making it creak. "Josh here said you put him in charge of my script. I think between he and I, we fixed the problems."

"It's a fascinating tale," Josh said quickly, handing the script to Debbie. "The only issue I see is how to market it to adults. I think we can get the horror crowd and the action crowd's attention. The issue is that there's a lot of drama in the film as well. Other antihero films like *Deadpool* and *Venom* relied more on humor coupled with darkness; the former was a success because it didn't pull any punches, and the latter got bad reviews because it did. Yet *Venom* still was a huge commercial success, because of its lead actor. Any more good and bad doesn't matter, so long as the audience can identify with the main character. Lose that and you're doomed. Word of mouth also counts for a lot. Mixed reviews are okay, but the horror and action audience is discerning, no matter what you've been told. If a horror movie isn't scary enough, that will go out over all the social media and in a week, sales will flatline. Same thing if an action movie doesn't have enough well-done stunts."

"We'll have good stunts, if I need to do them myself," Lash griped, showing his snake fangs. "And remember, no poof and the guy's a snake. I want a gradual and believable transformation."

Debbie groaned inwardly but smiled, placing the script on her desk and flipping to a random spot to skim a passage. "I'll read this over this week, and get back to you, Josh. But if I give the green light, do you have locations in mind?"

Joshua nodded. "Most of the action takes place in the South, primarily the Everglades swamp and the French Quarter of New Orleans. While the story begins in early 1900, those two places haven't changed. We can film most of what we need on a soundstage, then add in bits from the historical section of the city and probably a weekend in the swamp. But we could likely do it all in Louisiana."

"I can take you to the places it…um, things happened," Lash said reluctantly to Joshua, as his hand stroked the hilt of his serrated knife in his belt scabbard. "If you need details."

"You've provided enough details," Joshua assured him. "The mansion scenes from the night attack scene we can do here, we just need shots again of some Southern mansion from outside. I'll even wager that the actor that's playing Devlin in *Immortal Confessions* can be talked into playing a bit role in your movie, Lash."

"Good," Lash hissed. "I just want to make sure nothing is fake looking. I'm one of those horror fans you were just talking about, and I hate badly done shit."

"I wouldn't have signed on to work with you if I didn't think I could make your story come to life," Joshua said, looking Lash in the eyes. "I know you and I know Devlin. Which means I know better than that."

Lash nodded, pleased. "Glad to hear we understand each other." He moved away from the desk, towards the door. "Have a good day, ladies. Call me with issues, Josh."

After he'd slammed the door closed, Josh visibly relaxed in his chair.

"He make you nervous?" Sheila teased.

"He'd make you nervous, too, if you knew half the kills he's supposed to have made," Josh retorted, his eyes reddening. "My supposed immortality means nothing facing someone who knows all the ways there are to kill vampires."

Sheila started, then looked at Debbie. "He's a vampire?"

"Joshua is on loan from Devlin, to help with accuracy," Debbie explained hastily. "But we are prepared to offer you a job, Joshua, if you want one. I looked through the night attack scene you mentioned during your brief exchange with Lash just now, and it's good, really good. Tense, not too much gore, some close calls, and a horrific yet satisfying conclusion which I didn't see coming for the end. You have done previous work in films?"

"A little ghost-writing, a little film PR, but mostly marketing and finding locations," Joshua replied, opening his mouth slightly so his top fangs were visible. "I got turned back in the sixties, when Devlin realized that PR wasn't something that a modern vampire could do without." He laughed.

"We can't do without it, either. You're hired," Debbie said. "Whatever rate you were initially hired at to start, with additional bonuses if we hit our goals for Pandora this year."

"Agreed," Joshua said, standing. "I should be going now, though. Devlin wants constant updates on what's going on. I've been calling him once a day about noon to check in. He's pleased with my work so far, and I want to keep it that way."

"I know his position, that he's often up during the day," Debbie said as he went to leave. "But you're working days, Josh. How is that possible?"

"Prescription level sunblock, leaving late, and coming in early," Josh replied with a chuckle. "I'll have more trouble in the summer here, but I just may have to adjust my hours. I enjoy my work and am excited to do this." He leaned forward, as if conspiring. "It's exciting being part of Pandora and making films again. Mostly what I've done these last five decades for Devlin is greasing wheels, and as you know, he often prefers setting an example rather than playing nice."

"I do know. I didn't experience being the focus of his fury firsthand yet, and I wouldn't ever want to," Debbie replied.

"Nor I," Joshua said, opening the door. "Have a good lunch, ladies."

"How is it afternoon?" Sheila groaned. "Last time I looked at the clock it was ten."

"Our meeting didn't start until eleven," Debbie said, sitting in her chair. "Can you take care of Joshua's official hire?"

"Yes. Here are the new potential projects," Sheila said, handing Debbie five folders. "The scripts are in there, along with a very rough budget."

"Did you find a movie we could call *Dare to Tell?*"

Sheila made a face. "Not really, sorry."

"So what's a summation of each? I'll take these home and read them, but it'll take at least a week or two to get through them all, so I'd like to know which is your best bet?"

"Hard to say," Sheila said, after a moment. "Really, I like four of the five. I think they could be solid movies. But several scripts do need some work. You'll see that when you read them."

"Okay then," Debbie said nicely, frustrated inwardly. "Just start wherever you want and pitch. Go."

"Okay. Remember that you had said sometime last year that we'd had luck with paranormal movies, or films with at least a paranormal slant. How about a haunted house story, featuring a demon instead of a ghost?"

"The *Conjuring* series is already doing that."

"Yes, but in that series, demons are mindless evil that just seem to want to cause mayhem with no real purpose, like in those online articles we read together. The only reason it's a series at all is that it includes different evil witches/Satanists that keep calling different demons forth and not putting them back. What if ours was bound to a house, instead of to a person?"

"How would the demon get its 'soul-bites' that way?" Debbie questioned with a smirk. "Yes, I know horror fans won't know that insider joke, but they are going to expect possession and murder from a demon, at minimum."

"Anyone who dies there also becomes a part of the house/island and can't move on to either Heaven OR Hell. Imagine a place so cursed that you would be crazy to go there, so it's abandoned. But a group of kids goes there for some reason, of course, and mayhem ensues. Ghosts, murder, scares that only heighten as the story moves on, then ends with a big bang."

"Haunted house stories are always popular," Debbie mused. "They just remade *The Haunting of Hill House* into a series, and it's a hit, so I'm inclined to give this movie a green light. But I still don't understand how the demon is bound to the house."

"Remember all that talk of people summoning a demon? In most stories, the summoner immediately dies or is killed because they're generally portrayed in fiction as idiots who aren't prepared at all for what appears. But let's say that this one sorcerer, Latham, is prepared. He's smart, and he does a bunch of research, years of research, to make sure that what he's going to call out of Hell doesn't doom him. He summons a demon, an incredibly powerful one called Rigor, and immediately imprisons it, forcing it to build his island mansion. Rigor does that, but Latham further tricks him, asking him to ensure that the island cannot be destroyed, not by a bomb, or fire, not even a nuclear blast. The only way for that is for

Rigor to bind himself permanently to the island, as a demon can't be killed."

"But when Latham dies, the demon will be freed to go back to Hell, and the house falls down. Right? That's no good."

"The key to that is somehow Latham, with Rigor's help, made a lasting pact beyond death, some kind of curse made of layers and layers of heavy-duty magic. You go on that island, somehow you go off both the Devil's and God's radar. It's like a no man's land for anything living." Sheila smiled evilly. "And a warehouse for souls."

Sheila, that smile of yours is creeping me out, I half-expect to see shark's teeth. "But why would the demon do that?"

"To stay out of hell, permanently," Sheila said triumphantly. "And to get souls, a lot of souls. The more souls, the stronger the island becomes. I'm guessing also that the demon Rigor agreed to the pact knowing that the man and his descendants would eventually die, and the island would become the demon's own playground. I'm also guessing that the demon's not the only thing haunting the island, from the script. There are other demons there, those simple ones Shaker told us about that feed on fear, who began working on anyone that comes there. There are ghosts of the many people that died over the year: some sad, others vengeful and murderous. Plus there are a handful of demons that got there over the years through various means that are less powerful than Rigor, but also smart. For instance, one trick of the island is time, that it passes differently there. Another is the water. It freezes and thaws independent of season, to trap people there for the demons." Sheila shivered theatrically. "It's a great spooky story. We could really bring it to life with special effects."

"Hmm, it sounds like a good premise," Debbie said, nodding. "What's it called?"

"The Origin of Fear on Latham's Landing," Sheila said, making a face. "Too long, I know. But we can shorten it."

"Okay, good. Next?"

"I heard that Triss Vineyards has a new rare wine called

Incubus," Sheila stated. "We could come up with something to go with the wine, a story about a woman seduced by a demon mist, an incubus. Call the movie the same name." She handed Debbie the script. "It'd be cheap to shoot, like the demon island one, with all the scenes taking place in a house. The script needs work, but I think it would be easy to market and make a profit from."

Sheila's words sounded off to Debbie. *Since when had a film being easy to market or profit from been a reason to do the movie?* "Okay, I'll think about it. We'd have to be more careful than we were about *Hell's Gate* regarding the seduction scenes though. I confess, I don't think we could make it profitable because we'd have to cut it to a PG rating, and people who go to a sexy movie want to see some clothes come off."

"It might be worth it to check into making one movie, like this one, to try for direct to streaming or for a specific channel that's not on cable," Sheila said carefully, obviously unsure how Debbie would take it. "There's no worries about approval of content, because you aren't broadcasting it so just anyone can tune in, only selling it to a specific group that have already paid up front to have access to viewing it. That's what I meant, when I said *Incubus* would be easy to market and profitable."

"But who would we get to star in it?" Debbie said in confusion. "Do you have anyone in mind we could afford? We only have one star we can count on to work for below industry wages: Jett."

"There's a number of women who saw *Smoke and Ashes* with their boyfriends because of the number of scenes with his shirt off," Sheila said pointedly. "You give them a movie with him doing the full monty, you'll get people streaming."

But would Shaker want to do a movie like that? For some reason, Debbie thought not. *And do I want him to, knowing he's going to be my husband?* "I'll bring it up to Shaker tonight. I think it's doable, if we can find a hot actor willing to do it for a bargain price. Next?"

"Redemption has been a big theme in our movies that have been successful. There's a script here submitted by an unknown female author titled *The Sacrifice*. It's about a woman whose child is kidnapped and never found. She never truly recovers and becomes a recluse. Years later she steps in to save a child that nearly dies, after his mother attempts to kill him and herself. She saves him, but then the mother comes back when he's a young adult, repentant, asking to be forgiven and to be part of her child's life. The recluse doesn't give up the child, but she takes in the mother as well, and they live together happily ever after."

"That's it?" Debbie with sarcasm. "That seems like something that's made for Lifetime TV, not the theater. And there's no demons. Pass."

"It's written by a demon," Sheila said slowly. "Rack brought it to me, asked if we could do the picture as a favor to her. I said I'd ask you."

Without knowing who the demon was that submitted it, or what kind of power she wields, I can't risk offending her. "Send it back, tell her we'll consider it if she makes it more exciting, more of a horror film, and that she definitely has to make some kind of paranormal twist to it with one of the main characters, I don't care who. Maybe the child's paranormal or something, that's why the mother goes wacky in the beginning."

"Alright. You're probably not going to like this one either. *Hell to Pay* is a gangster movie, with a paranormal twist. A group of assassins—all of them paranormal in some way—go up against an evil spirit sent by a demon. Only three survive, but the thing they fought, some kind of sorcerous spirit called a Spiritwalker, keeps hunting them. It kills off another of them before the two that are left flee. They find a badass who has his own group of men and pledge their service to him if he'll help them destroy the spirit. He does, with a lot of bloodshed."

"Hmm, interesting," Debbie said. "Tell me more. How many people would we need?"

"If you have Jett in this picture as well, we'd need at least seven more good guys, total: the original group of six, and then the badass they run to. We'd need at least one bad guy, so eight total. The initial scene begins in the middle of the supernatural assassins getting slaughtered, so those actors could be recruited to play not only part of the assassin group that gets killed, but also the second group they turn to for help, as we can disguise the same actors with different makeup and costumes. The evil spirit monster could be done with CGI."

"What are the assassins' talents? Their supernatural ones, I mean."

"What you'd expect: a werewolf for brute force, a witch, a vampire, some kind of being that's half demon-half angel, and a fairy. And a demon."

"A fairy? Complete with wings?"

Sheila flipped some pages. "Doesn't say. She's one of the initial group that gets killed almost immediately."

"Hmm," Debbie said. "It's worth checking into, but I think we need to ditch the fairy. They just aren't badass enough. Add maybe another man who's a sorcerer, maybe another werewolf. Is the demon the bad guy?"

Sheila nodded. "He's vanquished by the end. They douse him with holy water or something. This is one of the ones I told you about that needs work; it needs a better ending. And the characters are very wooden, even given some great plot twists and dialogue."

Debbie made a face. "While I like it, we'd have to do a big rewrite to come up with a better ending, and more likeable, or at least empathetic characters. See what you can do."

"The last one is a simple romantic comedy, but it features a demon and a witch," Sheila said. "*What Matters Not.*"

Debbie skipped the face this time and went right to utter disdain. "What kind of a title is that? What's it about?"

"There's a white witch that's working hard to help her community, but her house gets vandalized, and her child's getting bullied. She decides to call on a darker magic and performs a few dark spells for personal gain. That attracts a demon, who tries to get her to do more bad things. But she ends up redeeming him, and they end up getting married at the end."

"Another lifetime movie, albeit for people who love and idealize demons because they don't know any real ones," Debbie said with a wry smile. "Pass."

"Okay," Sheila said, scribbling some notes. "Let me get working on the next actions, and I'll get back to you next month, after I have possible fixes and a sign off from the author on what we propose to change."

"Good," Debbie said with a nod.

"Action!"

"I hate coming home so late," Margery said aloud as she drove her Honda down the rural lane, rain streaming down the windshield. "Damn that new girl for not showing up."

A little kid darted directly in front of her, running hard across the street. Her brakes squealed as she pumped them, then stood on them. Just missing, the kid made it safe to the other side without looking as she swerved onto the side of the road, leaving a trail of black rubber.

"Damn kid. What the hell?"

Out of the dark brush on the side, hot on the kid's trail, some creature burst out running, too big to be a dog, too heavy for a deer.

"Hey!"

The creature ignored her, dissolving into the same shadows the child had, blending with the greys and blacks of dusk.

"Hello?"

"Help!" came a child's scream of terror.

Without a thought, Marge darted into the same shadows. Breaking through a layer of fog, she emerged to see the kid climbing a fence, and failing, her feet sliding on the wet chain link.

It's a little girl, her hair's just shorn like a boy. The thing was ten feet from him, watching as it stalked closer.

The hair went up on the back of her neck. *A wolf? Here?*

"Okay, "Debbie called out loudly to the director. "No bad wolves. We're going to get in trouble with the environmental people."

"OK, coyote-dog mix," the director called. "Make a note on your script, Voiceover, and action!"

A coy dog, wild, one of the biggest she'd ever seen. The dog half must have been a Rottweiler.

There was a growl from behind her.

Coydogs usually hunt in groups. Packs.

She lunged for the nearest weapon, a limb from the last storm lying at her feet and brandished it. "Come on!"

Images of lifesize coydogs attacked Marge from every direction.

"And Storm rides in?" Debbie whispered to Sheila, who nodded.

"Yes, the dogs start backing up, a few attack Storm kills a few, and the woman gets in a whack herself to one. We're going to add them later, CGI."

After the staged battle, Marge slumped, as Shaker appeared costumed as Storm. The woman hugged the little girl she'd saved, then turned to Storm. "How did you know? Who are you?"

"I saw your car at the road. Or should I say in the road? I'm Smoke Storm." He held out his hand, which Marge shook. "And I recognized the plate."

"I'm so thankful."

"Your motor's still running."

They all walked back to the rear of the stage, where the cars were. Storm turned to the woman. "I know what you are."

The woman convulsed and became a monstrous demon, and he

58

shot her dead, then turned to the little girl. "I told you to run in front of her, Lindsay, not almost get hit."

The little girl shrugged. "I didn't think the pack of dogs was dangerous, Storm."

"Be more careful."

"Okay, cut!" The director got up from his chair. "Jett, that was good, but I want to see some righteousness there. You're killing another soul-sucking bastard, sending its ass back to the fiery pit! You want the audience to feel that satisfaction with you."

"Okay," Shaker nodded agreeably, then caught Debbie's eyes as she stifled a laugh. *It's comments like these that you have to hear in person to believe.*

"Let's see it again. Places people. Action!"

"I do have to say, the final cut you did was better," Debbie said to Shaker, as they arrived home. "Bart is a great director."

"I always act wooden doing scenes where I'm executing demons, and I'm usually off the first few times with the lines, too. But it is one of the very few things I don't have experience with." He smiled. "Can't believe I'm learning something new after ten centuries."

"Do you have another scene to film tomorrow?" Debbie asked.

"Yes, some car chase with cars banging into one another and overturning and going through a crowd for the finale. I just have to be there to shoot Storm getting out of the car a little bloody. The stuntmen are doing all the stunts."

"Good. I have something to talk to you about." Debbie outlined the *Incubus* movie proposal. "Are you interested?"

"It would be easy," Shaker said. "She's right too, I get propositions constantly. I think we should do it."

Constantly? "But do you want to do it?" Debbie asked, trying to stifle an immediate flare of jealousy before Shaker sensed it.

"Yes, we should do it."

"We should," Debbie said, coming to sit on the arm of Shaker's chair. She rested her hand on his arm. "But that's not what I asked. Do you want to do this film?"

"No," Shaker said in a low tone. "I don't want to parade around naked for humans to get kicks from. I've never liked doing that."

"Then we'll do the movie, we'll just hire someone else for the lead," Debbie said. "Maybe one of the stuntmen who doubles as Jett. There's one other project I wanted to talk to you tonight about. It's the best of Sheila's offerings today and her favorite, even if she didn't say so. But the concept has a novel twist on demon pacts. It's about an island where a demon is summoned and then he's bound to that, so people come there but never leave, sort of like an Isle of Horror. Hey, maybe that's what we should use for the name—"

"Who submitted this script?" Shaker thundered, leaping from the chair with red eyes.

Alarmed, Debbie dug through her bag, pages falling out of the colored folders. "There's no name listed."

"No, we are not doing that movie." Shaker was breathing hard, nearly panting. "Find out who submitted that script. That was aimed at me, someone who knows the real me."

"What are you talking about?"

"That island is real. It's called Latham's Landing. And there is a demon bound there: my father."

~

Debbie pleaded with Shaker to explain, but he'd say no more on the subject. Finally he left, slamming out of the house. The next morning he still hadn't returned.

Debbie went from meeting to meeting, trying to focus, and

worried about Shaker. He hadn't answered any of her mental texts. *At least I know he's okay, as I'm not feeling any pain.*

Debbie's secretary rapped on the door, then pushed it open. "Ms. Deal, there's a phone call for you."

Debbie began to say take a message, then saw the woman's expression. "I'll take it in my office. Thanks everyone." She hurried to her office, then picked up the phone. "Hello?"

"Hello, Debbie."

Her mother's cool voice stopped Debbie, because there was only one reason she would be calling. "Hello, mother. Who's dead?"

"Your father. The funeral will be held this weekend. I'll expect you here on Friday." Click.

CHAPTER FOUR

"I didn't know your parents were still alive," Shaker murmured, as he leaned against the deck with her nestled in his arms. "There are no pictures of them anywhere in your home, and no photo albums. You never saw them at all last year, did you?"

"We're estranged," Debbie said tiredly, sipping some scotch. "Although I have to change that now, don't I? We were estranged, my father and me. My mother, well...we were never close to begin with.

"Do you want to talk about it?"

Debbie shook her head. "It doesn't change anything, to talk about it."

"Can you at least tell me where we're going then for the funeral?"

"A town in the Bible Belt called Sufferance. It's a pretty place actually. Picturesque. My family is one of the original ones that founded the town, and I have cousins there, and at least one uncle, my father's brother."

"Don't tell me that your father's the town minister?"

Debbie laughed. "No, but they are devout." She leaned back

into him with a sigh. "I'm not sure you should come with me. There are more religious artifacts in their home than on your set."

"Just symbols or objects that have been blessed?"

"Both."

"Bloody hell," Shaker rumbled. "Still, your fiancé can't not go with you. We'll just have to stay in a motel."

"There's no motel there. Sufferance is a historical town dating back from when the west was settled. "

"Then we'll rent a Winnebago." Shaker chuckled. "Why didn't you ever tell me this? I always thought you were from California."

"I told people I met out here that, because I didn't want to be who I was. I never told anyone, not Rebecca, not Sheila, no one. The whole point of leaving for college and film school was to get away from that and become someone else."

"I can understand that," Shaker whispered, nuzzling her cheek with his nose.

~

"I'm just glad that you hadn't been back here in twenty years," Shaker said joyfully, as he flopped onto the huge king size bed in the Presidential Suite. "They had time to build a Holiday Inn complete with restaurant, bar, and pool."

"I'm not sure we'll have time to try any of those," Debbie said nervously. "We've just got tomorrow and then we need to fly back on Sunday."

"We'll have time," Shaker said confidently. He gave her a leer. "Why don't you come over here and we can help each other relax?"

"Be serious, we have to shower and get back in the car," Debbie said crossly. "We're meeting my mother, my uncle, and my cousins for dinner."

Shaker made a face, then walked into the bathroom. Water began to pound the shower.

Debbie let out another sigh, then opened her briefcase, trying to decide what to wear. Then she looked into the mirror and saw her father's transparent form standing behind her. She let out a shriek.

Shaker was at her side in a split second, dripping wet and naked. The spirit disappeared.

"You saw him, right?"

Shaker nodded, going to the bathroom to grab a towel. "That was your father? He must have had an accident. He looks lost."

"Yes, he had an accident, a car hit his. But he's dead."

"I mean his soul's lost. It's normal, right after a sudden unexpected death. Souls aren't sure what's going on, most never think they could be dead. He'll figure it out eventually."

"But you said that souls are currency. Won't someone pick his up like it was a five dollar bill they came across on the street?"

"They might if he was advertising he was available to be harvested, but he's not." He paused. "A simplistic way to put it would be that he's like a baby wild deer: no scent for predators to find them by. But he's on a different plane of existence now and he can see me for what I am. I'd have no way to hunt him down if I did want to harvest him, unless he came right to me and stayed put long enough to harvest, but he'd be too afraid to do that."

"With good reason," Debbie said with an arch of her eyebrows. "You keep saying 'harvest.' What does that mean exactly?"

"It means that I'd teleport him into Hell, and hand him over to whomever's on duty. But that's not usually possible."

"You're doing it again, talking and saying nothing that explains any real facts."

"Okay. Demons can't just grab a soul and take it to Hell. That part of the human mythology about us is true. If it's someone we've been commanded to harvest, sure, but then the soul would have to have what's called a marker on it, where the human made a deal with the devil or a demon with their soul as the price. Demons can find someone like that anywhere they hide with very few exceptions. Also, if an order comes down from Heaven to Hell allowing us carte blanche with a particular soul. Sure, once in a while a demon can fool a soul into agreeing to go to Hell. But that's usually if it's a suicide, where the person is so fucked up mentally that they think they deserve to be damned." Shaker smiled evilly. "You might say that the Catholics help more than any other religion with all their talk of suicides having to go to Hell. Catholic souls are the easiest to convince, especially if they hadn't confessed recently. But Baptists like your family are almost as easy." He laughed.

Debbie ignored his barb. "You said something about animals knowing what you are. What about so-called evil animals?"

"You might have noticed that Lash is a snake, and he's not my best buddy," Shaker retorted, affronted. "That's all bullshit. Bottlenose fly or butterfly, bunny or bat, animals know me for what I am. They avoid me if possible. What they can't avoid, they attack. No animal is inherently evil."

"So us humans are the only ones that are stupid enough to think you could be anything but an enemy?"

"Come here," Shaker said gently. "You know me for what I am: your partner, your lover, and your protector." He hugged her. "Damn the rest, you're what matters, Mistress. Let me go get dressed, so we can be presentable at dinner."

Do not gulp the wine, or you'll be drunk before your dinner arrives. With effort, Debbie put down the glass and forced a smile back onto her aching face, then faced her cousin. "Tell me more about those butterflies you photographed?"

Her cousin beamed. "The five monarchs were clustered on this huge patch of milkweed, and the sun was just above—"

"Hello, daughter."

Debbie forced herself not to cringe, then made her smile more formal as she stood. Shaker also stood. "Mother." *Shaker, her name is Kallia, but call her Mrs. Tennison.*

"Did you order yet?" Her mother sat, then looked at Shaker, taking in Jett's handsome young muscular body and face. "Who's this?"

"I'm her fiancé," Shaker said with a nod of his head. "I'm sorry to meet you under these circumstances, and I'm sorry for your loss, ma'am."

Kallia Tennison stared at him, then looked away without answering to her brother, Debbie's uncle. "Stuart, go get the waiter and order me a gin and tonic."

Stuart nodded to Shaker. "Glad to meet you," then walked away. The cousins shifted uncomfortably.

"Can you tell me the funeral plan?" Debbie said directly. "Is there anything I need to prepare for?"

"The funeral procession will take place after the service at Church of Christ," Kallia said crisply. "You can ride with the family to the cemetery for the gravesite service, then we are going to the community center for the reception."

Sounds more like a wedding than a funeral, Shaker said in her mind. Debbie cleared her throat nervously, trying not to smile.

"The reading of the will is Sunday in a private meeting at ten in the morning." Kallia paused. "But don't expect anything, Debbie."

"I hope we can expect common courtesy," Shaker said mildly, though Debbie could feel how angry he was. "That's why we came here, Mrs. Tennison."

"Of course," she replied frostily. "I assume you're actually engaged?"

Debbie held up her left hand, showing the large Ruby and onyx ring. "Yes, we are. It just happened this past New Year's Eve. I haven't had time to plan anything and we hadn't set a date yet."

"You will have the wedding here," Mrs. Tennison pronounced, as if it were a royal decree. "Spring would be too soon and interfere with proper mourning, but a fall wedding would be doable."

Debbie gave in and grabbed her wine, taking a gulp. "We aren't sure we want to wait that long, or if we want something that formal."

"You are a Tennison, Deborah, and you will do your duty," her mother said coldly. "God knows, you've ignored it long enough, running off to godless California and starting that production company. We sent you to college to learn the law, so you could make something of yourself. Or become a business manager, to help with the family business. Instead you announce you're going into filmmaking—"

"What is the family business?" Shaker interrupted. "Social Climbing?"

"Flowers. All manner of cut flowers that we ship to florists and restaurants. Our family's been growing for close to a century now. Our faith goes hand in hand with our gardening."

"Excellent," Shaker said with a charming smile. "We'd like roses for the wedding. Black roses, with a few red ones mixed in."

Mrs. Tennison's mouth dropped open. "You can't be serious."

"Our favorite colors are red and black, as you can see by Debbie's ring," Shaker continued. "Which is why a traditional wedding just won't do." He smiled.

"Her dress will be white," Mrs. Tennison grated out. "And the flowers will be some shade of pastel, as will be all the decorations. That is tradition."

"No," Shaker said, standing and offering his hand to Debbie. "Our day will be ours and no one else's. Come on, let's go."

"Debbie, you get up from this table, and you can leave town immediately," her mother said. "We will strike your name from the family Bible, and you're dead to us."

Debbie looked at Shaker, then at her family. "I'm sorry you feel that way," she said, standing and taking Shaker's hand. "I will be at the burial tomorrow, because I'm here for my father, and it's my place to be there, whether you like it or not. Goodnight."

~

"Well, that could have gone worse," Debbie said, as she and Shaker eased into the Jacuzzi back at the Holiday Inn. "Maybe."

"I see why you don't visit your family," Shaker mused, stretching his toes out under the water to rub Debbie's thigh. "It's just as well you aren't going to the service. I can't enter a church. The gravesite burial should be okay, though I'll stand a fair distance from the priest."

Debbie nodded, her eyes closed, relaxing in the water.

"We haven't really talked about the wedding. Did you want something like a party, or something with just the two of us?"

Debbie forced a tired smile. "I want something very simple, with probably Sheila there as a witness." She paused. "Is there anyone you want there?"

"Rip would love to come, but like I said, he's often in trouble and might not be able to. Titus will want to come, and bring Leri, his wife. Other than that....there's no one else."

"Who would we get to officiate anyway?" Debbie asked. "Just a justice of the peace?"

"That would be best, so there are no religious overtones. Let me talk to Titus."

The way he said it made Debbie think he was more than a little familiar with marital vows. "How many times have you been married?"

Shaker frowned at her and didn't answer.

"How many times?"

"How many times have *you* been married?"

"I was kind of engaged to Henry, and a few other men before him, but I never went and actually tied the knot. Now answer."

"I've never said the 'til death do us part' to anyone," Shaker admitted. "Because I can't die. I really don't want to say it to you, either. I always found it grim."

"I think it's grim, too. Why don't we say 'til love and desire falters'?"

"Loyalty," Shaker said, after a moment. "Until loyalty falters."

Do you not want to say that you love me aloud? Debbie asked him mentally.

It's wiser not to. This must be thought to be another binding ritual, not anything more.

It is something more, though?

Shaker met her eyes. *You can see enough of my thoughts and feelings to know that it is.*

Debbie smiled at him sexily. *Tell me mentally, then.*

You're sexy and I want you, o' bride to be.

Don't tease. You haven't ever said it. I understand why, aloud. But if you feel it, say it.

Shaker chuckled mentally, even as he continued to watch her with a teasing smile. *You say it first.*

I love you.

Shaker blinked, as if he hadn't expected her to actually say it. A fleeting look of happiness graced his features, then he stifled a grin. *Very well. I love your resilience, your adaptability, your sexiness, your savvy, and your clever maneuvering. I didn't expect you to fall for me, even though I admit, I'm a real catch.*

No diversions tonight. Debbie crossed to his lap, then threw her arms around his neck. *I don't expect you to start quoting poetry. I just want to know you really want this, the real you that is caged inside all the rules you have to follow.*

Shaker hugged her tightly. *Yes, I want this. I want to be here with you.* He moved back, then began kissing her insistently.

"So you're in the mood now?" Debbie teased.

"In the movies, after a big emotional moment, sex is a given," he murmured. "Besides, it's what we both want."

"You're right," Debbie said, her eyes glinting happily with unshed tears, as she drew him in for a kiss.

∾

Debbie came awake with a gasp, clutching beside her for Shaker. But he was missing. She drew several deep draughts of air, then sat up in bed, her eyes focusing on the spirit of her father at the foot of the bed, staring at her. She let out a scream.

Shaker materialized near her, as the ghostly form of her father disappeared. "Shh," he said, sitting beside her. "He can't hurt you. He's just coming to terms with death. He'll pass on soon and be gone from this plane."

Debbie clutched at Shaker, fighting not to hyperventilate. "Can't you do anything for him?"

"I've just come from seeing my brother, Titus. He advised me not to attempt to help your father's spirit. If I were to lay hands on him, there's a chance I could send him to hell just from demon contamination. He said he's likely sticking around for his funeral. A lot of the newly dead do that, to say a final goodbye." He squeezed her tight, then let her go. "Why don't you get dressed, and we'll go have a good breakfast?"

"I admit that does sound good," Debbie said, getting out of bed with a yawn. "Mother is likely to have a lot of pretty ornate food at the reception that tastes like cardboard, so it's wise to eat well this morning." She cracked a weak grin.

Shaker smiled widely. "There are few problems that bacon can't fix, in my experience. And those can be handled with pancakes topped with copious syrup. Come, Mistress."

∾

Although Shaker and Debbie lingered over an elaborate breakfast, they arrived before the end of the funeral service at Church of Christ. "I'm just going to go in for a moment," Debbie said, over Shaker's protests. "Dad wouldn't care if I skipped his service, but I would like to speak to the pastor."

"Fine, but wait for him outside, where I can see you," Shaker cautioned.

Debbie looked at him strangely. "There's no danger here. It's hallowed ground, right?"

"Yes, inside the church and possibly also the grounds, so I can't follow you."

"I'll stay in sight," Debbie promised. She got out of the rental car, clutching her large black hat that threatened to fly off in the strong wind. With an angry grunt, she whipped it off and tossed it to Shaker, then hurried to the large double doors.

She felt a tingling in her legs as she walked to the door, as if electrical currents were coming up from beneath the ground. At first it was an annoyance, but it became stronger the closer she got to the door. She brought her feet down hard on the last few steps, trying to dispel the buzzing feeling in her soles, then pulled on the handle. It wouldn't budge.

It can't be locked. It's a funeral. Debbie tried again, then let go of the door. Suddenly, the door opened from the other side, as people began to pour out of the doors, some dabbing at their moist eyes. Quickly, Debbie pasted a smile on her face, as some of them began giving her their condolences.

Her uncle Stuart came out, as she hugged another well-wisher. "Your mother's been looking for you."

"I was in the back," Debbie lied. "I got here late and didn't want to make a spectacle."

"Where's your fiancé?"

"Waiting with the car."

"Good, for once you've done something proper," her mother said crisply, as she came down the stairs in her conservative black dress and small veil. "Come. The limo's just pulling to the curb."

Debbie forced a smile, then got into the limo with her mother and uncle. They rode in unpleasant silence to the cemetery, Debbie speaking to Shaker mentally.

I'll wait for you near the car, he said in her mind for the third time. *Remember, I can't come to you in there, so be careful.*

The only thing to fear here is my mother's nastiness. Debbie disembarked quickly, then straightened her skirt, following her mother and uncle to the grave where the casket was being unloaded, the pastor waiting expectantly. A few other mourners had followed them from the church, and were waiting to the side, held back by the pastor's wife.

Debbie stood awkwardly near the yawning hole of freshly dug earth, feeling the dewy grass soak her shoes, as the pastor talked about how her father had been such a pillar of the community. He closed with thanking her family for all they had done for others over the years. *Mom must have written that speech and asked him to say it.*

Her uncle handed her a rose, and she tossed it on the coffin, as it was lowered into the ground. *Goodbye Dad.* Turning, Debbie noticed that most of the other people had already left, and that her mother was speaking to the pastor, her uncle to the side looking uncomfortable.

"I understand you have some happy news," the pastor said, coming over to Debbie. He reached for her hand. Debbie jerked back, remembering the electrical buzzing she'd felt at the church, but the pastor's hand was just warm flesh as it clasped hers, nothing more.

Debbie smiled with relief. "Yes. I'm getting married."

"After the reception," her mother barked at both of them, walking away quickly to the limo, Debbie's harried-looking uncle in tow.

"We must obey the queen," the pastor quipped with a small smile. "I can talk to you tomorrow morning before or after Sunday Services, if you have some time."

Maybe I can ask him about demons. "Sure, Father, that would be great."

"Just John," the pastor corrected. "Or Father John, if you must.

I'm trying for a less formal and more friendly church. 'Less damnation and more salvation' is our online slogan."

"Mother must love that," Debbie commented, unsure what else to say.

"She's adjusting," Father John said. "Church attendance isn't what it was when we were young, sadly. The church has to be less rigid with believers to keep them." He smiled. "But this isn't a day to talk about church doctrine. I'm sorry for your loss. I'll hope to see you tomorrow Debbie. God bless you."

Debbie hurried after him, seeing Shaker talking to the pastor's wife near their cars. After saying farewell, Debbie got into the car. "How did you get in here?"

"Apparently the ground isn't hallowed, is the short version," Shaker said happily. "This isn't just a Christian cemetery, so they must bless individual graves. They're prohibited from consecrating the ground. It's hard to believe how fast faith has fallen in the last century."

"The pastor said as much," Debbie murmured, as Shaker drove them to the reception.

~

At ten the next morning, Debbie and Shaker went to the reading of the will. "I hope I'm getting points for all these things I'm going to that I don't actually get to attend," Shaker teased, as he sat down in the lawyer's outer office.

Debbie made a face at him, then went in. Her mother and uncle were already there waiting.

"Now that we're all here, let's begin." The lawyer formally read the will's beginning about debts being paid, then went on to bequeathments. "To my brother, Stuart Tennison, I leave my Porsche and my condo in Aspen, Colorado and a sum of five hundred thousand dollars."

Stuart looked visibly relieved.

"To my daughter Debbie Tennison, also known as Debbie Deal, I leave the sum of five hundred thousand dollars for use in her production company Pandora Productions, and my hunting cabin in New York." The lawyer put down the will, and picked up a small wooden box, handing it to Debbie. "And the contents of this box."

Debbie took it, then popped the lid. Inside were some photos of her father and her as a little girl, and a thin envelope with her name on it.

"The remainder of my estate and holdings I leave to my wife, Kallia." The lawyer made a polite smile. "We have some papers for each of you to sign. Mr. Tennison's estate is in very good standing, his final services were prepaid in advance, and much of what you had, Kallia, was joint, so most of it is formality."

"None of it a surprise," Debbie's mother said, standing.

"Oh, really," Debbie said, getting to her feet. "You told me not to expect anything."

"Yes, but not that you wouldn't get anything." Her mother managed a smile that looked like a corpse's grimace, all teeth. "The pastor said you were coming to see him tomorrow about the wedding. I'm glad you came to your senses." Before Debbie could answer, she strode out.

"I'm glad for you, Debbie," Stuart said, giving her a hug. "Your father was very proud of you, for breaking away and going after your dreams. He went to see all your movies, even the horror ones." Her uncle laughed. "He dragged me along. So I have to ask, is your fiancé that Jett Black, your action star? The one from *Smoke and Ashes*?"

"The one and only," Shaker drawled, as he stepped into the room. He offered his hand. "Glad to meet you."

"So, will there be a sequel? The ending seemed to indicate there would be."

Shaker nodded. "We've shot most of the scenes already, yes. Hopefully by Christmas."

"That's great news. Consider one ticket sold." Stuart hugged her again. "And I expect an invite to the wedding, niece. I don't mind coming to California, either."

"I'm sorry I haven't kept in touch," Debbie sniffled, suddenly overcome.

"I know why you didn't," her uncle soothed gently. "But I hope you will now. We're not getting any younger, as your mother likes to say."

"You're right," Debbie said. "I promise, I will."

Debbie gingerly approached the church, worried that she'd again feel the buzzing sensation coming through the ground up her legs. But oddly this morning the feeling was absent.

"Come in," the pastor said, opening the door. He took her arm and led her inside, then towards his office.

Debbie's relief at getting into the church was short lived, as the buzzing sensation came again up her legs, stronger this time, as if she were walking on electrified metal in bare feet. She stopped still. "Can we just sit here, Father John?"

"Of course," he said, indicating a pew.

"I'm not planning on having the wedding here," Debbie blurted out, as they sat. "Not because I don't like you, Father, but because I want my wedding to be my own." *And not here, God, now that electrified feeling is coming up through my back and ass.*

Father John nodded, as Debbie tried not to fidget. "I understand. I thought you might. But I do wish you'd reconsider. Your mother might seem strong, but your father's death has thrown her some. She's going to have a lot to do, running the company by herself."

"What about my uncle?"

"He's always helped out, but he's travelling most of the time, checking on big customers around the country. Your mother and father handled most of the day-to-day responsibilities. I know your company is important to you. But your family is important, too."

"I'm hoping to build a family, one of my own," Debbie said without thinking, then flushed, knowing Shaker had heard her. "This has all been a lot to deal with. I'm not planning on making any big decisions about my life this year, other than to get married. And I do have my own company to run, that I've put my heart and soul into." *The latter literally.*

The buzzing feeling suddenly increased. Debbie struggled to her feet.

"What's the matter?" Father John said, his brows knitting.

"I tell you, there's something here!" came an insistent voice. "I can feel it." Another young pastor came into view, agitated.

A large man was following him. This tall man stopped still, then swiveled his head to stare right at Debbie. "I feel it too."

He knows. Somehow, he knows. Shaker!

There was no response.

"Go in the back, I'll check the front."

The young pastor hurried back in the direction he'd come. The tall man headed right for Debbie.

Shaker!

Debbie headed for the door, making excuses to Father John of forgetting the plane was leaving early, anything to get to the door. But the tall man was faster and blocked her path.

Father John nodded. "I'll hope to see you soon, Debbie, but not too soon. You take care of yourself, and please let me know if you change your mind. Bless you." He turned and headed away. Debbie thought to call him back, but she knew it wouldn't be any use. *He might care about me, but he's not going to save me from a demon hunter.*

"Hello," the tall man said. "Your name is Debbie?"

"You already know that," Debbie said defensively. "Did you send those priests away?"

"Pastors," the man corrected. "And yes. One is a kindly old man who just wants to help people. The other can feel the demon bound to you and would kill you where you stand, if I hadn't shielded you."

"Why would you do that? Who are you?"

"I'm an angel, of course."

CHAPTER FIVE

"WHY WOULD AN ANGEL HELP ME?" DEBBIE SAID sarcastically. "I've never been what you'd call religious."

"I wasn't sent here for you," the man corrected. "I felt your father's anguish at his sudden end, and just came to push him in the right direction for salvation. Once on this plane, I heard the prayers of the young pastor, Father Matthew." He smiled, but it wasn't friendly. "He's what you'd call very religious, and because of that, favored."

"Favored?"

"Blessed. Specifically to be able to feel evil," the man said. "He can feel you. We only have a few minutes."

"Who are you!"

"Rafael," the angel said, not offering a hand. "Please consider what you are doing, Debbie. Marrying a demon—because that's what you must be considering, if you're bound to one—isn't something you can come back from."

Now that Father Matthew had gone, the buzzing Debbie felt was ebbing, but the electrified feeling remained, as she shifted her feet continuously. "Why are you concerned about me? I wouldn't think being married would matter, as I'm already damned being bound to him."

"Damnation isn't as simple as that," Rafael said. "Yes, you're doing evil, and you should stop. But I can see your soul isn't spoken for, so the bond you have isn't unbreakable. Is it new?"

"What is that buzzing I feel?" Debbie demanded, ignoring his question. "And if you're an angel, why don't I feel it with you?"

"We aren't demons, to announce our presence so coarsely," Rafael said. "That buzzing is a warning that you're around someone of real faith, someone who can likely sense true evil. I'd take that warning to heart." He looked up towards the altar. "He's coming back. You'd better go."

"Wait..."

Rafael pushed her towards the exit. "Think on what I've said. Consider if the life you're living is one you'll look back on with pride years from now, if you endure that long."

Debbie staggered out into the sunlight, then hurried to the rental car and got in, breathing hard.

Mistress? Are you okay?

Yes, just was telling the priest that we wouldn't be getting married here. It was a hassle.

All right. But hurry back. We have to catch that plane. I'm getting the bags to the car and checking out now.

Debbie looked over at the church grounds, then got out of the car, and went back onto the grass, sitting beside the sign. *Shaker?*

There was no answer.

The connection to him is broken on consecrated ground. Yet I can walk on it, even being bound to him. Something to remember.

～

"What are you doing?" Sheila yelled, as Debbie swerved suddenly into the church parking lot.

Debbie didn't reply, just hurriedly parked and dragged a still-protesting Sheila out of the car and onto the church grounds. "Call to Song or Harp. Or hell, both of them."

Sheila concentrated for a minute, then opened her eyes, surprised. "They aren't answering."

"Being on hallowed ground—a church, some graves, probably a pastor's home—does something to the connection between them and us. The demons can't listen in."

"I've never heard you refer to them that way before," Sheila said slowly, studying Debbie. "Has something happened between you and Shaker?"

"We don't have a lot of time," Debbie said, setting the timer on her phone for five minutes. "I really do have a doctor's appointment to get to after this, which was the reason I gave for bringing the car today to work. But I wanted to tell you what happened over the weekend." Debbie told Sheila about seeing her father's ghost, her experience at the church, and meeting Rafael. "That young priest or whatever he was, he was in league with this angel. He was like Cahill was; he could feel my connection to Shaker, using it like a dog with scent to find me. I think we're in danger."

"You are in danger," Rafael said, from behind them, leaning against the side of the church. "Even now he is looking into who was at the church that day. Sooner or later, he or someone like him will find you, if you don't renounce your evil."

"So you're the angel?" Sheila said angrily, walking up to him. "Who are you to tell us to do anything? You have no idea what we've been through."

"I'm not omnipotent, no," Rafael said. "But I can guess. You were both driven women in a man's corporate world, and you were tired of either using your body or flattery day after day just to keep pace, while weaker men advanced beyond you. So you took an old and easier path, not understanding the full consequences."

"Our path hasn't been easy at all," Sheila snapped. "You're the same as they are, Rafael. I don't remember any female angels talked about in the Bible—you're all male."

"You're correct, there are none mentioned."

"The Christian church, like almost all religions, is a male-dominated religion whose initial purpose was to keep the poor masses complacent, and in their place," Sheila stated. "It was formed to wrest the power from the female-centered Wiccan religions, labeling all women witches that didn't fall in subservient line. Don't give me crap about saving anyone's soul. The meek aren't going to inherit the earth. They aren't going to get anything or ever climb out of the gutter, because if you're meek you get shit on your whole life!"

"Suffering isn't something that anyone wants. But it is a part of human life."

"And why is that? Did you or your boss ever consider that the reason people turn away from religion is because they pray and follow all the commandments for years and nothing happens? There are no signs from God that he's even hearing them or sympathizing with their misery, much less going to bless them with good fortune. Debbie and I were raised as Christians, and neither of us are now, because praying and going to church every day didn't get us where we are. Instead we went into partnerships with beings that could help us, and what's more, were willing to work with us in the first place."

"You're not in a partnership," Rafael warned. "You're in a parasitic pact, as the host."

Debbie shivered, but shook it off, finding her voice. "Sheila's right. I appreciate your warning, Rafael. No, I don't like all the aspects of my "new relationship." But everything has a price, and everyone has their faults. Most every aspect of human life, as you refer to it, has rules to follow. Sheila and I are doing the best we can." She stepped closer to Rafael. "Keep your demon hunter away from us, or he'll end up dead. We don't want any fight with you or God, or him, we just want to run the business we both love and enjoy our lives. I don't think that's too much to ask."

"He is on a collision course with you, because of what you've chosen to do," Rafael said sadly. "I won't contradict what you've said, because it's truth and you're smart enough to see it. I can't speak for God's plan; I just play my part. But be wise enough to turn away before this runs its course."

Debbie's timer went off with a series of beeps, and she quickly stopped it. When she looked up, Rafael was gone, and Sheila was at the church door, tugging on it.

"Is it locked?"

"I can't open it."

Debbie tried it, also with no luck. "It's either locked or we can't get in. I'm guessing that we can't get in by ourselves, but if we were led in by a believer, we could. But you'd feel that electrical tingling, the same as I did."

"We need to talk to someone who's been through this before," Sheila said with a grimace, as she shifted her feet. "You're right, I can feel it too. There's obviously a few more rules we aren't aware of. But how would you be able locate someone who was once bound to a demon?"

"I'll ask Shaker tonight," Debbie said, "C'mon, I have to get you back so I can make that appointment."

"Do you think it's wise to tell him?" Sheila asked. "Although I don't see how we can keep this secret, even if we wanted."

"I don't see how, either. But we shouldn't," Debbie argued. "Bottom line is a demon hunter is on the move and coming for us. We need everyone at Pandora on alert. And ready."

∾

"You're in fine health," Debbie's general practitioner said, as he came into the room. "You're pregnant."

Debbie stared at him. "That's not possible. I've only had protected sex." *Except in dreams. No, damn it...that day before Shaker shared my dream. He asked me about protection, and I said no. Damn it!*

The doctor shrugged. "You must have had a condom leak. These are often very small, too small to notice."

"How long...um, how old is the baby...um, fetus?"

"Only three weeks, I'm guessing. I wasn't certain at first, your hormone levels are lower than normal. But we do see that sometimes in a, um...mature pregnancy."

Debbie's eyes narrowed. "You mean a woman who's forty plus."

"Yes," the doctor replied with a quick smile. "But that doesn't mean you can't have a healthy pregnancy and child. You should see your gynecologist as soon as possible, and also begin prenatal vitamins. No alcohol, if you usually drink, and no smoking. If you don't exercise, I recommend some light walking, to strengthen your legs, to prepare for the weight gain."

"I don't smoke," Debbie replied dully. *But I do need a drink.*

When Shaker came home that evening, Debbie was sipping a glass of wine and eating a huge bag of chips on the couch.

"Bad day?" he asked, setting down his keys and jacket.

"I met an angel who told me I was damned for being with a demon, and I'm pregnant," Debbie said crossly. "I'm not sure how more bad it could be."

"Bad enough for broken English," Shaker said, sitting down beside her and hugging her. "You're really pregnant?"

"Yes. Three weeks. Aren't you going to lecture me about drinking?"

"Humans have drunk while pregnant as long as there have been humans and alcohol," Shaker said. "You don't usually drink more than a glass, and you're always eating when you do. I think the last thing you need tonight is a lecture." He kissed her cheek. "Are you excited?"

"I don't know how to feel," Debbie murmured. "A baby is going to change our lives, mostly mine."

"Not that much," Shaker consoled. "We make enough money to hire a full-time nanny. Though we will have to get one that can be trusted. I'll ask Rack to recommend someone."

"No more demons!" Debbie shrieked, standing up and spilling the wine and chips as she pulled away from Shaker. "Didn't you hear what I said about that angel? Other hunters are going to come. One sensed me back at the funeral! I'm not safe anywhere, and it feels crazy to think about bringing a child into this situation!"

"Children were born in world wars, during famine and plague, and during genocides with much less scientific advancement, much more superstition, and less legal protection," Shaker said darkly. "Yes, some died, but enough lived to keep the population almost always growing. If you want to have this baby, odds are in today's world he'll be healthy."

"He?"

"Well, of course I'm hoping for a boy." Shaker beamed. "It would be the first one in my family for a long time. A very long time."

Debbie's eyes widened in horror. "He'd be half-demon?"

"There'd be something of me in the child," Shaker said evasively. "But your doctor told you a condom likely leaked. I haven't purposely been trying to impregnate you. Most of this baby will be Jett's child; probably his larger build, dark hair, and his blue eyes, or maybe your brown ones." He got up and walked to her, enfolding her in his arms. "I'm really happy for us. I know this was a shock, but I think it's a good thing."

"I do, too," Debbie whispered, clutching him suddenly as if her life were at stake. "I just didn't expect it this soon. We're going to have to get married quicker than I wanted."

"We can go tomorrow morning to the justice of the peace and start our honeymoon," Shaker said with a grin. "*Smoke and Ashes II* is finished. I'm not due on another set until mid-summer."

"Yes, but I'm not sure I want that," Debbie said slowly. "I have a full schedule at Pandora, Shaker. This is the worst possible time. I can't just leave with you."

"I knew you'd say that," Shaker said gently, giving her a hug. "But I wanted to offer, just the same." He cleared his throat. "And I know no one asks me, but in my breaks the past month, I penned a sequel to *Smoke and Ashes II*. I think it makes a good trilogy ending."

"Trilogy?"

"Think about *Star Wars*. There's a group of movies in one time frame, then it jumps to the next. We have the events of the first movie going right into the second, why not have them go from there into the third, like the Tolkien trilogies?"

"Putting yourself in some illustrious company," Debbie said with a smirk. "Have you had anyone else look at it?"

"Sheila's read the first half, and given me back a bunch of notes, most of them elaborating on scenery. She loved the dialogue. I want to begin shooting this month, before some of the sets and costumes we used for the second movie are stored. It'll save us both money and time. Can you give approval?"

Debbie drew back from Shaker, looking into his eyes worriedly. *Is something coming?*

Yes. I saw us trying to begin filming on this movie at the end of the year, and that it's never completed, Jett's series stops with two movies. I don't want that for myself or for Pandora. But if I shoot scenes this month and into March, maybe even April, I think I can get the vital parts of the picture done. The people playing the priest and the little girl have already said yes when I mentioned my idea to them, and everyone else from the first two films is dead, so we've got a good base.

"What about *Immortal Confessions*? That's slated to shoot most of the year, and it's just begun. We need all the stages for the different time periods."

"They worked on *Absolution* first, like you asked them to, while we were away," Shaker said. "Apparently its going really fast, supernaturally so."

"Are you helping that?"

"No, Rack is giving advice to the actor playing the demon, so when he's coming on for his parts, he's nailing them perfectly; evil yet sympathetic compared to the abusive human brother, the husband's rival for the heroine in the movie. Most of the movie is about empowering the female to stand up for what she wants and deserves. It's coming together nicely."

"So you think because that's going ahead of schedule, the vampire epic will also?"

"No, that's going to drag on, because Devlin's protesting every little change we ask for," Shaker said. "I have already called Joshua to ask him to have Devlin here nights, so the two of them can go over the key scenes or details from the previous day. I think when Devlin sees how much goes into a film, he'll work with us to get it right while still sticking to schedule. Or he'll call in some supernatural help to create the effect he wants. Either way, it's in our favor."

"Speaking of favors," Debbie said. "I hadn't chosen anyone this year for you. But I have been thinking of Henry. Titan Pictures has stayed off our radar so far, but today Henry sent me an email, asking why the stock deal was reversed. It's clear he thinks Pandora's in trouble, but I can't help thinking he wants something else. He also saw your real form at that party. Otherwise...choose whomever you feel would pose the least risk to you, and to what you and I are trying to do."

"Others also saw me at that party," Shaker said with a shrug. "I don't think Henry's a threat. But yes, I'll pay him a visit to see if he's eligible, so to speak. Thank you, Mistress. But what about the sequel?"

"Go ahead and start filming. What did you call it?

"*Destiny in the Ashes*. But I'm open to change that. Harp asked by the way that you stop at the Black Rose and use up the credit they still have for you," Shaker said. "Sorry, I keep forgetting to tell you."

Debbie nodded absently.

"What about Valentine's Day?" Shaker persisted. "It's our first being officially together, so I know I should do something grand, but I'm not sure what. It's this Friday."

How can so much have happened in two short weeks? "You could fill my office with flowers," Debbie offered, laughing. "Or how about a new car? Or adding on another room for a nursery to the house? I'm still not sure what we're going to do about that."

"All right, Shaker said, nodding. "But please stop by the Black Rose tomorrow. Harp was insistent."

～

Debbie paused before the smoked glass door emblazoned with the ebony rose. *You can do this. You need to do it: your hair is more roots than blonde, and your nails are a mess. It's stupid for you to have nerves at all, you're getting like Sheila.*

She pushed open the doors, then did a double take. The inside of the spa had been completely redone. Satin black curtains hung from the ceiling draped along all the windows and pooled on the floor, blocking out all daylight. Doors opened off the room, but all were shut. Light came from glowing balls of different colors hanging in space near the walls. A very old incense burner emitted a sweet smoke from a small corner table, the bed of hot coals beneath it glowing in the dim light. And a desk and simple notepad stood to the right of the burner, both empty.

"Hello?"

"Hi, Debbie," Song said, hurrying out of the first door. "Sorry, it's been slow today. We do most of our business at night now."

That explains Sheila's complaint about Song being gone a lot. "Catering to vampires?"

"Some, yes," Song said with a happy nod. "But also others that prefer no or little daylight. That's why we redesigned the spa. I also hoped that Sheila would come in, and didn't want her to recognize the place, trigger any bad memories, you know? But she never has."

"I encouraged her to," Debbie said. "It's beautiful."

"Thank you. So what do you feel like today?"

"What do you have? It's been so long I can't remember honestly what I had last time." Debbie laughed, wincing inwardly at the nervous giggle. *Relax already.*

"Well, we still have mudwraps; I recommend one of those. And we'll take care of your nails and hair, too. We also still offer massages with various oils, brow and lash tinting, and facials." She flashed a wicked smile. "But we have branched out, if you're feeling adventurous."

Debbie turned her head, looking at her with an answering smile. "I'm not sure how naughty I'm up to being. I just found out I'm pregnant."

Song's mouth fell open, then she jumped up and hugged Debbie, shrieking in glee. "What! I can't believe it, really? That's fabulous! I'm so excited for you and Shaker."

"Thanks," Debbie said, flushing. "I'm pretty nervous."

"Understandable," Song said, grimacing. "But don't believe all the bad things you hear about half-demon babies. There's a lot that can be done now to make sure that the birth is survivable."

It was Debbie's turn to gasp. "'Survivable?' What? What are you saying? No one's told me anything bad. Shaker didn't say anything!"

"Because he's a Big Bad, and he's got his brother Titus," Song said quickly, grabbing Debbie's hand. "Titus is a master of healing and Shaker's equal in magic. He'll be able to give you a very smooth pregnancy and delivery. It's really the delivery that's the issue, not the pregnancy. I'm sorry, I shouldn't have said anything." She quickly led Debbie into a room. "Here, please get undressed, and I'll sent in Xerxes to give you a massage and mud wrap. If you are interested, he can tell you about our other offerings." She got out a black robe from a small cabinet and laid it on the massage table. Before Debbie could protest, she was gone.

Well, you came here to relax. You might as well relax until you can talk to Shaker. Debbie undressed and waited in the room, the robe soothing in its thick soft terry.

A dark-skinned man came in, his mustache long and oiled, his dress just a toga. He bowed slightly to her, then indicated a bunch of oils.

He looks…Ottoman, as in Turk. "Lavender?" Debbie asked.

The man nodded solemnly, then gestured to the table. Debbie disrobed, then lay face down on the table, as Xerxes laid a warmed blanket over her. He snapped his fingers, and the soothing sound of lute accompanied by a waterfall flooded her senses. He began with her left foot, stroking and prodding her sore muscles.

Within ten minutes, Debbie was relaxed. By the time the massage was over, she felt like an overcooked lasagna noodle floating languidly in a pot of warm water.

Xerxes patted her hand chastely to get her attention, then put a few jars within her gaze.

"The rosemary-mint, please."

Xerxes then began spreading out a towel, then spreading mud over Debbie's body, the warmth suffusing her already relaxed body. She sighed happily, as she was coated, then wrapped in a body towel.

"Stay and rest," Xerxes said, surprising Debbie out of her stupor. "I will return in ten minutes."

"Um, are you going to do my hair and nails too?"

"Yes, after."

Debbie mused over his initial lack of speech, then began to doze. She stirred when Xerxes reentered the room and began to remove the mud with a warm washcloth.

When she was clean, Xerxes lay her robe within her reach. "I was told to tell you about our other offerings. Would you like to hear?"

"Yes."

"We offer facial rejuvenation. It lasts for about a month, but the effect is better than any dermal filler or facelift. But it's costly at five hundred dollars per application."

"Please go on."

"We offer glamours, mostly fairy magics. These last only at most a week and at least a day but are very effective. Mostly patrons ask for different hair or facial features, though sometimes they want to be truly someone else. The more change, the more expensive the potion. Prices start at fifty dollars and can go up to thousands."

"Why would someone pay that much?"

Xerxes smiled. "To follow a cheating spouse and not be seen. To entice a bored lover. To seduce a lover that refused the person in their true form. We've even had an older woman use it to look like a younger rival, to get her husband to admit where he hid some marital assets."

"Go on."

"The last option is our most popular, but most expensive. It's called Incubus. It's a lover that visits you in dreams, fulfilling your every desire. It will make you need more sleep than usual, but we have several people now that come back for it monthly."

Had this been why Sheila had proposed the movie idea of the same name, because her demons had mentioned a real life one they were employing at their spa? "I'm surprised they don't want nightly visitations," Debbie joked.

"They would, if we allowed it. But it wouldn't be responsible to do that."

"You'd probably get complaints from a lot of husbands."

"And wives," Xerxes corrected. "But it would be worse than that. The people would die from…overdose, so to speak. It can be quite an addictive…experience."

He's serious. Shit. "I'll pass," Debbie said quickly, sitting up. "Thank you for your time. I'd just like my nails done, and my hair. I'd like to go darker."

Xerxes nodded. "Of course. I'll take the grey out. Come with me."

I didn't realize it was so obvious. "Thanks."

Xerxes took her to another room which was a more traditional salon, where he did Debbie's hair, then her nails and toenails. When he was finished, Debbie stood, admiring her new darker tresses, then her neat red-hued nails. "Thank you. I feel so much better."

"Dark blessings be on you." Xerxes bowed, then opened the nearest door, leading back to the spa's front desk. Song was at the desk, talking to two females. They turned to look at her as she entered, then they looked at one another knowingly.

You're making me lose my happy thoughts, bitches. "Hi," Debbie forced out. "Do you know me?"

"We know of you," one said, but her tone was respectful, not snide.

Debbie waited, but the woman didn't elaborate. "I hope you heard good things."

"No," the other tittered. "But we like you much more for that. Your humanity is…refreshing."

"What are you?" Debbie asked bluntly.

"So rude," the other laughed. "But we enjoy that, too. We are goblins, from overseas. We just teleported in for the day. I'm Sylvia and she is Jezebel." The woman touched her arm conspiratorially. "You know how it is, trying to teleport in from out of town. You never know who might be standing in the spot you're going to, or be nearby, and witness you appear. Here, it's not a problem."

"I understand that," Debbie said with a smile, nodding. "So much has to be kept secret."

"We thought you might," Jezebel said with a nod. "Take care and be careful. There's been word locally of a young priest here in town searching. It's whispered he's hunting demons."

"I know of him," Debbie replied with a frown. "I'll be careful."

"Please see that you do," Sylvia said. "We are grateful for what you have done." She extended her hand, a card offered.

Debbie took it. "The Two Sisters. But it doesn't say what you do."

"Magic, of course! But only what we approve." Sylvia smirked, a large fang popping into view. "And we are extremely expensive. But if you need something done to perfection, we're the women to call."

"Thank you," Debbie said, taking the card. "I'll be in touch, if something comes up."

"More like something comes down," Jezebel said darkly, her eyes far distant on some unseen vision. "It's coming, Debbie. You'll want to call us before it does."

Debbie wasn't sure if this was a trick to elicit business, or real. She glanced at Song, the horrorstruck expression on her face galvanizing her. "When, and what is coming?"

"Your carefully built house of cards is facing a tornado," Jezebel intoned. "The first card will fall this summer, another by October. Act by then, or all is lost."

Debbie, unsure if she should reach for her purse to put a deposit down or brush off the warning as overdone theatrics had no time to do either before the two sisters disappeared. She wheeled on Song. "What the hell was that all about?"

"Nothing to do with Hell," Song said, holding up both hands plaintively. "Jezebel's always had visions, and people have paid her for hundreds of years for timely warnings. But Sylvia is not her sister, and I'm not even sure that's her real name. I'm not sure what they're up to, either, except here getting normal spa treatments, nothing supernatural."

"Are most of your guests now non-human?"

Song nodded. "It makes it easier, not having to hide what I am all the time. I really enjoy running the spa. Once I put out feelers for some help, we had several come in like Xerxes right away."

"What is he?"

"A faerie. That's 'ea', with an 'ie' on the end; no y's. Don't think they are either cute or sweet. They can be fearsome. He's very fair though, if quiet."

"He was very good," Debbie said, pulling out her wallet. "I should leave him a tip, actually."

"That's wise," Song said, taking Debbie's proffered cash. "The treatments you had used up half of your old credit. If you'd like to book now, I can set up another appointment with the same treatments to use up the last?"

"Yes," Debbie said with a happy sigh. "I'd forgotten how good it felt to be pampered."

"We have discount packages for six months, or a year; one treatment a month is the smallest," Song said, offering her a brochure. "Prices increase depending on what you would get. And for you…everything is half-price. I'm sorry it's not free, Debbie, but I have to pay my workers, so that's the lowest I can go."

"That's okay," Debbie said, touching Song's arm gently. "I appreciate the gesture. And yes, I'll take one of the packages with two treatments a month. I'll try to get Sheila back down here next month, in fact. She could use some time relaxing. She seems really stressed out lately."

Song forced a smile. "I hope you can, Debbie. That would be wonderful."

～

"Rack…er, Richard," Debbie said, as the demon walked into her office. "Show me what you've got."

Rack nodded once, then opened his bag, producing a bottle. Smoke curled up the sides of the label, and a pile of ashes was at the bottom. "Brimstone," he said, handing the bottle to her. "A deep red, peppery Shiraz mixed with a robust burgundy, not something you see often."

"I like that the letters appear to be burned into the label, like it's charred."

"Where there's smoke and ashes, there's usually fire," Rack said. "Go ahead and taste that, see what you think. If it's too unusual, I'll keep the label but just substitute a Malbec instead."

"And *Absolution*?"

"For that, I chose instead a white, as for everything else so far we've used reds. The bottle is also clear, to symbolize a redeemed soul. The lettering for that is silver on white paper in stark font, but we can change that, if you like."

"No, I like that quite a bit," Debbie said, studying the bottle.

"Take that home as well and taste it. Shaker knows his wine. He can taste it, if you don't like white wine."

I could, if he was home anymore at night, and wasn't exhausted when he was. Debbie pushed the thought away. "Sure, I'll do that. I have to be careful of my alcohol consumption anyway, I'm expecting."

Rack started, blinking rapidly. "You're pregnant?"

Debbie nodded, flushing. "Sorry, I seem to be telling everyone lately. I never thought before of how much carrying a child affects everything you do even before it's born."

"Yes, it does. But I'd caution you about releasing this information to too many people. I will keep your confidence, Debbie. But please, be prudent on what you say, and to whom."

"All right," Debbie agreed, slightly annoyed. "Do you have anything else for me?"

"No, as there are no other new movies on the schedule," Rack said smoothly. "Unless something has changed."

"Please see Sheila," Debbie said, thinking of Shaker's warning about the haunted isle movie. "She has a few projects we are probably going to green light by the end of the year. You might as well get a jump on wine selection."

"Very well," Rack said, with a pleased smile. "I'll get right on it."

～

Debbie yawned, then looked at the clock. *Damn, it's nearly nine-thirty. Where was Shaker?*

Feeling another twinge of nerves, Debbie looked longingly at the full wine rack on the kitchen counter. *Don't do it. You're expecting. And it's too late for a drink anyway, you've got to go to bed. You have to get more sleep, for yourself and the baby.*

Stifling another yawn, Debbie put aside her laptop and rubbed at her eyes. *Two hours, and not much to show for it, girl, except tired eyes. And you have to face facts: you're going to need some reading glasses pretty quick.*

Debbie hadn't thought much of her eyes couldn't even remember the last time she'd been to the eye doctor. But she'd always had 20/20 vision, no problems. And now…now the printed script pages and memos were slightly blurry. She could make out what they said, but how long would that last?

Debbie felt a sudden rush of panic and squashed it down. *Grow up, you're a big girl. You knew this would happen. All women go through this along with slowing metabolism, wrinkles, and grey hair. What did you think, that you'd be the one to somehow escape it?*

Debbie sighed, got up, and went to the bathroom, brushing her teeth before she surveyed her reflection in the mirror. *Yes, that's it exactly. I never thought it would happen to me. And now it is.*

Debbie grabbed a brush, and began tearing it through her hair, looking angrily for grey hairs caught in the bristles and finding several. Swearing, she threw down the brush, cracking the plastic handle. Gritting her teeth, she set the brush aside and grabbed the mouthwash, taking a mouthful. She was just swishing it around her teeth when a sudden noise came from the living room.

Her eyes bulged, and she spat it as quietly as she could in the sink, listening, too worried to call out. *Shaker! I need you!*

"Debbie?" came Titus's rumbling voice. "Are you here?"

It's okay, Shaker said in Debbie's mind. *Titus has brought Devlin to congratulate you. He couldn't keep the news to himself. And Devlin isn't a man accustomed to boundaries. Just be polite, please.*

Debbie's muscles went weak with relief, and she sat down on the toilet, suddenly near tears. With effort, she shook it off, wrapped a robe around herself, then went out. "I'm in here, Titus."

"Enchante, Deborah," Devlin said, stepping into view clad in jeans and a denim jacket. "How are you, lovely mom-to-be? I asked Titus to bring me by when he told me the news." He leaned down close to her waist. "Little child, blessings be on you. I will be most pleased to make your acquaintance."

His tone was odd, but so was him just coming to her home this time of night, no matter the reason. Why would Devlin care about a baby? *Shaker, what's this about?*

"I wanted to see you, is the real reason," Titus said kindly, taking her hands in his clawed ones. "Devlin just wanted to add his congratulations." He looked her over carefully, being obvious in what he was doing.

"Is there something you're looking for?" Debbie asked, glaring at him.

"Just to see if you're healthy," Titus said. "And you are. Please don't be alarmed, I'm just excited for you and my brother. Rip will be also."

"Well, thank you for the congrats," Debbie said with a firm smile. "But it's late, and I should get to bed."

"Of course," Devlin said with a nod. "You both need your sleep. Rest well." He left a small white bag festooned with silver ribbons on a nearby end table. "With my blessings."

"I have something else for you," Titus said. He whistled.

There was a deep chuff, and then from the nearest shadow, a large mastiff-type dog appeared, as if he'd been sitting there the entire time. His eyes were black, and his coat was black, his upright ears pricked attentively. But he was thin, almost gaunt.

Titus handed Debbie a collar made of matte hammered metal, lined with cloth. "Put this on him."

"What's his name?" Debbie asked, as she buckled on the collar. "There are no tags."

"Guardian," Titus supplied.

"Where did you get him?" Debbie said, excited but also worried

96

about taking on a pet when she already was overwhelmed. "What do I feed him? Has he had his shots?"

"This is not a mortal dog," Titus replied. "He truly will be a guardian to you, able to come out of any shadow when he is needed. He won't require dog food, just some meat now and again with water. He will not need any vet care. Shaker will show you what to do."

That sounds ominous. "Is he a demon?"

"A hellhound," Shaker said, as he appeared nearby. "Brother, you shouldn't have."

"Debbie needs a guardian, one that can be with her at all times," Titus said firmly. "Guardian will do that. Give him flesh and blood, the fresher the better."

Okay, I need a break now. "Thank you for your gifts," Debbie said politely. "I appreciate them. But I have to go lie down, I'm feeling pretty rotten."

"Goodnight," Titus said, taking hold of Devlin's arm. They disappeared.

Shaker petted the hound, who allowed it but had eyes only for Debbie.

"Aren't you going to say something?" Debbie said. "And where have you been?"

"Working," Shaker replied coolly. He headed into the shower.

Debbie swore under her breath, then climbed into bed. The hound climbed up beside her, and lay next to her leg, looking at her.

"I don't know anything about dogs," Debbie said, reaching out her hand tentatively to touch its sleek head. "Guardian. So you're going to guard me?"

The dog raised its head, inclined it slightly, then nodded.

Debbie froze. "You understand me?"

The dog nodded once.

"Can you talk?"

The dog shook its head, then whined.

"I have some meat in the fridge," Debbie offered. "Do you want some?" She expected the dog to say no after Titus's speech, but it nodded eagerly, dancing on the bed and whining.

She went into the kitchen, the dog trotting quick after her. She grabbed a handful of beef deli meat, stuck it on a plate, and put it on the floor. The dog wolfed it down, then looked at her hungrily for more.

"I'll get you some more tomorrow," Debbie said, putting down a bowl of water. The hound drank only a few swallows, then sat, looking at her.

"Come," she said, going back to the bedroom. The dog fell in step beside her.

When Shaker emerged, she was lying in bed, and Guardian was lying at the foot of the bed, sleeping stretched out.

"I suppose I can get used to it," Shaker allowed, as he climbed into bed.

"Looks like you're going to have to," Debbie said curtly, turning off the light.

CHAPTER SIX

MARCH

"I can't believe it's the last day of March," Debbie said, as she ushered Sheila into her office. I'm sorry again for not being able to meet with you on these sooner."

"We had a lot to think about," Sheila replied, as she and Debbie settled into their seats. "Okay, when I spoke to you last, there were five choices: *Incubus, Hell to Pay, The Sacrifice, Origin of Fear,* and *What Matters Not.*" Have you had a chance to speak to Shaker about doing the *Origin of Fear*? That's still my favorite." She smiled widely. "I shortened the title, I think its catchy. What do you think?"

Debbie was uneasy to admit the personal information Shaker had told her, and since his flat outright refusal, they hadn't spoken more on it.

Say nothing of what I told you, Shaker said quickly. *Not to anyone. That movie must not come to pass. All that will happen if it does is that people will seek out the real island the script you were given was based on and feed the evil that's there.*

Shouldn't you want that? Debbie asked him.

I have an idea who wrote the script. Ask her who was the author.

"Debbie?" Sheila said. "Are you asking Shaker now?"

"He wants to know who the author is."

Sheila rifled to the top page. "Sonny Morning."

"Sonny Morning," Debbie repeated.

Reverse the words, Mistress.

"Morning Sonny," Debbie said slowly.

Morningstar.

Debbie stopped breathing, sitting very still. *That can't be.*

Other demons have come, wanting to be a part of Pandora. Why should the devil be any different?

I don't pretend to know the devil's mind, Debbie thought, trying to control her breathing. *But why would he do this, and not ask you himself.*

He has his own mind. But we can't be sure it's him, and not some other demon pretending to be him, wanting us to do this for some purpose of their own. It may well be the forces at the house itself that sent us this script, to draw more victims into that waiting spider's web.

"Should I come back, Debbie?" Sheila asked in exasperation.

"No, just give me minute!" *Then why not do this?*

I would think if this came from the devil, that it would come through more official means. All he would have to do is send word that this was his will, and I would agree. But as I said, I can't be sure. I advise not to act on this, to wait and see if a missive does come, or if someone else sent it, for them to reveal themselves.

Who else could it be?

I have enemies. Mostly people who would love to see me jump in fear from a trick they orchestrated. But I do have a few who truly hate me. Those like Azaroth, who I sent back to Hell. He might have networked and done this. Do nothing.

"Debbie!"

"Don't do anything with that picture, for now," Debbie said quickly, standing and walking around to try to settle her frantic nerves. "Shaker says he won't star in it. He's afraid the author is someone he knows that has a grudge."

"Well, I already bought it," Sheila snapped. "I get a say in things here, too, you know."

Debbie looked at her oddly. "Of course you do. I'm not saying that you're wrong in wanting to do it, it's perfect for Pandora. Shaker's just adamant that we don't make it this year. But if you bought the script at a good price—"

"For a song," Sheila snapped again. "I had to act, the author sent a follow up missive, saying he'd offer it to Angel Pictures if I didn't."

"Angel Pictures? I never heard of them."

"They're our new rivals," Sheila said bitterly. "They bought up both *The Sacrifice* and *What Matters Not* before I even got back to the authors. They are focusing on television for now but are already making entreaties into getting their own studio, to branch out into direct-streaming movies."

"And they wanted *Origin of Fear?*"

"Yes. They wanted *Hell to Pay*, too. I bought that, too. We've asked the author for a rewrite to alter the main characters the way you wanted. She's agreed, and said she'll have it for us by end of October, if not sooner."

"That's fast," Debbie commented, deliberately not making it clear whether she was speaking of the author or Sheila's purchase of the two films. "Very good. Well done. I'm sorry if I held you up."

Sheila shot Debbie a dark look. "I just need to do my job, Deb. I feel like I have two bosses now, you and Shaker."

"He's less boss than adviser," Debbie said carefully. "But he's been right before in the past. Schedule *Origin of Fear* for next summer, and *Hell to Pay* for the spring. Put out both for auditions for not only the cast, but a lead actor. We should finish on *Destiny in the Ashes* by then."

"I looked over the script Shaker did, but he only let me read the first half, and shooting is supposed to begin tomorrow.," Sheila complained. "I would feel better if I knew how it's supposed to end."

"I'll talk to him. But I thought it had already begun shooting? He's been going early to work the past two weeks and coming home late, saying how tired he is as soon as he gets home."

"Well, he hasn't been coming here," Sheila said, her tone malice-laden. "All we have been shooting is *Immortal Confessions.*"

She is definitely changing, and not for the better. But how to say that? I can't. "That's enough for now," Debbie said too brightly. "I'll talk to Shaker and ask him to give you the rest of the script ASAP."

"Good," Sheila said, offering up her second natural smile. "I'll get to work." She stalked out of the office.

Debbie sat back down in her chair, rubbing her temples. *I trust Shaker. But what has he been doing that he isn't telling me about? And what can I do about Sheila? I've got to do something!*

There was a knock at the door. "Ms. Deal, there's a gentleman to see you, your ten o'clock appointment."

"Send him in please."

A middle-aged man appeared, his trimmed beard and long sideburns the only thing out of current fashion. "How do you do?"

"Hi, I'm Debbie. Please have a seat. Thank you."

"I'm John. Shaker told you I wanted to invest."

This is the one with the house that's haunted that Shaker told me about. "Yes," Debbie said, shifting uncomfortably in her chair. "He said we could shoot a few scenes we needed using the outside of your home, The Chalet?"

"Yes, as long as you don't go inside the house, I am fine having the film shot there. You will also not give credit to me at the end of the film or mention the exact location to reporters. Just tell them it was filmed on a stage here."

"I can't do that," Debbie explained. "There will be others that know here—cameramen, etc.—that scenes were shot there. If I make a big deal about concealing that, as in lie about it, then someone will notice that, and blow it up into a media frenzy. Often, it's better to hide in plain sight, as the saying goes."

"Very well," John said gruffly. "I was just trying to avoid unpleasantness."

"I'm not sure what you mean."

"My house was famous some years ago for disappearances," John said, his smile dark and deadly. "It's not anymore and I'd like to keep it that way. I also am eager to help Shaker out, for his help in return. But my wife and I enjoy our solitude, and the company of close friends. Others, well..." He chuckled. "They still disappear on occasion, if they come seeking thrills we are not...predisposed to."

"Are you what Shaker is?" Debbie asked, half hoping he didn't answer.

"I am what he is," John answered, after a moment. "Or more specifically, what he was. Do you know what that means?"

Debbie took her notepad, and drew a pair of wings and a halo, then an arrow pointing down.

"Yes," John said. "You might say I'm a special case, in that I never left this plane. I can't be killed, or banished, only rendered temporarily...out of the action."

"Why?" Debbie blurted, before she thought. "Sorry, you don't have to answer that. It's none of my business."

"Because there is more than one way to disagree with a master," John said carefully. "As well as more than one disagreement to bring to the table. I chose a more diplomatic route with a lesser... insubordination. I got a lesser punishment. That's all you truly need to know."

Damn straight it is. "Thank you," Debbie said quickly. "I'm grateful for your help. Now did you have a specific picture you wanted to invest in? Or just in Pandora in general?"

"I like what you are doing for my kind," John said, ignoring the question. "I thank you for that. But please be careful in how you portray us. We truly aren't souls waiting to be saved, no matter what Shaker may have told you. We just want to have our own lives, and not feel like we are damned no matter what we do. We don't want to be portrayed as simple evil beings who can't behave or build anything worthwhile. But we do expect to be treated fairly and with respect. And nothing we give is free."

"That is actually exactly what Shaker told me," Debbie countered. "And we are being careful with the scripts we choose. In fact, we are rewriting several now for release next year to make the demons featured in them less, um…pure evil."

"I'm not saying that some demons aren't that way—base creatures of evil," John said, putting his hand up. "It is a path of the normal human seduction with those ones; terrify with evil power, then alternately bestow gifts of favor to make you believe you are still in control." The man grinned. "But you are not in control, not at all. And the truth was, you never were, Deborah Deal. Shaker has always been in control. And that is best, for the male to protect what is his."

God save me from chauvinist demons. "We are in a partnership, but I do take seriously what he has to say, as I'm sure your wife does. Her name is Victoria, I believe?"

John smiled and inclined his head, as if to show he was impressed. "Victoria was her great-grandmother. You mean Madeline. She is my wife, my one and only, heart of my heart."

"I'm sorry, yes, Madeline. You love her?"

"Yes," John said, his tone becoming soft with emotion. "She is my reason for being able to face the always-increasing pace of the world, so different now than what it was."

He's not afraid to say he can love. But he's also relatively free from punishment, by his own words. "I'm sorry, but I have to ask again, did you want to invest in a specific movie, or the company in general?"

"In *Immortal Confessions*," John said curtly. "I know Titus only by reputation, but I know he works for Devlin, who I have heard much about over the years. The picture will be a success, because Devlin will stop at nothing to make it so. There could not be a safer investment."

My urge is to tell him nothing in film is a sure bet, but that's not wise, for myself or Pandora. "I certainly hope it will be a success. And I'd be glad for you to invest in the picture. Do you want that information credited in the film? You would be named as a producer."

"Yes, I think Madeline would like that very much." John nodded in approval. "We watch a lot of movies at home."

"Then I'll arrange it. Did you have a sum in mind?"

"A hundred thousand. And the use of my mansion to represent Devlin's home." He handed her a check made out to that amount.

A hundred thousand. I knew he was rich, but I expected more. "Very well, I'm glad to have you on board, John.

"You are invited with Shaker also for dinner, if you are free some evening," John said, handing her a card. "I'll provide a feast for you both."

"Thank you," Debbie said. "I'll tell Shaker tonight. I'd love to see your home and meet your wife."

"Wonderful," John said, rising from his chair and offering his hand. "We look forward to seeing you both."

～

"How did the shooting go at The Chalet?" Debbie asked Joshua, in the next staff meeting.

"No problems. In fact, we were able to do all of the takes relatively quickly, in the space of a few days. That part of *Immortal Confessions* is done."

"That's some good news," Debbie said. "Anything else?"

"Sheila asked that you come down to see Jett's filming of *Destiny in the Ashes.* She said there's some issues to work out."

~

Debbie got out of her car and hurried down the path, zeroing in on the noise of the film crew through the trees

"Debbie!" Sheila called, motioning her over. "Good, you're just in time."

"Okay, people, places! Get to your places! Alright, anytime now, Cassandra, start the voiceover."

A woman began speaking, her tone reminiscent of a sepulcher. "The two girls were being held for ransom, held in an abandoned basement of a house that was only foundation, nothing visible above earth. Concrete and cinderblock, left there cold and ignored for years except for adventurous kids years ago. But as more had turned to video games and cells, the structure had been forgotten in its isolation. While there was a stack of rotted wood and a bare earth fire pit, the vent was structured in a way beneath some trees so that if you were careful, no one would see the smoke, or know anyone was there at all."

"This sounds like that Alex Cross movie, the first one...*Along came a Spider*," Debbie whispered to Sheila.

Sheila nodded. "Yes, but the kidnapping spot being in the woods is the only similarity."

Shaker strode onto the set, dressed in his battered jeans and denim jacket, his shoulder length black hair mussed, his bright blue eyes determined. A gun was on his hip, a flask of water in his hand.

Sheila leaned closer. "Backstory here is that the girls have been missing two weeks. Storm finds out about them by accident, a priest who had mentioned the kidnapping during a holy-water pickup. A parishioner has confessed, and he doesn't want to alert the police."

"Aren't we going to have a problem with religious discrimination or something from Catholic organizations?" Debbie asked.

"No, we'll have the ghost priest come down firmly on the side of telling authorities and condemn the live priest. Legal says no issues."

Shaker continued on the set, kneeling to read the trail.

"Smoke gets the guy to the police and kidnapper/ransomer confesses but demands that he be released or that he won't reveal the location of the girls," Sheila whispered.

"Damn that son of a bitch," Shaker swore. The cell in his pocket rang, and he answered it. "I'm at the forest. But there's no sign any person's been here. There's a lot of ground to cover, most of it forest with only rutted ATV trails. If only I had a better idea of where he's hiding the girls."

"The priest had an idea of where the girls were, but he wasn't sure exactly," Sheila supplied.

"He said that the ransom's going to be paid. That's what's being said around town. I haven't heard anything from the parents, as I haven't talked to them," Shaker said angrily. "But the girls will be dead by then. They've seen their captors in the now three weeks they'd been held. Hostages remember a face, everybody knows that."

"You see the problem?" Sheila asked pointedly.

"Yes," Debbie nodded, wincing. "You need to cut the dialogue, redo it. Maybe cut this whole scene's dialogue, just have him silent in the woods looking around with background music to increase tension. How many more of his scenes are like this? We should stop shooting until you redo the script. How old are the girls?"

"My thought exactly. Five and seven years old."

"Wait!" Shaker shouted. He took off running.

"Cut!" Bart yelled. "Okay, that's good for now. Cassandra, you get up on the end of the path over there and be ready in five."

The film crew broke down, moving fast to shoot the forest from a different angle.

"Storm meets up with an amateur sleuth that has also deduced where the girls were being held," Sheila explained. "That's

Cassandra. She's out of shape, a smoker that has to keep stopping to catch her breath."

A voluptuous young woman came into view about fifty yards away, near an old access road going up from the corner of a semi-clearing. She stopped to look at a bird, a nuthatch hanging upside down eating something, then focused on the edge of a foundation behind it, almost invisible in a heap of ferns and moss. She stopped dead, then began inching closer quiet as she could, visibly shivering slightly. She took out her phone, then swore.

Not too pretty, but interesting looking. "Who is the actress?"

"Cassy Knight, a.k.a. Selma Joya."

Cassy hurried behind a tree, hiding. She put her hands under her armpits, and moved her feet, as if trying to warm them, looking anxious.

The surface trapdoor opened behind the foundation remains. A six-foot hulk came out, solid as a linebacker and built as if he could take a full clip and not drop. He looked around as if he'd heard Cassy, but she'd approached from the back of the foundation. He looked around briefly, then headed out in the opposite direction.

Quickly, Cassy hurried to the door and opened it. The two little girls were tied up there waiting, their eyes huge and scared. Opening her pocketknife, she sawed through the ropes. Urging the older girl to follow, she carried the younger out into the now steadily falling snow.

"This is good, but why isn't Storm doing this rescuing?" Debbie whispered.

"Because we need Cassy to get us some female audience. Remember *Kickass*? That would never have done as well without Hitgirl."

Debbie nodded. "You're right. The plot seems to be great, it's just that dialogue. Yes, please rewrite the dialogue, or cut it or something."

Sheila nodded. "Glad to hear you agree. I'll start it next week. By the way, Storm has the final battle with the main bad guy you just saw walk offset. There's some really good action there, a long chase scene that ends near a house, a lot of blows exchanged where it seems the bad guy could win. That part doesn't need any help, it's pure gold."

"That's a relief," Debbie said, nodding. "And thank you, Sheila."

Sheila smiled, and for a moment, she was the old Sheila in her warmth and twinkling eyes. "You're welcome."

Just as Debbie was about to leave, another little girl peeked at her around the edge of one of the fake trees. Debbie was about to wave, then her smile froze on her lips. *Celia. The ghost of Amanda's child, her former secretary whom Shaker had targeted and removed.*

"Killed, you mean," the little girl said, moving closer. Her expression was hateful. "You killed my mommy."

From Sheila's shadow, Guardian rose up, stepping quickly in front of Debbie and growling. The ghost stopped in its tracks, then hissed. The dog's hackles went up, and it bared its teeth, showing a mouthful of unnaturally long serrated fangs.

Celia hissed again, then disappeared.

"You're a good dog," Debbie said, patting Guardian's head.

"When did he get here?" Sheila asked, looking with surprise at the dog. "I didn't know you had a dog."

She didn't see the ghost. No one did but me. "A wedding present," Debbie explained. "Early. His name is Guardian."

"That's great." Sheila knelt, holding out her hand. "You're big. Hi, Guardian."

The dog ignored her, and everyone else, still looking in the direction where the ghost had been.

"So is he good protection?"

"The best."

~

Debbie turned this way and that in front of the mirror, looking at her reflection. *Damn it, this looked fabulous on that Victoria Secret model.* She fluffed up her hair, pouted sexily, then sighed and made a disgruntled face. *But she's probably seventeen. And not pregnant.*

Ever since Debbie had found out, she'd been eating all the things she usually didn't allow herself: burgers, milkshakes, ice cream, chips, and pretty much anything she had a craving for. As a result, she'd gained five pounds. All her clothes still fit, but they were tight. And this bright red sparkly negligee with the cut out sides and padded bra that had been sitting in her drawer for over two months, waiting for a night when Shaker was actually home, was now just a little too small.

Debbie touched up her makeup, then frowned at the crow's feet and worry lines on her forehead. *Even my face has smile lines now.* She held up the jar of face cream, glaring at it balefully. "You're not doing your job."

She touched up her face with a little more foundation, then wrapped her robe around her, shivering slightly. *I long for the days when I didn't get cold so easily.*

I'm home to warm you, Shaker's mental voice said teasingly. *I'll be right in, Mistress.*

Debbie smiled, then looked once more at her reflection. Maybe it was time to treat herself to some facial rejuvenation. *I'll think about it.*

"Think about what?" Shaker said, coming into the room. He grinned, taking in her outfit. "Wow. I hope you'll think about it, because I'm thinking about it right now. In fact, it's all I'm thinking about."

Debbie stretched back on the bed languidly. "You like?"

"I do," Shaker said, reaching for her. "Especially the no panties part." He kissed her roughly, sliding his hot hands down her sides, the electric connection they made on her cool flesh making Debbie sigh.

"Lay back," Shaker murmured, running his hands up to cup her breasts, then push the padded material down to bare the soft flesh. He cupped the cool flesh in his hot hands, squeezing slightly.

"You feel wonderful. So warm…mmm."

Shaker rubbed her nipples, pulling her breasts out of the cloth so they stood at attention. He lowered his mouth to the succulent nubs, teasing first the left one, then the right one with his tongue.

"My turn," Debbie said, trying to get up.

Shaker pushed her back, then spread her legs, rubbing her clit. She groaned as his fingers made lazy circles, her center warming as her juices began to run.

"My turn," Debbie said more insistently, pushing up against him. She helped him out of his jeans, then his jacket, playing her hands across his tight abs. Shaker moved, flexing the muscles under her hands.

"I love when you do that," she said, kissing his chest.

"Good, I have another muscle I want to flex for you," Shaker teased.

Debbie lowered her eyes to half-mast, then licked her lips as she gazed at him. She lowered her head to his erect member, tonguing the silky flesh, then the small cleft. Shaker groaned, then gasped as she licked the length of his cock, then put her lips around the head, working the tip of his cock back and forth in her mouth, flicking it with her tongue. He pushed up, straining to enter, and she let him, taking the length of him as he plunged into her.

Shaker thrust up twice more, then stopped her. "Please, I want to be inside you, Mistress."

"Stop asking," Debbie said harshly. "Start taking what you want. Say it!"

Shaker looked at her for a moment, then grinned widely. "Get over here now and please me, woman!" He grasped her about the waist and pulled her astride him, holding her in place as he slammed up into her. Debbie let out a cry, then moans as he pushed into her again and again.

"I love to watch you ride me," he said gutturally, as she bobbed above him, panting. "I love how your breasts move every time I enter you."

Shaker moved faster, and then he was coming, spurting into her, his grunts both desperate and possessing.

"Mmm," Shaker said, flashed a smile, then rolled over on top of her. He pushed in deeper, and Debbie let out a fresh cry.

"No, I'm not done with you, not by a long shot," Shaker said, cupping her buttocks as he pushed his hips tight to hers. "You're mine. All of you is mine, and I want you to know it."

Debbie closed her eyes, giving herself up to the sensation. *You feel so good...*

Say it!

The mental shout was a like a slap, snapping open Debbie's eyes. "Deeper," she commanded, meeting his gaze. "You want to show me I'm yours? Make me yours."

Shaker smiled, doubling his efforts, sweat making his taut flesh gleam. He reached under her leg, pushing back her ankle as he bent her leg, then thrust again. Debbie let out a grunt of pain, the tip of his penis bumping her cervix.

"That's what I wanted," Shaker grunted, moving faster, his thrusts complete. "That last...goddamn...inch!"

"Ooh!" Debbie groaned, as he hammered into her. The feeling was strange, but as she felt him sheathe all of himself again and again within her, the feeling of pleasure grew.

Shaker shuddered, then came again. He took a deep breath, then again moved Debbie, this time to her knees on all fours. With a quick press of his hips, he was back inside, again thrusting.

"You make me so fucking hard for you," he rasped, clutching her breasts as he thrust. "Seeing you in your office, in your tight little skirts or slacks, thinking about outfits like these under them. Watching you nibbling on the end of a pen in a meeting, thinking about you tonguing my cock. Watching you bend over to get something and imagining bending you over your desk and spreading your legs and pumping into you until I come!"

Debbie's heart was racing, her arousal like a cat in heat. She matched Shaker thrust for thrust.

"And you want it too, don't you? I see how you look at me with that teasing smile. You're thinking about the same thing I'm thinking, my pants around my ankles, your legs wrapped around me, my cock inside you." Shaker groaned again. "You're so wet, because you want it so much. Say it!"

"I do want you," Debbie panted. "I want your big hard cock. Make me come, Shaker."

Shaker stopped for a moment, then began pistoning into her, holding her tightly. Debbie came screaming, writhing under Shaker, his screams echoing hers a few seconds later.

As she lay trying to catch her breath, he resumed his thrusting. Shockingly, the feeling of another climax began to build.

"What, you can't…"

"I can," Shaker said possessively. "And I am."

Close to a half hour later, Debbie wiped the drool at the edge of her lip, then got up from the bed, unsteadily making her way to the bathroom with her hands out to the sides, fingers spread wide. She checked herself for spotting, then went back to bed, again walking carefully to spare her throbbing core.

Shaker stirred when she lay next to him, bringing her into his arms. "Sore?"

"I feel like I've been snaked, if you'll excuse the crudity. Holy shit, Shaker."

Shaker laughed. "Demon-ed, oh yes. You did say to take what I wanted and not ask."

"I did," Debbie said happily, burrowing into his warmth. "And it was wonderful."

"Yes, it was," Shaker said, his embrace tightening around her. "You are wonderful, Debbie."

"Thanks."

"And I like your crudity," he went on. "I like that you aren't afraid to say what you feel and think, even if it's inappropriate. You surprise me in good ways. You make me laugh. I like that best of all."

"More than me nibbling the end of a pen?"

Shaker laughed, then kissed her cheek. "I like it all. And I like that you keep it all for me."

"About that," Debbie said seriously. "Who are these people 'constantly' propositioning you? I'll fire them, man or woman."

Shaker laughed again. "Mostly not people I work with, my dear. People who wait on me in stores, who have seen my movies, or my face on a celebrity rag." He caressed her hair. "You have nothing to worry about."

"Why is that?"

"Because all I am, the real me, is all for you," he said gently. "The good bits and the bad bits. You will not reform me, my sweet. But you certainly have shown me a different perspective."

Debbie thought to ask him what was going on that he was being so forthcoming about his feelings, but her phone beeped.

"You should get that," Shaker said, swinging his legs over the edge of the bed. "It's probably Sheila, asking if you've asked me yet to let her rewrite *Destiny*."

Debbie cringed, her euphoria fading. "I'm sorry, but I listened to the lines you did when I visited the set. It does need work. The plot is solid, even your direction is great, but she's right, it needs editing."

Shaker made a face but nodded. "Alright. But if she wants to cut scenes, I want at least a say in how and which ones, ok?"

"Ok." Debbie keyed in her password. "It's not Sheila. It's someone I've never heard of." She passed the phone to Shaker.

He took it, and then nodded, answering it. "Yes. Please bring it right over." He repeated the house address, then hung up. "Toss on some clothes."

"Why?" Debbie said, even as she began dressing.

"You remember you gave me some ideas?" Shaker said, pulling a shirt over his head. "I acted on them."

Debbie blinked, then took Shaker's offered hand. He led her

upstairs and outside, where a brand new black Subaru Outback was being unloaded into their driveway.

"What is this?" Debbie said, astounded.

"Your new car," Shaker said, taking the keys from the attendant. He handed them to her, then signed some papers. "No sports cars for you, mom-to-be. You're going to have to settle for a suped-up station wagon. Happy belated Valentine's Day."

Debbie laughed, then ran to her new car. She climbed in and started the engine, loving the purr and the new car smell. "This is fabulous," she called, opening the window. "It's even got a smart screen."

"I'm glad you like it," Shaker said, resting his upper body in the opening. "It's got all the most recent safety features, so it'll stop and slow down automatically even while driving if you are about to hit something. And there's a panic button, if you need to call for help."

"Pretty high-tech," Debbie said, looking at all the buttons. "I love the mix of black and steel."

There was a woof from the backseat. Debbie looked in her rearview mirror to find Guardian sitting there, tongue lolling happily.

"He approves," Debbie said.

"The commercials do say 'dog tested, dog approved'."

"I don't think they meant hellhounds," Debbie said with a smile. "Thank you, it's wonderful. But I feel bad I didn't get you something. With everything that was going on, I forgot about Valentine's Day."

"You are giving me something, in less than nine months," Shaker said, kissing her. "It's I who still owe you to be square."

The next morning, Debbie arrived in her office to find every surface covered in bouquets of red roses. The air was heavy with their potent scent.

"Wow," Sheila said in awe, as she poked her head in the door. "Some guys still get it right."

"With a little prompting," Debbie added, touching several of the red velvety petals in a caressing motion.

"I thought Jett looked well-satisfied this morning," Sheila cracked. "You must have not told him about the rewrite we need."

"As a matter of fact, I did," Debbie said, rounding on Sheila. "And he agreed, he just wants to be allowed input if you cut a scene, which I agreed to. So please furnish him with any scenes you've rewritten, and he can start shooting those. We'll work in the order you rewrite."

Sheila's eyes narrowed, but she nodded. "Works for me."

"Hey, how about lunch?" Debbie added, turning back to her desk. "We haven't caught up in a while on anything but work. Are you free?"

There was no answer. When Debbie looked out of her door, Sheila had disappeared.

~

"I'm telling you, she's changing," Debbie said to Shaker later that night. "Is there anything you can do about it?"

"No," Shaker said. "A little ruthlessness is a good thing. She might just be jealous, you know. You have a new car, a bundle in your oven, an office full of flowers, and the most eligible bachelor since Valentino…or even Rhett Butler."

"Your opinion of yourself knows no bounds," Debbie quipped, as she put her arms around Shaker. "But you're right. I didn't think about that. Maybe you could say something to Song? Harp doesn't seem to care that much about making Sheila happy."

"He cares about protecting her, but you're right, he's not very romantic. Yes, I'll mention something. But Song is more thoughtful in general; she may have come up with her own ideas."

Debbie nodded absently.

"One last thing," Shaker murmured. "You mentioned building a nursery. But I don't think we need to add on. We can just convert one of the guest bedrooms. I can do that, but I need to know what to do?"

"It's your baby, too," Debbie managed, trying to blink back tears. "What do you think the room should look like?"

"Peaceful," Shaker said. "Someplace to feel safe."

"I agree. But what colors? What kind of images, or just solid colors?"

"I've heard Winnie the Pooh is a good choice," Shaker ventured. "And gender neutral."

"Heard from who?" Debbie asked, curious.

"Devlin," Shaker grudgingly admitted.

"He has a baby?" Debbie said in confusion. "He's a vampire. What the hell?"

"Nothing to do with Hell." Shaker laughed. "He got lucky and found a mortal who was both able and willing, no small thing. They used Pooh for their nursery."

"Why haven't I heard this before?" Debbie said, turning and focusing on him. "No wonder he was so keen on congratulating me. It's odd that you never said anything."

"Devlin and the mother have had a rocky relationship, so to speak," Shaker explained. "Yes, they are together now in a committed relationship, but...its complicated. Just don't mention anything to him or anyone else about it, all right?"

"Wait, his whole movie he's so adamant about is about losing his love Anna, and then pining for her for eternity and punishing his brother forever after," Debbie said, irritated. "That doesn't fit with him being in a relationship now with a baby."

Shaker smiled at her knowingly. "Love changes people, Mistress. Forever is a long reality. Would you have imagined you would be engaged and pregnant this time last year? Or be happy to be doing either?"

Debbie frowned at him. *Well...no.*

"One of the tools of survival is moving on," Shaker said softly, hugging her. "Enjoy the moments you have to the fullest, but don't dwell on them when they're gone. Believe that more moments are coming, if you do what you can to make them happen."

"Did all your centuries teach you that wisdom?"

"No, Debbie," Shaker said, kissing her lips. "You did."

CHAPTER SEVEN

APRIL

"Tell me why you wanted an April wedding?" Debbie's uncle Stuart said, as he rehearsed walking her down the aisle the night before the wedding.

"Because I'm going to have a baby." Debbie said with an exhausted sigh. "And as much as I don't care about this family's traditions, I do want my child to have two parents, and one name."

"So you're going to go with Debbie Black? Really! I didn't think you'd change it."

"I wasn't going to. I've used Deal for so long it feels more like the name I was born with than Tennison. But then I decided it really didn't matter. All that matters is really committing to Jett and our child. It's less about independence, and more about the bigger picture."

"You're sounding nothing like the young girl who vowed she didn't need anyone but herself to make her dreams come true," Stuart teased. "You didn't just turn into a woman, you turned into a smart one."

"Well, I was a very smart girl, what did you expect?" Debbie said with a laugh.

"Okay, quiet!" Harp yelled, looking uncomfortable and very pissed off. He was dressed as a priest, standing in front of the unmarked altar, Song and Sheila beside him unable to keep the grins from their faces.

This has to be a dream. "Where is the justice of the peace?"

"Jett asked me to officiate," Harp said, his hands clenching a small unmarked book that obviously wasn't a true Bible. "After you announced you were going to get married, I began studying up on what it took to officiate. I got my license to marry, so it'll all be legal."

"The question is did they already do a prenup?" a snarky voice called. "I object, otherwise!"

Debbie turned, appalled, watching a sleazy-looking dyed-blond that was poured into a spangly spandex dress walk haphazardly down the aisle. *What the hell?*

"Unfortunately not yet of Hell," Shaker murmured to Debbie. "Jett's sister, with all of his same weaknesses." He turned to the woman, offering her a smile that was bared teeth. "Rhonda, we're just thrilled you could make it."

"Well you haven't changed a bit," Rhonda said drunkenly, staggering over to Shaker and throwing her arms around him. "You're still an asshole."

"Well, he's my asshole," Debbie said cuttingly, pushing Rhonda off Shaker. "We've never officially met, but I'm Debbie, the bride."

"Sister-in-Law!" Rhonda crowed. "Always wanted one. Not." She let out a cackle.

"I suppose it's too much to ask that you brought Daryl along with you?" Shaker said. *That's her husband, who from Jett's memories usually keeps Rhonda in line,* he said to Debbie mentally.

"The fucker left me," Rhonda snarled, her heavily made up face turning mean. "Emptied our bank accounts, too."

Okay, this is probably really rude of me, but she's my choice for this month, Debbie thought to Shaker. *Just please do it before the wedding tomorrow.*

Shaker swiveled his head and looked at Debbie in utter shock, then burst out laughing.

"Don't you laugh!" Rhonda yelled, lunging toward Shaker. "I'd have come asking for help before now, except for Brady. It's about time you helped your little sister."

Song stepped in front of Sheila, just as Shaker did the same to Debbie. Rhonda's heel stuck in the carpet and she went sprawling on the floor at their feet.

"Enough already, Rhonda!" came a thunderous voice.

Debbie looked past Jett's flailing sister. A tall, thin man was coming down the stairs, his expression murderous. He pulled Rhonda to her feet, then sat her in a chair in the first row. "Sit down and mellow out, right now." The man flashed a smile at Debbie, and then came over to her. "I'm Brady, Jett's brother."

"Younger brother," Shaker amended. "As if she couldn't tell."

He does look like Jett with his blue eyes and black hair, except not as handsome. And much younger, yes.

Only a few years, but he doesn't have the addictions Jett had. In fact he's been the rock of the family, since their parents were in the car accident. "I wasn't sure you were going to make it," Shaker said aloud. "I know it's short notice, but I wanted you here."

Brady stepped in and hugged Shaker hard. "I'm your brother, of course I'd make your wedding. Now do I get to be the best man?"

"Sorry," Shaker said quickly. "But I didn't plan on having one."

"Why not have two?" a rumbling voice called. "I can share the honor with the groom's earthly brother." Titus walked in, his reddish countenance, red eyes, and black short horns visible. Debbie shot a nervous look at Shaker.

Relax, Brady and Rhonda can't see through the glamour he's wearing. "Brady, Rhonda, this is Titus, a longtime friend. He's in the same business I am."

"Glad to meet you," Brady said uncertainly. "I'm sorry, Titus, but Jett hasn't talked much about you."

"He's been there for me when I needed him," Shaker supplied, resting a hand on Titus's back. "Too many times to count."

"That's certainly the truth," Titus grumbled good-naturedly. "I think of him as my brother, in spirit. He's always getting into scrapes I need to drag his ass out of."

Debbie stifled a laugh, as Brady shook Titus's hand, his expression intrigued. "Where did you meet? Did you do a movie together?"

"It'll have to wait," Titus said smoothly, stepping past Brady. He reached out, just catching a passed-out Rhonda as she threatened to take a nosedive into the carpet. "This little flower's wilting. Jett, why don't you and I help Brady get her back to their hotel?"

"We don't have one," Brady said reluctantly. "We thought we'd get one once we got here."

"I'd have you stay with us," Shaker said quickly, "but Rhonda looks pretty bad, and we've got our hands full with the wedding."

"She wasn't too bad until Luke left," Brady said with a sigh, eyeing his prone sister. "I've been meaning to tell you, but I hated to dump this on you. I know you've had your own problems."

"I thought her husband's name was Daryl?" Sheila said, offering her hand. "Hi, I'm the maid of honor. Sheila."

"Good to meet you. And yes, that's right. Her boyfriend was Luke. She called him that, but really they were drinking buddies. He cleaned up his act last month and told her to get clean or he was leaving. She didn't…and he did. Since then she's been on a perpetual bender."

"Why don't I take care of her tonight?" Titus offered, hoisting Rhonda into his arms. "Brady, you should catch up with your brother. Jett's got a lot to share with you."

"I can't ask you to do that," Brady said quickly. "God, you're all going to think Debbie's marrying into a terrible family. We're not all like it seems."

Yes, they are, or more precisely were, Shaker said to Debbie. *The parents died in a crash because they'd been drinking and driving. Jett and Rhonda got the same genes. Brady is the only one that's somehow immune.*

"It's okay," Debbie said to Brady quickly, patting his arm awkwardly. "Wait until you meet my mother. You're going to think the same thing."

"Technically speaking, she may not make it," Stuart inserted meekly. "She has vowed not to, but I hoped she relent, and I'd get a last minute call from the airport demanding that I pick her up. But now I'm not sure."

"That's alright," Debbie said with a false cheerfulness. "I have the people that care about me here, old family and new. But now let's go retire for the evening, it's a big day tomorrow."

～

Brady went home with Debbie and Shaker, with Sheila following with Titus, Rhonda, Harp and Song. Rhonda was still passed out half on Song's lap, snoring softly.

"Are you sure I'm not putting you out? Damn, this day seems like it's been just as embarrassing as possible."

"Brady, it's okay," Shaker assured him for the second time. "We have a guest room, and like Debbie says, she expected to spend tonight at Sheila's so we can honor tradition. All that superstition about the bride not seeing the groom until the wedding takes place."

"But you're sure that you're okay to deal with her?" Brady asked Titus. "She usually wakes up groggy and repentant. That lasts until her first drink. She'll tell you she's quitting, but it won't last."

"I'm sure," Titus assured. "I think she'll sleep most of the night. Any problems, I'll call Jett."

"Come on," Shaker said, clapping Brady on the shoulder. "Come in and tell me how you've been. Or maybe that will wait. You're exhausted, I can tell."

Debbie watched the two walk into her home, then glanced at

her demon brother-in-law-to-be. "You sure this is a good idea, Titus?"

"You want a perfect wedding, don't you?" Titus said, as he backed her car out of the driveway. "Well then, let me arrange one."

~

"Good thing I got a house with three bedrooms," Sheila griped. "Plus a fold out couch. Debbie, I put you in the guest bedroom nearest the bathroom. Rhonda can go in the one next to you."

"I can take the couch," Titus said, casting a baleful glare at Harp.

"No, I'll take the couch," Harp said quickly.

"Don't be ridiculous, you can sleep with me and Song," Sheila said.

"Thank you," Titus said dismissively. "Now children, the way I see it, we have two choices. I have already given Rhonda a small sedative that will make her sleep through the night. I can either put a temporary spell on her to keep her sedated tomorrow, so she doesn't interfere with the wedding…or Song can possess her."

~

"You can't seriously be suggesting this as the right course of action!" Debbie yelled.

"Calm yourself, please," Titus said, putting his hands up. "I'm just saying that Rhonda is a female version of Jett, the way he was before Shaker possessed him. She'll betray us eventually, because she'll ultimately see something she isn't supposed to. She's got a very weak will, if Brady is telling the truth, and he looked too exhausted by her not to be. Yes, spells can be used to fight addiction, but with someone who has multiple addictions like this and no interest in fixing them, magic isn't a long-term solution."

"But I had no idea Jett had a sister or a brother, so he must not keep in touch with them," Debbie argued. "How much of a concern would she be if she's never around?"

Titus gestured with his hand, and a doorway appeared. Debbie and the others stared as Shaker came walking through, the furniture of her living room visible behind him before Titus closed the doorway with another brief gesture.

"That's not teleporting," Sheila breathed, her eyes round as plates. "That was something else."

"A magical doorway, just what it looked like," Titus said in a bored tone, but his expression was proud. "It takes finesse with magic to make one, not just knowledge."

"Plus a good deal of power," Shaker added, with a nod to his brother. "I can't stay long, but Brady was almost asleep on his feet. He passed out before he could even shower and undress. I left him snoring on the guest bed." He turned to Titus. "I know what you're thinking, and if you can get the others to agree, I'm in. Brady has been taking care of her, and it can't last much longer. He's nearly out of money and energy. That means she'd be coming to us for whatever she can get, and it's more than we can or want to handle right now. So either I harvest her as Debbie asked me to do, or Song possesses her."

"Are you strong enough, is the question?" Titus said, turning to Song. "You're young to be trying it. But in the condition she's in, she won't put up much of a fight."

"Can you just possess her, if she's unwilling?" Sheila asked, staring at the snoring Rhonda.

"I'm surprised that you care what we think, and aren't making the decision for us," Harp said bitterly to Titus.

"For this to work, you all have to be on board one-hundred-percent. That means all of you. I have not been out of Hell so long because I went around issuing commands with no thought for those carrying them to fruition." He turned to Song. "Are you willing?"

"Yes," Song said, licking her lips nervously. "I want to try it. Shaker can harvest her if it doesn't work."

"Yes," Shaker said. "I'm in."

"Harp?" Titus asked.

The younger demon nodded. "Yes. But we'll have to explain her role reversal."

"It will be taken for a blessing," Titus smiled evilly. "And it will be one, for everyone here."

~

The next morning, Debbie and Sheila were downstairs having breakfast when the new Rhonda made her appearance. While her face was pale it was freshly scrubbed, her hair damp and smelling of shampoo. "I helped myself to some clothes. There wasn't any luggage…of mine."

"How is it?" Sheila asked looking out of the corner of her eyes watchfully.

"I feel ill from withdrawal, with a hangover as topping," Song admitted, sitting heavily in the chair. "And she's wailing inside me, fighting me. I didn't think she had that much strength."

"She'll soon give up," Titus said, materializing near the kitchen sink, startling Sheila and Debbie. "It's normal for that to happen in the first day or so. Once she realizes it's not going to get her anywhere, she'll grow quiet."

"But is she always going to be back there in my brain, chattering about like a squirrel on meth?" Song griped, rubbing her temples. "I can see why her husband left her."

"Now, now," Titus chided. "You are Rhonda now, Song. You have to have always been Rhonda. Part of the joy of possession is taking on all of the person's previous and current sins as your own."

"Ugh, that sounds terrible," Sheila commented. "I wouldn't want to be punished for something I didn't do."

Titus laughed, a great rumbling sound. "People so easily

possessed aren't usually stellar pillars of the community, Sheila. We take what we can get."

"Hey, I didn't know we were on a first name basis," Sheila teased with a grin.

"I take the liberty with all those people whose lives I save," the demon said cheerfully, stifling a yawn. "And this is early for me, so you'll have to excuse my informality. I'm linked to a vampire, remember."

I can't believe I'm listening to this conversation on the morning of my wedding, Debbie thought surreally, standing. "Shouldn't we hurry? It's nearly seven now, and the wedding is at noon. We need to get dressed, and do our hair, and still make it to the church."

"Not to worry," Titus said, with a wave of his hand. "I am here to make sure this day is as perfect as possible." His red eyes glittered. "Go get ready, lovely bride. Your demon awaits."

Debbie paced the office of the courthouse, checking her reflection in the mirror every few minutes. Sheila, Song, and she had donned their gowns after arriving, then the two bridesmaids had left to check that everything else was okay. Debbie's uncle hadn't come by yet, but he wasn't due for another half-hour.

I'm afraid to wrinkle my dress if I sit down, but my feet are already hurting. Why did I think I should wear heels? How stupid!

Because it's your wedding day, and you wanted to look pretty, a throaty mental voice that wasn't Shaker's said. *Understandable, if unwise.*

Who's there? Debbie thought, pushing away her fear.

Titus, came his reply. *Do not speak of this to the others. I am outside the door but will not enter, lest Shaker view you from my mind, and bring you bad luck. He is nervous this morning, and I've already had him break into my thoughts a few times.* He laughed, the rumbling sound unsettling in her mind.

This is crazy. What do you want, Titus?

Just to assure you that all will be well today. I will speak to you after the ceremony. There is something we must discuss. But here is your uncle. Good luck, Bride-to-be.

There was a knock at the door. "Debbie, it's Uncle Stuart. Can I come in?"

"Of course, it's open," Debbie called, feeling for Titus, but he was gone. She opened the door. Stuart came in, fixing his tie. "Sorry I'm late, I seemed to hit every red light this morning. The more I hurried, the more I seemed to slow down. "

"It's okay, you look great!" Debbie said, giving him a hug.

"You are the one that looks great, um, beautiful," Stuart said, pulling back from her and looking her over. "This isn't what I expected after what you said to your mother, but it's perfect."

Debbie looked one more time into the mirror, the heavy satin of the floor-length classic ivory bridal gown swishing as she moved. "I didn't know if I wanted lace or any beading, but once I saw this, I knew I loved it. You don't think it's too glittery?"

"It's perfect. What made you choose ivory?"

"I knew I didn't want white, and I also didn't really want a colored suit, or some kind of other dress. I wasn't sure about the veil either, but I wanted a tiara, and to have my hair up. I always wanted that, when I was little."

"Then I'm glad you got it," Stuart said happily. He extended his crooked arm. "Are you ready?"

"Yes. But Sheila and Rhonda aren't back."

"We'll go see where they are. Come on."

Debbie nervously went with him, going through the door into the long hallway of offices. *I'm glad they let us use these conference rooms to get ready.*

Sheila was with Song waiting in the doorway to the room the ceremony was being held in, both of them holding sprays of red roses, their red heavy satin dresses copies of hers with black and red beading. "Stay right there," Sheila called to Debbie. "Shaker and

Brady are late, but on their way. Harp's up at the podium, getting ready."

"Do you have the ring?" Debbie called back to Stuart.

"Got it right here in my pocket."

Are all brides this anxious? Debbie examined her bouquet again, looking at the red roses arranged around one single black and red one, the long satin black and red ribbons trailing down from the large bow that tied them together. *I like the black and red, but I can't believe we actually did that for our wedding colors. It's kind of obscene. My bridesmaids look reminiscent of an old-time brothel.*

"They're here! Get the music started."

Debbie heard music began, but it wasn't the music that she'd expected played from a stereo system. This was real music played on instruments. And there was the scent of wildflowers. *What the hell?*

Courtesy of Hell, came Shaker's teasing thought. *Come, my bride. Come to me.*

Debbie and Stuart walked out, then stopped, as they watched Rhonda walk down to the podium. But it wasn't there anymore. In its place was a shimmering magical portal door, a forest glade beyond, where Harp waited near a huge standing stone, Shaker and Brady and Titus beside him. Near them a string quartet played on the grass, the musicians outfitted with tuxes. All were visibly demons.

"What the heck is that?" Stuart stuttered.

"Just an illusion," a woman said lightly, as she walked up and touched his shoulder. Her long brown hair was in an elaborate braid, her dress authentic Victorian peasant, shades of violet that seemed to undulate. "Walk through, they are waiting."

Sheila walked to the shimmering portal door, then through it onto the grass.

Stuart relaxed, then he walked through with Debbie. Immediately the cool dewy air hit her, and she was glad of the heavy dress, even as her shoes immediately soaked through.

The woman in purple followed them, then stopped just inside the portal as they continued on. *She must be holding it open.*

Leri is holding it open, in case we are discovered, Shaker said. *You look beautiful, Debbie.*

You look very handsome, too. She smiled then laughed. *I can't believe that we're doing this. Where is this?*

Do you like the setting? I wanted it to be a surprise. There is no place on earth more magical than here.

Stonehenge is not what I expected. Debbie looked around at the massive rocks, enclosing them in a set of circles. *Wait, aren't there more stones here than there are supposed to be?*

Titus and I worked with Rip most of the night to bring them here and set them into place. We cut and shaped them with magic those weeks in March, when I told you I was shooting the sequel to Smoke and Ashes II. It took a lot of time, but I wanted you to see it as it once was, before man and time ruined it.

Stop talking to one another, Titus broke in. *You're supposed to be getting married. You can talk later.*

Debbie giggled, and Stuart shot her an odd look. They made their way to the altar.

"Who brings this woman?" Harp called.

"I do," Stuart said. "She comes of her own free will."

Debbie went to stand before the stone. Harp brought out a chalice with a cavorting naked woman engraved on its side and handed it to her. "Who brings this male?"

"I bring myself," Shaker said, stepping to Debbie's side. "I come of my own free will."

Harp handed him a large dagger, the burnished blade gleaming, a cavorting demon engraved on the jeweled handle. "Who stands with this couple, as witnesses to the vows they will swear?"

"We are with them," Brady, Stuart, Sheila, Titus, and Rhonda said. "We stand as witnesses."

"Male and female, assume your positions, and speak your vows."

Shaker and Debbie turned to face one another. "You are my chosen one," Shaker intoned, brandishing the dagger. "I will protect you, cherish you, fill you, and give my life for you if need be. My happiness is your happiness. Let our union last until loyalty should fade."

Debbie bowed slightly, holding out the cup with both hands to Shaker. "You are my chosen one. I will nurture you, comfort you, lie with you, and respect you. My happiness is your happiness. Let our union last until loyalty should fade. *And love,* Debbie added mentally.

Shaker set the length of the dagger into Debbie's cup.

Harp raised his hand, palms held up. "This male and female are now joined. Let the forces of this sacred place help cement their bond with loyalty and give them lasting happiness. May their power together be greater than their power alone." He lowered his hands. "You are husband and wife. You may kiss the bride."

Shaker grabbed Debbie, and kissed her until she swooned, as the onlookers clapped and whistled.

"You forgot the rings, doof," Sheila said to Harp, as she handed Debbie Shaker's ring.

"Sorry," Harp said, looking mortified.

Brady produced a shining red-gold ring, then handed it to Debbie. "I think this is yours."

Debbie slipped it on, then gave Shaker his ring, which was plain gold, which he slipped on.

"If you're done, we should get out of here," Leri called. "Rip says he can't keep the tourists out much longer."

Back at their home, Debbie and Rip toasted their union. "Are you sure you don't want to go out to dinner?" Debbie asked, as she removed some cold cuts from the fridge.

"No," Shaker said, scanning his phone. "The paparazzi have

been looking for us the whole morning. There's a lot of speculation about where we are. One rag's even posted a cash reward for a validated sighting. As much as I'd like to teleport you to a secluded beach, or one of the nicer restaurants in Paris to celebrate, we should stay in."

"We'll have to appear sometime," Debbie prodded gently. "And we never even talked about our honeymoon. Now it's here. Did you plan something? I didn't."

"No," Shaker said, turning his phone off. "I'm neck deep in scenes that still need doing for *Smoke and Ashes III*, and you've got your hands full prepping for the early release of *Absolution*."

Debbie looked at him oddly. "What are you talking about? That movie doesn't release until September."

Shaker let out a breath, then turned to face her. "It's going to release early for some reason. Trust me."

Debbie's face turned an ashen color. "Is this part of what you saw, when you looked ahead for us?"

Shaker nodded. "Yes. If there's anything you need to do to prepare for the picture marketing-wise, start doing it."

"Okay," Debbie said slowly. She sat down in her wedding dress on the couch, food forgotten. Guardian appeared from the shadow she made, coming to sit at her feet with a confused whine. Absently, she gave him some of the cold cuts, which he wolfed down voraciously.

"I'm sorry," Shaker said, coming to sit near her. "I didn't mean to upset you."

"I want to ask you what else you saw," Debbie whispered, her expression terrified. "But I don't want to know, either. Because you said there were good and bad things."

"Yes," Shaker said, hugging her. "I wish I could tell you that there were only good things. But I can't."

"I know," Debbie said, turning and clutching him.

"Come," Shaker said, picking her up in his arms, the train of her long dress whispering as the satin shifted. "You need a nice warm bath."

Hot water scented with soothing lavender comforted Debbie, as Shaker finished lighting candles around the bubble-filled tub.

"You must have got some products from Song."

"She, Harp, and Sheila got us a gift basket from the spa with your favorite things, plus a few surprises. Why wait to try it?" He blew out the match, then climbed in, groaning as the water engulfed him.

"Yes, this is just what I needed," Debbie said, her eyes closed.

"You and me both," Shaker said, reaching out to clasp her hand. "Happy honeymoon, my Mistress." The couple stayed like that together, until the water cooled.

Later that night, Debbie nestled close to Shaker. "Are you going to be disappointed if we don't do it tonight?" she asked tentatively.

Shaker snorted.

"That's not an answer," Debbie said, a smile playing about her lips.

"No," Shaker whispered. "I like this, just being here with you." *I haven't done this much* his mental voice came tentatively.

Cuddling?

Yes. Or just being with someone and not having to be anything but myself.

Good. I want you to be happy. I want us to be happy.

Shaker hugged her but didn't reply. Just as she was drifting off to sleep, he said, *So do I.*

Debbie stirred. "Mmm?"

Shaker's hand covered her mouth, bringing her out of her

stupor. *That's why my vow was loyalty. In other words, it's an oath of allegiance. I made it before God and the devil in a place of power purposely, so that both would hear, and take notice.*

Why? Debbie thought sleepily, as she drifted off again.

Because they are the only two beings I must answer to. Stonehenge predates Christianity by thousands of years. It's a place of power that only needed the stones to be complete again. The vow we swore there today cannot ever be broken. Now, because of that, neither of them can ever ask me to harm you.

CHAPTER EIGHT

MAY

THAT NEXT MORNING, WHEN DEBBIE AWOKE ALONE, SHE recalled Shaker's last words. *Instead of the comfort he must have meant them to be, they're frightening. I'm not anybody to warrant either of those beings' attentions...and I wouldn't want to be.* She rubbed at her eyes, exhausted. *I was having another nightmare, but I can't remember it. Nightmares should be outlawed on the night you get married.*

Debbie's cell phone beeped. She grabbed it up, then looked at the mass of texts, glanced at the clock and swore.

An hour later, she was just pulling into her spot when Sheila met her in the parking lot.

"This is the first time you've got me cornered before I got to the elevator," Debbie joked. "It must be bad."

"It is bad," Sheila said. "I'd have called, if it wasn't the day after your wedding. I know I told you that you were crazy for not going on a honeymoon at least for a couple days, but now I'm really glad you didn't."

"Walk with me," Debbie said, hurrying to the elevator. "What's up?"

"Joshua's dead."

Debbie stopped in her tracks. "Dead how?"

"His apartment was broken into. He was staked. Before that, his head was cut off."

"Has Devlin been in contact?"

"He's sent Lash after whomever did it. He said he'll be in touch as soon as he knows more. And that we'll get another of his "people" by tomorrow night, to act as a new liaison."

"Great," Debbie said under her breath, jamming her fingers on the open button. "That police detective will come back around snooping. We were doing so well, no deaths of anyone on set."

"Well, that's the bad news. Someone leaked a picture of the body, and it's going to be splashed across the evening news."

"Can Devlin do damage control?"

"He says he could but said he "elects not to.""

"What the fuck?" Debbie said harshly, tossing her briefcase down near her desk. "He 'elects not to'? Why the hell not?"

"Because the papers are leading with the story, giving publicity to his movie. The press are using the vampire connection, saying that there's a wacko out there who's against our movie, killing people associated with it as he thinks their vampires. You know the old line, that no publicity is bad publicity. And he's right. We've had more hits on the movie title on our site that any movie we've had up on the site so far, including *Smoke and Ashes* or its sequel."

Debbie looked at her a moment. "Could Devlin have arranged this?"

"I don't think so," Sheila said, clearly shocked. "He wouldn't kill one of his own people."

"He would do anything for that movie to be successful."

He didn't do it came Shaker's mental comment. *Devlin takes his role of protector of this country seriously, most especially to his own staff. He'll be taking vengeance in blood and flesh, as soon as he finds out who did this.*

Who do you think it was?

136

Vampire hunters. Likely the Van Helsing group.

"Shaker thinks it was vampire hunters," Debbie said to Sheila.

"Harp and Song do, too," she answered. "I didn't know there were such things."

"There are demon hunters," Song said, as she came in the office door in her new human body, squeezed into a much too-tight sweater and short skirt. "Why wouldn't there be vampire hunters also?"

"What are you doing here?" Sheila asked, flushing. "Especially dressed like that?"

"It's my first day," Song said nervously. "As my new self." She turned to Sheila. "I don't...look like I did. So I wanted to get some pointers from you to see what I should change, and what I should keep. My old clothes don't fit, obviously. This is the only thing I could squeeze into."

Debbie smiled inwardly, even as she waited for Sheila's response.

"What you looked like before was good," Sheila said slowly. "But yes, this is a more, um, full-figured look. Maybe get some larger sizes."

"I could figure out that for myself," Song snapped, her eyes narrowing. "I want to know if you like your women busty, or leaner. I can lose some weight, along with getting fit. But I can't help being a few inches shorter."

Sheila hugged Song, then kissed her. Debbie looked away, embarrassed but smiling.

"You look happy," Sheila said tenderly. "That's what matters. Be healthy, and the rest doesn't matter to me. Ok?"

"Ok," Song said, blowing her a kiss. "I'll see you later. I have to go do some shopping. Brady is still sleeping in the guest bedroom, he was up late talking to Harp."

"Talking about what?" Debbie called after her, but Song didn't answer.

"She's nervous," Sheila explained, as she closed the office door. "This is her first possession."

Debbie looked at Sheila, then began to howl laughing.

Sheila stamped her foot angrily. "This is serious. She's really nervous. I'm trying to be supportive, but I'm kind of weirded out, too. It's like having your lover in bed, then you glance out of the corner of your eye and get startled seeing a stranger."

Debbie was crying now, wiped at her watery eyes, trying to catch her breath. "I know that," she managed finally. "I went through the same thing with Shaker last year. It's just that sometimes I feel like I'm in a movie instead of making them."

"Yeah, I know the feeling," Sheila said wryly. "But we are still making them, and since you didn't take time off, I need your focus."

Debbie wiped her eyes again with a tissue. "Okay, go ahead."

"First of all, *Immortal Confessions* is still shooting. But with this killer on the loose, I think we need to increase security."

Debbie nodded. "Yes. Do that. Talk to Mr. Minor and hire a few more guards."

"Next, there's been gossip that Titan Pictures is plotting something."

"That's nothing new. They're always plotting something, they make movies."

"Aren't you a master of wit this morning?"

"Mistress of wit, actually."

"I'm giving you a pass, but just today, Mrs. Black. Anyway, I'd like to make sure all of the bookings we've done are double-checked, and that promotions are scheduled for all releases this year. I know it's early, but I don't want to wait and then find out all we can get for the release weekend is one screen in Des Moines."

"I think that's a good idea," Debbie agreed, thinking of Shaker's warning about *Absolution's* early release. "But you'll have to pay upfront. How's our capital?"

"Remember, Devlin offered to bankroll several of our other movies if we consented to do his, plus he put up the money for his," Sheila said. "While we aren't made of dough, we have plenty to lock in screens, and more importantly, ads. Devlin wants a lot of ads for his movie, and I want to start booking those. Also, we have the final designs for the movie posters to approve, a media package to prepare complete with a short clip, and also the official trailer."

"Devlin have any thoughts on what he wants in that?"

"He does." Sheila flashed up a pad of paper filled with delicate writing. "He furnished me with ten pages of notes. I have to get with Adeline and see what scenes we can splice together from what we've already filmed, and what scenes will need to be shot early to get this perfect."

"That sounds great," Debbie said. "I think you could've gotten along without me after all."

"Nope," Sheila said, standing up. "Because Henry's here downstairs, with several of Titan Pictures' legal team."

"What do they want?"

"Remember when you took the stock public, then we undid that? Well, they had shares of stock. They're suing us."

Debbie walked into the conference room, Sheila at her left shoulder, Catarella and Giorgio at her right. Henry and his team followed.

"Please have a seat," Debbie said, sitting herself. Sheila, Giorgio, and Catarella followed suit. "What is it you want?"

"As Sheila might have told you, we are putting forth an injunction," Henry said. "As shareholders, we should have had the right to vote on the stock-buyback before you went ahead and did it."

"There's no legal precedent for that," Giorgio scoffed. "Don't waste our time or yours with this nonsense. Now do you have anything to discuss or not?"

"Yes, a few things," Henry said nastily, glaring at Debbie. "The money that you paid for the stock that you bought back from us was insufficient. The price of the stock is now double what it was then. We demand the difference."

"Buying back company stock can—and usually does—inflate a company's share price and boost its earnings per share. But none of that matters, as Debbie is the only one now who has shares of Pandora stock. In any case, what happened was the norm, not something you wouldn't have seen coming."

"What we see is Debbie getting rich off our good-nature last year," Henry sniped. "What kind of lucrative executive bonuses are you assigning yourselves this month?"

"That's none of your business," Debbie said coolly. "You were compensated for your efforts."

"I'll say one more time, do you have anything worthwhile to discuss?" Catarella stated. "None of this is worth the time this meeting is taking, much less legal fees from either side. You know this, Henry. So get to the point."

"Very well. We want to make another offer to buy Pandora."

"Why?" Debbie sputtered. "You know I'm not going to sell to you. This company is everything I've worked for."

"It was, but there's good reason to think it's not now," Henry said, his eyes glittering. "You just got married, and gossip says you already have a baby on the way."

There was a collective gasp from Catarella, Giorgio, and Sheila. Debbie flushed.

"I see that my source was right," Henry said, smirking. "You should take some time off, Debbie, start that family you've put off for so long."

"Call security to see Henry out," Debbie said coldly. "The only thing I've put off too long was throwing you out of my company for a second time, Henry. Get lost."

"Remember, my offer still stands," Henry said, tossing a folder to her. "There's an undated contract. You can fill it in when you change your mind."

"Get out!" Debbie said, standing.

"Hope to hear from you soon," Henry said, then turned, his team following him out.

"I do not deserve to have this happen the morning after I got married," Debbie said, staring after him with hate.

"He's just desperate to derail you and this company," Catarella assured. "But I will meet with him alone from now on. If anything comes up that could actually be a real issue, I will notify you."

Debbie nodded. "Good." She made her way back to her office, where to her surprise, Titus was waiting.

"I thought better of interrupting your wedding night," he intoned. "How is the hound working out?"

Debbie nodded, her smile faint but genuine. "Guardian's a great dog. I forget he's not real sometimes."

"He's the spirit of a real dog," Titus corrected. "And if you were attacked, he could attack whatever it was more effectively than a real dog."

"I wouldn't want him to be hurt, though. He's already getting to be more a friend than a defensive measure."

"Like Shaker?" Titus asked pointedly, studying her.

"Is this really what you wanted to talk to me about, if I really love your brother? You were in my mind, you must already know the answer."

"No," Titus said with a shake of his head. "Whatever is between you and he is between you, and none of my business. I wanted to talk to you about Devlin's movie."

"What about it?"

"I'd like you to make my role less villainous."

I must have missed a few pages of script. "I'm not sure what you mean."

"The big climactic battle at the end. I'm opposing Devlin, and I killed someone important to him, you might say the heroine of the story—"

"Anna?"

Titus looked at her as if she were incompetent. "No, she was dead before then. Haven't you read the script?"

I really, really should have taken today off. "I haven't read the entire script, only seen a synopsis, and a few scenes here and there as they were filming. Truthfully, I didn't know you were in *Immortal Confessions.*"

"I'm only in the end. Shaker is as well, in his true form. We had to battle at the end, and he bested me, as he usually does. Devlin's going to insist on accuracy, but it would be best for us all if you altered the story and made only one demon part of the final battle: myself, fighting on Devlin's team instead of opposing him."

"If you know he's not going to go for it, why even ask me?"

Titus stepped closer, folding his arms across his wide chest. "I know you know of my relationship to Shaker, but that's not widely known outside of a small trusted group. It would be better for us all if you take steps to keep it that way. Familial relationships are dangerous tools in the hands of enemies."

"Why are you asking this of me and not Devlin?"

"Because he won't listen to me. I know Sheila simplified the script some, so it would fit into a three-hour movie. Tell him you must simplify the end for the same reason."

Debbie looked up at him and flashed a forced smile. "You know, honestly, I don't care. If you recommend this for safety reasons, then I'm fine with it. Just go to Sheila and tell her that I said it was okay, see if she's willing to agree."

Again, he wore the same look, as if she were inept. "Aren't you the CEO?"

"Yes, but she's been prickly about that lately," Debbie said, seizing the opportunity. "Speaking of which, um…do you have something that would help her to resist, to um…"

"Be less evil?" Titus supplied with a knowing smile.

Debbie nodded. "She's changing. I can see it."

"Yes, she is. But there's nothing that can be done about it, especially with her being bound to two demons. One would be better."

"It's too late for that now," Debbie protested. "She can't just send Harp away."

"Hmm," Titus said thoughtfully. "Very well, I'll go and see her now." He disappeared.

"You're welcome!" Debbie said loudly, annoyed.

"Then I'll enter," a smooth voice drawled.

Debbie looked to her doorway, where a dashing yet dangerous man was lounging like a great cat watching its prey, his brown hair in a short ponytail. "And you are?"

"Nathan, but you may address me as Nate," he said, flashing his vampire fangs. "Devlin sent me. We go way back, though I'm not mentioned in his movie."

"How far back?"

"My state—and it *is* mine—is called the Volunteer State, because so many of us volunteered to fight in the war of 1812. I got my fangs on a battlefield, and used them on a few more afterwards, until Devlin recruited me for his new government." Nate smiled. "Things were a lot simpler then."

"Do you have experience in film, like Joshua?"

Nate shook his head, still smiling. "But I do have experience in show business." He moved his hand in a graceful motion, long talons appearing. "And unlike Joshua, I have experience in killing and covering it up, a skill I hear you are sorely in need of at Pandora."

Shit, what did you get me into, Sheila. "We can't have any more deaths here."

"Rest assured, you will not. Any that must happen will be disappearances only." Nate inclined his head, then with a sexy smile gave her a courtly bow that would have been almost romantic, except for his talons, bared fangs, and bright red eyes which made him terrifying instead. "Devlin asked me personally to see to this, so that there would be no more problems. I would not have left my seat of power, otherwise. You may rely on me."

Debbie nodded, then forced another smile. *Work with what you have.* "I'm glad to hear that, Nate. Joshua was coming in some days to watch the shooting or compile questions/issues and speaking to Devlin at night about them for clarification and direction. You can do whatever works for you to accomplish this, but there will be staff meetings you will need to attend once a month during the day."

Nate wrinkled his nose. "Daylight, ugh. No worries though, I've a demon of my own. I can teleport in to the meetings. As for Devlin, yes, I'll review with him at night. Can you have a tape of each day's scenes made for me to play for him? That would be easiest, so he can review and tell me anything that looks wrong." He laughed richly, then grinned. "Sorry, I meant a DVD or perhaps as a file on a USB stick? I forgot which decade I was in for a moment there."

"Yes. See the director Bart," Debbie said, scribbling a note quickly and handing it to him. "Give him this. His office is down the hall, to the left. Please also come to the next meeting, it's in a few days."

"Here is my email and other contact info," Nate said, producing a card.

Debbie took it gingerly from between his talons. *One end actually looks as if it was dipped in blood.* "Thank you."

"Adieu," he said, then left by the door with a swagger.

I need a break. Debbie was about to call for takeout from her office when she heard a tap at the door. Shaker stood there in his Smoke outfit, smiling, a large tray of steaming Chinese food in his hands.

"I heard about Henry's visit and thought a lunchtime indulgence of fried food was in order."

Debbie's stomach growled loudly. *It's definitely time for lunch.* "Your timing is perfect," she said, beckoning him to sit down at her small conference table. She kissed him on the lips, then helped him lay out the food.

"So you met Nate?" Shaker asked, as she swallowed down the fried rice and noodles.

Debbie nodded, her mouth full. *He was scary but all business.*

He's a ruler under Devlin, state level. I often think Nate has the mettle to hold a country of his own, if he only wanted the responsibility.

Debbie swallowed fast. "Should I have reason to worry?" *About Devlin, I mean.*

Shaker shook his head. "Nate's never made a grab for more power in over a hundred years, I don't think he will now. But remember always that he's who Devlin calls in when Lash balks at doing something. And that's saying a lot, because there are only a few things Lash would refuse to do."

"Such as?"

"Kill innocents. Murder as a means to an end. Torture for the sake of inflicting pain, not for information or discipline. Nate would do all three with a song in his heart."

"Why would Devlin call him in to be our liaison?"

"Because Joshua was mild-mannered and very PC. He likely tried to talk his attacker out of killing him. Nate will respond with lethal force from the first provocation. He also despises hunters of all kinds and may decide on his own to hunt Joshua's murderer down himself, which he has the right to do. Devlin is right in assuming we shouldn't have any more issues now that he's here."

Debbie shoved an egg roll in her mouth. "It's ridiculous how much I eat anymore. I'm hungry as soon as I stop eating."

"That's a good thing," Shaker commented. "As we've been invited to The Chalet tonight. I'll pick you up here at five, and we'll teleport home to change, then we'll teleport there. Dinner's at six."

"Is there any way we could postpone?" Debbie asked wearily. "You wouldn't believe the day I've had, and I still haven't checked on any of those bookings or other decisions we talked about."

Shaker shook his head. "John's very selective about his guests. If we cancel, we might never be invited back. He's an important ally, Mistress. We can't afford to lose him."

"All right," Debbie said, stuffing another roll into her mouth. "Then I'd better get back to it. See you at five."

~

"It's like something out of a gothic tale," Debbie whispered, as they approached the great carved oak door of The Chalet. Lights were on all over the great house, shining out into the night. Surrounding the house, there was only blackness as far as her eyes could see. *Must be forest. What a great setting.* "Almost like we stepped back in time."

"Inside is likely much more modern," Shaker said, knocking on the door with one of the great iron knockers. *But it's good you wore the ballgown and I, a tux.*

A woman in an old-fashioned maid's uniform answered, then curtseyed, her eyes vacant. She didn't speak but pointed the way ahead as she shut the door behind them.

The long hallway was lighted, sconces high on the walls holding candles. But ahead, the room at the far end was lit with electric light, a crackling fire in the large fireplace.

"Evenings here can be quite chilly this time of year," John said, getting up from the hearth. He shook Shaker's hand, then bowed to Debbie. "Good to see you again, Debbie."

A woman in an elegant lace dress with a full skirt hurried into the room, and over to Shaker. "Hello, I'm Madeline." She did a full curtsey and took John's arm. "We're so happy you could join us tonight."

"You must both be famished after a full day," John said. "Please come, we will serve dinner now."

Shaker and Debbie followed them into a long, dimly-lit ballroom. In the center a wide but smallish table that seated four had been placed. The huge crystal chandelier above it was lighted, illuminating the parquet floor and the carved wood chairs, but it left the edges of the room shrouded in darkness. The table was bare except for place settings, and two buffet tables were on either side of the main one, both laden with food.

"Please, help yourselves," John said, handing Shaker a plate. "Shaker, you're with me. Debbie, please follow Madeline."

Debbie looked at Shaker then at the offerings on the table. The one nearest her and Mad held all manner of fine foods, from several high-end varieties of caviar to simple devilled eggs. The table nearest John held platters of different meats, some steaming and some on ice. *Flesh. And likely not just animal.*

Averting her eyes, Debbie followed Mad to the other table, and began loading her plate. "You must try some of the eggs," Mad said, taking three. "I know they aren't proper dinner fare, but I enjoy them so."

Debbie took a few, nodding. "I like them, too."

"Your dress is lovely."

"It's one of the period costumes from *Immortal Confessions*," Debbie admitted. "Shaker favors it, so I borrowed it for the evening."

"Then I must applaud your costume department. Their attention to detail is to be commended."

After the couples were seated, several more vacant-eyed servants appeared from the edges of the ballroom, bringing varieties of wine and glasses. They returned to the shadows when done, disappearing.

Shaker and John didn't speak, steadily eating with no conversation. Madeline smiled at Debbie frequently, but made no effort to converse. Unnerved, Debbie also focused on eating, the only sound the clink of their silverware. *What a beautiful but odd night.*

After they were finished, Shaker nodded to John. "Wonderful, not that I would have expected anything else, John. It's an honor to be in your home."

John inclined his head as if this was also some sort of ritual. "It's our honor to have you both here. But I'm sure Debbie would like a tour. Ladies, if you'll excuse yourselves?"

Madeline stood, and pulled out Debbie's chair quickly, forcing her to stand. "Come, Debbie. I'd love for you to see some of our innovations."

So we're dismissed? All right. Debbie smiled at Shaker, then followed Madeline out.

The next hour was filled with slow walking, as Madeline showed her the libraries, the kitchens and pantries, the living rooms, other dining room, and hallways of other rooms which weren't being used at the moment.

"John's study is in one of these," Madeline said, as they walked. "But that's his space. I don't enter it."

Debbie looked at the other doors, wondering what else was behind them. Noises of something alive and sentient shifting within as they passed by some of the closed doors were discomforting. "Are you ever afraid here?"

"I was, when I first came here," Madeline tittered. "The place had a bad reputation, and I didn't know John then. But we've made a real home here."

"So there are no ghosts?"

"Oh, there are many ghosts," Madeline replied. "Just none that mean us harm."

"You mean there are literally spirits of dead people here, haunting your house?"

"Of course," Madeline said. "Where else do the dead go after life is done?"

"How about Heaven or Hell?"

"I think that some that die go there," Madeline said after a moment. "But others don't want to, for whatever reason. So they find places like this that attract them, and they stay, because they can. Maybe some of them are afraid to pass on, because of what they did when they were alive."

"Are you afraid of death?"

"Of course not," Madeline said, as if it were preposterous. "I'm not going to die, though."

"Why not?"

"Because I want to stay here with John, and he has the power to keep my spirit here with him."

"Aren't you afraid to live forever and see everything you know change?"

"More afraid to face judgment. I've done a lot for love, over the years."

"What about redemption?" Debbie said to Madeline.

"You mean is it possible to enter Heaven, to be forgiven your part in murder and mayhem for the riches of the mortal world?" She snorted. "Perhaps. Certainly many former Mistresses and Masters would like to believe so. I don't think so myself."

"Aren't you worried about your soul, if you think that?" Debbie persisted. "I'm going to have a baby soon, and I'm worried about my child's safety. When it was just me with Shaker, I didn't think about it, even when we had some close calls. But now, I can't stop from wondering about it."

"I think Shaker would do anything he could for you and your child," Madeline said. "I don't know him well, but it's obvious that he dotes on you. And the stories you told at dinner of your wedding and the lovely things he did for you to celebrate your first lover's day were deliberately beautiful and extravagant. I'm sorry that doesn't sound like a better compliment." She laughed nervously. "I don't get out much to talk to people."

I didn't tell any stories at dinner. We didn't speak! Shaker said nothing! "John said you don't like to leave here."

"I don't," Madeline said with a shrug. "I have a computer, to see all I care to of the world. So much hate and anger, and it just seems to get worse every year. My days are full of making The Chalet a home for myself and John." She smiled, and suddenly Debbie heard Madeline's voice in her mind. *You didn't speak, you thought, Debbie. I'm able to tune into your thoughts, just as John and Shaker were able to have a conversation with their minds during dinner. I hope you'll forgive the intrusion. It was obvious you were nervous, so I thought it would be better to just keep silent, see what kind of conversation you would like.*

Debbie laughed nervously, trying not to panic while she tried to remember if she'd had any rude thoughts while she was eating that everyone had 'heard." "Well I'm glad I didn't think anything rude. I'm not used to being overheard in my own mind."

"My apologies. John and I speak much of the time with our minds to each other, so it's seemed second nature to do so with you both, who share a similar relationship. I will stick to spoken words now that I know your preference for them. But you asked how I keep myself busy. I read, I surf the 'net, I sew, I decorate, and I garden in the warm months. When John is away, I have our friends if I'm lonely."

"Your friends that live locally?"

"Spirits mostly," Madeline said, emitting another nervous laugh. "I feel so odd to be discussing this with another person. I never have before. They live here, of course. They aren't all human, or I should say they weren't all human, when they were alive. But they are content to dwell here. They enjoy our love."

Debbie kept the smile pasted on her face, unsure of what to say, the replies coming to mind both offending and dangerous to utter. *Who knew what was listening in the confines of this house?*

"Quite a few entities, to be sure. We have a few cats, also," Madeline went on. "We've never had a problem with mice, but I had cats growing up. They didn't care for John at first, but they grew to tolerate him after a little while."

"I'm glad you're happy," Debbie said finally. "We have a hellhound, ourselves. Shaker and I have had our share of troubles. Nothing we did to one another, just the vast differences in what we are. It's hard to overcome."

"Think of yourself as multicultural," Madeline said with a wink. "I read extensively, so I know how hard it is for someone like you and me to get anyone else who has read the modern fiction about demon love to understand the reality. They think we are deluded, some kind of patsy for loving immortal beings. They don't understand love comes in different forms. That doesn't make it any less real."

Debbie paused, then told Madeline about the angel Rafael, and all he'd said, and Cahill's attack the previous year. "That's what I'm worried about, Madeline. That someone will come after me and kill my child because they think its evil."

"No child is born evil," she said, hugging Debbie tightly. "But you're right, that you shouldn't let down your guard. Could you somehow make it known the child is not Shaker's? Possibly a sperm donor?"

Debbie blinked at the abrupt change in subject. "I'm not sure," she said slowly. "Shaker's very proud he's going to be a father."

"It will be safer if the child isn't thought to be his," Madeline said firmly. "I'd advise you to put another name on the birth certificate as the father. And to announce publicly that you had a sperm donor. The child's welfare must be first and foremost, at all costs."

"You speak as if you had a child of your own," Debbie said curiously.

Madeline smiled strangely. "Come. We must rejoin the others. John is calling to me."

"How do you hear other's thoughts when you aren't bound to them?" Debbie asked, as they walked. "I didn't hear anything as we ate from any of you."

"I hear yours only when you project a clear thought. I can't hear feelings or general impressions, because we don't share a bond. I mostly saw your memories of your wedding and courtship as pictures projected in your mind. Reach out to someone, and you'll be able to get snippets at first, then in time mental pictures and clear thoughts."

"Will it work with anyone?"

"Anyone who's not crazy," she tittered. "They might be able to tune in and hear you!"

"Thank you. I'll have to practice."

Madeline took her hand, walking much faster. "Please come. John is strangely adamant we return immediately."

Debbie was hurrying after her when she felt a sharp pain in her lower back. She stopped fast, unsteady in her heels, then another hit her stronger than the first. She rocked backward, then fell sprawling. Pain was now clawing at her insides, as if something was trying to break free.

"Shh, shh," Madeline comforted, holding her. "Shaker and John are coming. Just remain calm and breathe!"

Guardian came trotting out of the shadows, whining. He paced back and forth, panting nervously, then sat on his haunches and began howling loudly.

Debbie groaned, then another ragged spasm hit her, and she blacked out.

Debbie awoke in Shaker's arms on the floor, her dress stained with blood. She looked at Shaker, speechless. *Did I lose the baby?*

"Titus did all he could," Shaker said. "I'm sorry. I'm sorry for us both."

Debbie began to cry in long hitching breaths.

"Come Mistress," Shaker said, gathering her prone form in his arms. "It's past time you had some peace."

Debbie sighed happily, munching another handful of potato chips from the family-size bag. She wiggled her toes underneath the huge fluffy comforter, awaking Guardian, who looked around, then put his head back down.

"I'm glad you're relaxing," Shaker said, as he brought in two glasses of wine. "Let's do some wine-tasting. Here, I opened some of the different vintages Rack's given you; this is that Timeless, for Devlin's movie. I think its excellent. But is that what I think it is?"

"A Steven Segal movie," Debbie said with a grin, taking the glass and sipping. "It's a guilty pleasure. I love watching him kick ass. I'm just about to the scene where he takes on the entire bar in this one."

"I think you were in the majority in the days he was a major star, he made a lot of action movies."

"We should have some scenes like this in your sequel," Debbie said. "By the way, have you shown Sheila the end? She keeps asking me for a full script."

"I'll write in a bar scene, just for you," Shaker teased, easing under the comforter with her. "But I am not taking on an entire bar, that's ludicrous."

"It's fun."

"Yeah, if you're watching," Shaker chuckled. "In real life, someone's going to get in a few solid hits, maybe a few someones. I'd rather incapacitate them all with magic before they even know I'm there. It's much less risky."

"But less exciting to watch," Debbie said with a frown.

"No arguments there. I don't want to ask, but we should talk about what happened. Are you feeling better?"

"Yes," Debbie said reluctantly. "Some. Well, physically I am. Reality is settling in. I feel like me being pregnant was just a dream. And now that I'm not, I am free to go back to work, to how our lives used to be."

Shaker watched her, not speaking, his mind blank.

"But that feels so cold to say. Even though it makes no sense at all, I want my dream back. Even with all the panic and worrying and stress about being a good mom or even having a healthy child...I just want my dream back, Shaker."

"We can have another child," Shaker said carefully. "Jett's fully functional; I checked. I know that sounds clinical, but I wanted to make sure after this happened that it wasn't something to do with me. And your doctor said you were healthy. So we'll try again."

"But is that what you want?"

"I want us to have a healthy child." He lifted her chin, making her look at him. *I foresaw that we would have a child together. Don't despair.*

Debbie smiled and clutched him, as he hugged her.

CHAPTER NINE

JUNE

"THE FIRST CARD WILL FALL THIS SUMMER, ANOTHER BY October. Act by then, or all is lost," Debbie murmured, looking at the legal document in her hand. "That's what Jezebel said. I should have retained them both then."

"To do what?" Sheila said groggily, from the gurney next to her. "And where am I?"

"Emergency ward," Debbie said, grabbing onto Sheila's nearest hand. "There was an explosion on set, one that wasn't orchestrated by our people. You were caught in the blast."

Sheila glanced at her wrist, taking in the medical tag there. "Then why am I breathing?"

"Harp. He was looking through your eyes, he said. He noticed something and teleported in but couldn't get you out in time. But the table that would have killed you speared him instead, you just got thrown a fair distance. He's at the Black Rose, being tended by Xerxes, who apparently is well-versed in demon anatomy. All you had was a broken arm. They gave you a shot already, for the pain, and stopped your bleeding."

"He's some kind of faerie, I think," Sheila muttered, touching her bandaged arm. "But why am I here, and not at the Black Rose, too?"

"Because they don't have the power to heal you. You need stitches and have multiple breaks."

"They do, too." Sheila struggled to get up. "And magic is faster, I could be back to normal by tonight. I'm not staying here."

"They can't spare the power to heal you," Debbie hissed, forcing Sheila back down by grasping her injured arm. Sheila cried out in surprised pain, cringing back. "Harp's pretty bad off. He said you still hadn't fed them, Sheila. They've been subsisting on some kind of magic the spa is generating, he wasn't specific."

"That's Incubus," Sheila groaned. "It lets them suck soul power, in small doses. I can't believe you squeezed my broken arm!"

Shaker mentioned something about that kind of spell to me, I think. Am I far gone, that it no longer seems so reprehensible? "Song said when you woke, to talk to her mentally, and designate at least three people. Harp will need that many to survive this." Debbie leaned closer, her eyes scanning the hallway. "Sheila, those were her words. Do it now, before you pass out again. The doctor's coming back any minute to give you a sedative and prep you for surgery. Or you might wake up with no demons at all."

Sheila closed her eyes for a few minutes. "Done," she said, opening them. "Song said she will go and take care of it."

A doctor and a nurse strode up. "Hi, you're Sheila?"

"Yes, she is," Debbie supplied, standing up.

"Yes," Sheila said groggily, then recited her birthdate and full name when prompted. The nurse gave her a sedative, then wheeled her away.

Debbie sat down and went back to reading the letter. *Titan Pictures sued us for what we did to move the stock back to private. Henry's effort was crap, a junk lawsuit, but we had to spend money to answer it. Now they are trying to accuse Jett of fondling some starlet-wannabe.*

"Debbie?" Shaker said, walking up to her.

Debbie looked up into his bright blue eyes with relief, as she stood and hugged him. "I'm glad you're okay."

"That priest was behind this," he whispered. "Did they take Sheila in?"

Debbie nodded. "She'll be in surgery for a few hours. Her arm was pretty bad."

"I'd prefer to get Titus to take a look at it, or even Leri," Shaker murmured. "But he's busy with Harp. I've never heard of someone creating a bomb where the parts used were blessed, but that's what he did. And it worked, too. If Harp hadn't been only grazed, he'd have died."

"Isn't there anything you could use as a defense against holy items?" Debbie asked, as they walked out to her car.

"Nothing that's known," Shaker mused, buckling himself in.

"But the blast also hurt some innocent people," Debbie went on, pulling out into traffic. "Our Spring picnic was ruined. I had to cancel it for this weekend. Doesn't that count against the priest? I mean with God?"

Shaker winced slightly. "No. The people working were Pandora employees; because they are working for us, they are considered guilty. Maybe not as much as we are, but definitely not innocent. The priest hurt people, he didn't kill them."

"The more you tell me, the less I understand the rules of Heaven," Debbie said darkly. "Hell's laws seem harsh and mean, but at least I see the logic in them."

"There is logic in both," Shaker said with a sigh. "Don't forget that God and the devil are supposed to be at war. But the devil was given dominion over the earth, while God reigns in Heaven."

"I still don't understand," Debbie complained. She passed him the letter. "By the way, Jett supposedly raped a woman in his trailer. We're going to have to see a lawyer and figure out an alibi."

"He did it," Shaker said, after a moment. "I accessed his memories. He was high at the time, and this woman had just sold him some drugs, but wanted twice the price. So he told her he'd screw her as part of the deal. She initially said yes, then got pissed off when he came and left her wanting."

"Did I tell you lately that I'm glad you cleaned up his bullshit?" Debbie said in exasperation. "The only reason he wasn't killed for his stupidity was because you took over. He would have made my human donation list before the end of last year."

"Yes, Jett has…I have made much better decisions this year," Shaker said with a toothy smile. "And speaking of donations, it's past time. So who do you nominate?"

I told him to make his own choice. Why hadn't he? "I take it Henry was a no?"

"Henry would have been fine last year, but he's found Buddhism since you broke his heart. His faith is new, and it's strong. Sorry."

"Then let's go out for dinner," Debbie said, eyes narrowing. "And see who volunteers themselves."

~

"Well, the waiter was nice, the food was great, and in spite of them being out of tiramisu, I can't complain of any service we had here," Shaker said, sipping his espresso. "So what now?"

"You tell me," Debbie said, swirling the last dregs of her wine in her wineglass. "Should we frequent the ghetto, see who we can rustle up there?"

"Not recommended," Shaker said with a frown, as he laid cash on the bill, then closed the leather booklet. "While you might find people who won't be missed there, they usually can defend themselves. I can't risk my flesh while filming is going on. We're better off going back to the hospital."

"For what? Someone dying?"

Shaker nodded.

"But that angel I met, he was trying to guide my father's spirit to Heaven. Aren't you risking running into one of them?"

"Hospitals have angels, yes, but it's rare. There are far more often demons there, haunting the corridors waiting for spirits to leave their bodies. I just may have to push ahead of a few colleagues," he said, standing up. "Besides, Sheila's there, we have perfect cover for visiting. Let's go."

"Now, you go and ask at the desk about Sheila," Shaker said, as they entered. "I'll go to the bathroom, then head upstairs. Get Sheila, then come after me."

Debbie looked at him in surprise, as he hurried away. Shaking her head, she went to the main desk. Before she could ask, she caught sight of the doctor.

She ran up to him. "Excuse me, I was here with a friend with a broken arm. Can you tell me what room she's in?"

The doctor looked like he didn't recognize her, then nodded. "Broken arm? Oh yes, the film executive. Yes, she's upstairs with her brother."

Debbie's eyes widened. "She doesn't have a brother. What room?"

"Miss, I really—"

Panic suffused Debbie. "What room!"

"304, take the elevator at the back, and head to the left—"

Debbie took off running, as she shouted to Shaker telepathically. She took the elevator, then met Song coming out of the stairwell with Xerxes. "Hurry," Song said, falling to her knees and jerking. "He's trying to exorcise us!"

Xerxes began running and Debbie followed, giving him directions even as she labored to keep up, swearing when her high heel cracked suddenly. Grabbing the shoe in one hand, she took the other off and ran in her bare feet.

Xerxes burst into a room on the left, interrupting the priest in mid-chant. Sheila was on the bed tied down with restraints, a gag in her mouth. The fanatic brandished his bible as if it were a sword. "Come no closer!"

Xerxes reached out and grasped the priest, then both of them disappeared.

Debbie hurried to unbind Sheila, ripping off her gag. "Can you walk?"

"Hell yes, I can walk! Get me the fuck out of here!"

Debbie helped Sheila up from the bed, then the two of them hobbled out the door together. They made it to the end of the hall, then into the elevator. Xerxes did not reappear.

Song met them at the ground floor. "Come, Mistress," she said, taking Sheila's arm. "We must get you home."

"Did you feed?" Sheila said, as they hurried to the door.

"Ma'am!" the front door receptionist yelled. "Ma'am, you can't just leave!"

"Bill my insurance!" Sheila yelled back, not stopping.

"Ma'am!"

Shaker pulled up in Debbie's car outside. "Get in!"

The three piled into the car, and Shaker took off.

"Thanks for your help back there," Debbie said sarcastically.

"There was nothing I could do against a priest," Shaker defended, as he wove in and out of traffic. "And I was too weak to risk getting an injury."

"Did you feed?" Sheila and Debbie both said at once.

"Yes," Song and Shaker both said together, then looked at one another.

"Harp is better, but not mobile yet," Song said, stretching her hands so talons formed briefly before disappearing. "I'm back at full strength."

"Good," Debbie said quickly, not wanting to hear details. "Shaker, are you?"

"Yes, but I ran into your angel," he said darkly. "Which is the only reason you aren't still there, Sheila. He went after me, and I led him outside, then in a chase teleporting around the city." He paused to swerve around a car and dash down an exit that loomed up suddenly out of the dark. "He was guarding the priest."

"What about Xerxes?"

"He teleported the priest to Asia, to the mountains, before he went back to the Black Rose," Song said, after a moment, reading from her phone. "He's sure that the guardian angel will retrieve the priest before he freezes, however. Then he says they will likely return. He's giving his two weeks notice. Ugh."

"Those two are going to be a problem," Sheila said. "Hell, they already are. We're going to need some kind of a security detail."

"We need some kind of defense against them," Debbie said, after a moment. "Security is fine, but all that can do is alert us, not take an offensive."

"There's no defense against holy men or faith in general," Song complained. "That's why we always lose once we come to someone's notice. The only way to survive is to leave and go somewhere else to start again."

"We can't leave, so we have to fight," Debbie said. "Moreover, we have to win. You say they have blessings and faith, so even just normal human guards on the payroll will be overcome, if it comes to a confrontation. Can't we counteract that with some kind of curse?"

Shaker looked at her in surprise. "You're saying get around the faith, not challenge it overtly. Yes, that might work here."

"You need liquid sin, or something like that," Sheila said suddenly. "Something to overwhelm the good with evil."

"You're thinking like a demon," Shaker said with approval. "And you raise some good points. Let me get with my brother and see what we can come up with."

That night, Debbie, Sheila, Song, Shaker, and a sick-looking-but-recovering Harp gathered in Debbie's large living room.

"Where is Titus?" Debbie said.

"Devlin keeps him pretty busy, especially in the evenings," Shaker placated. "I communicated the information to him. He is probably taking the time to research it."

The doorbell rang.

"Who could that be?" Debbie said, rising nervously.

"It's Rip," Shaker said gruffly. "Which means there's a problem." He stalked to the door and opened it. Standing there was a smaller version of Titus, with a more reckless expression and a shock of spiked black hair. "What's going on?"

Rip looked at Debbie. "I'm sorry I didn't make the wedding. I heard it was nice. I'll bring you a gift as soon as I've got a steady gig. I'm working for Devlin now—"

"Rip, where is Titus?" Shaker demanded, not letting him in.

"Devlin needs him tonight. He sent me to tell you he can't make it."

"He couldn't just come and tell me himself? It would have taken five minutes! He's not dealing with the kind of emergency we are!"

"It's an emergency," Rip said in a low voice. "Titus is handling operations. He asked that you be available on standby, if needed."

Shaker looked at Rip for a moment. "Like 1975?"

"Pretty close."

"All right," Shaker said, letting his shoulders fall in defeat. "I'll be here all night."

"Thanks bro." Rip disappeared.

"Damn it," Shaker swore. He flopped on the couch.

"What was all that about?" Sheila asked. "What happened?"

"Something's happened to Devlin," Debbie said, sitting near Shaker. "Hasn't it?"

"To men like that priest, vampires are just as bad as demons," Shaker explained. "And wereanimals, like the bears that guard Devlin, or snakes like Lash, they're not much above us in most fanatic's estimation. I should have thought of it. The priest likely contacted other hunters in this state to get information about us.

Devlin's movie has been in the news, they made the connection he was involved with us. It's a usual hunter tactic, to have several attacks at the same time on multiple targets. Usually at least one succeeds, and there's confusion with everyone involved."

"Is he hurt?" Sheila asked, worried.

"Rip wouldn't have admitted if he were," Shaker responded, shrugging. "But I'm guessing it was a close call, he's likely under house arrest until Lash takes care of whomever attacked."

"Why don't we hire Lash to take out the priest?" Sheila asked. "He's supposed to be able to get to anyone, right?"

"I'm not sure Lash would take on someone an angel was supporting," Shaker cautioned. "But even if he would, we can't really afford him. Besides, even if we did, we'd make a martyr. There would be another believer who would come to avenge him. No, we need to arrange an accident for this priest totally unrelated to us… or some kind of diversion."

I could afford him, with the money my father left me, Debbie thought. *I'll leave that as a last resort, though.*

"Diversion?" Sheila echoed.

"On a scale of truly encompassing evil…we aren't, plain and simple," Shaker clarified. "We need to give that priest another target, something he thinks is worth going after more than us."

"None of these are real solutions," Harp griped, shifting painfully. "We can't be part of a production company promoting ourselves and hide at the same time. Song, our spa is likely going to be another target. I thought we were here to discuss magic?"

"There is a spell to break down a person's will," Shaker said slowly. "But I don't see a way to administer it when we can't touch the priest. We'd have to get someone with no demon connection to do it for us."

"I can see if I can convince Xerxes to return?" Song offered meekly.

Shaker shook his head. "What we need is someone not tainted by a demon who also is skilled enough to do complex magic."

"Who is willing to help us," Debbie added. "For a reasonable fee."

"Leri could do it," Shaker said, after a moment. "Titus's wife, you met her at the wedding. She's married to a demon, but she's not bound to him. But she'll ask for a favor in return."

"So grant her one," Harp said in exasperation. "We're facing oblivion here."

"Whatever she'd ask for isn't something we'd want to give her," Shaker warned. "But you're right, in that I don't see an easier way out. I'll go now to find her." He hugged Debbie, kissed her cheek and disappeared.

Debbie bit her lip, and walked to the window, watching the stars as the group behind her bickered about what to do about Xerxes's departure. As she watched, the figure of a little girl came out from behind a tree in their yard, then waved up at her. *It's Celia again.*

"Guardian," Debbie called.

The hellhound trotted out of the blackness of the hall closet, then took up position near the window.

Celia's grinning face rose up in front of the window, as she touched the glass. The hound lunged at the window, the ghost retreating with a stymied hiss.

Debbie closed the drapes, sealing out the wraith, then went to her bedroom, curling up with Guardian beside her. She hugged the dog, and finally drifted off to sleep.

~

Early the next morning, Debbie opened her eyes to Shaker, who was sitting on the side of the bed near her looking into space. "What is it?"

This is being kept under wraps, he said mentally. *Do not speak of it aloud or mention it to anyone. Hayden, Devlin's estate, was attacked last night. Devlin and his little girl escaped, the house sustained minimal damage, and about a tenth of his guards were killed before they repelled the vampire hunters.*

Is that worse than it sounds? Rip made it sound like it was Armageddon last night.

The hunter groups combined their strength and attacked together, something they have never done, much less to Devlin himself. Over half of the attackers died in the battle last night. He will enact a terrible price from those that were captured for this; word is he and his brother Danial are hard at work doing that this morning. But there's more. Devlin's lady love, Sarelle, was essentially kidnapped by a fellow vampire of Devlin's standing, Michael. He's saying he did it to save her from the hunters, but that he stepped in so easily at the exact right time to snatch her from harm smacks of an elaborate plan. I believe Michael means to keep her a prisoner.

Debbie took a deep breath. *That shouldn't be that difficult for Lash to handle, right?*

Lash was also taken hostage last night.

Debbie felt the first stirrings of real fear. *But he's an expert. He'll be able to break them free?*

He likely could get free himself easily, but he won't leave Devlin's lady there. Again, this whole thing stinks of intricate planning, maybe something months or years in the making.

But Lash's been in situations like this before, hasn't he? He's another one of you that's decades old.

Lash was only taken as a hostage once and it wasn't for ransom, it was so his enemy could torture him before killing him. That is the closest he's ever come to death, and he survived because of sheer luck. No, this isn't the norm.

"Damn it." *Can you help them?*

Shaker didn't answer.

"Shaker?"

"Titus got forced into Hell," he said, letting out a breath. "He's out and back in Devlin's service, but he's resting."

"How could this happen?" Debbie said. "I mean, how could vampire hunters have arranged that?"

"They had help, likely from Michael's camp. He must have a demon of his own of some power. Or," Shaker paused, looking over at her to catch her eyes with his own gaze. "The devil not only allowed it, he authorized it."

"Why?"

"Because Titus is happy here on earth with his family around him. While he does much evil in Devlin's name, it's not the length and breadth of evil that is expected of him, you might say. He's been in Devlin's service a long time. The devil might have called him in for a warning to remind him of his purpose here on earth."

"That is unfair and horrible. Titus has only helped us."

Shaker grimaced. "That's likely what the devil tortured him for. Anyway, I'm telling you all this only so you know that Titus says that Devlin is inconsolable over the events of last night. He's holding it together for now for his kid, but I'm not sure how long that will last. You may get messages saying that the movie is cancelled."

"He can't do that," Debbie breathed. "We'll be ruined. That movie has been the focus of our entire year!"

"I'm telling you this because I want you to keep doing that movie, at all costs," Shaker said firmly. "Titus said he talked to you about the film, then to Sheila. She has an alternate simplified script she made using his notes and ideas; use that. The changes are minimal but will be effective. Ignore any missives from Devlin to the contrary. In fact, ignore any messages you get from him and don't take his calls for now. Okay?"

Debbie nodded. "All right. Will Nate still be liaison for us?"

Shaker shook his head. "He's gone back to his state on Devlin's orders. The whole vampire hierarchy is in an uproar; Devlin's home was not the only one attacked; attacks have happened all over the world. The hunters will be decimated country-wide as soon as the vampires regroup. But until that threat is dealt with, we're on our own. But we'll be okay." He patted her arm. "I have someone coming to see you tomorrow who will help, his name is Terian."

"Damn it, we've got to get going. Catarella has that meeting with both of us this morning."

"There's no rest for the wicked," Shaker said, getting to his feet. "Let me shower, and I'll be ready in ten."

~

"Mr. Black, thank you for coming today," Catarella said with a glint in his eye. He turned on a digital recorder. "Debbie said she briefed you on what your accuser is saying. So what's your side of the story?"

"That the sex was consensual, that we were both high at the time, and that it was her idea," Shaker said.

"Well, that does put another spin on the events." Catarella took some notes, then looked up. "Will you testify to that under oath?"

"Yes," Shaker said.

"Can anyone corroborate your story?"

Shaker named several people. "They initially introduced us at the party preceding the event in question. They knew I was into drugs, and that she sold them."

"This may be more cut and dry than I anticipated," Catarella said, obviously pleased, making more notes. "Let me get back to her attorney, and I'll also contact these two people, and make sure they'll back up your story. I'll call you later in the week."

"Thanks," Debbie said, as he left. When they were alone, she said, "What did Leri say about a spell to defend against the priest?"

"She said she could redirect the priest, but that she couldn't guarantee he'd go for it. She's done enough black magic over the years that she's got her own aura of evil, so she's not willing to get too close, especially as it would attract more attention to Devlin, not to mention Titus."

"Did she advise something else?"

"Yes. Relocating."

"That's crap," Debbie said angrily. "How is it that Devlin has been master of a country for over a hundred years and had a demon all that time and he doesn't have angels and demon hunters after him?"

Shaker looked at her strangely, then nodded. "That's right, you read the script of *Immortal Confessions* and put the rest together. But you're wrong. Devlin has weathered many attacks by preparation and planning, but some were just pure luck. Lash has saved him more than a few times, but it's Titus and the magical aid he's given Lash that have helped Lash to win over Devlin's enemies over and over. Devlin's graveyard—yes, his estate has its own that covers several miles—is teeming with the bodies of guards who have fallen in his service defending him. Most of them died because they didn't have that same magical help which Lash always took."

"Then what we really need, instead of more magic, is brute force," Debbie said slowly. "You are close to Titus in magic; you could enchant someone, give him some kind of magical armor. We've got demons to protect us, but we need someone to go on the offensive, someone non-demon they can't see coming." She paused. "Lash is a hitman, one of the best you said."

"The best, currently."

"Well, who's second best? Can we hire them, put them on retainer?"

Shaker stared at her in amazement, then laughed richly. "I do love your ruthlessness, Mistress. And no, we could not afford them, either, not that the current #2 would take the job anyway. He fancies himself a good guy."

Debbie furrowed her brows. "A good killer? And we can afford someone, I can use that five hundred thousand my father left me."

"It's of no consequence. You're right that we need some more muscle." Shaker stood. "You're also right that we can afford it with your inheritance. Anyone in the top ten would likely be able to do what we need done. But we also need strategy. Terian can recommend some additional security precautions, and he'll likely recommend someone who is Ranked to take out the priest. Not in the top five, but in the top twenty. If he recommends several people, hire them all."

"Can we afford several, plus whatever this Terian charges?"

"It's your life, Mistress, maybe all our lives. Pay whatever they ask for."

~

Debbie was in her office the next morning when her secretary buzzed her. "There's a Mr. Terian here to see you."

"Show him in, Kaitlyn."

A tall man with reddish-brown eyes walked in, dressed in a suit and tie, his hair in a short ponytail.

"Hello," Debbie said. "Please have a seat, Mr. Terian. I understand a mutual acquaintance set up this meeting.

"Yes, he said you were having some security issues," Terian said, opening his briefcase. "I'm from Solutions, Inc." He took out a laptop, opened it, and began typing. "And it's just Terian. Can you tell me how many employees you have that have access to your office?"

Debbie answered him, and the following fifty-something questions he asked detailing Pandora's operations. When she was done, he typed a few more notes, then sat back in his chair.

"You're a very accessible boss," he said finally. "That's good for your employees, but not good for your health, Ms. Deal."

"Mrs. Black."

"Sorry. Mrs. Black. I'd advise a security guard next to your door in the hours you're here, and at home stationed outside, perhaps living on premises whenever Sh...um, your husband is not with you. This person you select should be hard to kill, if not immortal."

"Are you available?" Debbie said bluntly.

Terian smiled but shook his head. "I'm a partner in the firm I'm here representing, Solution's Inc. I was asked to do a consult on recommendations to keep you more secure. No, I'm not available."

"Can you recommend someone that can start in the next twenty-four hours? I'll need a guard for my VP, Sheila, as well," Debbie interjected. "She's been the main target so far, not me."

"Yes, I was briefed on what happened. I understand she's also got a bond of her own?"

"Two."

Terian's eyebrows raised. "Really. That's seldom done. And likely what got her the attention. Your attacker may have followed you out here, but the stronger concentration of demon he's sensing coming off her because of her double bond is what's got him focusing on her instead of you."

"Can he be taken out?"

"Not by me, or my partners," Terian said. "But there are a number of people I can recommend."

"Good. What else?"

"I'd install a card-driven passcode system, and put locks requiring one on every door. That won't stop people getting in if someone lets them in, but it will cut down on unauthorized visitors."

"What about cameras at all the exits and entrances?"

Terian shrugged. "You can do that, but it's a waste of money. You're not going to prosecute these people, and they aren't out to get evidence on you. You're both at war. They will kill you if they have a chance. I'll tell you straight, if that priest comes here to get you, you're not going to get a visual of him. The path will magically clear of random people, and they might not remember even letting him in. The cameras would just stop working."

"Shaker mentioned something to that effect. It sounds utterly ridiculous. We make movies here, we aren't in one."

"You are working to further demons on earth," Terian said softly. "To show them to be beings that would be fair partners, if demanding ones. That's not going to get you any favors in Heaven.

You are lucky that you don't have angels coming here in a posse out for your heads."

"I didn't set out to do anything but run a production company," Debbie said, miffed.

"I have seen signs up within your office celebrating the Year of the Demon," Terian commented.

"Those are from last year," Debbie said weakly. "We had a lot of demon pictures come out that were successful, and it seemed like a good marketing plan."

"What's done is done. Get those passcards in place, and I'll get you some names. That's a good start." He paused. "Off the record, my own personal recommendation would be to donate some of your proceeds to a local charity and be highly visible about it. Also, I'd diversify your films so that they focus on more than evil beings."

"We are not planning any demon films for next year," Debbie said slowly. "The only one that features a demon has it as the main villain."

"Good," Terian said, nodding. "I'd say if we can get you to the new year in one piece, you'll be fine." He stood, then held out his hand. "Don't worry. Danial and I are very good at what we do."

Debbie shook his hand, her brow furrowing. "Danial? Devlin's brother?"

"The same," Terian said, losing his smile.

"Sorry," Debbie said quickly. "The name is just unusual, so I wondered."

"No, it's I who should apologize," Terian said awkwardly. "I should have made it to your wedding. But I have a new baby myself, and she's a handful." He smiled again. "I understand you're expecting yourself."

Debbie blinked. "How did you know that? Who are you?"

"I'm Titus's son by Leri," Terian replied formally, his tone cool. "Shaker's my uncle. So you're my aunt."

I have a nephew. Debbie couldn't resist the smile coming over her face. "Really. I had no idea Titus had any children. Are you a demon, too? You must be, right?"

"No, or I'd never have gotten this job," Terian laughed, handing her a few sheets of paper. "Danial hates demons. I'm only half demon. Leri's a dark faerie."

Debbie nodded. "That's right. Sorry."

"No problem, it gets confusing." Terian packed up his laptop, then headed for the door. "I'll send you a bill. But I would recommend you hustle to get things in place. That priest will try again, and soon."

"And no, I'm not pregnant…anymore," Debbie said, biting her lip hard. Tears formed in her eyes anyway, and she leaned against the desk for support.

"I'm so sorry," Terian said, dropping his laptop and rushing to her side. He helped her sit in her chair. "Miscarriage?"

Debbie nodded, then began sobbing. Terian hugged her, then handed her some tissues from her desk. "I don't have any good words for you," Terian said finally. "Just that if you try again, to make sure you have a cesarean. Plan on it."

"You say you're a half demon. Was your baby's mother human?"

"100% human."

"And she delivered safely?"

Terian nodded. "Titus was there, he ensured a safe birth."

"Then maybe it's just me," Debbie said bitterly. "Maybe the problem's me."

"I'm sure that's not the case," Terian said uncomfortably, patting her hand. "Do you want me to call for someone?"

"No," Debbie said, pulling her emotions in with effort. "Thank you for your advice, I'll follow it. Send me those names ASAP, please. I'll feel better when we have someone here."

"I'll do that," Terian said, picking his bag back up. "Thank you for your time." He hurried out of the office.

CHAPTER TEN

JULY

"Are you sure that you want to stay in today?" Debbie called, as she made coffee. "There's a lot of celebrations going on, and it's a gorgeous day. We should have had the company party for the fourth this week instead of last week."

Shaker embraced her from behind, the feeling of his erection pressing against her buttocks drawing a moan from her suddenly parted lips. "Yes. 'In' is where I want to be." His fingers reached down, pushing up her negligee as he thrust lightly with his rigid flesh. "But was your heart set on going out?"

"No," she said throatily, turning her head. "'In' sounds great to me." She kissed him hungrily, licking his lips, then darting her tongue inside to taste him.

"Mmm," Shaker said. He lifted her, then sat her on the counter. With a sexy smile he began kissing her again, working his way lower until his head was between her legs. "Spread 'em, princess."

Debbie let out a giggle, then arched her back, as his tongue began to move in circles around her clit. He teased the soft nub, sucking gently, then backing off when she began to writhe and pant.

"Stop teasing," Debbie gasped. "Take me."

"You had only to ask." Shaker stood, and moved between her legs, bringing her forward hard to accept his manhood. He began thrusting in long, fluid strokes, as Debbie gripped his muscular back, her legs wrapped around him.

"Feel good?" Shaker murmured, as he kissed up her throat, not slowing his pace.

"Don't stop," Debbie groaned. "Give me all of you."

Shaker lifted her from the counter, then still kissing her carried her to the nearby loveseat. He sat, letting her straddle him.

Debbie pushed down hard, closing her eyes as she felt him slide further inside. She began to ride him, smiling down at him possessively.

"That's right, baby," Shaker said, watching her. "Make me come, baby. I want to hear you scream my name."

"Really?" Debbie murmured, not stopping. "Well, I want to hear my name too, baby."

"Ready when you are," Shaker teased, as he thrust faster.

"Sorry, but you'll have to wait. I'm enjoying this." Debbie moved slower, contracting her muscles, sliding up and down his rigid shaft. Shaker's response was to thrust up hard, his mouth going slack, as she rode him.

"You like that, baby?" Debbie purred. "Working that big hard cock of yours with my wet pussy?"

"Hell yeah," Shaker grunted, gripping her hips. "Take it, woman."

Debbie lowered her upper body down, her hips working harder as her climax neared. She pushed closer to Shaker, letting the burst wash over her body as she screamed out his name.

"Debbie!" Shaker grunted, then roared. "Debbie!"

~

"You know we're missing Sheila's party," Debbie said mischievously to Shaker, as they lay in bed together, Guardian snoozing on the floor all stretched out. "She said something about a barbeque."

"I know, but I wanted to spend the time just with you," Shaker said tiredly. He hugged her. "The days of work are starting to get to me." He chuckled. "I've never had a full time job for months before. I see now why people snap sometimes, just because they spend so much of their waking life working. I get home and fall into bed, instead of ravaging you. I wanted to feel like myself again." He kissed her cheek. "Did you think about what you wanted for your birthday? It's coming up fast."

"I'd rather not celebrate it," Debbie said uncomfortably. "Especially as I'll probably need my new reading glasses to find the cake to blow out the candles."

"Not likely. The cake's going to look like a Christmas tree, it'll have so many candles."

Debbie smacked his chest irritably. "Don't say that, even if it's true."

"Sorry. But I would like some pointers like you gave me for Valentine's Day so I know what to get you."

"All right, I'll think of something," Debbie said absently.

"You need to focus," Shaker said, pulling her on top of him. "On me. It's time for round two."

~

"I'm trying to help you, ma'am—"

"Then actually help me!" Debbie screamed into the phone. "Stop telling me why you can't do what I need and start telling me what you can do for me. *Absolution* is scheduled to come out in September! You can't seriously be telling me now that you have no record of not only the booking for the theaters, but nothing for the name of the movie itself!"

"I'm sorry, Ma'am. I've looked under your name, Pandora Productions, your associate's name, your various actor's names, and the name of the movie, and we have no record that you ever called and booked a release in September—"

Debbie gritted her teeth, then took a deep breath. "Alright, please check then for the following movies, starting with *Immortal Confessions* for November."

"Yes, ma'am, we have *Immortal Confessions* for November of this year. And we have *Smoke and Ashes II* slated for release in January of next year. But those are the only two movies we have booked for Pandora Productions. I'm sorry."

This can't be happening! Debbie forced herself to breathe. "Alright, thank you." She took another deep breath, then called Sheila on her intercom, leaving a voice message. "Please come to my office ASAP as soon as you get this."

Close to a half-hour later, Sheila arrived. "I'm sorry," she said, as she hurried in. "Today's been one problem after another, and all of them aren't normal."

"I know!" Debbie yelled, banging her hand down on the desk, fighting her urge to smash something. "Every theater I've called says that they never heard of *Absolution*. They have no record of bookings. So we are screwed."

"No necessarily," Sheila offered. "Since the success of *Smoke and Ashes*, we opted for regular releases in theaters. We can do a small limited release for *Absolution* instead. We never thought it would be a huge money-maker anyway."

Debbie's brow furrowed. *Sheila hadn't ever said that before, she'd stressed the importance of the picture for its literary promise.* "Yes, we can do that, but not in September. That's a hard month anyway for releases, everyone's thinking about either hurricanes or the start of school."

"Yes, we'd have to release *Absolution* now, at the end of this month, in order to get any of the literary crowd to pay attention. August is too late, everyone's either outside or on vacation."

The early release Shaker talked about...that I forgot all about, because of my miscarriage. "Can we have it ready that fast?"

"Yes, if we cut some scenes," Sheila said sharply. "The visions of violence that the demon sends the husband, to try to get him to murder his wife. But if we do that, we might not get the teen crowd. Much of the movie as it stands has a lot of dialogue, and not much action. We cut these dream sequences, it might be considered too tame by anyone younger than fifty. We can just forget any profit. The most we can hope for is breaking even—"

"Sheila, are you serious?" Debbie asked as cordially as she could manage. "You've seemed harder and harder on this movie all the time. You were one of the reasons we did the picture, because you thought it was a great story. What is up with you?"

Sheila glared back at Debbie, then deflated suddenly. "I just want us to have a good first release for the year. You remember *Hell's Gate* last year, what a debacle that turned out to be. *Tinderbox* wasn't much better. I didn't want another train wreck."

"I don't either," Debbie said. "But we're between a rock and hard place. Let's call an emergency staff meeting in an hour to notify the team. We're overdue anyway because of the July 4th holiday."

"Okay. I was going to ask you what you and Shaker did," Sheila said. "Harp, Song, and I had a barbeque."

Did you feast on burgers or people? "We stayed in bed."

"Trying for another baby?" Sheila asked with a wink.

"No," Debbie said, with a small smile. "We talked about it and decided to just be happy together. And if we get pregnant again, so be it." *And Shaker told me we'd have a child, that he foresaw it. I have to trust in that.*

"I think that's a great attitude," Sheila said a little too brightly. "I'll see you in an hour."

"A great attitude"? Ugh. Debbie shuffled her papers, then went back to her office.

"You have two messages," her secretary said. "One didn't leave a number, said they would call back. The other was from Terian, he said for you to see your email, he sent you some contacts."

"Great, thanks." Debbie hurried into her office and brought up her email. Terian's message was at the top.

Mrs. Black,

Here is a list of three people we'd suggest for the job of guarding you. I've listed their skill sets and contact information. Contact for Phenom, the company that can set up your passcodes and card system is at the bottom. Thank you, and we look forward to working with you again in the future.

Terian

Solutions, Inc.

First things first. Debbie looked at the clock, then picked up the phone and called Phenom. "Can I have your new clients' department?"

~

"Thank you everyone for attending this emergency meeting," Debbie announced, striding in to the conference room the next morning. "I have some announcements, then I need a fast update on everyone's work." She paused a moment, noting if everyone was there, then did a double take as Nate was there, sitting in Joshua's old seat. He gave a little finger wave and smiled at her, but this time kept his fangs hidden.

"First off, I've contracted with a company Phenom to put in a badge system. This has nothing to do with paychecks. It's simply to increase security."

"Do the police have any leads on who killed Joshua?" Adeline asked.

"We are not being kept in the loop on the police investigation," Debbie responded. "All I can say is that there have not been any more murders reported." As Adeline tried to speak again, Debbie talked over her. "There will be at least one onsite guard who will patrol the company during normal business hours, along with Mr. Minor. We may go with two. These will be introduced at the next meeting."

"Speaking of introductions, my name is Nate, and I'll be the new liaison for *Immortal Confessions* to the client," Nate said. "I have Josh's notes and have been working to catch up with the tapings you have done. So far, the client is on board with what you have done."

"All of it?" Bart asked skeptically. "Forgive me, Nate, but I'm used to getting a page of corrections every morning, which is why this movie still isn't finished."

"The client is being more understanding of our work schedule," Debbie said. *Brace for it.* "Especially as we will be releasing this movie in September, a full two months early."

Everyone but Nate jumped up, exclaiming all the various reasons they couldn't make the new deadline.

"Settle down!" Debbie shouted. "Take your seats. This isn't a choice, this is survival. Titan Pictures seems to be on a rampage lately. They have increased pressure, and I assume brought to bear influence on the theaters we work with, causing a slew of problems, the worst of which is having all the theaters and advertising venues we had scheduled misplace our bookings. The only way to fix this is to use the bookings *Absolution* would have had for *Immortal Confessions*, and add to them, which requires more money."

"We are also having cash-flow problems," Sheila uttered. "Adeline reported that a Trojan horse was uploaded to our website a few weeks ago. We fixed it, but several people were infected from downloading our movies, and they spread rumors on social media that our site wasn't safe to visit. We are working to correct that, but another virus was uploaded this morning. So we can forget about any download dollars for a while. Additionally, the person we booked our ads with on television left the company. Turns out he's been embezzling money from his clients this year, including ours, and not scheduling any ad space at all. We hope to recover those funds as we have paperwork backing up our claims, but that will take time. We are going to have to spend more money now to get the ads we need."

"I'm sorry, but I have bad news also," Carolina said. "A water main broke and flooded one of the lots. The set itself wasn't being used, but we were using it for storage for the costumes for *Immortal Confessions*, as there were so many. All of them were soaked. The peasant clothing and men's clothing is undamaged, but the various women's gowns were made of silk, and all of them were ruined. We're going to need more funds, and in a hurry."

Debbie gripped the edge of the table with her fingers in frustration. *How much of this was bad luck and how much was Henry, or the priest? I could infuse the company with my inheritance to see it through, but I can't, I may need it to pay for more security.* "We have the cash to handle one of these crises, but not to handle them all at the same time. We either release *Immortal Confessions* in September, or we sell Pandora to Titan Pictures. Do any of you want that? Well, I don't either! Please sit down and listen."

There was a shocked silence, then her staff took their seats.

"We plan to release *Absolution* early, to a small number of theaters. *Immortal Confessions* will take its scheduled ad space and theaters. Sheila, what's the release date for *Absolution*?"

"Last week of July. I met with Bart before this meeting and he's set to cut the scenes we haven't shot yet. It'll require some re-editing. But we'll be ready in time."

"Good. Thank you, Bart. Adeline, put together a short week-long social media package to give this movie a boost and create some awareness of the film, as it's not going to get much in the way of advertising. For now, disable the download part of the site, and refer anyone looking to purchase our movies to Amazon."

"All right," she said, furiously scribbling notes.

"Stacey, I know it's a lot to ramp up, but I hope with less revision we can have *Immortal Confessions* ready on time. Where are we in filming?"

"We've got only half the picture shot, because of all the revisions," she said weakly. "I'm sorry, Debbie, but we've been forced to redo several scenes multiple times, and several more the client still doesn't like even when we have incorporated his suggestions."

"I will handle that," Nate said firmly. "I have a different view than Joshua on how to get this particular job accomplished." He handed Stacey a folder. "The scenes within from the movie are fine to be shot as is. The client has made several notes: follow them and my notes of clarification, and those are okay to go to the final version, with no further client review." He handed her another single piece of paper. "There are several that the client feels must be approved personally: these are they. I will attempt to have the client come in for those scenes, so that he can give live direction, to reduce wasted time on everyone's behalf."

"Are you crazy?" Bart said to him from the doorway, where he had just appeared. "We can't have a client in here while we're filming, especially this client. I've read more than a few of his comments. While he's direct, he's often cruel. If he offends any of the stars, the movie's lost."

"Be that as it may, I'd advise my suggestion is the only way to get this picture done on time," Nate said, not backing down. "This was something I was going to recommend, when we had most of the fall to shoot and reshoot. Now I think it's crucial."

"Let's try it," Debbie said, holding up a hand to silence Bart. "Nate, you are responsible for his conduct when he is here. I know his first language is French, ask him to use that exclusively. You can translate for him in a nice way to the actors on set, if there's a correction to be made in real time. Agreed?"

"Good solution," Nate said with a nod. "Agreed."

"Bart?"

"All right, we'll try it."

"Nicole, I have the final script for *Smoke and Ashes III: Destiny in the Ashes*," Sheila said, handing her a packet. "Here's a copy I had made. Please check it against the first two movies, and give Bart your changes, if there are any."

"None so far," Nicole said, flipping through it. "Though I was beginning to wonder if it had an ending."

"How is that movie coming?" Debbie asked of the room. "*Smoke and Ashes III*? Anyone have anything to say?"

"The plot that I read seemed good, and the scenes I saw that were shot were well done," Nicole said, looking at Sheila. "There were a few problems with continuity, and I proposed fixes for them. They are reshooting those scenes this coming week. The next week we'd have needed the rest of the script, so I'm glad I was finally provided a copy."

"We've only been able to shoot half of *Smoke and Ashes III* because of all the issues with *Immortal Confessions* anyway," Bart supplied. "If we ramp up on the vampire movie to finish it in time, we'll have to halt work on *Smoke and Ashes III*."

"That's fine," Sheila said, glancing at Debbie. "We're way ahead of schedule on that anyway, it's not supposed to come out until the following year."

She wants to know why we're shooting it at all now, and I can't tell her that Shaker said he had to because he looked into the future. "Good," Debbie said. "Anyone have any questions?"

There were none.

"All right," Debbie said. "Let's get to work. Please shoot me an email if anyone thinks of anything else."

～

"You can't be serious!" Debbie shouted. "I spoke to your office at the beginning of this month! You can't possibly be telling me now that you found our lost reservations now that it's the last day of September!"

"Ma'am, I'm just telling you that we've got Pandora Productions listed as one of the companies slated to provide a film for release this September. *Absolution* is the name that's listed, and I know you had a limited release of that earlier this month. Because of that, we're calling to see if you are planning to change films, and release something else in September."

"Let me get back to you."

Ten minutes later, Sheila was in her office sitting across from Debbie, Harp, Song, and Shaker standing nearby, all of them pissed. "Stinks of demon," Harp snarled.

"No, I think its Henry," Debbie said. "He orchestrated this somehow, knowing that we'd move *Absolution* up for limited release. He also knew if we cancelled the September slot now, we'd get downgraded for the next year from green status to red."

"What are you talking about?" Shaker asked.

"Just slang Sheila and I use," Debbie said wearily. "Production companies book theaters ahead of time. They agree to a certain amount of screens and a general run numbering two weeks to two months, most of the time the shorter end of that time period. Everything is planned out in advance. We called last year to get the fall slot for *Absolution*. But the theater doesn't want to show movies that were released earlier in the year in a fall slot, not unless they're guaranteed moneymakers, which *Absolution* isn't. So if we don't release a new movie to take the slot in September, we've got to back out of the slot, which leaves the theaters scrambling for a movie to release in the sudden vacuum. Usually, what they can get and release in time isn't a money-maker, and they lose revenue. The theaters don't like getting burned, and they'll make us pay for that in our next releases, by shortening the runs or offering us last pick of dates."

"We'll have to release *Immortal Confessions* on double the screens we planned," Sheila said heavily. "We've got nothing else ready. We're gambling the future of Pandora on a vampire movie, I can't believe it."

"Henry was counting on that, to put our epic against his studio's epic."

"An *Escalation,* indeed," Shaker said, his angry eyes burning hot as coals. "A well-played one." He turned to Debbie. "I will go to Devlin now, tell him what has happened, to make sure he is okay with this. We will need all of the extra power and pull he has to get this done. We need to fill those theaters."

"But you think we can do it?" Debbie asked him.

Shaker nodded. "With a little help from Hell." He disappeared.

"Come on," Debbie said, grabbing her coat. "We need a break, Sheila. Let's head over to the Black Rose. I bought a package deal last month...no wait, it's been several months now. I wanted to take you, as a treat."

Sheila shifted uneasily. "I shouldn't. I still need to read through the rest of Shaker's sequel. He finally got me the last half this morning."

"You can read it over the weekend," Debbie said, ushering her friend toward the door. "We've been working nonstop today. And we're going to get some drinks and chocolate beforehand!"

"You were right," Sheila smiled lazily, as Debbie poured the last of the wine into her glass. "We really needed this."

"The year is more than half over, and this is the first time we've really had a night off," Debbie pronounced. "If we aren't working our asses off, we're fighting supernatural forces."

"Above and below," a voice intoned snarkily. "Licentiousness and debauchery."

Debbie and Sheila looked up to see Henry, his puritanical face stern in judgment. "What the fuck do you want?" Debbie swore. "Haven't you caused us enough trouble with your bullshit?"

"Just to say hello." He smiled meanly. "I heard you're having some trouble with your bookings, so sorry to hear it."

Henry did this! "You son of a bitch!"

"Could you be more of a petty-ass twat?" Sheila drawled, her eyes glittering with malice. "Your retort's not even up to par with a popular high school girl's. Why don't you go away and grow some balls?"

Debbie burst out laughing, spewing her mouthful of wine over the table.

"You know, I never knew what Debbie saw in you," Sheila taunted. "You're not handsome, you're not clever, you can't even throw a verbal punch. I'm so glad she found Jett, he treats her like a princess." She smirked. "He really knows how to take care of a woman, if you get my meaning."

Henry's face suffused with rage and embarrassment. "You wait, you bitch, you're going to get yours."

"Oh really?" Sheila challenged, staring him down. "And you're going to be the one to give it to us, are you? You'd have to get it up first, you pompous prick."

Debbie laughed, expecting Henry to stalk away, or maybe have a heart attack, his face was so purple. What she wasn't expecting was for him to pick up the empty bottle from the table and smash Sheila in the head with it. The glass connected with a heavy clunk, Sheila flying sideways to crash into the nearest table.

Debbie shrieked, then lunged for Henry, grabbing the bottle as she fought against him swinging it down onto Sheila's prone form. "Help!"

There was an instant when Debbie was sure no one would come, her grip slipping on the blood-covered glass, Henry's angry expression looking over her, his teeth locked together in a rictus of rage, other customers backing away from them in fear. Then waiters were there prying her and Henry apart.

"Stop!" "Call 911!"

Debbie went to her knees, cradling Sheila's battered face. Her friend's eyes fluttered once, then she went still. "Help!" she yelled. "Someone help us!"

~

Debbie sat slumped in the hospital chair, her head pounding with the wine she'd drunk, a sour taste of defeat in her mouth. When someone sat beside her, she expected Shaker. Instead she looked into the tearful eyes of Song.

"How are you still here?"

"She's in a coma," Song said, dabbing her eyes. "She's not dead. But it was close enough that her heart stopped in surgery twice." She paused. "My brother's gone, Debbie."

Debbie wiped at her eyes, trying to think coherently. "Can we summon him back?"

Song shook her head. "No, the bond was severed. Mine is gone, too. I can't feel Sheila anymore. She's not responding to my mental prompts, either."

"How are you still here?" Debbie asked again.

"Because I've got Rhonda's body," Song whispered. "It's enough to hold me here. Harp's already been called out of Hell by another master. I won't see him again for a while."

The finality in her tone was crushing. Debbie tried to muster sorrow but felt too numb. "I'm sorry," she said lamely.

"They're letting her go home in a few days," Song said, standing up. "I'll be back to get her then. Until then, I've got to work on the house, put in a few ramps for her wheelchair."

"Wheelchair?" Debbie gasped, snapping out of her inertia.

"Only for a while. They said she should wake up soon, the damage wasn't bad. But there are small fractures to her skull that need to heal. She'll need someone until she's okay."

"But your bond is broken," Debbie said, looking around to make sure they weren't overheard. "That priest is still around. Why stay?"

"Look, we might be on the wrong side," Song said curtly. "But Sheila was only ever good to me. I care about her. I'll stay until she's well. If she wants me to leave after that, I will. And you're a bitch to say that to me now, of all times, after everything we've gone through together." She stalked away.

She's right, I shouldn't have said what I did. Debbie watched her go, then felt Shaker touch her mind. *Mistress?*

Why aren't you here? Sheila's been hurt.

Shaker came from around the corner, his eyes focused on her.

What took you so long? Debbie stood, extending her hand.

That's not me! Run!

Debbie's smile froze, and she staggered backward, into Sheila's room, pulling chairs behind her. "Get back!"

Shaker's form modified, becoming that of Rafael. Debbie let out a breath, and grabbed a rolling tray table, putting it in front of her. Guardian materialized from the shadow of the bed, crawling out from under it to snap and bark, as he maneuvered between Debbie and Rafael.

"I'm not here to harm you," the angel intoned. "Just to give comfort to Sheila. Call off your hound, before he gets sent back to Hell."

"Why would we want anything from you?" Debbie hissed, as Guardian growled at her feet. "All you've done is hunt us."

"Because you're doing evil," he corrected. "My mission here is comfort."

"What evil have you seen either of us do that merits your attention!" Debbie shouted. "The world has dictators and mass killings and serial murderers and child rapists and sex trafficking and you're here, spending time and energy on us? No wonder the world is the devil's playground, when you angels are all acting like idiots! You have real power and you're standing around, waiting for someone to give you orders instead of doing something! Stop patting people on the head and preaching the dos and don'ts of life and start actually saving some lives!"

"You know, I've faced a lot of humans bound to demons, and others that did evil. You are the rudest one who's shown me the least respect."

"What respect should I show you? You talk about forgiveness, but all you do is condemn. You're worse than a demon, Rafael; you're a hypocrite."

"Whatever you think of me, I am here to warn you," Rafael said. "As you might know, the demons Sheila was bound to were sent back to Hell. She'll recover in time. Your bond with your demon is still active, and the priest knows this. He'll try for you soon."

"Then you'll be guiding his soul to Heaven shortly," Debbie retorted. "Thanks for the warning." *Neither of them know that Song is still here. We need to keep it that way.*

Rafael nodded, and disappeared.

CHAPTER ELEVEN

AUGUST

Debbie lay in bed, blinking back tears. *Why does it matter if I cry here? No one can see me. And I can't let them see me anyway, until the swelling of my face goes down.* She reached up to her face, feeling again with her fingers the unnatural hardness of dermal filler over her cheekbones just under the skin. *I hope it softens a little in time.*

Guardian nuzzled her hand. When she didn't pet the hound, it slunk away into the nearest shadow and disappeared.

I'm here, Shaker said softly in her mind, as his strong arms gently enfolded her. *What's wrong, Mistress?*

It feels like everything. I just can't do this anymore. On top of everything else, Nelson and Jeremy resigned today, saying they didn't feel safe working at Pandora anymore. I don't think they'll be the last. I'm just so tired of trying to make people get along, spin proverbial script thread into gold profit.

I don't understand, he replied. *Pandora is doing well, better than last year at this time. Yes, we've had problems, but we're getting them under control.* He paused. "I'm sorry I wasn't there when Sheila got hurt. Rip had got himself in trouble—remember, I told you he was a male demon version of Rhonda—and I had to get him out. Otherwise they were threatening you."

"Who?"

"Some Satanists who knew enough to dabble but didn't have any true faith in their false god. Don't worry about it, they're dead. And you don't need to give me any selections for this month now, either."

Debbie wiped at her face angrily, wincing as she touched her puffy face. *I thought I really planned out what I wanted for Pandora, and myself. I thought I had the best plan possible to get there. And nothing's happened.*

Much has happened. Shaker kissed her forehead, the brief heat comforting in the cold room. *It may not feel like it, but we are making great strides. Don't lose heart, Mistress.*

"What if we do all this, have gone through all we did, only to end up with nothing we wanted?" Debbie whispered, her voice cracking on the last words.

"What is it that you want that you don't have?" Shaker asked.

"I don't know…" Debbie started, the words becoming a wail. She began sobbing.

Shaker held her until she stopped. *Explain,* he said in her mind. *Don't speak aloud.*

Debbie grabbed for a tissue. *I don't know what's wrong with me. I was always proud to be one of the founders at Pandora. I loved being the center of attention, that my decisions were what made the company successful, built it from nothing. But lately I've been feeling like it's a huge weight on my shoulders, one I want to be free of. I don't want to get any more crisis calls. I don't want to be the person that has to step in and smooth things over or use some demon magic to create a last minute miracle that saves us from ruin. But if I gave that up for some other career, I think I'd be bored and upset that I wasn't right in the middle of the action. How can I want to leave this company that I gave so much of my life to build?*

You just need a vacation, Shaker soothed. *Everyone needs a break from time to time.*

But I can't take a break, Debbie replied bitterly. *We are in crisis mode right now with Sheila in the hospital indefinitely. My phone rings, I have to answer and deal with whatever it is. There's no break from that.*

There is, it just comes with a high cost. Shaker hugged her. *I can briefly stop time.*

Debbie snorted, then turned to face him. *You're powerful, Shaker. But even God and the devil can't stop time.*

"I'm not talking about "The Hellbound-Train," Shaker sniped, pinching her behind so she jumped. "It's called Day in an Hour. It's a major spell, and I'll be exhausted for the next day after. But I can give you some hours of peace with it. It's less about stopping time really than it is speeding up the time for one person: you."

"You're saying that my perception will be that hours have passed, and for other people, it will be seconds?"

Shaker nodded. "More like minutes for them. You'll get 60 hours, while an hour passes for them. But this will also take a toll on you, unless you use those sixty hours wisely. I'd advise using at least half of the time to rest. If you don't, you'll snap back into real time like you're coming off a college Spring Break of cocaine-fueled all-nighters."

Debbie grimaced. "Why did you suggest this, if it's got so many side effects?"

"I just want to make sure you understand what you're getting. All magic has side effects, some are just worse than others. This spell was made years ago because a battle disaster needed to be averted, and a messenger had to make it fifty leagues to give warning. It worked, the warning was given in time. But both the boy and his mount died of exhaustion right after."

"Did you create this spell?"

Shaker nodded.

"Why is magic so…heartless? Because its black magic?"

"Demon magic, you mean," he corrected. "And no. Magic is manipulating the world around you in unnatural ways to get what you want. There's always a tradeoff for that manipulation. Black gets better results, because it's more ruthless in what is traded. White magic is simple magic that usually lasts much less and has far weaker effects because what is traded is not supposed to hurt anyone. Demon magic is just black magic that often uses souls as a powerbase."

It always comes back to souls. "That's an additional reason why demons want souls?"

"The boss downstairs used to want souls because they were a kind of magic currency, and to power Hell, as I explained previously. But souls are also a source of power that can be used in magic to strengthen a spell, and it's plentiful. You might say it's the most a human has to offer a demon." Shaker nuzzled her. "All fleshy pleasures aside."

"What else can be used to strengthen a spell?"

"Old artifacts from ancient times, especially from someone who knew magic. Sometimes wizards or witches would imbue objects with power."

"Their power?"

"Sorry, I should have said energy. Energy from their own life force, or life force or souls stolen from others, or even captured as they died naturally. A soul is really a person's life force, their life energy. Once harvested, it can be stored indefinitely. Think of it as a battery that never expires."

"But it can be drained?"

"Easily. Humans can die that way, so can non-humans." Shaker studied her. "What did you do to your face?"

"Please tell me I look younger," she said self-consciously.

"Yes, you do," Shaker said, turning his head this way and that to look at her face. "It looks very good."

"I decided to try some facial treatments, because thinking about my birthday this year really was making me feel older. I can't do anything about my nearsightedness, or my hair going grey, but I could do this. So I did."

"Did it hurt?"

"Yes," Debbie said. "They injected some collegen into my nasolabial folds."

"Sounds naughty," Shaker teased.

Debbie smiled just a fraction. "And also something onto my cheekbones. I heard the woman ahead of me referring to it as her "face prop." Then Botox for my forehead lines." She tried to knit her brows together, moving them slightly. "I've had to try to knit my eyebrows for the last few hours, they said if I didn't do that, there was a chance that the fluid could paralyze part of my eyelid or eye."

"Talk about magic having side effects." Shaker laughed. "I think you have a fair share of those with no magic. I'm surprised you didn't just go to Song for a glamour."

Debbie flushed. "I didn't want to ask you to do anything like this for me. It seemed petty." *And I wanted it to last for months.*

"I'm all about indulging vices." Shaker laughed. "But you shouldn't feel badly at all. You did something that made you feel very good."

"It cost a small fortune."

"So what?" Shaker said. "You do look a good five years younger." He kissed her gently. "I'm happy for you, that you took some time for yourself and did something, just for yourself."

Debbie hugged him. "You're a good husband, you know."

Shaker hugged her. "I know. You're a good wife." He fumbled at his pocket. "And since you didn't give me any ideas, here's your birthday present." He handed her a small ornate metal box.

"This doesn't look like it came from Kay's," Debbie teased.

"It didn't," Shaker said, affronted. "No wife of mine is going to wear mass-produced jewels."

"You sure this is safe to open?" Debbie asked, looking at the heavy engraving. "It's brass, and that looks like an ancient warning."

"Will you just open it already."

Debbie opened the curved lid. Inside were simple ruby drop earrings, easily a carat each, with red gold posts. The gems shone like stars in the room's weak light. "They're beautiful."

"Put them on."

Debbie bit back her teasing of asking him to say please and put on both earrings. Getting up from the bed, she went to the dresser mirror and looked in. "They're lovely."

"I'm glad you like them," Shaker said happily, hugging her around her waist.

"Thank you. They must have been expensive."

"I called in a favor for the gems, but yes, they were expensive to have made," Shaker said proudly. "I never had money of my own before, really. Sure money I stole, but nothing that I ever worked for myself. I like that I can buy you things."

I forget the differences in us sometimes. "I didn't mind when you couldn't. That getaway you took me to last year on the beach was lovely."

"I'd like to take you there now, and spend the next week in your arms," Shaker said softly, "But I can't."

The way he said it made Debbie turn and look at him. "Why not?"

Shaker pulled some papers from his back pocket. "I need your social security number." He grabbed a pen.

Debbie recited it, then tore the papers out of his grasp the moment he finished inking the last digit. "Life insurance?" She gaped at him. "Are you going to die?"

"No, but Jett likely is," Shaker said softly, taking the papers back. "One of the images I saw was a funeral. You were standing there crying, and I wasn't there beside you."

"That could be nothing! You weren't at my side at my father's funeral. That could have been the image you saw!"

Shaker shook his head. "No, the colors on the trees were fall.

194

I'm guessing that's what Jezebel meant when she mentioned that prophecy to you about something bad coming in October."

"Are you sure it's not Sheila?" Debbie said, biting her lip.

Shaker shook his head again. "No. She was to the side of you, with another woman. So she will recover in time."

Debbie let out a breath, relieved. "That's something."

"Sign this," Shaker said, handing her more papers. "This is a power of attorney, living will, and health care proxy."

Debbie scanned the paperwork. "This says no resuscitation."

"I have no idea what might happen," Shaker said patiently. "I'm covering all the bases. Catarella suggested this, to be prudent."

"What's going to happen, if Jett dies? Will I ever see you again?" Debbie bit her lip hard. *Don't cry now, pull it together.*

Shaker touched her cheek, gently caressing with his fingers. "Almost certainly. But I don't know what's going to happen, Debbie. Titus's getting recalled to Hell is too soon for me not to take that into consideration. If somehow I'm recalled to Hell...well, I'm not sure when I'll get out again. It could be years...or decades. By then you'll likely have a new life, one I'm not part of anymore."

"Don't say that!"

"This is how things are, how they have always been," Shaker said dispassionately. "I knew this was how we would end, if we were lucky." He laughed mirthlessly. "You had better call one of those protectors that Terian recommended tomorrow, first thing."

Debbie reached out a shaking hand to slap Shaker in her rage and despair.

Do it! Shaker said in her mind.

Debbie stilled. *Shaker?*

"I'm a demon and demons can't love, you mortal fool," Shaker mocked, a sneer spreading over his face. "Human women are all the same: easy prey."

Debbie slapped Shaker with all her strength letting out a scream of fury.

Good. Say nothing! Shaker glared at her, rubbing his face, yet his words in her mind were loving. *I'll visit you in dreams.* He stalked away.

Confused, Debbie watched him go, then collapsed into tears.

~

The next morning, Debbie awoke alone. Shaker didn't answer her mental calls, no matter what she said. She finally dried her tears, wincing as her face was still sore, then drove to work.

"No calls," she said to her secretary. She locked her door, then pulled up her email, moving to Terian's message. *Might as well try them in order.* "Hi, is this John Wickman?"

"No," a curt voice said. "This is Alan Freeman. John moved out last week." Click.

"Great," Debbie muttered to the dial tone. "Okay, next." She dialed, then listened to the phone ring…and ring. *What the hell, they never heard of voicemail?* "So much for you, Fallon Jericho."

She went to the last name on the list. "Van 'Gore' Gorello. Okay." She dialed, then was about to hang up when a man answered, his words too slurred to understand.

"Hello, Mr. Gore?"

"Nope," the man said, his tone suddenly professional. "Hold on."

Finally. Debbie waited, then another man picked up. "Yes, this is Gore."

"Hi. This is Debbie from Pandora Productions. Terian recommended you to me."

"Yes, the woman in pictures who was having trouble with a stalker," Gore replied.

"A stalker with a bible with plans for an exorcism."

"Yes, those are the most determined kind." Gore laughed. "Do you have a location of where he is staying or working out of? What's his name?"

"No. His name is Father Matthew. But he's also got a guardian angel named Rafael watching over him."

"The archangel Raphael, mentioned in the Bible? He's pretty powerful," Gore said skeptically.

"I don't think it was that famous angel, no," Debbie said after a moment. "but hell, who knows."

"Hmm. Haven't heard of him. Well, first of all, a guardian angel is one of the good guys. Because of that, they aren't able to take human life, as a rule. While they can send evil like demons back to Hell and act to defend holy men, they don't get involved in the affairs of man." He paused. "What that means is if this priest goes after you and not the demon, which is how most hunters banish demons, then the angel can't help him. Moreover, the priest can be killed if he attacks you."

"You'll kill him?"

"I would have to follow you, to be there at the right moment. But it can be done, yes."

"Do you, um…take care of the body after?"

"I'd assumed your demon would want it?" Gore said. "To eat?"

Taken aback, Debbie stammered. "Umm, I…"

"Sorry, just kidding, I know they can't touch holy men for food. But they can possess them briefly, if they're dead. Have him walk the guy out and into the path of a car, that's the easiest option."

He's cold. But that's what I need, a cold killer, albeit a trustworthy one. "How much?"

"I'd charge a thousand a week, if you booked me for this job," Gore said. "Usually I'd ask for twenty-five large for a hit, but this is babysitting, with an easy kill. The priest would have to adhere to no-magic/no teleporting/no magical weapons. It'd be a vacation of sorts for me. Plus the way Terian told it, you were a relative, so he, um, encouraged me to give you family rates, which I am."

"Thanks," Debbie said uncertainly. "You must be good friends with him."

"Nope, never met the guy. But I know the man he works with,

Danial Racklan. That vampire can hold a vendetta for centuries, it's said. And he's a crack shot. I'd like to be on his good list, not his bad list."

Devlin's brother. "He's someone to be respected."

"Damn straight there, honey. Not long ago he was doing the same jobs I do now, and just as good at it. Word is he's taking an open-ended vacation right now from Solutions, Inc., but he'll be back. Who knows? Maybe next time he's hiring, he'll give my resume a look."

Shaker said Devlin's cemetery was teeming with dead guards. Does Danial have a cemetery of his own, too? Why the hell am I thinking about this? "When can you start?"

"Tomorrow will be fine, if you're okay tonight. I'll need to make some arrangements. Do you have a spare room I can stay at your home? I'll bring my own food, a small fridge, and TV, and my DVD collection. Do you have internet service?"

The ramifications of being under 24-hr guard hit Debbie. *So much for romance, not that Shaker and I are speaking right now.* "Yes. And yes, we do. Please come to my office tomorrow and bring everything you need. I'll write you a check, if that's okay?"

"Yes, with business clients, that's fine, as long as it's company issue. Lock your doors and I'll see you tomorrow afternoon."

The day passed uneventfully, Debbie's mental missives to Shaker unanswered. As she was shutting down her computer, she decided to call Song.

"Hi, Debbie."

"Hi. Listen, how's Sheila?"

"No change so far, though I am reading to her," Song said sadly.

"Listen," Debbie said on a sudden whim. "I hired a live-in guard. He's starting tomorrow. Why don't you come and stay with me for a while? That way you don't have to pay for extra security, and I'd be glad of the company."

"What about Shaker?"

"He's working all the time," Debbie said in a false cheerful voice. "I'd really like the company. Plus the priest thinks that both Sheila's demons are gone. He's still around, if he discovers you, he may try to end her coma...permanently."

"Gotcha," Song said. "I'll pack now, and we'll be over soon."

"How will you transport her?" Debbie asked suddenly.

"Levitation is easiest. I drape a sheet over her, and pretend I'm pushing her on a cart of some kind. No worries. See you soon."

Debbie hung up the phone, then shook her head, smiling. *Too funny.*

That night, Song and Sheila arrived, the latter looking asleep, if pale. Debbie got them settled in the spare bedroom, then went and opened a bottle of wine. *Just one glass.*

"Please pour one for me," Song said from behind her. "I really like the taste of wine."

"You sure?" Debbie asked, as she poured a second glass. "It's pretty sweet. It's a white, the one slated for *Absolution's* release party that never happened."

"Demons can't eat anything but flesh and blood, unless they use magic," Song said, taking a large swallow. "I never knew the things I was missing. I can see why my people are so big on possession."

"Rhonda a.k.a. you look great," Debbie complimented. "That's a fetching hairstyle."

Song laughed, then touched her light blonde waves. "I wanted something softer and less punk than the bright red." She turned around. "What do you think?"

"I think the looser clothes look much better, especially the long skirt," Debbie said with approval. "Titus was right, it was a blessing."

"You know, I was so intimidated, meeting him," Song said, taking another gulp of wine and giggling. "I've been hearing stories for decades, but never thought I'd be on his team."

Should I tell her about him being forced into Hell? No, Shaker said not to. "He's been very helpful, especially at the wedding."

"Yeah, I keep waiting for what he and Shaker did to Stonehenge to get discovered." Song laughed. "Titus put some kind of invisibility spell on the added rocks, with Shaker's help. It'll fade in time, but they didn't say when. The humans are going to flip out."

"They probably will." *It's odd, her not including me in that statement.* Debbie sipped her wine, to settle her nerves. "So how is the Black Rose?"

"Good!" Song said proudly. "I did get Xerxes to come back, and we hired another masseuse, a witch called Hannity. She's quiet, but very good, like he is. Business is doing well." She took another swallow of wine, then held out the glass. "May I have some more?"

"Sure," Debbie said, pouring another.

"I'm just anxious about Sheila," Song said. "I've been teleporting back home to see her every hour when I'm working, just to check on her, do the physical therapy, and make sure she gets her feedings."

God, I should have thought of all this, and helped out with home-care. "Intubation?"

"No, I'm using a bit of magic, to teleport the food into her. Titus showed me that spell, too. It's a reverse of one he created, to be able to eat food he can't digest, to get it out of him." She made a face. "Otherwise we get sick, if we aren't possessing a human host."

Debbie drained her glass, then poured another. *I'm not sure what else to say. Wait, Madeline said to listen. Perhaps I can get a clue of what she'd like to talk about.* Debbie concentrated, and for a moment, there was nothing. Then came a barrage of Song's mental thoughts at the volume of a whisper.

I'm glad Sheila's not dead, but what if she dies? Will I go back to Hell or be able to stay? Is Debbie going to charge us rent? I can pay some if we sell the house, but if Sheila comes back, she'll be upset. And I'd have to lie, get some kind of paperwork or something... Song's rambling thoughts went on and on in loops, worries about money, about what she should do next, about her brother Harp, what was going to happen at Pandora, then back to money.

"Listen," Debbie said, putting down her glass. "I'm afraid, too, and not sure what to do. You both should stay here with me for a while, until at least another month or so passes. Hopefully Sheila will wake up. Shaker said he had a vision she would."

"He said that? Really?" Song hugged Debbie, then drank the rest of her wine in one long swallow.

"Another? We killed this bottle, but there's more in the cabinet."

"No, I'd better pace myself," Song said with a grimace. "Rhonda still isn't past her addictions. When I drink, she usually tries again to fight me for control. Besides, I should get Sheila fed." She put down her glass. "Do you want me to make you something? I'm a decent cook."

"I've no idea what I have in the kitchen," Debbie said, opening the fridge. "Lots of red meat for Shaker that's maybe past expiration, some fruit and vegetables that have seen better days, and a bunch of box refrigerated meals for one."

"You should eat better," Song chastised, filling her wine glass with water. "Go and relax. I'll fix something in a few minutes."

Song called Debbie in a half hour later. There were two heaping chopped salads, a small baguette on each plate, and a piece of pie with two forks. "That's to encourage us to finish the salads," Song laughed. "I zipped out to the store. Dig in."

"This is delicious on its own," Debbie said, after a few bites. "Wow. You're a great cook."

"This isn't technically cooked, but I know what you mean." Song giggled. "But I can cook, yes. I'd be happy to buy food for us, and also cook for you, in payment for letting us stay."

"Sure," Debbie said, clinking her glass with Song's. "It's a deal."

Debbie fumbled for her phone, looking at the clock. *Damn it, I overslept. Stayed up too late talking to Song. Then nightmare after nightmare, waking up to find out I was still inside the dream. I may have to get some pills soon if I can't get some restful sleep.* She grabbed the phone as the last ring ended. "Damn it!" *At least I saw the display read Pandora.*

She hit the return call button, then waited.

"Pandora," her secretary answered. "How may I help you?"

"Hi, it's Debbie. I'm sorry, I overslept. I'll be in shortly."

"Oh hi, I just left you a message. There was a woman in here looking for you. She looked very young."

It can't be Celia's ghost, and you're insane for thinking of that first. "What was her name?"

"She didn't give it, but she's called before, I recognize her voice. She left when I said you weren't here."

Uneasy, Debbie looked at her watch. "I'll be in shortly. If she comes back, call security."

Debbie hurried into the kitchen, breathing a sigh of relief when she saw Song was already up and had made coffee.

"Good Morning! What would you like for breakfast?" Song asked. "I'll go shopping today, if you'll give me a list of your favorite foods."

Her cheerfulness is bracing in the morning, but I'm glad not to be alone. "Any kind of pasta, salads like you made last night, any kind of bread, pizza, most chocolate, and soups, if they aren't cream ones."

"Wow, you're quick on decisions," Song said, jotting down notes. "But that makes sense, you're a CEO. Okay, I'll get some of everything."

"You sure you have time for that?"

Song nodded. "Teleportation makes it all possible. No worries." She flashed a smile.

Debbie nodded, gulped her coffee, and hurried to the door.

As soon as she walked into her office, her cell went off again.

"Bart, what is it? This is a bad connection?"

"That's because I'm covering the phone with my hand," he hissed. "Please get down here now, your client's here talking to the actors, giving them all kinds of odd pointers in English, not French, and we're going to shoot Anna's death scene in a few minutes and Nathan's not here yet—"

"Damn it! I'll be right there."

Debbie ran out of her office, right into Stacey. "I'm coming, Bart just called."

"Actually, Jett asked if you could meet him on set," Stacey asked. "We're shooting the big battle at the end of *Smoke and Ashes III*, and he said he wanted you to see it."

Shaker, did you really ask for me?

There was no answer.

Damn you for not answering me! "I've got to handle a problem, but tell him I'll be there as soon as I can," Debbie said, pushing past Stacey. She hurried to the set of *Immortal Confessions*, running into Nate as he came out of the men's bathroom.

"Sorry, I know, Dev usually never gets up this early, and he didn't call me," he said, before she could speak. "Obviously, this is an important scene for him. He wants to make sure that it's perfect."

Nicole raced up to Debbie as she and Nate arrived. "I'm so glad you're here. Bart said he called you."

"Do you understand what the vampire is feeling here?" Devlin thundered. "He has built up an entire life, put everything he had into it, and it's come to ruin. He's been nothing, and he knows what that feels like. He thought he'd never feel like nothing again. But he's lost everything."

"He hasn't though," the lead protested. "He's got his friends, his allies, and he's smart and crafty, not to mention powerful."

"Not compared to the enemies he's facing. He's looking at imminent doom, maybe unending torture. So he screams out his frustration to the heavens, before planning a last-ditch offensive."

"So what's the problem?" Debbie said to Nicole. "What he's saying seems to be valid, and it's not offensive."

Nicole gestured to the stage. "Well, he thinks that the lead should, um, sing at this point. Not scream."

Debbie glanced at Devlin, who was still animatedly talking to the lead actor, as they pushed into the stage area. "Sing what?"

"Well, that's part of the issue. The client's recommending some lyrics from an older song that no one knows set to music he wrote. The song was never popular, and it doesn't fit the period at all. But he's not backing down. The actor's about ready to refuse to sing."

"Do you understand?" Devlin said loudly to the lead actor. "He looks at the events that he's manipulated in place, all his accomplishments, all the near misses where disaster was averted, and he's hit by the fact that none of it matters. What always mattered was how much he loved her, and that she loved him back just as much."

The actor shifted, affronted. "I do understand that, I've studied hard for this character to bring him to life. But I don't see how a song at this time is better than the heart to heart talk he could have with one of his allies—"

"Let me handle this," Nate said, touching Debbie's shoulder. He moved almost in a blur to the stage, coming between Devlin and the lead. "Hey, you didn't wait for me. You know the rules, Dev."

"I want this song," Devlin said peevishly. "I wrote out the lyrics. I accept that the whole song is too long. But I want this excerpt of it in there."

"Then we'll figure a way to make it work." Nate turned to the lead, a copy of Devlin in looks and build, but far less menacing and commanding. "Can you sing these?"

"That's what I've been trying to explain," the man said, his tone almost velvety, again a copy of Devlin's. "This voice is doable, because I've been working on it for months." His voice raised in pitch, also becoming more coarse. "When I have to shout or talk loudly, I can lose it and use my normal voice. But I can't sing. There wasn't anything in the script deal about having to sing."

"Anyone can sing," Devlin scoffed, looking down his nose at the man. "All actors should be able to sing."

"I'm telling you, I can't," the lead said, growing angry. "Especially when I'm wearing my prosthetic fangs. So you'll have to get someone to sing for me."

Devlin was about to reply, when Nate bumped his shoulder. "Why don't you give him a sample of how you want him to sing it?" He motioned for the accompaniment, the sound people who he'd just been speaking to who were now scrambling to adjust their machines, as the beginning of a haphazard tune began playing from the speakers.

Devlin glared at Nate, enraged, as if he would strike him, then wheeled around, striding for the stage. A sound tech pushed a microphone at him, but he pushed it aside, knocking the man into another who caught him from falling. He reached the middle of the stage, took a deep breath, and began to sing.

Judging by the look of the organ grinder
    You'll judge me by the fact that my face don't fit
    It's touching that the monkey sits on my shoulder
    He's waiting for the day when he gets me

But I don't need no alibi, I'm a puppet on a string
    I just need this stage to be seen
    We all need a pantomime to remind us what is real
    Hold my eye and know what it means
    Will you be a friend of mine to remind me what is real?
    Hold my heart and see that it bleeds?

·   ·   ·

His voice was perfect, flawless in its depth, polished...and brimming with the pain of abject loss, heart-ending pain which had no end and no beginning, as it was all-encompassing. Devlin was drowning in it, his audience pulled down with him.

He finished the last note, his expression anguished. Nate clapped loudly, then everyone followed suit. "Did you get that?" he said to the sound man, who nodded.

Damn, he's right. That song adds to the scene, gives it power, even if the words are funky. Debbie hurried up to the stage. "Wow. I didn't know you could sing like that. And I must say, as the studio head, we are not going to get a better rendition, even if we hold auditions." She paused. "Please consider singing the songs you want included in this movie. You composed the score, so I'd leave it to your good judgment to decide where they fit."

Devlin looked at her, his eyes red, though with sorrow or anger, she couldn't tell. "Just this one." He stalked away, and Nate hurried after him, with a "go on shooting" to Debbie.

"Well," Bart said happily. "Let's keep going. Get that song fragment copied, at least three copies." He turned to the lead. "You'll take one home with you, until you can lip sync to it perfectly, understood?"

Debbie hurried out toward the set of *Smoke and Ashes III*. She tripped once, then pushed open the set door. As she entered, a thought from Shaker slammed into her.

GET OUT NOW!

Debbie stumbled and went to one knee, as an explosion rocked the set, knocking her on her ass and taking the wind out of her as it obliterated most of the sound stage. Guardian appeared from the smoke, the dog biting gently into her shoulder, and dragging her backward outside, as the front wall collapsed right where she had been. She lay gasping, Guardian standing over her, then the world went black.

~

"Wake up, Debbie."

Debbie opened her eyes to see Jett sitting beside her on the couch. Shaker's red eyes flashed momentarily, then the sharp blue of Jett's eyes returned.

Jett's dead, this is a dream. "Shaker?"

"I can't stay long, there are means of monitoring dreams, and you're fair game, having been bound to me," Shaker said, touching her arm. He brought her closer, hugging her. "We were never... forthcoming about our feelings, but I knew how you felt about me. And you were not wrong in how I felt for you." He kissed her warmly. "I knew what we had was different in those last months of our first year together, when your safety became more to me that just that of my Mistress. I hadn't ever had a real relationship, where I was a partner to someone. I hadn't ever had someone really love me just for me. Thank you for that."

"I love you," Debbie said, clinging to him. "There has to be a way for us to be together."

"There isn't," Shaker said sadly. "I knew this was impossible from the first, but that didn't stop me wanting it. It didn't stop me wanting you."

"Look, can't you petition God, or something? You were one of his original angels, you said."

Shaker shook his head. "I have done too much since that time, to ever be forgiven." He hugged her tightly. "God will not intercede. And Satan can't be held off forever. He had a hand in this somehow. He must be made to think that you are nothing to me and that I'm the same evil killer I have always been, so that you can have a good life."

"I don't want a good life, I want a life with you!"

Shaker pushed back from Debbie, making her look at him. "I could whisper the endless platitudes of a thousand romantic scenes from history, but that still wouldn't give my feelings for you justice." His expression was one Debbie had never seen before; determined, but also pleading. "I love you. Yes, I'm saying it now. I was stupid to not have said it before. I want to protect you, and there is only one way: go back to Hell willingly and sever our bond. If I take the fall, all that I have done in your service will fall back on me alone—"

"No!"

"That ghost will stop hunting you. The nightmares will stop. Demon hunters will stop targeting you. Your soul will be cleansed. Pandora is successful now, you don't need me like you did, Debbie! This is the only way out."

"No," Debbie said resolutely, taking Shaker's hand in hers. "I pledged you my heart and soul and I make good on my promises. We're in this together; we're partners. I'm not backing out to leave you in a pile of shit, Shaker!"

"You must let me do this, or we are both doomed," Shaker said, disentangling from Debbie and standing. He began to pace. "I have thought of different scenarios, even made discreet inquiries of several powerful allies of mine, to try to come up with a better solution. This is the only way."

"We can fight! How can you not want to fight for what we have?"

"I don't fight battles I can't win," Shaker replied, exasperated, stopping and turning to face Debbie. "The more time goes on, the more apparent our love is going to be to the forces of Hell. Satan will be amused at first, then he'll use it to control me."

"I thought he already controlled you? Isn't he the master of all demons?"

"Hell is not well ordered, no matter what the *Inferno* and modern television series says. The point of Hell is disorder and chaos. The goal of demons is to spread that chaos all over the world, because it leads to suffering, fear, and a lot of bad times." Shaker let out a breath. "Satan isn't really the problem. It's other demons, or enemies of mine. You remember what happened to my brother, Rip. How they used him to get to me?"

Debbie nodded. *They knew he was your brother, so they tricked him, and then you had to bail him out. But that won't be me. I'm not a liability!*

"That targeting never stops. It will start happening to you, Debbie. I can't put you in that position if I love you."

"So you're giving up because of what might happen?"

"What will happen," Shaker said sadly. "There is a goblin witch I know who has the gift of premonition. You already met her: Jezebel. She contacted me a week ago, told me she had valuable information to sell. I thought it had to do with Pandora. Instead it was about me."

"What did she see?"

"Me back in Hell, then summoned back out. She wouldn't give me specifics, other than to tell me that I was bound to a sorcerer, and that he would 'force me to betray and hurt someone I cared for as if they were my family'."

Debbie took a shuddering breath. "And you think she meant me? She could be lying!"

"Jezebel never lies about her visions, not to her customers. She knows if she did, no one would trust her foresight." Shaker swallowed. "And in the hundreds of years I have known her, she has never seen something, and not had it come to pass."

Debbie sank back down to the couch, terrified. *Don't throw up, it won't help.* "How does your leaving help us, if we can't advert this?"

"For me to be back in Hell, I either have to break the bond myself, or you would have to be killed," Shaker said quickly. "If I break the bond and go back willingly, you won't be killed. The future isn't written completely, Debbie. Jezebel only gets glimpses."

"Say we do this," Debbie said slowly. "What about the second part of this prophecy? 'betray and hurt someone you care for'. Who does that refer to?"

"I don't know. It can't be Rip or Titus, they are my family. You are my family via marriage to Jett. So I'm not sure what that means. She may have gotten a glimpse of us being intimate, and then me hurting you because I'm forced to, and come up with that warning as a description."

"Could she have seen the events in reverse order, that Satan forced you to hurt me and betray me, then you're back in Hell when I die?"

Shaker shook his head, then sighed and shrugged. "I don't think so. Jezebel is usually very specific in repeating what she sees, to try to maximize something that will be recognized, so her visions can command a higher price. I've been involved in hearing ten or so of her visions through the years, and the order of what she sees has always been correct."

Involved how? "But these ten visions, they were all more or less right?"

"No. They all came to pass exactly how she said they would. What happened wasn't always how others or I surmised what she foretold was going to happen though. She rarely gets names. For example, there are a lot of sorcerers, that could be anyone. What's sure is that someone of power is looking for me. You're going to die unless I relinquish you, because they'll kill you to make me available to be bound to them."

"What if it's a heart attack or something! You leave me, and I might die anyway!"

"You're not going to die. I'll surrender myself to the priest tonight. Trust me." He kissed her quickly, then disappeared even as she reached for him.

Debbie blinked her eyes, then sat up. Guardian was beside her, whining. Smoke was still billowing from the demolished set, along with the smell of cooking meat.

Those are bodies cooking. Jett's body. Debbie turned and vomited her morning coffee on the pavement, then used Guardian to pull herself upright. Bracing herself on a nearby trash receptacle, she began dialing 911.

~

"Can we go over it again?" Detective O'Hara asked.

"How many times do we have to go through this?" Debbie protested. "I was busy at the other set, with my director, the actors for the film, the client who funded the picture, and his liaison."

"And is that normal, to have a producer there onsite watching filming?"

"It was a stipulation of his investing in the picture," Debbie said for the fifth time. "I am not usually there myself, but I had gotten a call from my director asking me to be there, there were some issues about a scene. We worked them out with the liaison's help—"

"This Nate you mentioned."

"Yes. Then I hurried to the set where *Smoke and Ashes III* was being filmed, because I'd had Stacey, one of my staff, come and tell me that Jett had requested my presence."

"Jett, your husband, didn't tell you of this before? No cell phone message or text?"

"No, we hadn't been spending a lot of time together," Debbie said sadly. "He's been working a lot, we had to reshoot a lot of the scenes."

"And you're sure that's what he was working on?"

"What are you saying? That he was having an affair?"

"Well, I understand that you just had your VP's ex-girlfriend move in with you earlier this week."

"Along with my VP, who is very ill," Debbie said pointedly. "Sheila will recover. But yes, I'm happy to have Rhonda there." She glared at O'Hara. "You are aware that Rhonda is my sister-in-law? I think it's in very poor taste to insinuate something was going on between us."

He held up his hands. "Hey, I only meant that Jett and his sister didn't get along. I pulled her records, she's had some substance abuse problems. Maybe she slipped off the wagon, and he decided he couldn't handle it."

"Why don't you concentrate on the facts? Do you have any idea what killed my husband?"

"ME says it's too early. We have people coming to test the site for both arson and explosives." He paused again. "I understand you had another bomb go off a month ago? Pandora's racking up the body count again this year."

"We're done," Debbie said in disgust, standing up. "You have any more questions, you can talk to my lawyer."

"Sit down, Mrs. Black. I still want to know why two movies are shooting at the same time. Your director Bart said that's unusual, as in it never happens. Several other people on your staff told me the same thing."

"Because they weren't really shooting entire scenes on the set Jett was on today, just filling in dialogue that we changed," Debbie stated. "We're in a rush to get *Immortal Confessions* done, now that we're releasing the movie early."

O'Hara put away his device, after making a last note. "Okay, we're done. I'm sorry about all that's happened to you." He paused. "I was one of the officers who interviewed Henry, I know he was behind what happened to your VP. Please know we're going to put him away for a long time."

"That won't wake Sheila up from her coma," Debbie said tiredly. "Goodnight."

As she drove home, thoughts crowded her brain, yet she couldn't concentrate. *Shouldn't I be more upset? It's because I know Shaker's still alive, that he can't die. If he's alive, there's always hope for us. But how are we going to finish the third movie now? Maybe I can get Brady to play Smoke, just for the scenes we need to film, having him facing away from the camera? Fuck, I'll have to call him, tell him that his brother's dead. God, I'm going to have to plan a funeral, too. I'm a widow now, and I've been married less than six months. The papers are going to have a field day with this entire mess. And my mom's going to be furious.*

Debbie parked her car in the garage, then went inside. Instead of Song's cheerful welcome and the smells of cooking, there was only silence.

Something is wrong. "Guardian," Debbie called.

The hellhound slunk out from behind the couch, then began wagging his tail. Debbie petted him, then went to the kitchen, and put some meat in his bowl. As he was eating, she looked on the counter for a note, but there was nothing.

"Debbie?" a rusty voice said weakly.

Debbie turned. Sheila stood there holding onto the door handle, looking as if she might collapse at any moment. "Sheila!" Debbie rushed over, hugging her friend. "You're awake!"

"I feel like shit warmed over," Sheila said. She looked at her body. "And I gained a few pounds. What were you feeding me?"

"Song, she's been taking great care of you," Debbie said happily. "She's going to be so happy that you're awake."

"I can't feel her," Sheila said, with a panicked expression. "Where is she?"

"I'm not sure," Debbie said, sitting at the kitchen table. "I expected her to be here. Sit down, there's a lot to bring you up to speed on."

~

"I'm so sorry about Jett," Sheila said, when Debbie had finished. "So you can't feel him?"

Debbie shook her head. "Nothing."

"I'm going to try Song," Sheila said, feeling for her phone. "I'm worried now. It's getting dark. She's not answering my mental texts." She looked around. "Have you seen my phone?"

"Who knows where yours is." Debbie handed over her phone. "Use mine."

"She's not picking up," Sheila said, biting her lip.

There was a knock at the door.

"Damn, I forgot, that's the bodyguard I hired," Debbie said, standing. "Wait right here."

There was a screech from outside the door.

"That's Song!" Sheila dashed for the front door, throwing it open. The priest stood there, eyes burning with righteousness, a cross in his hand still smoking. Rhonda was on the floor, unconscious, her hands and chest smoking. The stink of sulfur surrounded them.

"You bastard!" Sheila said, launching herself at him. He pushed her back, the cross connecting with her flesh. There was a sizzling sound, and the sharp smell of burned flesh. Sheila let out a shriek, then fumbled back, her arms crossed over her chest.

Damn it, why didn't I get a gun for my purse? Debbie ran for the kitchen in search of a knife, Sheila following, the priest in pursuit.

"We haven't done anything!" Sheila stated, backing away as the priest advanced.

"You might not have, but your demons did. And you're guilty by association."

"What has he done, except protect me?" Debbie shouted. "It's you and others who have attacked us!"

"Strife follows evil."

"He said he is giving himself up to you. Sheila, run and get help! Guardian!"

The priest stopped, confused. "What?"

Sheila grabbed Debbie's phone and staggered out of the room. Shaker materialized in front of Debbie, as Guardian emerged from under the kitchen table, growling. "You know I'm not Jett," Shaker said, advancing with his hands up. "But I was. All of this was my doing. You've won. Now leave her alone."

Guardian sat in front of Debbie, still growling at the priest.

"That must be a demon dog," the priest exclaimed, brandishing his cross again. "What kind of trick is this?"

"No trick," Shaker said wearily. "You know I can't touch you." He got on his knees, submissive. "Do your rites, send me back."

"You can't be serious."

"I am." Shaker turned toward Debbie, but kept his eyes averted. "Go, Mistress. Hurry."

The priest lowered his cross to Shaker's head, shouting out some Latin. Debbie took a breath, then felt a searing pain as something was wrenched out of her. She dropped to her knees, shaking hard, as Shaker disappeared, screaming loudly as he began to burn.

"Stop it! Shaker!"

"You're not leaving either." The priest pulled out a gun, holding it on Debbie. "You'll just get him out of Hell the moment I'm gone, won't you? If I leave you alive."

"You bet your ass I will," Debbie snarled. "And then I'm getting a gun to kill you."

Rafael materialized by the shoulder of the priest. "Let the women go. You have the demons; they are vanquished."

"No," the priest said sternly, his finger on the trigger. "Not until she's destroyed. She'll just summon him again. I can't leave her alive."

"His marker is no longer on her soul," Rafael urged. "You did destroy his manifestation on this plane. Reach out to her, what do you sense?"

The priest glared at him incredulously. "No demon removes a soul marker, ever! They never let go willingly."

"But this one just did. If you kill her now, you're guilty of murder."

The priest ground his teeth, then lowered the gun to her temple. "Leave, Rafael. Now."

I'm going to kill him. Debbie grabbed a paring knife, then struggled to her feet, trying to get to the priest. Rafael intercepted her, a gunshot sounded, and her world suddenly faded to blackness.

When Debbie awoke, she was alone. She wept there on the cold floor, then pulled herself together, making her way into the living room. Sheila was sitting on the edge of the couch, looking almost too calm as she sipped from an almost empty wineglass.

"Is it you? Really you?" Debbie said, grasping the doorframe for support.

Sheila nodded. "Come and sit down." She poured another glass of wine. "I feel like Swiss cheese. The burn on my chest isn't healing, and I've lost Song, too. If I didn't know she was really still alive somewhere, I'd be devastated."

"Shaker's alive, too," Debbie said, sitting down and taking the glass. "But I've lost him. Our bond's broken." She rubbed her eyes. "What happened? Why aren't the police here?"

"Because your bodyguard, Gore, showed up," Sheila said with a smile. "He was a few minutes behind the priest, but he figured out what was going on. He shot the priest as the angel went to catch you. The angel glared at him but didn't do anything but vanish." She sipped her wine. "I helped Gore wrap up the body. He left with it."

"What about Rhonda?"

"Sedated for now, another thanks to Gore. He had some heavy-duty sedatives with him, probably for questioning people, who knows. But when Rhonda wakes up, she won't be Song anymore. I'll have to try to figure out what to do. I'm having a glass of wine first, to settle my nerves before I call and dump this on Brady."

"You and me both," Debbie said, holding out her glass. "Because I've got to tell him about Jett, too. Pour."

CHAPTER TWELVE

AUGUST/SEPTEMBER

"Rack, you can't be serious. There has to be some way to get Shaker back."

"You could try to summon him out," he said finally. "But there's no telling if you'll get him specifically." He stared at her, incredulous. "It's the middle of the night. I thought you called me because you needed help getting rid of a body, not to ask about this."

Were you hoping for a late-night snack? "I called you because you're the only other demon I know, and I don't have a way to get in touch with Titus." *Because he's not responding to any of my mental texts, and even as desperate as I am, I am not ballsy enough to call Devlin's home and demand to talk to him.* "There must be a way to get him specifically out. Aren't you upset at all he's back in Hell?"

"Shaker's never inside long," Rack assured. "He's wily, and he's devious." He gripped her arm. "But you pay attention to this. Because of how it ended with you, he likely won't be back, Debbie. He truly cared for you, and you'd be a target just like he told you, if you were together again. If you really care for him, you'll leave him alone, let him work his own way out of this."

"That's not a help! Would you leave your wife, if you were in Shaker's position?"

"Yes," he murmured. "But she would be wise enough to let me. We'd find each other when her mortal life was done."

"How?"

"Maybe we'd both be in Hell. Maybe in purgatory? I don't know, and I don't care. I believe that I'd be able to find her, after death, after our being bound, even if that bond was broken. The true hell would be being alone without her."

It is Hell, being here alone. "Fine," Debbie said, picking up the phone and dialing. She shifted her feet back and forth as it rang, then was picked up.

"Hayden."

"Hi, this is Debbie Black. Can I speak to Titus? It's about his brother."

"Just a sec."

After about five minutes, Titus answered. "Hello, Debbie?"

"Titus, Shaker's back in Hell. That priest got him before he was killed himself."

"I know," Titus rumbled. "He told me what he was going to do. But the priest is dead? That's good for you, you'll have a respite, at least."

"Aren't you upset?" Debbie's voice rose. "You were sent back, and you got back out the next day. Can you get him out?"

"No."

"What the fuck do you mean, 'no'? We have to get him out!"

"Shaker's old enough to make his own plans, and he wouldn't appreciate me interfering in this."

"But he's being tortured!"

"And he'll be punished more if I try to intervene, and I could wind up myself back in Hell. Look, I know you don't understand, you're a mortal of forty or so. To you Hell is the worst possible outcome, the realm of horror stories, the threat used to keep you in line your whole life. To us, it's our hometown. We don't like it there, but we know how it works and how to navigate it. Shaker's resilient, the most hardcore demon I know. He'll be fine. Now get some sleep, you're going to have a busy day tomorrow planning Jett's final arrangements."

"Don't you understand I have to do something, Titus!"

"Why don't you pray? Goodnight."

"Damn it!" Debbie slammed down the phone, cutting off the dial tone. It was then she realized Rack had left.

Guardian whined, then looked at the lapping waves, keeping well clear of the water. He looked longingly back at the dark hunting cabin, then at Debbie. She turned and looked at it too, then shook her head. *Don't be tempted to go in. You see enough reminders of Dad, and you might lose your nerve.*

Debbie knelt next to him, removing the metal collar. "I free you, good dog. Thank you for protecting me these last months. And if there is anyone listening to my prayers, I pray that you go straight to Heaven, because there's nothing I can think of, ever, that should condemn any dog to Hell."

Guardian shuddered, then stretched, falling over on his side. He twitched once and was still. Up from his gaunt body rose a misty form of a small collie-like dog, panting happily. He looked at Debbie, barked once, wagging his tail, then vanished.

Debbie looked at the lake in the setting sun, then threw the collar out into the waves. It plunked into the water with a heavy sound, sinking fast.

Just like I will.

Debbie took a breath, then waded into the water, letting out a gasp at the feeling of icicles stabbing into her legs. In a few moments, she became numb, then waded out further, watching the sun get swallowed down.

"I have to do this," she said aloud, her eyes tearing.

Shaker may have released me, but just because he's not answering doesn't mean he can't still hear me. He'll be able to claim my soul and get out of Hell. Or else I'll find myself there with him.

Debbie waded out farther, until only her head was above the water. She looked down at her hands. *I can't feel them.*

There was a splash, and then hot reddish arms encircled her.

Shaker! Debbie turned stiffly in his arms, even as they teleported to the shore. She looked up into the concerned eyes of Titus.

"This will not help him," Titus said, wrapping her in a towel. "Though I know why you did it. Don't do it again."

Debbie ached to throw the towel back at him, but she was shivering too much. "Who are you to tell me not to!"

"Shaker asked me to look out for you. He shared some of the details of what he foresaw."

"I want him to have my soul. He can use it to get out of Hell."

"No. Because he's already out," Titus said sadly. "I checked with some people I know. A powerful warlock has him, one who'll stop at nothing to get what he wants. He would use me, or you, or anything he needed to as a means to further tie Shaker to him."

"I can get him free, if he has my soul to bargain with."

"You can't. The warlock would take your soul instead, as property of his demon. He'd be within the law to do this. You'd sacrifice yourself for no real gain."

"We can't just leave him there to be tortured!"

"He was happier with you than I have ever seen him," Titus said, embracing her. "He did things I wouldn't have believed he would ever do. Don't make his actions in vain."

"I can't just let him go!"

"What about your company? About Sheila?"

Pandora. I did everything I did because that company was the most important thing in the world to me. And now I can't think why I ever thought that way. "Sheila can run the company and she has Song to take care of her. At least Song should be easy for her to recover."

"No," Titus corrected. "The person who took control of Harp

got Song as well. That I do know, as it's an associate of Devlin's they now work for. Both of them are doing fine."

Debbie shook her head. "No way. Song would never leave Sheila willingly."

"She didn't have enough strength to hold onto Rhonda's body; she's too inexperienced. The host personality is back, and Rhonda's awake and babbling about demons. She's locked in Mossberg Sanitarium. Brady admitted her this morning."

"How do you know all this?"

"Because when Brady's plane landed this afternoon and he couldn't reach you, he called Sheila and she tried Devlin's looking for me. I heard from her just as I felt you let Guardian go. You're lucky I was able to look through his eyes as he left to get your location." His eyes flashed, fires burning in their depths. "You freed him and tossed that collar I created in the water like it was garbage." He turned to the waves, and stretched out his hand, the collar flying up from the water, to land gracefully in his hand. "Do you know what that hellhound cost me?"

"I wouldn't have thought you would be a supporter of eternal servitude," she said spitefully.

Titus pulled Debbie to her feet, then grasped her by the shoulders firmly and shook her. "Everything you and my brother worked so hard for is going to fall apart, if you don't snap out of this and start holding it all together again. Do you understand? Is that what you want? Do you think Shaker busted his ass all this year using that Day in an Hour spell over and over because that is what he wanted?"

So that's why he mentioned it…and slept so much in the time he was home. "No," Debbie said, closing her eyes and biting her lip hard so blood came. "No, I don't."

"Are you ready to get back in the ring and fight?"

"No," Debbie said, pulling the towel tighter. "But I'll do it. You're right, it's what he wants."

Titus looked at her approvingly. "You are a good wife, and a fine woman, Debbie. Come. I'll take you to Sheila now."

~

"I'm glad you're okay," Sheila said, hugging Debbie hard. "I was worried."

You were right to be. "I'm sorry about Song."

"Rhonda's been admitted as an inpatient," Sheila said, wiping at her eyes. "Brady's been great. My insurance is going to cover it."

"How?" Debbie stammered.

"We were going to get married," Sheila said, digging for a tissue. "Damn it. Can never find one when I want one and the rest of the time they're falling out of my purse." She dug one out and wiped her eyes. "Anyway, I had Brady sign her name, he's used to doing that after taking care of her for months. Harp had gotten the marriage paperwork all ready right before he got called back to Hell, so he'd already signed it. I just signed it and backdated it."

"But why do that for Rhonda? Song's gone."

"Because Song might be able to come back," Sheila said hopefully. "Titus says he knows the person who has them and that they're being used as nannies, if you can believe it. The kids are some kind of supernatural crossbreeds, they're maturing very fast. When the kids are adults, they'll likely be freed."

"What if they aren't?"

Sheila glared. "I care about her and I want that chance. I know she wants it too, without having to ask. Wouldn't you do the same, if Shaker only had to put in a year or two?"

"Yes," Debbie admitted. "But Titus said for him, there's no chance of that."

"There's a chance as long as Shaker's still alive, and he is," Sheila said, taking Debbie's hand. "Let's go home."

~

Debbie lay in bed awake, turning over restlessly again and again, unable to get comfortable. *I've been awake for hours now. I am never going to get to sleep.* She sighed, then got up and went to her medicine cabinet, looking around. But all the prescription meds were missing.

Damn you, Titus. Or maybe it was Sheila. Stymied, Debbie sat on the edge of her bed. *I need to relax.*

Seized by sudden inspiration, she got up and crossed the room to the closet, rummaging in the back. *There it is!* Debbie pulled out a velvet bag, then took the lifelike phallus back to her bed. Lying down, she spread her legs, then began playing with herself, imagining Shaker with her, his hands on her.

He touched her thigh, running his hands up to her womanhood, softly stroking as his mouth found hers, seeking hungrily. He tried to push inside, but she tensed up. "Relax," he whispered, pushing down her nightgown to cup her breasts, squeezing possessively. "Let me in."

Debbie made herself relax, as Shaker rubbed the head of himself on her opening, then bore down. He eased inside slowly, unrelenting, then began to move back and forth, her channel becoming slippery as their breathing became more ragged.

Shaker paused, then rolled over. "Ride me, baby."

Debbie splayed her hands on his thick chest muscles, taking every inch of him she could as he held her hips. "Come for me, baby," Shaker grunted, moving her faster.

Debbie felt her climax begin, that sweet release so nearly within her grasp. "Yes, oh yes, God yes please! Yes, yes, yes!" She went limp, panting, post-coital bliss suffusing her body. She was just easing up to clean the dildo when there was a crackling noise, and an old man appeared at the foot of her bed. She let out a scream.

"So you're why he was so reluctant," the hooded old man grated, leaning on his staff, his long robes a dusty grey and black.

"Get the fuck out of here!" Debbie shouted, grabbing in her nightstand for Lash's throwing star.

"Stop," the man intoned.

Debbie's arms and legs froze, her muscles unable to move.

"What makes you so special that he would fight me for you? An unremarkable human woman whose best years are behind her?"

"Nothing," Debbie snarled. She closed her eyes and focused. "Our Father, who art in Heaven, hallowed be Thy name—"

"Silence," the old man uttered, and Debbie's mouth muscles froze as well. "I'm no demon, so that will have no effect. I predate Christianity, as well."

Shaker's new master, the sorcerer. I'm screwed!

"Why would he go back to Hell for you?"

"The choice of serving of my own free will," Shaker growled, appearing behind the wizard. He slapped the staff away, then pinned the old man's arms back. "Let her go, Cyrus. Right now."

Energy shot out of the wizard's hand, crackling and hissing as it slammed into Shaker, the demon's mouth tightening in pain. There was the stink of burning flesh. "Let go of me. I command you!"

"You burn me bad enough and I'll be worthless to you! Let her go!"

Cyrus closed his eyes, and a crackle of energy surrounded him, knocking Shaker away to slam into the nearest wall, cracking it. He slid to the floor, stunned.

"Mere child with horns," Cyrus said with a wave of his hand. "I will peel your skin for this, Shaker. But you're right we have more pressing matters. And I have learned all I needed to." He turned to Debbie, catching her eyes as he smiled a ghastly grin. "Good to meet you, Shaker's wife." They both disappeared.

"Debbie!" Sheila said, bursting into the room.

A sleepy Brady was behind her, eyes bleary. "What the hell happened?"

"Just a nightmare," Debbie said, hugging Sheila. "I'm sorry I woke you. It was so bad I fell out of bed."

And hard enough against the wall to crack the wallboard?

Debbie blinked at the odd thought, then realized it came from Sheila. She concentrated. *Sheila!*

Her friend recoiled as if slapped. *Debbie?*

Get Brady out of here. Shaker was here, that new master of his found me. He tried to protect me, but that wizard is some kind of metahumanoid that's older than Jesus, he tossed Shaker aside like he was a child.

Sheila staggered, then caught herself. She turned to Brady. "Why don't you go back to bed? I'll stay with her for a while."

Brady nodded, yawning, and headed down the hall. Sheila closed the door and sat down hear Debbie. *Tell me everything, including how you knew we could talk this way.*

∿

"So Titus was right then," Sheila said, when Debbie had finished speaking. "There really is nothing we can do to free Shaker, and he can't free himself."

"For now," Debbie said bitterly, resolution in her eyes. "Only for now. But we are going tomorrow to talk to a priest or some other religious person, get some blessed knives. And I'll also call Gore, to get us each another gun....and a hefty supply of bullets."

∿

"I'm surprised you came here," Debbie said carefully, as Gore walked into her office the next morning. "But I'm glad you saved me a trip."

"Just to collect payment," Gore said good-naturedly, with an easy smile. He put a paper bag on her office desk. "And to make the delivery in person. I also need to ask if you want to continue the arrangement. I thought not, with your problem taken care of."

"It won't resurface, will it?" Debbie said coolly.

"No," Gore said. "All taken care of." He paused, looking at her.

Debbie waited a moment for Shaker to say something, then swallowed hard, realizing he wouldn't. *It's just temporary. I'll get him back, I will.* "No, I don't think I'll need live-in services now. But can I call on you again, Gore, if something else arises?"

"Of course. I encourage repeat customers. Well, those who pay promptly, anyway."

"How much do I owe you?" Debbie said in a direct manner. "I know what you quoted, but I didn't even get you settled. Yet you did the job, even went over and above, so to speak. And you made arrangements to give me live-in service that now you'll have to cancel. So I thought I should pay you for the first week, at least. Plus whatever the charge is for the delivery."

Gore nodded. "That's fine. Easiest job I ever did, in truth. But yes, that's my minimum fee. And that friend of his might decide to pay me a visit in retaliation, so I have to consider that. As for the delivery, that's seven. Sorry to charge so much, but you didn't just ask for the two, you asked for legitimization. That's where more than half the cost was. But I threw in the 2 blessed knives for free."

Debbie wrote a check for a thousand dollars, made out to Gore for "security services," and handed it to him, along with seven thousand dollars in cash. "Here you go."

"A pleasure," he said, tucking it in his back pocket. "Please call, if you need any help in the future." He put up his hand in a half wave, then left.

Sheila came in the door a few minutes later. "You look like you're holding up."

"You saw me this morning, that's not headline news."

"You know what is? Stonehenge. They've discovered extra rocks suddenly in the formations. It's all over the news."

"Sounds like a mystery," Debbie said, not looking up.

"I never mentioned this, as I was having them enlarged," Sheila said, handing a packet to Debbie. "I snapped a few pictures as you were coming down the aisle, and when you were saying your vows. I thought you might like to have them."

"That's thoughtful of you. Put them on the desk, please."

"Look, we're friends, so I'm just going to say it. I think you should talk to someone."

"I have you to talk to."

"And I have you," Sheila said, smacking the desk with the flat of her hand and startling Debbie. "But I'm still having trouble coping. I'm having a lot of nightmares whenever I sleep. Those feelings I talked to you about last January, about being evil? Well, I still have them, but they're stronger now.

"Shaker and Titus said it was because you were bound to two," Debbie murmured, her eye on the still open door. "Give it some time. It's only been two days."

"Think about it, is all I'm saying. And yes, people are gossiping about you, like you worried about. They say your marriage was a sham, just for publicity, and that's why you're already back at work."

"You know, I've never understood that," Debbie barked, her eyes livid. "I'm supposed to be so distraught that I can't come to work. To do what, stay home and cry? If I do that, we're lost, I need to be here preparing for the launch of *Immortal Confessions* later this month!" She took a deep breath and fought for composure. "We really need to focus on Pandora, Sheila. Our friends are gone temporarily; hopefully they'll be back. We have to believe that, and not give up hope, or sit around being angry about what happened."

"I am angry about what happened," Sheila shot back. "But no, I'm not going to sit around waiting, either. I'll see you at the meeting this afternoon." She walked out.

Debbie rubbed her eyes, then went back to her emails. More than half of them were professional condolences. She quickly typed up a thoughtful generic reply and began pasting and sending.

About halfway through, right before lunch, a new email popped into her inbox. *Sender unknown?* The subject was Guardian Dog. Debbie clicked on it.

. . .

When I looked into the future I didn't just see good things and bad things I saw you and I saw your love for me and I saw what you would do for me when the time came because I knew that your love might wax and wane but your loyalty would not and because it would not, that I can trust you more completely than I could trust anyone. I can't stop what is going to happen, but I have changed it and you have given me by loving me: a home which I never had before. I can't give you everything else I would like to, and I can't promise you anything more than I have. But thank you, Mistress.

Debbie sniffled, wiped at her filling eyes, then hit print. She took the page, and folded it, putting it in her purse. Then she deleted the message from her email and deleted items folder.

～

"Hello everyone," Debbie said, as she walked into the conference room where her team was assembled. "First of all, thank you all for your condolences. I loved Jett very much, and it's literally hell without him. But he cares, um, cared, very much about his movie he was working on at the time of his passing, and I'm coping by being here, working on his greatest passion." Debbie paused, looking around. "Having said that, we should discuss *Immortal Confessions* first. Are we ready for release?"

"The trailers are all done and uploaded," Adeline said in a soft tone. "The social media campaign has started. Ads are up, yes, all of them. I verified the bookings for the talk shows again this morning."

"Good, we can't afford another issue, even with Titan Pictures being on good behavior recently," Debbie said. "Bart, are we done?"

Bart shook his head. "No. But we're pretty close, just have to re-shoot some dialogue. We should be done by end of this week, then it's a work weekend marathon to cut it in time. But we have been editing as we finish the scenes and splicing the movie together as much as we can. We did cut a bunch of scenes, so the picture is now estimated to be a lot shorter, just over two and a half hours, instead of three and a half." He cleared his throat. "The client agreed to shooting them after release, and including them on the DVD as an extended version release."

"Good. Audiences usually can't sit still for more than three hours anyway. At home, they can hit pause. Anyone have anything else to add for this picture?"

No one spoke up. It was then that Debbie noticed that Nate was missing. *Well, he is finished with his part in the picture, he probably went back to Tennessee.* "Okay, do we have any numbers on *Absolution?* How did we do at the box office?"

"Pretty well, actually," Sheila said from the doorway, as she hurried to her seat. "Sorry I'm late, but I wanted the most up to date info. We released this movie back in July, at the end of the month. It did a fair job for the few theaters that showed it, but the reviewers really liked it, especially because it wasn't that violent on screen, but alluded to the violence instead." Sheila shuffled some papers, then pulled one out. "One reviewer said *Absolution* was a thinking person's horror movie. Another said it reaffirmed his faith that humanity was still both moral and capable of forgiveness."

Not what I expected...some truly good news. "That's great. DVD and streaming sales?"

"Interest is there, but it's small," Adeline put in. "We're gotten inquiries about purchase. Sheila's right, the movie is trending at eighty-percent fresh on Rotten Tomatoes, which is pretty good, given it's got forty reviews, which is also a surprise. And yes, before you ask, that's a large number of reviews for a limited release that hasn't been out long."

"Very good. Okay, what about *Smoke and Ashes III?*"

"Well," Stacey said slowly. "We've got the footage that Jett finished before his passing, which is substantial. If we hire a lookalike to stand in for him, and shoot from the side or back, we should be able to finish it."

"Bart, Nicole, what about a sequel?" Debbie asked. "Is continuing the series possible, given the script of this third movie? Or are we stuck at a trilogy? I haven't read the ending, so I'm asking if you can possibly move scenes around so we can have a sequel."

Bart looked at Nicole, then they both looked back at her. "Can we see you privately?"

Uh oh. "Sure after the meeting," Debbie said, her stomach twisting. "We're done here for today anyway, unless someone has questions to raise."

"I do," Adeline said, standing up. "And I think I speak for all the people here. Are you going to do something about what's happened this year? We've had several people killed here while working from explosives. These aren't some malfunction of special effects, they seem to be someone with a vendetta planting bombs. I'm starting to think I should look for another job for safety reasons, like Jeremy and Nelson."

"I was going to raise that question myself," Stacey said, looking uncomfortable. "There's been another killing by that vampire fanatic. They found the remains this morning."

Suddenly, Nate's absence took on a new possible meaning. *Shit, Nate, you scared me, but I liked your no-bullshit attitude.* "I'm sorry, I hadn't heard of that. Who was the victim?"

"Some loner based up in Washington. He's a vampire fiction writer who pens books writing as a vampire who hunts vampires. He was beheaded and staked."

"That man had no connection to Pandora," Catarella said calmly. "Or to movies or even to this state. It could well be that he ran afoul of some gang operating there that decided to copycat the original crime."

"Catarella's right," Rack agreed. "The passcard system keeps all vendors in shipping/receiving. I also authorized an additional camera to be installed there. The police did find a connection to one of the techs shooting with Jett the day he was killed. The camera shows this tech using his own passcard to let in another man about an hour before the bomb went off. The man signed in as an alarm system consultant, but Phenom has never heard of him. The tech has been fired, and a copy of the tape and signature given to the police."

"Thanks for telling us, Rack," Adeline said, sinking into her chair and visibly relaxing. "That makes me feel a lot better."

"Sorry you are just now hearing this, Debbie," Rack apologized. "But I didn't want to disturb you in your grief."

"Please see me later this afternoon," Debbie said, holding his gaze. "I want a full briefing, and to see a copy of the tape. Well done. Very well done." She looked around the room. "We're done for today. Thank you."

Everyone rose, except Bart, Stacey, and Nicole. Debbie closed the door, then turned to them. "What is it?"

"Did Jett have some kind of premonition?" Stacey blurted out, her eyes wide.

That's exactly what happened. "Why?"

"The script, well, it's set up to write Jett out of the series," Bart said, holding up his open hands. "He shot all the scenes needed for the film that were close up; we really can get a stand in to finish it. With minimal shooting time, which is so rare that I feel like it can't be accidental. This movie ends by Jett dying, and passing off the torch to the little girl Lindsay and...damn it, the character that the new actress Cassy plays, I can't remember the name—to carry on in his stead. Given that he died right after, it feels like more than coincidence."

Debbie blinked tears out of her eyes. *I can't believe the lengths you went to, Shaker.* "Couldn't that be a fluke?"

"I didn't say anything to the police," Bart retorted harshly, looking at her searchingly. "But there was a camera mounted back from the set, just enough so that the footage shows a good view of Jett saying his lines but it's not obvious he's on a set. None of my guys mounted it there, I asked them. And I didn't do it. But someone did."

What? "That camera must have been obliterated in the explosion."

"It was!" Bart said more loudly. "But it was set up to feed over the Internet to a recording system. We have the final minutes of footage, where as part of the script a house blows up with a mortally-wounded Storm inside, killing him. The bomb that killed Jett was in the house, we have the camera panning back and then the bomb goes off. Almost like whomever planted the bomb also planted the camera. Someone taped your husband's death!"

Could it have been Father Matthew? Could he have wanted the tape, to see if Shaker would rise up out of Jett's body after the explosion killed his human body? "Someone was targeting Jett. They went to a hell of a lot of trouble to get him. Maybe they wanted to capture their handiwork?"

"I'd believe that, if the recording didn't feed onto our production tapes. That's where the footage went. As far as I can see that was the only place. This goes beyond normal behavior." His eyes narrowed. "Jett didn't know enough about cameras to do this, in my opinion."

No, but Shaker would have been smart enough to do this. "I'm not sure what to say," Debbie offered. "I don't know the ins and outs of the actual film being shot. Yes, it's possible that Jett knew something was up, but why would he send Stacey to tell me to come there if he knew he was about to die? Our marriage was happy." She took a deep breath, remembering. "I thought I heard him shout as I entered to get out, trying to warn me."

"About that," Nicole murmured. "Stacey says she never said that Jett was looking for you the day of the accident, that she wasn't anywhere near your office though she didn't report that to the police. So you might want to check the tapes, if there's any more cameras that Rack put in place that he didn't tell you about."

"That's right," Stacey murmured.

She thinks Rack put the camera there. "Do either of you really think I had something to do with my husband's death?"

"No, of course not," Nicole said, standing and coming over to her. "He did love you, and you loved him, it was obvious when you were together. I said what I did because someone probably did tell you that morning to go to the set, and you thought it was Stacey. It would be better for you to find out who it was, so you can get them to back up what you're saying to the police."

"I'll check," Debbie said. *If it wasn't Stacey, then I was told to go there to die along with Jett. That priest might not have been working with only an angel; he might have had more help.*

"Rack, I'm glad you put the camera in," Debbie said without preamble, as he walked into her office. "Did you put in any more?"

"Yes. There's one watching your door with a view of the hallway, another watching the front entrance, and several watching the side doors. I had Phenom add them, when they installed the passcard system."

"You didn't have any on set? And you wouldn't know how to wire one to record digitally in another location?"

"I didn't have any on set. And I didn't wire the camera that shot Jett's final take. Bart already asked me." Rack glared at her. "I would have saved him, if I was anywhere nearby."

"Sorry," Debbie said, holding up her hands. "I have to ask as we don't know who put it there. Show me the hallway recording you have from that day right before the explosion. I also want to see the footage that was shot right before the bomb went off from the mystery camera, and the recording that you gave to the police of the suspect."

"Alright." Rack hit a few keys on his laptop, then turned it to face her.

Debbie saw herself walk out of her office, looking preoccupied.

She was on the phone, talking. She hung up, then turned, talking to someone behind her. "That's Stacey. I can't understand why she'd say she wasn't there."

"Because that's not her," Rack breathed. "Look again."

Debbie let out a gasp, watching onscreen as her figure hurried down the hall, moving out of the camera line of sight. Revealed was the small figure of a ghostly girl, wearing a ghastly look of pure hate. "Celia."

As she watched, the ghost faded from view and disappeared.

"Ten to one, the police watch this, they won't be able to see her," Rack murmured. "You were lucky. She meant to kill you. How did you run afoul of a ghost?"

"Shaker killed her mother."

Rack widened his eyes, then nodded in understanding. "That'll do it. You might want to see a priest, get a blessing, now that it won't hurt anyone."

"That's on my to do list tonight."

Rack typed a few more keys. "Here's the secret camera."

Debbie watched as Jett ran after a large man heading to the fake house. He tackled him, and the two went down scuffling. The villain brought his knife up, sheathing it in Jett's lower chest. Jett let out a grunt, then punched him. "This is all staged fighting, part of the scene," Rack explained, fast-forwarding as the two combatants wounded one another, fake blood spilling out of hidden bags. "Here's where it gets interesting."

A bloodied and battered Jett staggered out from under his fallen opponent's body, looking about to die at any moment. He reached out to the camera, expression pleading but resolute. "I love you. Be a good girl, Lindsay. Give 'em Hell." He turned suddenly as if he heard something, then his face whipped around to face the doorway, mouth opening to scream something as the set of the house exploded outwards, enveloping him in a ball of fire. The recording abruptly stopped.

"That's where the camera got fried." Rack closed the video. "You said he tried to warn you?"

That was Jett, not Shaker. Shaker's not dead. Compose yourself. "We hadn't talked for days, really," Debbie admitted, bracing herself on the edge of her desk. "He just cut me off and didn't come home at night. This would have been the first time I saw him in days." She sighed. "I feel like I have ten pieces of a thousand-piece puzzle."

"Here's the video of the tech letting in that mystery guy," Rack said, pulling up the last video. "Do you recognize him?"

Debbie watched as a furtive man let in another, and both of them walked off screen, accompanied by the safety manager, Mr. Minor. "Yes, that's the priest who tried to kill me. Fire Mr. Minor, if it hasn't already been done."

"Here's what I think happened," Rack said slowly. "And yes, I fired Mr. Minor this morning. The priest set both of the bombs. He knew Jett was possessed, and wanted to kill the body, figuring rightly that the man's mind was gone. After that was done, he went to your home, planning to wait for you but finding Song, who he'd also have been able to sense was a demon in a human host. He banished Song from her human body, maybe calculating that Rhonda was still able to come back, or that she was just a lot less powerful foe. Sheila's tie to Song being broken was a big enough shock to waken her, or maybe she was going to wake up anyway. Then you're both there with no protection, so he tries to make it neat and tidy by taking care of you, too."

"Celia sees him plant the first bomb, and that he's back making another to kill Jett. She tries to get you to go get blown up along with Jett. Shaker warns you in time, so you don't. Odds are he did see some part of his last moments, if he looked into the future. He might have recognized your dress, your hair, something from the vision."

"Then who planted the camera there?"

"Probably Shaker. He might have thought you could use the

footage. Or he might have thought you could use it to prove his death for the insurance."

"You know about that?"

"Of course, he asked me who I used for life insurance, and I told him I didn't carry any policies." Rack laughed. "But then I don't have a human host, either."

"Why would I need footage of his death?"

"There's usually a suicide clause, and he'd just brought the policy. I'd say he did this to make sure you got the money. He's worked harder this year than I've ever seen, Debbie. He was trying to tie up loose ends for you, so you'd have it easier when the time came."

Debbie blinked her eyes over and over, then wiped at them. "I know. He did so much…I don't know what to say."

"Don't say anything. Just change your story to getting told by someone, not Stacey. Leave the rest. And go collect that insurance."

"I should promote you. Want to take on security duties?"

"No," Rack said reluctantly. "I'm already stretched too thin between the vineyard and here. You should hire someone, though. People are scared. We still might get attacks."

Say this nicely. "Why? Sheila and I aren't um, tainted anymore."

"Because demons work here. It's not over yet, not by a long shot."

～

"You have a phone call from a Mr. Dalcon."

What can Devlin want this early in the morning? I hope not more crazy rambling. "Please put him through." Debbie picked up the phone. "Hello, Devlin."

"Good morning," he said cordially. "Because for the first time in months, it is one. My lady is at my side once more." He paused as if waiting for Debbie to say something.

"That's wonderful news," she replied quickly. "I'm glad to hear it."

"Lash has also returned. Now that my house is once again in order, I can turn my attention to other matters. I will make some calls and call in some favors today so *Immortal Confessions* becomes the blockbuster I want it to be."

"Honestly, Devlin, I'm not sure if it will help," Debbie said carefully. "We made good use of your money for advertising and our promotional strategy, if rushed, was sound. Five separate trailers are available on YouTube. Anyone who's registered at Fandango or Regal or Loews or any other theater chain fan club has gotten emails saying they'll earn extra points on their account for watching all of the trailers, more for seeing the movie. Our social media has been sharing pictures and interviews of the stars for the last two weeks, and we'll up that with new content until the movie's been out in theaters for several weeks. The main talk shows have the stars again being interviewed about the movie the first week it opens, usually both the male lead and one of the two female leads, sometimes several supporting actors. All of the trailers also have been shown on TV on the most watched channels."

"Which is excellent," Devlin commended. "But I have seen ads for *Escalation* as well on those same TV channels, and online. It's marketing is also sound."

"True. But we made a very good movie. I think *Immortal Confessions* can hold its own against *Escalation*."

"That would be true, if I were content to let it compete fairly," Devlin said mirthfully. "But I play to win, Debbie. I am not going to sit by and watch all that I've worked for not reach the lofty heights I aspire for it. Especially when I know that Titan Pictures has not played fairly against me from the beginning. They sabotaged us several times, and if I had not been distraught, I should have dealt with them then. Be assured, there will be an escalation, and that it will happen today." He paused. "Thank you for all you have done. Adieu."

"Goodbye." Debbie hung up the phone, then wasn't sure what to do, after hearing Devlin's speech. She went for an early lunch, grabbing some takeout as she read a few new unsolicited script offers.

Returning, she was greeted by Catarella, looking one-hundred percent the demon he was. "Can you believe it!" he chortled. "This is just perfect!"

"What?"

Sheila came running up behind him. "Haven't you heard? Henry's been arrested."

"He was out on bail?"

"Yeah, our great justice system. But yes, arrested again! The executives of Titan Pictures apparently get up to some wild parties on their supposed "teambuilding" weekends. And those parties include cock-fighting, which apparently this year morphed into dogfighting."

"I don't believe it," Debbie uttered, then shut her mouth, looking around her quickly. "Since when?"

"There's a full investigation pending. The California SPCA was alerted to some dogs that were being kept chained on some property without access to food and water. When they went to rescue them, the dogs went after the animal rescue team. Turns out these were trained attack dogs, and several were pretty scarred up from previous fights. On the premises was a fighting ring, and also records from fights that took place earlier this year, as well as the graves of deceased dogs."

"My God that's disgusting," Debbie said angrily. "Titan Picture's CEO did this?"

"His signature is on some of the paperwork. He's denying everything of course. But the coup de resistance is that there is also a video that released on YouTube, it's gone viral and the views are climbing. It shows the last few minutes of a dogfight where a dog is killed, and the CEO is there with his cronies, and the two male leads from Escalation, congratulating the winning dog's owner."

"Holy shit."

"Exactly. The SPCA is calling for blood and a boycott of the movie. So is PETA, The Humane Society, Best Friends, and at least a dozen others. Twitter is going crazy, as are the rest of the social media platforms." She paused. "People are cancelling their pre-bought tickets in droves. Titan's stock has plummeted ten percent already, and I'd guess it will fall double that at least, as more details come out."

Devlin did this somehow. Debbie remembered Guardian's last look at her, and felt tears welling up in her eyes. *Compose yourself.* "Will you get together some legal paperwork for us, to say that we will sponsor the rehabilitation of the dogs that were rescued?"

"I will. That's a perfect response for us." Catarella looked at her strangely. "I never took you for an animal lover."

"I'm a new convert." Debbie smiled at him and walked away.

"Congratulations!" Devlin said to Debbie, as he clinked her glass at the release party for *Immortal Confessions.* "Our movie is a complete success."

"It's broken *Escalation's* back," Sheila crowed. "You were right, Devlin, we've got a blockbuster." She laughed. "Ever given any thought to a sequel?"

Devlin knitted his brow, then turned to look at her, his smile growing wider. "You know, I do have an idea about that. I'll send someone to you in a month or so."

"But where is your lady?" Debbie asked, eyeing Titus, Devlin's lone companion for the evening. "I only ask as I was looking forward to meeting her. She must be so proud of you, of all you've accomplished."

Devlin parted his lips as if he was about to say something, then touched his tongue to one of his upper fangs, as if thinking better of it. "She just went through an ordeal and is not ready to be in crowds yet. In fact, as much as I looked forward to this moment of triumph, I must be leaving early, to return to her." He smiled. "I will bring her to meet you soon, when she is ready." His smile widened. "This is a night for all of us to celebrate. And I look forward to seeing what other pictures you have in the works. As I promised, I'll fund at least two others, given I am allowed to read the scripts."

"That wasn't a condition before," Sheila said delicately, glancing meaningfully over to meet Debbie's eyes.

"Just to confirm that you are not coming up with some vampire hunter hero, to vilify my kind," Devlin laughed. "Nate also sends his regards. He has his hands full right now, so won't be back, but wanted me to tell you he enjoyed his time at Pandora."

"We enjoyed him," Debbie replied. "I'm sorry, but before you go, I have to ask: did you find out who killed Joshua?"

"That is what is occupying Nate's time right now," Devlin said, losing his mirth. "Be assured, we will. I take it personally when someone directly reporting to me is killed in my service, no matter the reason or by whom."

"I liked him very much as well," Debbie said quickly. "I hope you get justice for Joshua."

"We will," Devlin reiterated. "I'm sorry as well for your losses." He kissed her hand. "I hope in time, your loved one will return to you."

"Thank you," Debbie said warmly, dabbing at her eyes again.

"Please, before you go, take a picture or two with the poster, and the stars? Sheila asked Devlin. "I know you said you are needed at home, but this night won't come again. You may want to remember this night a century from now."

"Always thinking ahead, dear Sheila," Devlin teased. "You are right. Let us do that right now."

"How are you feeling?" Titus said, when Debbie and he were alone. "You look much better. I'm sorry I didn't attend Jett's funeral, but I thought it would raise more questions."

"It's fine," Debbie said. "It was a media fiasco, and no one who knew him was there except me, Brady, and Sheila. Well, um, I mean, who knew Shaker." She paused. "Jett didn't have any real friends, just admirers."

"I'm glad you're back in the saddle, so to speak."

"You were right. I need to focus on holding things together here, and hope that when Shaker's able, he contacts me." *Should I tell him about the email, or that sorcerer's visit? No, he'll just tell me to let Shaker sort it out, which is what I'm going to do.*

"He'll find a way to contact you soon, to tell you he's okay," Titus assured her, patting her shoulder. "I'm sorry, but Devlin is calling me to take him home. Have a good night."

That Friday, as Debbie was packing up to leave for home, her secretary buzzed her. "There's a woman here to see you."

"There's no one on my calendar for this evening," Debbie said slowly, scanning the empty page of her virtual appointment book.

"I've got her on my list," her secretary said pleasantly. "She's the one that's been calling you for weeks. I'm buzzing her in now, Mrs. Black."

Titus! Debbie screeched mentally, her fear building. There was no answer.

Song! Debbie screamed telepathically. *Can you hear me?*

There was a subtle shifting, then came Song's weak mental whisper *Debbie?*

Please help me!

Hold on. I'm coming.

Debbie hurried to the door and locked it, but it was thrown open, a young woman with long wild-looking red hair dressed in jeans, a T-shirt, and hiking boots coming into the room. While there was no heavy black feeling that she was a demon, an air of menace surrounded the woman.

Song materialized, took one look at the woman, and promptly disappeared again.

Oh shit! Debbie went for her desk, scrabbling for the gun. The woman held up her hand, and Debbie froze still, her fingers around the gun's handle.

"Stop," the woman said gently. "I'm not here to hurt you. I'm here to save you."

CHAPTER THIRTEEN

SEPTEMBER

"Who are you?" Debbie demanded, not lowering the gun.

"My name is Myrrh," the young woman said. "As to who I am, I'm a half-breed. Half-fairie," she winked, her blazing blue eye when it opened turning purplish red. "Half-demon."

"Why are you here?"

"You are in need of security," Myrrh answered. "I'm here to answer that."

"Why?" Debbie said, cocking the gun.

"I could be all mysterious and play games, but I'm not going to," Myrrh said, stretching out her hand. Debbie's gun was wrenched from her hand, flying into Myrrh's grasp. "We have a lot to do, and not much time. Please gather your things, Mrs. Black, and I'll escort you home."

"No," Debbie said, leaning against the desk. "I don't know who you are, and I have my best friend staying with me. She's just becoming herself again. I'm not going to risk her life—by bringing you home," Debbie finished, as Myrrh let go of her arm, and stepped into her kitchen, heading straight for the fridge. "How did you do that?" Debbie demanded. "There are wards on this place!"

"Shaker got recalled to Hell," Myrrh said, opening the fridge door. "So any spells he did were broken when he departed. I see you have a ton of meat in here. Do you mind if I help myself, it's looking pretty dated?"

"Debbie?" Sheila called, walking into the room as she toweled her hair. The sight of Myrrh stopped her in her tracks. "Who's this?"

"Myrrh," the woman said with a wave of her slender fingers. "Good to meet you."

Sheila brought out her gun. "What do you want?"

"Don't make me take it away from you," Myrrh said without looking up. "Just put it away. If I wanted to kill you, you'd be dead already." She turned to Debbie. "I saw on the news that you're footing the bill for those dogs that were rescued. Do you like all animals, or only dogs?"

"I used to have a hellhound, but I set him free," Debbie said, sitting down at the table with a sigh. "That was his meat, not Shaker's. I think he went to Heaven, so I'm glad. But nights like these I miss him."

"I can get you another," Myrrh offered. "But they'll cost you." She looked at Debbie oddly. "I never met anyone that set one free before."

This is all too much, all of it. "Help yourself to whatever food you want in the fridge," Debbie said, standing up. "I'm going to take a shower."

"Thanks," Myrrh called, piling up a plate.

Debbie went into her bedroom, Sheila following. "Who the hell is she?"

"Some kind of half-demon, half-fairie who came to protect me. I didn't invite her, she just teleported us both here. Now you know as much as me." Debbie undressed, then climbed into the shower. When she emerged, Sheila was still sitting on the bed.

"Song came to see me."

"I saw her briefly," Debbie said, sitting beside her and taking her hand. "Is she okay?"

"She says she's fine, that what Titus told me is true; she's a nanny to a part vampire child named Sharon, and Harp's bound to Elijah, Sharon's sister." She sniffled. "She told me she didn't expect me to wait for her, that she'd be gone at least a year, maybe two. But she said she'd be able to visit more as the child grew up, that the kids were both maturing abnormally fast."

"What did you say?"

"That I loved her, and I'd wait for her," Sheila said, wiping at her eyes. "And that I'd protect Rhonda, so she could return to a host." She smiled. "She couldn't believe I forged the marriage certificate, said that no one ever had done anything like that for her before." She sighed happily. "She said she'd come back as often as she could to visit me, hopefully when the kids were sleeping."

Some hot demon sex sealed that pact, I'll guess. Debbie hugged Sheila happily. "I'm happy for you, I really am."

"I'm sorry for you," Sheila murmured. "But Shaker could come back in a different body, couldn't he?"

"He could if he could get away from that sorcerer," Debbie said, reaching for a tissue. "But I don't know if he can. I still remember him screaming, Sheila, it was awful."

"He's free," Sheila murmured hesitantly.

Debbie gasped, then pushed away from Sheila, staggering to her feet. "What do you mean? How do you know?"

"Song said she heard about it from another demon who was fresh out of Hell. Shaker had just brought in the soul of some powerful guy called Cyrus; it earned him some praise and renown, as the guy was ancient, and had been calling forth demons for years, but always disposing of them when he was done using them, before they claimed his soul, because demons can't kill their own masters. But Cyrus was killed, so Shaker got it."

"But...that's wonderful!" Debbie said excitedly, spinning a few times in happiness. "He can come back to me. God, I was so worried!"

"He's already bound to someone else," Sheila said in a low voice. "Some woman."

Debbie's mouth dropped open, as her shoulders sagged. "What?"

"That's all I know," Sheila said hastily. "Song swore me to secrecy, but I told her I had to tell you. She said that was fine, but then changed the subject and refused to tell me any more."

"Why!" Debbie shouted. "He's my husband, God damn it! Why am I just now hearing this from you, not from Titus, not from Devlin, not from Rip, not even from Song! I've been worried for close to a month now Shaker was in pain, and there was nothing I could do, and no one could be bothered to tell me he was safe!"

"Because Shaker likely has some plan," Myrrh said from the doorway. An enormous crow was perched on her shoulder. She slipped it another piece of meat, which it gulped down. "He always has some plan, Debbie."

"That bird's not going to crap on the floor, is he?" Sheila said, looking nervous.

"He's not just a bird." Myrrh gave her an indignant look. "He's one of my souls. The others are roosting outside, for now. But they'll come in when it gets cooler, not that it gets truly cold here."

"Who are you that just moved yourself in?" Sheila said, standing to put her hands on her hips. "We don't know you, and you have no one to vouch for you."

"Bloodsong saw me," Myrrh replied with an evil smile. "Ask your demon lover about me, when she comes tonight to lay you."

Sheila started. "Wait, how do you know that she—?"

"It's not only goblins that have the power of foresight," Myrrh stated, turning and leaving.

"Of all the damn witches, we get a sarcastic one," Sheila uttered, then whipped around to look at Debbie. "You're just going to bed?"

"What else should I do?" Debbie said, plumping her pillow.

"There's no one I could ask who I trust now to tell me the truth about Shaker. Song appears to be the only demon that is on our side anymore; hopefully she'll fill us in on this Myrrh if she visits you tonight." She turned off the light. "Let me know when she gets here, if she'll talk to me, that is."

～

"Debbie?"

Debbie blinked her eyes, then sat up in bed, turning on the light. Song was sitting beside her, again in her slender woman guise, with red and black hair.

"Hi," Song said uncomfortably. "Sorry for earlier today, I just—"

"Never mind. Who is this Myrrh?"

"They call her a lot of names. Dagger Maiden, She Who Waits, those are the most used. I don't remember the others."

"Why those names? What do they mean?"

"I can't tell you if any of this is true, but it's what I was told. She was raised by a group of natives here in America, around the turn of the century. She didn't want to be a mother or something. She was trained as a warrior by her adopted tribe, that's where the first name comes from. But when she came of age, the demon part of her started to show itself. She was a sorceress with a lot of power, but she didn't have a lot of experience. The tribe called on its neighbors, and the shamans all came together, and bound her into rock. That's where the second name comes from; the legend of a monster buried in rock that was waiting for the right time to break out. And I guess she did, because here she is."

"Can we trust her? You are obviously afraid of her."

"She could have killed you easily," Song placated. "I'll guess that Shaker asked her to watch over you, maybe even paid her to. Or maybe Terian recommended her, and she expects money. You'll have to ask." She shifted nervously. "As for me...I'm bound to someone else now, Debbie. They command my actions. I'm allowed here now for very short periods, but that could be taken back, and I don't want to risk that. If I get injured, the child I'm bound to will feel it, and there'll be a harsh punishment for that. So yes, if there's any kind of attack, I won't be able to lift a finger to help either you or Sheila. I'm sorry."

"Hmph," Debbie said contemptuously, even as she understood Song's rationale. "What about Shaker?"

"He's in the same boat I am; he can't risk being involved with you, and getting hurt," Song answered. "Don't think he doesn't care, when you know he does." She touched Debbie's hand. "I believe he's trying to find a way back to you, Debbie. Have faith in that." She let go and stood. "I'm sorry, but I have to get back to Sheila, and say goodbye. I only have a few moments left before I'm missed back in Europe." She hurried out of the room.

Debbie followed her a few steps, meaning to demand answers, then stopped, catching sight of Myrrh out on the deck, a murder of crows attentively surrounding her. She walked to the sliding glass door and opened it. The crows readjusted their stances, watching her intently, but didn't fly away.

"Feel better now?" Myrrh asked coolly.

"No," Debbie said, coming to lean on the deck near her. The crows moved with a hiss, then shifted their heads, studying her.

"I'm surprised you aren't afraid of them."

"Should I be?" Debbie said, holding her finger out to one. "They seem intelligent, and they're very handsome." The crow cawed once, straightened up, then hopped onto her finger.

"Bawdir likes you," Myrrh said with a smile. "But he's often a sucker for flattery."

"What are their names?"

"I'm not going to tell you, as you won't remember anyway," Myrrh grumbled. "It's takes time to tell them apart."

"Fine, be that way," Debbie said with a shrug. "I wanted to offer you the guest bedroom. Your crows are welcome to come in, if they behave themselves."

The murder all cawed and flapped their wings, as if irritated.

"Tonight they will stay out, to get the lay of the land," Myrrh said. "But you mentioned hellhounds. Would you like another?"

Debbie sighed. "Yes, I would. But then I'd probably free that one, too, before too long. You said they were expensive."

"They are...for demons," Myrrh said, looking over at Debbie with a smile. "Fairies have a few other ways to get one that...aren't. You're not what I expected."

"What did you expect? For that matter, who told you to come here? Was it Shaker?"

"I've never met him," Myrrh said, petting one of her crows, which shivered in delight at her touch. "But I've heard of him. He's a powerful demon."

"I thought you weren't going to be mysterious and play games?"

Myrrh laughed. "You're a direct one. I like that, reminds me of myself. Okay, Terian told me some time ago you were looking for a guard. I called but wanted to talk to you before I just showed up, see if I wanted to be your guard. I don't usually hire myself out like this; when I do, it has to be for someone I deem worth protecting. But you were never in your office when I called, and your secretary wouldn't give out your cell. So I stopped by twice, but again, you weren't in your office. I began to think you were just avoiding me."

"Why would I avoid you?"

"Then I heard about Jett dying, and decided I'd try one last time. And there you were finally."

"Are you Ranked?" Debbie asked bluntly.

Myrrh looked at her with new respect. "Ah, so you know about that. No, I'm not. I'm not an assassin. I'm a sorceress, as you already likely heard from Song."

"Can you fight?"

Myrrh laughed. "I know I look young, but I came of age close to a hundred years ago, Debbie. I could fight in my youth; I was trained for it. I stick to magic now, it's a lot safer. But what you're really asking is can I protect you, and the answer is yes, I can."

Debbie opened her mouth to ask more, but Myrrh held up a hand. "Get some rest, Debbie. You're dead on your feet. Everything else can wait until morning. Nothing will disturb your nights from now on." She smiled. "Unless you want them disturbed."

~

The next morning, Debbie slept in, secure for the first time in months that she was safe. In the morning, she turned over to find not one but two small, lean black hounds sleeping near her. Startled, she shifted away with a yelp. Both dogs cowered back, eyes wide.

"Shh," she said offering a hand to the nearest one. "You don't have to fear me. I know you understand my words. Would you like some meat?"

As Guardian had, both dogs leapt up, whining excitedly, whip tails wagging madly. Debbie laughed, then led them to the kitchen, dividing up the remaining meat into two bowls. "Damn, Myrrh and her crows must have had hearty appetites. I'll have to get some more meat later today."

The dogs cleaned their bowls, then sat, watching her.

Myrrh walked in dressed in a long black robe, one of her crows on her shoulder. "I see you found them."

"What are their names?"

"You can name them," Myrrh said. "But choose good ones, so they'll stay."

Debbie petted the nearest one. "They don't have collars."

"That's because I didn't buy them, I stole them," Myrrh answered with a grin. "Helped them escape Hell. The collar you're referencing is a magical tool, to keep the spirit bound to you once it leaves Hell." Her smile faded. "And no, I won't make some for you."

"I don't want you to," Debbie said cuttingly. She turned to the dogs. "If you stay, stay because you want to. I'd be glad of your company. Tell me your names."

Both dogs studied her, turning their heads this way and that, then looked at Myrrh, who rolled her eyes. "Lazarus, Charon," she said. "Leave us for now. Debbie will call you, if she needs you. You are to come when called."

The dogs nipped at one another, then began chasing each other in play. They ran into the shadow of the trash can and vanished.

"They'll be back," Myrrh assured. "But you will have to call with your voice, and loudly. There's no mind link."

"Thanks," Debbie said happily, making some coffee. "Truly. I feel better this morning than I have for months. I'm sorry, but we should have talked about it last night: what's your fee?"

Myrrh looked at her oddly. "Let's say a hundred thousand for the rest of this year. Then we can renegotiate, if you need my services beyond that."

Steep, but at least I can pay it. "Agreed. Will you live here?"

"I'll stay with you sometimes, but I have my own home to tend to," Myrrh said, her eyes far away. "But you'll have the dogs, and I'll leave a few of my souls to guard you. They'll also defend you, if needed."

What can birds do against anyone? "Why do you call them your souls?"

"Because they are literally my souls," Myrrh said proudly. "They were once beings that worshipped me as a goddess of sorts. They're bound to me. Call it my demon heritage, if you will."

"Do you still see your parents?" Debbie asked. "They're immortal, right, being fairie and demon?"

"I never knew them," Myrrh said darkly. "Only what they were." She smiled bitterly. "I heard Song tell you my history. I must have been a huge disappointment, to have been abandoned. I always imagined it was some forbidden affair that created me, so they had to get rid of me before they were discovered."

Should I share? Screw it, I want to. "I wasn't close to my parents, either. I lost my father back this spring, but I hadn't talked to him in years. My mother considers me an utter disappointment; she didn't even come to my wedding."

"That's...pretty bad," Myrrh admitted. "I didn't know you married Shaker's host."

"I didn't marry his host, I married him," Debbie said proudly. "It was at Stonehenge; he even redid the rocks, so they would be as they once were. We were so happy that day, even though I felt it was rushed. I was sure I was going to be a mother, and a wife. Now I'm a widow—"

"So you decided not to have the baby," Myrrh asked bluntly.

"No," Debbie said, aghast. "Why would you say that?"

"You just seemed like a tough career woman, everything I heard about you. Having a baby is a lot of work, especially on your own."

"Are you a mother?" Debbie snapped.

"I never wanted to be," Myrrh admitted, looking for the first time shy. "Faerie women have a hard time creating life without a lot of magic. I never met anyone that wanted me to have their baby, either."

"Neither did I, until Shaker," Debbie said sadly. "But I miscarried." She kicked at the table leg. "That's why I'm upset he hasn't contacted me. I know it's cliché, but I don't have that much time to have another baby. I want us to have another chance before it's too late."

"What else?" Myrrh uttered, petting her crow.

"What else what?"

"You want Shaker back in your life, and in your bed. What else? If I'm going to guard you, I need to know your goals."

"I had a guard before and he never asked me any of this."

"He was a male, wasn't he? Ranked?"

"Yes."

"They don't think of the big picture," Myrrh said contemptuously. "Only their own bottom line. Tell me about him first, then, and everything he did for you. Leave out nothing."

"Gore isn't bad, but he's also barely in the top twenty," Myrrh said when Debbie had finished. "He's also not to be trusted. He knows the inside of your home now, so it would be a good idea to change it up, even just move some furniture around."

"You're making it sound like he's an enemy."

"He's got the potential to be; he's a killer for hire."

Aren't you? "Ok, I can do that."

"I'll also strengthen the wards on this place, so no one can teleport in or out, except for myself and Titus."

"You know Titus?" Debbie said quickly.

"Of course, he's my kin," Myrrh said. "We're related on the demon side somehow. He's very big into genealogy."

"Then you and I are kin," Debbie said slowly. "By marriage. Titus is my brother in law."

"Well, why do you think I'm here protecting you?" Myrrh said with a wave of her hand. "C'mon, get dressed. You can tell me more as we make some food runs. We need a strategy for Monday and next week. We'll go from there."

She's holding back a lot, but I do feel what she is telling me is the truth. "What about Sheila?" Debbie said as she stood.

"She's going to need more sleep. Song spent most of the night here, by the sounds I kept hearing."

Good for her. "Okay, I'll be right there."

"Okay, so tell me the problems that you're facing," Myrrh said, as she drove Debbie to the grocery store. "I'll make a mental checklist. Getting Shaker back in your life is one. That may take some time, depending on this woman who has him. But if Song can get a regular furlough, I'd guess he can, too. What's two?"

"Two is trying to run the company without Shaker," Debbie

murmured, as she looked at the murder of crows following them in the driver's side mirror. "I depended on him for his contacts, his counsel, and his protection. I didn't realize how much I was running the company with him until it was all back on my shoulders. We're also at a loss for another star. I'm going to have to hold auditions and hope someone shows up. But we've had trouble with security, and others of my team have quit; the latest person is Stacey, who was supposed to be coordinating our films. She gave her notice yesterday."

"So Pandora's needs are number two on the list," Myrrh said. "You also need a new star, which you can probably find without too much trouble; that's three. Will you want Shaker to possess this person eventually?"

Debbie hesitated. "No. Shaker hated being Jett, he was always in the magazines for something, or getting photographed. He enjoyed making the movies, but I think it got to him, all the acting and being someone he wasn't. I never asked him if he liked it, but I think now, looking back at the comments he made, he thought it was just another role he had to play." She blinked back tears. "He probably was relieved when Jett was murdered, so he could stop having to act."

"Stop crying and hold it together. That's an order, Debbie. Four?"

She's harsh, but what I need right now. "Four through seven are new team members to get us back to full potential," Debbie mused, wiping her eyes on her sleeve. "As for eight, well, if you're only staying around until the first of the year, then that's plenty already to accomplish."

"Terian said if we got you to the end of the year of the demon, which is this year, then you'd diversify your films for next year," Myrrh said. "Then you'll likely be safe again with no guard required. The priest is toast, the angel's been gone since then, and you've fired the other security rifts."

"There's still a ghost hunting me," Debbie said, and began

telling her about Celia. "The hound I had kept it at bay, but it's gotten bolder each month."

"I'll lay it to rest."

"You can do that?"

"Of course. We just have another stop to make."

~

"Go in," Myrrh cajoled.

Debbie hesitantly went up the stairs of the church. Being a Saturday afternoon, the doors were closed, and no one was around. Debbie grasped the handle with a half-hearted tug, expecting it not to budge. Instead, the door opened smoothly, and she stepped inside. She approached the side of the altar, where candles were lit for those who had passed. She put in a donation, then lit one.

"You weren't on the list," she said tentatively, then cracked a smile. "But I'm sorry, Jett. This light's for you. You weren't a good man, and I still think that Shaker made you a much better one in the time he was with you. But please forgive me if you think I wronged you. And I hope you are at peace, for what happened to you."

In succession, Debbie made more donations and lit candles, naming off the people she knew Shaker had harvested, including Amanda. As she closed the brief prayer for her former secretary, there was an angry hiss from behind her. Debbie wheeled around, lit taper in her hand. Celia was there with glowing yellow eyes, her grin ghastly.

"You think you can light a few candles and be forgiven?" the ghost shrieked. "You will not be."

Remember what Myrrh said. "I'm sorry," Debbie said, not backing down. "But I didn't kill you. Stop haunting me and be at peace. Your mother waits for you, Celia. Pass on and go to her."

The ghost reached out, slashing at Debbie with her ragged nails, ripping four bloody furrows down her arm. Debbie yelped and staggered back, dropping the taper and clutching her bleeding flesh. From outside the church, twin howls sounded, angry and stymied.

The hellhounds. But they can't get in! Likely Myrrh can't either!

The ghost picked up the still-burning taper, which began to glow like a branding iron. "You're not sorry. But you will be. Oh, you will be!"

The twin doors slammed wide open, as Myrrh appeared, moving slowly as if slogging through knee-high mud. The murder of crows wheeled frantically in the sky behind her, cawing madly, diving toward the church, then away. In her hand was a ball of green fire. The ghost turned to her, screeching, claws outstretched.

"Go back to the grave, little girl," Myrrh commanded, her blue eyes flashing. "Go back willingly, or I'll end your haunting here. What remains of you will join my murder, until you have atoned for your crimes."

"Demon!" Celia growled.

"You are becoming one, in your hate," Myrrh intoned. "As such, you are fair game to me. I owe no allegiance to Heaven or Hell. Go back to the grave!"

Celia hissed, then launched herself at Myrrh.

"Have it your way." Myrrh threw up both hands, the green fire shooting forward to engulf Celia, who screamed shrilly as she writhed in the eerie flames. The girl split in two, one misty form disappearing, the other solidifying and darkening as it shrunk, becoming a baby crow.

Myrrh stepped forward, scooping up the stunned bird. It pecked at her, and she smacked it on its head sharply, causing it to wobble. "Behave."

"What is going on out here!" a fat pastor said loudly, as he hurried out from the back. "I'm trying to teach a catechism class!"

"Sorry, Father," Debbie said contritely, as she hurried out after Myrrh. "We were just leaving."

Myrrh walked to where her murder was whirling and swooping, then tossed the little crow up into the air. It plummeted, then caught itself, flapping madly as others of the murder took up position beside it, helping it to climb into the sky.

"Is it over?" Debbie asked, as she petted her two ecstatic hounds.

"Come on," Myrrh said uneasily, striding to the car. "Others with ability nearby likely felt that. We have to get going."

"Did you steal her soul?" Debbie asked, as she let both dogs into the backseat, then got in. "Celia's?"

Myrrh gunned the vehicle away from the curb. "Another spirit had attached itself to hers; possibly her mother, maybe someone unrelated. That spirit was angry, really angry. It fed on your fear and guilt, got stronger. It was Celia's essence that disappeared and passed on. Whoever the angry spirit was, they are now one of my souls."

That night, Sheila and Debbie sat in the living room with the two dogs napping near the small fireplace, drinking some wine and eating chips, as Debbie filled in Sheila about what had happened. Myrrh was absent, but had left two of her crows behind, which were sitting on top of a bookcase, watching intently for any dropped snacks.

"You're going to make them sick," Debbie said, as Sheila tossed another into the air. The two crows both dived, the smaller one grabbing the chip and gulping it down.

"She didn't say not to feed them," Sheila retorted, tossing another chip. "I can't believe you never told me about Celia haunting you."

"You couldn't see her," Debbie said with a shrug. "Even if you might have believed me, what was the point?"

"The point was, you say I'm your best friend." Sheila put down the wineglass. "But you've kept me kind of at arm's length this year."

"That wasn't just me," Debbie countered. "We were both busy

with our significant others. And you seemed jealous of Shaker's influence on me."

"I felt like I had two bosses," Sheila admitted. "I told you as much."

"You were right," Debbie said, taking Sheila's hand. "I didn't realize how much I was deferring to Shaker until he wasn't connected to me anymore. I was afraid of making mistakes, so it was easier to go along with what he suggested. I'm sorry for that."

"I'm sorry, too," Sheila said, hugging Debbie quickly. "I didn't realize how much Harp and Song were distracting me until they weren't there, either. One or the other was almost always in my mind, asking about this or that, unless I was having a conversation with someone. Away from work, one of them was always with me, twenty-four-seven. Having two lovers was exhausting, because while Harp didn't care if he had much of my attention, he did care about sex. It was all he thought about."

"I had no idea," Debbie said, then burst out laughing.

"You laugh, go ahead!" Sheila said, throwing a pillow at her friend. "But he kept me up past midnight sometimes. Sometimes he even pretended to be Song to get more sex, and I didn't realize it until he came…"

Debbie laughed so hard she howled. Sheila hit her with the pillow again, then began laughing herself.

"I miss Song very much," Sheila said, taking a sip from her glass. "But I don't miss Harp and his demands. With everything that's happened this year and last…I'm glad we all got a break from one another."

"So are you still going ahead with planning to go back to Song in a year or so?"

"I love her, and I want to be with her," Sheila said firmly. "But would I bind her again? I don't know." She paused. "If it was the only way to be with her, maybe. I miss the telepathic connection; it might be worth it for that. You must have realized by now that the one you and I shared temporarily had disappeared."

Debbie nodded. "I tried it with you the night Myrrh teleported me home, to warn you, and I couldn't."

"So what about Shaker?"

"Haven't heard from him," Debbie said sadly. "It's been a month now."

"I know, I can't believe fall's passing so fast," Sheila sighed. "Tomorrow's the first day of October." She sipped her wine. "I'm just glad that *Immortal Confessions* is a success."

"Did Devlin tell you he was thinking of a sequel?"

"I did hear him mention that, at the release party," Sheila mused. "Maybe next year will have to be the year of the vampire." She laughed.

"How about year of the ghost, instead?" Debbie offered. "You wanted to do that movie *Hell to Pay* and *Origin of Fear*. Both of those stories focus on ghosts, right?"

"Demons and ghosts," Sheila said, thinking. "As bad guys. Are you really thinking of doing another Smoke and Ashes movie, beyond finishing Jett's third installment?"

"No. I'm taking Terian's advice to diversify. We'll do those two movies you bought next year, and also bring out Jett's final movie. We still need a new star, anyway. Which reminds me, I need to call Brady tomorrow, see if he'd be willing to stand in for Jett."

"He's coming tomorrow to visit Rhonda with me," Sheila suggested. "I'll bring him back to the studio with me, so he can see you, if your afternoon is open?"

"Yes, that'd be great."

"Do you mind if I stay here for a while?" Sheila asked tentatively. "My house is huge and empty now. But I don't want to impose."

"Yes, please stay," Debbie answered quickly, offering a sad smile. "I feel the same. It's from us having constant company. Sudden quiet is unnerving."

"Good," Sheila said in relief, leaning back into the couch. "I like Myrrh, too."

"Like her, or like her?" Debbie asked meaningfully.

"Didn't I just say I'm recovering from being with a sex addict?" Sheila said crossly. "I meant just like her like a person to talk to. But she is very beautiful, though."

Debbie smiled. "Yes, she is."

~

That night, as she was drifting off, Debbie heard something. One of her dogs stirred next to her, growling softly.

"Myrrh?" she called.

No it's me, a familiar voice said in her mind. *I'm back, Debbie. Can you let me in?*

Shaker?

Yes. The sheer yearning in his tone was unmistakable. *So you know it's me, we got married at Stonehenge and you had a single black rose in your bouquet of red ones. You asked me to look ahead into the future at the beginning of this year and I did. Please come and let me in. There's a ward on your home now so I can't teleport in.*

Debbie was up and moving, pushing past the dogs as she threw open her bedroom door and hurried to the front door. She shoved back the locks, then threw herself into Shaker's waiting arms.

CHAPTER FOURTEEN

SEPTEMBER-OCTOBER

DEBBIE HUGGED HIM HARD, HIS PENETRATING WARMTH soothing. *You're here. You're really here.*

Shaker kissed her passionately, his hands roaming her body. He made to step into the house, then stopped, stymied. "Who did you get to ward the house? I can't even step in, so it can't have been Titus."

"A fairie called Myrrh. She's some kin of Titus's...um, I mean ours."

Shaker pulled her close, teleporting them. They arrived in a hotel room, a sleeping figure on the bed. *Brady,* Shaker said in her mind, as he scattered some dull powder over the sleeping figure. *Now he'll sleep until dawn.*

"Why are we here?" Debbie asked, as Shaker lay down next to Brady, and rolled into him. Brady's body twitched slightly, then sat up, his eyes flashing red briefly before his lips curved into a seductive smile that was a twin of Jett's. *He really does look like a younger version of Jett.*

"Because I want you, I've missed you, and I need you," Shaker said, taking her in his arms. But this time he didn't kiss her, he just held her as if he'd never let her go. "I'm sorry for how I had to leave you, and that I had to leave you at all."

"Why are you possessing Brady?"

"Because I know you wanted a child, and I want to give you one," Shaker said softly, caressing her cheek. "I've been watching Brady, and he's pretty much celibate, but everything works. I've slipped into him before at night, with him none the wiser, to make sure he'd be safe to use."

'Safe to use'? I've been worried for Shaker because he hasn't contacted me, and he's had enough time to be planning sex? "Why didn't you let me know you were okay?" Debbie accused, taking a step away from him. "Sheila got told by Song that Cyrus was killed a week ago, at least!"

"I'm sorry," Shaker said, bringing her to the bed to sit down. He put his arm around her. "If you know that, then you'll know I'm bound to a new Mistress now. I needed time to figure out her schedule, so that I could see you without being missed."

"Does she know you're married?"

Shaker shook his head. "With her, I'm a model demon, playing the role to the hilt. She got into this for the same reason I did, to free herself from Cyrus. It's not like you and I, Debbie." He hugged her again tightly. "I don't want her to know anything about you. She can be jealous about what she thinks is hers."

"But you are hers," Debbie said weakly, swallowing hard.

"Yes," Shaker assented, separating from her. "She can command me, and if she summons me at any time, I'll have to go do whatever she wants me to do. But so far, she's busy with her own life; there are already weeks she doesn't talk to me or call for me. I gambled that tonight it was safe to come and see you." He hugged her again. "I didn't want to come to you and be pulled away before we had enough time to talk."

"Did you really want to talk?" Debbie said sarcastically, gesturing to his almost naked body. "You're not dressed just for talking, are you?"

"Why are you so angry with me?" Shaker murmured. "Do you think I wanted to leave you, to get burned by that bastard sorcerer, for any of this to happen? I was sure he'd take you prisoner that night, after your thoughts of me led him to you."

"I'm glad you're okay," Debbie said, hugging him tighter. "I was so scared for you, the night you and he appeared in my room. How did he find me?"

"You were calling for me mentally, as you climaxed," he said lustfully. "I couldn't help it, I also watched your thoughts of us having sex, and enjoyed myself. Cyrus was a great one for patrolling dreams and invading minds, and he caught me. Before I could sever the link, he'd discovered you."

"So you could hear me, all those times I was calling for you?"

Shaker nodded. "I could always hear you, ever since we were bound. But I didn't dare answer you, for fear of him discovering you and using you against me. After he found you, I knew I had to get free, no matter what it took."

"But you didn't answer me for weeks this year. How long exactly were you working for Cyrus?"

Shaker let out a long breath. "He summoned me out of Hell years ago, and bound me as his servant, but with pure magic, not a pact of flesh. I had no say in serving him. But he let me do what I wanted, and never called on me or asked me to do anything, to the point I found myself wandering around your studio the night you and I first met. I didn't understand his motivations at the time for possessing me and not utilizing me, but I do now. He'd foreseen a lot of events that revolved around Devlin and Titus. He wanted someone on his team who would be able to best Titus, when he finally decided to play his hand."

Debbie remembered Titus's words in her office. *We had to battle at the end, and Shaker bested me, as he usually does.* "But you averted that battle?"

Shaker nodded, his mind reaching out to touch hers tentatively.

I love my brothers, and I don't want anything to happen to them. And I love you, Debbie.

"Then say it aloud."

"I love you, Debbie," Shaker said, hugging her tight.

"I just can't believe this is really you. For all the times you were so careful not to say what you felt, all the times you said you worried someone was listening. You always said it was the devil."

"Cyrus," Shaker said, his tone furious yet respectful. "Saying his name was enough to get his attention, always. Even my picturing him in my mind was enough, sometimes. He ordered me back to his side late this summer, saying it was time. I resisted going to him, until he nearly pulled me out of Jett. I couldn't mention him to you, ever, much less tell you the real deal. That's why I gave into the priest, let him send me back to Hell, knowing Cyrus would feel my death through our bond, and summon me out of Hell again, like Jezebel had foreseen."

"Why didn't Cyrus die when you did that?"

"He's more than human, he was able to protect himself." He touched her cheek. "Otherwise, the priest would have gotten me, probably. And you would have died from my deathblow, when I was sent back to Hell, because the pain and shock you felt through our bond would have been too much."

"And it worked."

Shaker nodded. "He's dead now and locked in Hell." He smiled, letting out a deep breath. "I'm really free."

"You're not free," Debbie said pointedly. "You're bound to some woman. What's her name?"

"Nope, not going there," Shaker said impishly, his smile fading. "She's a good Mistress: relatively immortal, has masses of her own guards, has two lovers already, and hasn't asked me to do anything for her that was hard."

Debbie's eyes narrowed. "Did you have sex with her?"

Shaker rolled his eyes. "Yes, in her dreams only. Cyrus was

watching me always, but he was a terrible prude. The only way I could contact her was through her dreams, and—"

"So you had sex with her only once, to get free?"

"No, she commanded me another time since then in her dreams to make love to her," he said bitterly. "I did as ordered." His eyes were glowing from anger in the dim light. "And if she orders me again to do it, I will, in dreams or in the flesh. Don't condemn me for what I've got no choice in."

"Did you enjoy it?" Debbie snapped at him.

"Yes," he shot back. "I was missing you and thinking that—"

"I don't want to know what you were thinking," Debbie said tiredly, standing up.

"She doesn't want me," Shaker said with a sigh. "I tease her with licentious words, and she likes that, it makes her feel virtuous to reject me because I'm a demon. She wants me to want her. But it ends there. Underneath there's no longing for me or fantasies about me, Debbie. I don't have fantasies about her, either."

"Our bond was severed, but the mental link can be made again between us," he murmured, drawing her in for a kiss. "We don't have to be bound to share that, Debbie." He pulled her down onto his lap, reaching his hand under her nightgown to slip between her legs, even as she tried to push him away. "My fantasies are all about you. That's all they have been about for months now, ever since I knew I was going to have to go back to Hell!"

His hand found her soft mound and began stroking. Debbie's lips parted to protest, but Shaker silenced her, slipping his tongue into her mouth.

I want you, wife, his voice growled possessively in her mind. *I have wanted you for months, I hated having to turn you off for days to work on that last movie, to pretend to be Jett and exchange pleasantries with shallow people who meant nothing, to not come to you all the times I felt you thinking about me and feeling sad. I'm here now, with you. How can you not want me?*

I do want you, she responded, parting her legs slightly so he could cup her moist womanhood. *But you hurt me, the things you said when you left, even if I understand why now.*

I'm sorry. His lips moved down her throat, as his, hands shoved down his boxers. *I'm sorry I hurt you. I was so afraid you'd be hurt in that blast. I was afraid Cyrus would hurt you, that the priest would, that someone else would and I wouldn't be here to stop them.* He moved lower, going to his knees beside the bed as he pushed up her nightgown to her waist.

"Shaker, please," Debbie breathed, as she felt him slip his tongue inside her. She ran her hands through his black hair, as he teased and licked at her swollen clit.

"You're so wet," he crooned, drawing back for a breath. "Tell me you missed me too."

"Yes, I missed you," Debbie gasped, as she felt him plunge his tongue inside her again. Her hands gripped his head, as she pushed up against his probing tongue, opening herself to him. "That's why I touched myself." *Why I almost ended myself.*

What? Shaker drew back from her, bringing her into a sitting position, his expression incredulous. *What did you do?*

Debbie couldn't look at him. *I thought if you had my soul, you could break free from Cyrus. So I tried to give it to you.*

Shaker hugged her hard again, pulling her tight against him. "Don't ever do that," his whispered brokenly. "Don't ever. Please, tell me now that you won't."

"You sacrificed yourself for me," Debbie sniffled. "What kind of wife would I be not to do the same?"

"I sacrificed my host body, and my manifestation here on Earth. That's not the same." He kissed her forehead. "Promise me now that you won't ever try something like that again, no matter what happens."

"All right."

"I'm not worth your life," Shaker whispered. "Or your soul. Don't ever barter those, not for me."

"You bartered yourself to Cyrus for me," Debbie said softly.

"Okay, we both did what we had to do," Shaker amended. "But that's done. I'm coming to you now as someone that loves you, to be with you however I can. Do you want me?"

"Yes," Debbie said, kissing him hard. *Take me now.*

Shaker pushed her back on the bed, moving into position between her legs, he pushed forward, his hot erection sliding deep. "I've wanted to be inside you so much," he groaned, beginning to thrust.

I wanted you to, Debbie said, pulling him atop her. She grabbed his ass, pulling him deeper.

Lightbringer, you feel good, Shaker groaned, thrusting faster. *I fantasized about this so many times in the last weeks, coming to you, telling you everything, then taking you, making you mine again!*

Come, Debbie said, quickening her pace. *Make me yours!*

Shaker let out a bellow, then clutched her, twitching as he shot his load. He clenched his buttocks a few more times, then relaxed. "Don't you move," he ordered with a smile, then rolled off her.

"And why not," she said coyly, as she watched him strip off the boxers from one ankle.

"Because I'm not finished," Shaker said, lying beside her, his eyes lustily roaming her body as he touched himself, tugging on his penis. His semi rigid cock filled out and he was again atop her, pushing inside with a groan. "I didn't think about this so long to have it end so soon. I love how wet you are for me."

"That's your come," Debbie murmured sexily.

"You said make you mine," Shaker growled, as he rolled onto his back. "Come and claim me. I want to hear you scream."

Debbie shook her head, instead getting onto her knees. "Come and get me. Make me scream."

"Don't have to ask me twice," Shaker said, pushing up from the bed. He grabbed her hips, pulling them tight back against his, and began to pump for all he was worth. Debbie clenched her vaginal muscles, tightening around him like a glove. Shaker shuddered, then pumped harder, coming again with a shout. He eased down on his back, breathing hard.

"Out of juice?" Debbie teased.

"This body is," Shaker said apologetically. "You'll have to give me a moment."

"No," Debbie said gently, taking his hand. "Come out of him."

Shaker looked at her oddly. "Why?"

"Because I want you, the real you. That's who I love. That's the only male I want inside me right now: you, Shaker. Get over here."

Shaker reached up a hand to caress her cheek, then got up and moved to the chair in the room. He stepped out of Brady's body, then carefully covered the man with one of the blankets from the bed. Stepping to the bed, he sat down, then maneuvered onto his back, his large swollen penis erect and quivering. "Come to me."

Debbie went to him, taking a sharp intake of breath as she eased his huge phallus inside her. Her already slick flesh accepted him, then she began to move on him.

His clawed hands reached up to grasp her hips, as he thrust up. Debbie let out a cry, feeling him touch her cervix.

You feel so good. I've wanted you so much, You're the only one I wanted inside me, just like this. Take me, Shaker! Take me!

Nothing existed in those next moments but the motion of her body together with Shaker's, both of them moving toward climax. Strangely, though Debbie was maddened with excitement, her orgasm built slowly, the exquisite sensation finally washing over her in an easy wave, not the tidal crash she'd been expecting. But when it was over, she felt utterly spent, and weak as a kitten, almost shivering.

"Don't stop," Shaker murmured. "Please don't stop. Keep moving." *I need this. I need you.*

Debbie did as he bade and kept rocking on him. Again the feeling built, but this time it was massive, crashing over her and wringing scream after scream from her parted lips. She sagged down on him.

Again, he whispered gently, moving her hips with his deft hands.

The next orgasms were different, almost mini-shocks that required little effort, but were much smaller than the first two. Finally, after five, she splayed her hands against his chest. "I have to stop."

"I'm out of practice myself," Shaker groaned, pulling her down close to him.

Debbie snuggled into the heat of him. "I've missed you, did I tell you?"

"Yes, but you can tell me again," he rumbled happily.

"I missed you."

"I missed you, too."

"I don't want to ruin the post-coital bliss," Debbie said drowsily. "But why don't we just go back to my house?" She looked over at Brady in his chair, feeling a stab of guilt. "We should give him back his bed."

"This was the most action he's likely seen in years, if not his whole life." Shaker chuckled. "But you're right, he's deserving of more respect." Shaker slipped his loincloth back on as Debbie dressed in her nightgown, then picked up the sleeping Brady, laying him under the sheets as Debbie helped tuck him in. "Thanks, bro." Taking Debbie's hand, he teleported back to her backyard.

Immediately, crows surrounded them, cawing raucously.

"Good we have no nearby neighbors," Shaker drawled. He addressed the nearest crow. "Where is your mistress?"

"Here," Myrrh said, stepping out from beneath a tree, another crow on her shoulder. "You must be Shaker."

He bowed. "Thank you for taking care of Debbie in my absence."

"You're welcome," Myrrh said. "I'm assuming you want me to allow you access?"

"Yes," Shaker said politely.

Myrrh murmured some words, then turned away, heading back into the shadows. "Go in."

I'm not sure she likes me, Shaker said mentally, as he followed Debbie inside to her bedroom.

She saw me very upset over you. Or she might blame you for Celia. Debbie told him quickly about the ghost, and Myrrh's solution.

"Inventive, harvesting that malevolent force," Shaker said in approval, as he snuggled in bed with Debbie. "She's clearly a force to be reckoned with, one I'm glad is on your side."

"Are you staying tonight?" Debbie interrupted. "I'd like you to, but I understand if you can't."

"Yes," Shaker murmured, kissing her nose. "As I said, my new Mistress doesn't call for me often. But if she does, I have to go immediately. If you wake up and find me gone, tonight or the next or whenever, don't worry. I'll return as soon as I can."

"Are you moving back in?" Debbie said, trying not to smile.

"If you'll have me," Shaker said with a grin. "I don't want to be in the way, and I know you're busy." He hugged her again. "I'm not going to be waiting here when you get home, demanding your attention. But we are married, after all."

"I knew it, it's about sex," Debbie teased.

"No, it's about me wanting to be with you as much as you'll let me." Shaker sighed happily. "But I have to sleep now, I'm exhausted. Tomorrow is another day."

Debbie snuggled into him, and promptly fell asleep.

The next morning, Debbie awoke alone. She was disappointed but showered and got dressed. As she walked into the kitchen, she heard Shaker's booming voice and Sheila's laugh. *He's still here. I didn't imagine it all.*

Of course not, Shaker answered in her mind. *I just wanted to let you sleep. Come out, I've made breakfast.*

Since when do you cook?

Since my new Mistress, who showed me how, came his defiant reply.

Debbie entered the kitchen, where Sheila was eating a pile of cooked meat. Song was also there, her red and black hair a haphazard mess, her face one big grin. *Looks like we all got lucky last night.*

"Have some sausages," Sheila said. "They're fabulous."

"So it's all meat?" Debbie said, grabbing a handful of bacon from a heaping plate, then some sausages.

"I'm making the eggs now," Shaker said, cracking several into a skillet. "That's it, this is all I know how to make. I'll have to watch some cooking shows and build up a repertoire."

"Protein is the breakfast of champions," Song purred, tickling Sheila, who shrieked.

"Wait, where are the dogs?" Debbie asked curiously. "Charon? Lazarus?"

"New dogs?" Shaker asked curiously. "What happened to Guardian?"

Debbie ignored him, moving into the living room. Behind the couch, the two hellhounds were cowering within the slim shadow, looking at Debbie fearfully.

"You can come out," Debbie said, tossing some bacon into each dog. "No one will hurt you."

"On the contrary," Myrrh cautioned from behind her. "They're right to be afraid. They're escapees from Hell. You've got two of Hell's soldiers in your kitchen."

Debbie turned to Myrrh in desperation. "Can you fashion collars for them that look like that battered metal that won't hurt them or bind them to me?"

Myrrh flashed Debbie a grin, then waved her hand. Now both dogs appeared to be wearing beaten metal collars. Charon and Lazarus came out tentatively, still whining nervously.

"I see," Shaker said from the doorway, making no move toward the dogs. "I'm glad you have them, in case." He turned to Myrrh. "Your doing?"

She nodded.

Shaker held up a hand in a quick motion. "Song and Sheila won't overhear us now," he stated. "I know of you, Myrrh, enough to know that you never hire yourself out to be someone's bodyguard. Why are you really here?"

"I have my reasons," she said.

"I'm sure you do," Shaker said, a ball of black fire forming in his hand. "Tell them to me. Now."

Myrrh held up her own hand, and a ball of black fire with red glints formed there, burning furiously. "We war with Hellfire, you'll burn this house to the ground with all of us in it. Do you want that?"

"Stop this," Debbie said, stepping between them. "Shaker, she helped me where there was no one else. Terian told her about the job. I've hired her as a live in guard. Myrrh, Shaker's not an enemy, he's an ally. Further, he's my husband."

"You don't need the money," Shaker said to Myrrh, ignoring Debbie.

"Yes, I do," Myrrh said angrily, her one eye turning purplish-red. "When you're the widow of a vampire with a large estate to keep up, you need to work for cash now and again. The government of this country doesn't make allowances for mystical beings, that they don't have to pay taxes. Prices go up each decade. My souls need to eat, as do I. You can't use magic for everything." Her tone was pure bitterness. "Even a treasure hoard doesn't last forever."

"True," Shaker allowed, still studying her. He flexed his fingers, the fireball disappearing. "I meant no disrespect. I'm grateful for all you have done, Myrrh."

The sorceress also flexed her fingers, her fireball disappearing. "Neither did I. I'm just uneasy around full demons. You remind me what I could be, if I step wrong."

"No offense taken," Shaker said sarcastically. Then he chuckled. "I take your meaning, and you're wise to beware." He nodded to Debbie. "I'd better get back. Come back when you're ready."

"He's different now," Debbie mused, when Shaker had gone. She petted the dogs, who were still peering about anxiously. "He's lighter somehow." *And I don't think he'd have left a hearing ward in place to shut him out back when we were bound.*

"Because he's no longer dependent on you." Myrrh moved to the window, opening the curtains. The dogs jumped up, barking at the crows roosting in a row on the deck railing in the sun, their eyes almost closed. "Lazybones."

"It'll be a relief, us meeting on even terms this time," Debbie said.

"You aren't on even terms," Myrrh said gently. "He's bound to another, one whose existence he depends on to stay here. The burden has just shifted off of you." She rested her hand on Debbie's shoulder. "But you're right, it's as equal as you two will get. I hope it works out for you."

Debbie turned to look for Myrrh, but the sorceress had disappeared. Debbie turned back to the deck, but the railing now was empty, only a few black feathers floating on the breeze in the noonday sun.

~

The next week at work was busy, with hardly a breather for Debbie. She got to work early and stayed late, coming home to fall into bed after a quick shower. Finally, on Friday, she left early with Sheila, taking her friend up on an invitation to the Black Rose.

"I should've come in when Song was here," Sheila said, admiring the new trappings as they waited for service. "This is beautiful. I hope Xerxes keeps it open."

"You can tell her tonight," Debbie teased.

Sheila's face fell. "She won't be coming. The kids have some social event they need to be escorted to. Or maybe that's the father, and the kids are staying home with the demons, I'm not sure."

"Where's the mother?"

"Dead, killed by vampire hunters five or six months ago."

Debbie shifted uneasily. "I'm sorry. I've gotten used to Song being around again."

Sheila narrowed her eyes, as if she might say something nasty. Then her face softened. "Me too, though she isn't around as much as Shaker. He must have gotten a sweet deal this time."

Debbie looked at her quizzically. "Is there some problem with you two?"

"No," Sheila mumbled. "Well, maybe."

"You're kidding, after all the pining you did over her? What the fuck, Sheila?"

"Hey, you're just as touchy as I am," Sheila sniped back. She banged her fist on the table. "Hey, where's the service? We need to relax!"

"Ladies," Xerxes intoned, coming out from the back. "What can I help you with today?"

"We need the full works," Debbie said, catching a glimpse in the mirror. "Color, cut, manicure, pedicure, massage and wrap."

"I'm sorry, but I can't do both of you today," Xerxes said, looking pained. "I can do the hair and nails for you both, or the massages and wraps."

"Color," Debbie said anxiously. "My roots are showing. And my nails are all grown out, too."

"You first," Xerxes said, beckoning to Debbie. "Sheila, come in the back too, I'll apply your color second, then switch off, to get you both done."

"So much for our big afternoon," Sheila said grumpily, following them in back.

"So we'll come back next Friday," Debbie placated, as she sat in the chair and Xerxes combed out her hair. "That's a good idea anyway. The next day is Halloween, that's the night of our company party. We missed the spring festival, I want to go to the party."

"Why?" Sheila griped, as she picked up a magazine.

"Because I like to dress up. Just cut off the dead ends, please, Xerxes. Same color as last time."

Xerxes did as she asked, then applied the dark brown color. But when he went to Sheila, she shook her head. "Make me a redhead. A dark rich red."

"Alright," Xerxes said neutrally, showing her some shades.

By the time he applied Sheila's color, Debbie was having her hair cut. When her friend walked into the nail salon and sat down as Debbie's toenails were drying, Sheila wasn't recognizable. "What did you do?"

"Just lavishing some of my ill-gotten gains on myself," Sheila said, looking into the mirror and fluffing her newly long red hair. The face looking back was Myrrh's, except more stunning, with solid green eyes. "Just a glamour. I wanted to surprise Song tomorrow. This will last until then."

"Haven't you had enough of being mistaken for someone else?" Debbie hissed. "You're going to get hurt, Sheila."

Sheila's mouth dropped open, then her eyes flashed a momentary hazel as she sprang up. "Forget the fucking nails," Sheila snarled. "I can't believe you brought that up now, and here, of all places! I'm moving out tomorrow, Debbie. And if you don't stop telling me what to do, you'll be getting my notice, too." She stalked out.

Debbie looked after her, mystified, then settled back down, as Xerxes went to work on her nails.

When Debbie arrived home, Shela's door was closed. But boxes lined the entryway, and some were piled up in the foyer. *I guess she*

was serious. But maybe it's for the best, with Shaker and Song being around more. We'll want our privacy.

Shaker was waiting in the living room, the two dogs lying attentively at his feet. "I found their weakness," he said, feeding one something grey and red. "Fresh squirrel."

"Ew," Debbie said pointedly, turning and leaving.

I didn't kill it, just noticed it get hit, so took advantage. Shaker came after her. "Sheila came home in a mood, and just started packing. I helped pile some of the boxes in the hall." He shut the bedroom door. "Is it me? Does she not like me being back?"

Debbie shook her head. "I think she'd like some privacy to be with Song. After you left, we had a heart to heart. She admitted to me she still felt, um...evil."

"But you don't?"

Debbie shook her head again. "I feel normal. Yes, I did start to feel nasty sometimes this year. But that stopped." *When you left.* "But she's back how she was, if not worse, now that Song's back in her life. We had a fight at the Black Rose, and she actually threatened to quit."

Another reason it's for the best that I broke our bond. Shaker sat down on the bed. "We need to get her into a convent, the sooner the better. I know of one, too, as it happens, that has a recent open bed."

Debbie snorted. "You've got to be kidding. There's no way she'll go."

"You need to make her go," Shaker urged. "Or else you may be summoning her out of hell if you still want her to work at Pandora."

"You told me months ago that there was nothing we could do, that it was no big deal if she was more ruthless!"

"Because putting her in a convent then would have broken her bond with Song and Harp," he said, exasperated. "We needed them as a functioning unit. And none of them would have permitted it.

They would have turned against us. Now…it hurts no one and it will reverse what is happening to Sheila. I feel a blackness to her. She needs to be prayed over for a few days, and to be away from Song."

"Song cares about her."

"Song cares about staying out of Hell," Shaker insisted. "The kids are teens now and will soon be able to make a choice to keep their demons or release them. If they release them, its back to Hell. She may be pushing Sheila to bind her. Or they might already have done the deed."

"That can't be. Song said a year or two."

"Be that as it may, I have seen the two children, and they are no longer children."

This is crazy. "Okay, so how do you think we should do this?"

"I'll teleport you to the convent. You get her to the doors. I'll take care of the rest."

"All right," Debbie said, heading into the bathroom. "I'll be out in a minute, I need to shower and change. When should we do this?"

"Tonight, the sooner the better."

So much for showering. Debbie yawned, then splashed some cold water on her face. *I can't believe that I'm on this rollercoaster again.* She emerged from the bathroom to find Shaker missing. Pulling on some sweatpants, she went in search of him.

Myrrh and Sheila were sitting in the living room like twins, birds perched on most surfaces, the two dogs in hiding behind the couch. *Their hiding is all I needed to see to know Shaker's right: Sheila's turning.*

"I was telling Myrrh the news of me leaving Pandora," Sheila said nastily, setting down her glass. "And trying to convince her to come and work for Song and me."

Shaker appeared, clasped both Sheila and Debbie around the wrists, and teleported. They arrived on a wooded path, moonlight shining down.

"What are you doing?" Sheila shouted, tearing free and running away.

She's calling for Song! Shaker shouted. *Head her off before she teleports!*

Debbie darted after her. She finally caught up with Sheila, the two of them leaning against a tree trunk, breathing heavily.

Go for shock value. "You're turning into a demon," Debbie said. "All those thoughts of evil you've been having all year? Well, I should have listened and got you help. I'm here to do that now."

"No!" Sheila shouted, drawing her gun, and leveling it at Debbie. "I'm not. And I'm not going in there—"

Myrrh materialized behind Sheila, then touched her head, catching her as she collapsed "Hurry," Myrrh said to Debbie, tossing her the gun. "We have a little way to go yet."

The threesome hurried down the path, arriving at a gate in front of a huge stone building. Myrrh opened it, and Debbie followed her to a large wooden door, and knocked.

The door was opened by a nun who looked weary beyond measure. "Yes?"

"This woman is being pursued by a demon," Myrrh said. She passed Sheila's unconscious form off to another pair of nuns. "Dalcon sent us. Please pray over her and save her soul."

"Another one?" the nun said with concern. "Well, Mr. Dalcon did pay a great deal of money. Very well. Come back in a day or so. She'll recover by then, if she can." The door was closed.

Myrrh grabbed hold of Debbie and teleported her home. Charon and Lazarus came out at once from under a small end table, whining and wagging their tails.

"Sit down," Myrrh said kindly, pouring them both a drink. "You need it."

"First I need answers," Debbie said angrily pushing the glass away. "How did you know what to say? What's Devlin got to do with this? Why were you even there? Where did Shaker go?"

"I knew you'd had a fight when I saw her packing. I was also…

flattered but uneasy to see her wearing my likeness. It's unwise to go around with my face when you don't have anything to defend yourself with besides a gun. I caught some of what Shaker said to you aloud, about her needing to go to the convent. So I followed you. It's good I did, or you'd be dead."

Debbie grabbed for the drink and took a swig, remembering Sheila's wild look. "She wasn't kidding with her gun."

"No, which means she's already pretty far gone. But the nuns will do what they do best: pray." She sipped her wine. "As for Shaker, his Mistress called to him. He had to go." Myrrh put the glass down. "I'm not coming down on him, Debbie. But I'd advise you not to teleport with him from now on, because there's no guarantee he'll stick around to get you back. And I wouldn't count on him being there for you, because he can't promise that."

"But you will, at least for now?"

Myrrh nodded. "Yes."

~

"Where's Sheila," Lash asked, standing suddenly in Debbie's doorway the next morning. "We had an appointment. When I went to her office, her secretary sent me here."

"I'm sorry, but Sheila's taking off a few days." *To try to regain her humanity.* "What did you need?"

"She called and left me a message while I was on a job, saying there was some movie she wanted me to do for her."

Sheila, you are dead for leaving me here to deal with this. "Can you give me some details? She hadn't told me yet that the script you were working on with Josh was ready." *Joshua died, though. Had anyone stepped in to take his place? Probably not.*

"That's because it's not ready," Lash growled. "He kept telling me to fix the ending, make it happier with a broad and a kid. I told him life isn't like that for people like us. He said film was fake, that it was selling stories and hope, not reality. I'm not sure I like that."

"I'm sorry, but I'd recommend you take his advice," Debbie said. "People do care a lot about happy endings now, even just happily for now endings. You don't have to end it with a kid and a wife though, just a good friend, or on a happy note. What he said about hope, I'd take that to heart."

"Okay," Lash said after a moment. "So what's this about *Hell to Pay?*"

It took Debbie a moment to realize that Lash was talking about Pandora's upcoming project. "Oh. It's an action fantasy movie about a group of supernatural assassins going after a bad ghost. They get killed except for a couple, and those go to find a badass, who then goes after it with his men and them. Havoc ensues and more die until they end the ghost."

Lash was silent.

Debbie finally looked over at him. He was pale, and his human eyes had turned to snake pupils. "What is it?"

"Who gave you this script?"

"Sheila acquired it. We asked for a rewrite, which the author did. I honestly wasn't told she was considering you for this movie, even just as a consultant. Or were you interested in producing it?"

Lash didn't answer."

"Lash, what is going on here?"

"You tell me," he said angrily, rounding on her. "Because that's not a script, it's a chunk of my life you're describing. The badass you describe is me. The ghost was a Spiritwalker, a mortal's soul that a sorceress turned free of its human flesh to kill. We got it finally, but not without friends of mine dying."

"We didn't know," Debbie said slowly. She turned to Sheila's folder on *Hell to Pay*, searching the notes. *Lash as Badass?* was written on the second page, along with *weresnake—lead into Lash's movie?* underlined twice. "It looks like Sheila thought you'd be a good fit for the badass in the movie, and that she could tie it into the movie you're making based on your life. There's nothing else here, no notes about how she thought this new script was based on you."

"But it is," Lash hissed softly. "It was a bad time I'm not really keen to see it up on the silver screen, either. Who is the author?"

"Jared Valeras," Debbie said, reading quickly. "No one we've dealt with before."

"That's because that's my father, and he died back in the 1920s," Lash hissed harshly. "Someone's playing games here, Debbie. I don't like it."

"Neither do I," Debbie said, meeting his eyes. "Shaker expressed similar concern over another script we purchased. The author of that one was someone from his past, and its subject was a painful reminder, like this is for you. Can I hire you to find out who is doing this?"

Lash nodded. "Yes. No fee, I need to get to the bottom of this for myself. But I'll tell you what I find out."

"Agreed."

CHAPTER FIFTEEN

OCTOBER-NOVEMBER

"Hi, Debbie."

Debbie blinked, pasting a quick smile on her face that turned genuine when she saw it was Brady. *I can't tell who he's supposed to be, but I like that bare chest under his black leather jacket.* She was glad of her mask, as heat suffused her face, remembering the night in his hotel room. "Hi there. Happy Halloween."

"Your Victorian dress is beautiful, but I almost didn't recognize you under the mask. This is a fabulous party. That Incubus wine is something else."

"Thanks, I lost a bet with Sheila, so she picked out our costumes. My first choice was going to be a witch." She raised her glass and clinked his. "It's a great wine. We're lucky to partner with Triss Vinyards."

"Sheila told me to come over, said you had something to ask me."

"Yes, I wanted to know if you'd be willing to stand in for Jett," Debbie said carefully. "He was working on a movie when he died, and he finished all but a few scenes."

His expression was pure surprise, and somewhat endearing.

"But I'm not an actor. I've got no experience. You must have stuntmen who could do what you need."

"We do, but I wanted to ask you if you were interested. As you might know, Jett wrote this movie himself. It's the only movie he wrote, and it was very important to him."

"I didn't know that." Brady was quiet for a moment, then nodded. "Sure, I'd be glad to. Since he died, I've felt angry, like I should have done more for him. This I can do."

"We can schedule it around your trips here, if you like? I know that you've been visiting Rhonda regularly."

"Not for much longer," he grimaced. "They have her doped up most of the time, because she raves whenever she's lucid. I'm very grateful to Sheila for taking care of my sister. I thought it was sudden, them getting together. But now I wonder if all Rhonda's acting out her whole life wasn't because she was gay all along and didn't know how to act on it."

Debbie bit her lip to keep her expression serious. *Do not laugh. For all you know, Rhonda was rebelling against something.*

"I wanted to thank you, too," Brady said, taking her hand. "You really straightened my brother out. He wasn't much of an older brother most of my life, and we were never close. You helped him become one. Thank you for that."

While Debbie agreed, Brady's praise made her uncomfortable, knowing the reality of Jett's fate. "I loved him very much."

"Did you get the insurance yet? I'm asking because he told me the night before your wedding, if anything happened to him, I was supposed to make sure you got it."

I want to ask him to let go of my hand, but it feels awkward to say it. Debbie nodded. "Yes. I have it in an investment account." She smiled. "Now it's my turn to be crass. Did you get your share of the inheritance?"

Brady nodded. "Yes, but I'm not sure why he didn't leave all of it to you. Did you know he was dividing his estate between you, me, and Rhonda?"

"No," Debbie said, shifting her feet, and pulling her hand away from Brady to casually adjust back her wig. "But I think he tried to be fair. Like you said, he'd changed this year. He wanted to be the brother he hadn't been, and that meant taking care of you two, not just me."

"Family should take care of one another," Brady said with a smile. "Which is why I'm moving out here."

"What?" Debbie said, almost spilling her drink on a passing Spartan and his dominatrix witch.

"I need to be closer to Rhonda. And I need to be closer to you. Jett loved you more than anything. I promised him I'd look out for you."

"That's really not necessary," Debbie said quickly.

"I think it is," Brady said seriously. "I'm not looking for a handout, Debbie. I made this decision before you asked me to be in Jett's movie. I've already quit my job and lined up a few interviews out here. I still have to find a place, though."

"You're welcome to stay, if you need a room for a few days," Sheila offered, as she came up to them. "I'm sure Debbie has room, too."

"I've got a roommate," Debbie said quickly. "She's got practically a flock of birds, and I've got two dogs, but if you don't mind that, sure."

"I may take you up on that," Brady said, giving her a winning smile.

There's so much of Jett's smile in it. "Okay."

"I need to steal Debbie," Sheila said. "Sorry."

"That's okay," Brady said, setting down his wine. "I need to go anyway, I have an early day tomorrow. You two be good." He headed off into the crowd.

"He's looking hot," Sheila said slyly. "I think he's been working out."

"Will you stop?" Debbie chastised, flushing again. "I'm going to take you back to that convent, you need more prayers."

"Don't give me that piety. You were looking at his chest, not his face." Sheila laughed. "So he said yes?"

"He did. But that was before I knew he was moving out here. Why did you volunteer my place?"

"Well, Shaker's back," Sheila said with a shrug. "Brady's cute. He's a ringer for Jett, hell, he's even a few years younger. Don't you want to set up house again?"

"How can you say that?" Debbie retorted, incredulous. "Brady's a good guy."

"Don't get all moral with me," Sheila said, her eyes flashing. "Really, this year you've had a stick up your ass constantly, Deb. You never had any trouble making the ends justify the means before."

"Yeah, and maybe I should have," Debbie said cuttingly. "And you should've too."

"You know, just fuck off," Sheila snarled, turning and disappearing into the crowd.

Debbie took a deep breath, mock-widened her eyes, and let it out. 'Unbelievable."

"I daresay so," a man's voice said from behind her. "You're much more attractive in person than your Linked In picture allows."

Debbie turned to the stranger, taking in his walnut sun-streaked hair and pale blue eyes. "Then I guess you're in luck. And you are?"

"Gabriel Gray, at your service," he said with a sexy smile and a flourish of his hand. "That's my stage name. I'll be on your director's calendar as Gabriel Vassago. I'm coming tomorrow for an audition for *Hell to Pay*."

Had Sheila already put out a call for actors? Well, I did give her the green light to schedule it for next year. "Good to meet you."

"I'm glad to meet you. This is a great party."

He's gorgeous, but he's not the father of wit. "Please enjoy yourself. I look forward to your audition tomorrow." Debbie turned and headed for Myrrh, who had just appeared near the door, beckoning to her. "What is it?"

"He's a demon," Myrrh said, pointedly looking back at Vassago.

"I didn't feel anything?" Debbie said curiously. "Are you sure?"

"Yes. You're used to cohabiting and being bound to one, so you stopped registering the intuitive threat. We call it demon-blind."

"He said his name was Gabriel Vassago. He's auditioning tomorrow."

"Vassago could be just looking for a job, and heard about Pandora. Or he might want to step into Shaker's shoes."

"I'm not looking for a lover."

"That doesn't mean one's not looking for you," Myrrh said with a smirk.

"Very funny. You and Sheila can just—"

"She means me," Shaker said, leaning over Debbie's shoulder to kiss her cheek. "Sorry I'm late. How's your evening?"

"Wonderful now you're here," Debbie said, hugging him. "Myrrh was just telling me there's a demon here."

"Where?"

Debbie went to point, but Vassago had disappeared. "Apparently someone who is auditioning for me tomorrow."

"Where did you get that ring?" Shaker asked suddenly, looking at Debbie's left hand, where a lustrous flat pearl and two tiny seed moonstones on either side rested on her middle finger.

"Remember that box my father left me in his will? Well, I finally opened it, and inside was this ring. He just wrote that it was an heirloom of my family, and to wear it with his love."

"Good, I was worried." *Why aren't you wearing my rings I gave you?*

Because I'm not sure I should. We need to talk, Debbie thought to him reluctantly. *I want you in my life, but I'm not sure how to make it work, with you needing to be on call all the time to another woman.*

Tonight I'm all yours. Would you like to dance?

Debbie nodded happily, going into his arms.

~

Debbie blinked, then sat up. *Where am I?* She was still dressed in her costume, but her head was heavy, as if she could sleep at any moment. But there was a restlessness in her body. *I'm at Pandora, in the lounge the actors wait in to audition.*

There was a noise down the hall. Carefully, she got to her feet, then teetered on her heels towards it. She reached the door and threw it open.

There on the edge of the conference table was Sheila, her skirt hiked up around her waist to bare a garter belt and black stockings. Between her thighs was Vassago, pumping for all he was worth.

He's fucking her. Debbie watched them, breathing harder, as Vassago pushed Sheila back on the table, ripping her lacy bodice down the front, her breasts spilling out to be grabbed by his greedy hands, his mouth claiming first one nipple, then the other as Sheila writhed under him. He let out an eager growl, then grabbed her ass, pulling her forward as his movements intensified. She let out a howl, wrapping her legs around his pistoning buttocks, then came hard, moaning loudly, his coarse grunts punctuating every time he slid deep. The air in the room was rank with the smell of lust and the coarse sounds of heavy breathing.

Vassago turned, then smiled. "Debbie. Good to see you." He turned, then moved away, heading to the door. Sheila weakly pushed herself to a sitting position, her arms over her torn dress.

"What the fuck are you doing?" Debbie demanded.

"Taking an audition," Sheila said dreamily. "As far as I'm concerned, he's hired."

"You've lost it," Debbie said in disgust. "Give me your resignation tomorrow." She strode for the door, but was stopped by Vassago, who had returned, his clothes in place.

"I'm honored to have her support." Vassago's eyes were lowered, his tone confidential. "But it's you I need to convince, Debbie. Please, let me begin."

"Begin what?" she said, backing away.

He moved faster, like a blur, catching her hand, and pulling her close. "My audition."

"Let go of me!"

"Stop struggling," Vassago whispered gently. "I'll not do anything to you that you don't want me to do. But you do want me to do something to you, don't you?"

Debbie's heart was beating wildly, her breaths pants as he backed her toward the conference table. "What do you mean?"

"You know exactly what I mean," he said, his lips brushing her ear. "You were watching us. You liked watching us, because you imagined she was you, on your back."

"I did not!"

"I can smell your excitement," he murmured, his breath hot on her throat. "Do you know how to tell a woman really's in lust?" He leaned into her, and she staggered in her heels, falling a bit against the conference table, his hand quick as it slid between her legs. "She parts her lips." His hand slid under her panties to cup her thatch, then rub gently on her engorged clit, which was swollen and protruding. "Both pairs." Debbie let out a gasp, trying to steady herself against the table, as he rubbed gently, her face flaming as she felt her moisture soak his fingers. "So warm and wet," he whispered, his lips inches from hers, his fingertips just gently pressing into her, teasing.

"No…what are you doing…I…."

He rubbed her clit in lazy circles, then raised his glistening hand between them. "Here's the proof, milady."

Debbie scented her own excitement, and let out a groan, then a sharp intake of breath as she was lifted onto the table, and felt his hand stroking her once more.

"So warm, so inviting. Lay back, Debbie. Lay back for me."

Debbie lay down, spreading her legs wide, the first sweet kiss of his lips making her cry out, grasping his head as his hands splayed possessively on her inner thighs, spreading her wide for his probing tongue. She felt the first stirrings of climax, then he raised his head.

"Bare your breasts for me."

Debbie shrugged out of the jacket, then pushed down her strapless bustier, baring her breasts. She raised them in her hands, her breaths abrupt with relief as she felt him take them in his mouth, sucking gently, then biting the nipples.

"Please," she whispered. "Take me."

Vassago smiled, then opened his pants, his large erection springing forth. He took it in his hand, rubbing the leaking tip on her opening, as she begged him to enter her. Gently, he pushed in, then withdrew, teasing her for moments that felt like hours.

"Please!"

Vassago pushed in deep, sliding the length of his shaft home. Splaying his hand on Debbie's upper thigh, he cupped her ass with the other, his strokes long and rhythmic.

"Why...does it feel...so good...Ohhhh...Ohhh!"

"Because you want it," he purred, quickening his movements. With a few guttural grunts, he came, then pulled out.

Debbie felt like she would cry, to have the seduction over so soon and with no climax. But Vassago shook his head with a small smile, then brought her to the lounge, where he sat down on the couch, beckoning.

Eagerly she straddled him, the feel of his still-hard cock slipping inside her making it unbearable not to move. She began riding him fast. Not to be hurried, he grasped her hips, again making the strokes long and slow, sliding over and over the too-swollen clit. Too soon, she was coming, the tidal wave larger than any she'd crested before, the orgasm mind-blowing as she screamed out her release. After she lay twitching, her eyes fluttering, the sensations still shimmering through her body. "What did you do to me?"

"Just gave you a taste of paradise," he said gently. "Rest now."

Debbie awoke in her bed, her body aching thoroughly. She rubbed her eyes, then laughed at herself. *Of all the people to wet dream about, some strange demon who'd she'd have to face on Monday, and maybe for months, if he was any good. Ugh.*

She looked over and breathed a sigh of relief that Shaker was there beside her, then went into the bathroom. As she sat down on the toilet, she felt wetness, and grabbed some toilet tissue, thinking it was her period. To her surprise, it was her own come, coupled with the rank smell of semen.

She burst out of the bathroom, demanding of a just waking Shaker, "Did we have unprotected sex last night?"

"You did," he said, his nostrils flaring. "But not with me."

Debbie stared at him. "What?"

"I'm guessing your Vassago is an incubus, likely the one that's been working at the Black Rose. He's probably convinced Sheila that she should do that movie she was thinking about back in the spring."

"If he's that good, she should," Debbie breathed, remembering. She cast a miffed look at him. "Why didn't you save me?"

"I awoke when you began moaning, but I checked your dream, and you were enjoying yourself." Shaker smiled. "I could tell he was there and what he was, but you weren't being harmed." His smile faded. "But be cautioned, if you go back for seconds, he will take a bit of your energy next time. This was a freebie, because he was auditioning, in his own way."

"Hell of an audition," Debbie said, sighing. "But yes, I'm a believer, too." She sat down on the edge of the bed. "Are you upset? You don't seem to be."

"An incubus's main power lies in his ability to seduce. It's inherent. I'm not upset, because it's very rare that any female can resist."

I feel like I should yell at him for not stopping it, but I'm really glad he didn't stop it. "Why didn't you intervene?"

"Because Pandora does need a new star. Vassago's got the charm, he's got the looks, and he's got the sex appeal." Shaker kissed her cheek. "I admit, I watched a little of your action, got me horny as Hell." He reached for her.

Debbie moved back, out of reach. "I'm not sure I like being targeted. That's what he did. Sheila's besotted with him."

"Shh," Shaker said, coming to sit near her. "You had some good sex, and it was sex both of you enjoyed. If you and she hadn't experienced it firsthand, you might not have believed that he had any power and passed on hiring him. It seems he really wants this opportunity."

"Should I worry about getting pregnant?"

"No. His mind touched yours, not his flesh. Yes, you have the scent of his come on you, but that will dissipate; it's a manifestation of his visiting you, not real semen." He kissed her throat. *But I'd be happy to provide you with some, if you've a mind this morning to let me.*

"Don't you have to be running off?" Debbie said pointedly.

Shaker frowned at her, then seemed to look into the distance. "You're right, that I'd be wise not to start something and get interrupted." He squeezed her hand. "Besides, you wanted to talk this morning. That takes precedence over my carnal appetites."

Ignore his quip and launch straight in. "I like you here with me. But I don't see how we can have any kind of life if you're never sure how long you're going to be around."

Shaker frowned. "Doctors are on call, and they still have lives."

"Yes, but they get vacations, too. You don't."

"There are a lot of times when my Mistress is with her lovers, or at some planned event that's well guarded, like last night, where I'm sure not to be needed. Those times I'll be here with you, if you're free. Other times, I will have to be absent, and yes, there may be some periods with very short notice." He squeezed her hand. "I love you and I want to be in your life. I didn't say what I did and marry you because I was bound to you at the time, I did it because I wanted to, because you're who I want. That hadn't changed."

"My feelings haven't changed, either," Debbie said, squeezing back. "But I have to know, is it always going to be like this?"

"No," Shaker said. "My tentative plan is that once she gets used to our arrangement, that I'll ask for a more set routine to be available. She's fair and reasonable so far, so I think she'll agree. Yes, there may be emergencies, but those should be few and far between."

"Okay," Debbie said, kissing him.

"So you'll wear my rings?"

"Yes, once you get her to agree to your plan."

His tone was grudging. "You drive a hard bargain."

"It's one of the reasons you love me, remember?"

"Very true," he said, pulling her close for a kiss.

CHAPTER SIXTEEN

NOVEMBER-DECEMBER

"Well?" Debbie said to Rack, as he came into her office. "Will there be an Oscar nomination for Cahill?"

Rack smiled. "I don't think so. But I am hearing that Jett may be up for a posthumous Critic's Choice award."

"No! Really?"

He nodded. "Remember what I said about a death of both meaning and opportune timing? Well, it's coming together perfectly."

"That is fabulous news. Are you all ready for the *Smoke and Ashes II* release party?"

Rack nodded. "You mean in regards to the wine, yes. I'm sorry I got you worried about a possible shortage, we'd just misplaced some cases."

"Good."

"I also heard that you hired Vassago, and that you're planning on filming a Netflix–exclusive series called *Incubus*."

Debbie nodded, opening her email. "Yes, end of next month. If you have any more of that Incubus wine, it's a good plan to lay aside some casks for the that release party as well."

"I will." Rack paused. "I wanted to talk to you about Sheila."

Debbie shut her email and gave him her full attention. "What is it?"

"She's been really on edge lately. I heard that she moved back into her own place, and Song's a regular visitor." He took a breath. "I think you need to assign her an assistant."

Debbie gazed at him coolly. "Are you recommending yourself?"

"I've seen this before with others, and it ends the same way, in violence," Rack said, not backing down. "There's an ominous feeling to her now, as if she's becoming a demon. She needs an assistant now to learn her role, so when she eventually combusts, we all don't go down with her."

"That's my friend you're talking about," Debbie said angrily.

Rack was unruffled. "And this is your company, one you sacrificed for. Make plans now, before it's too late."

Debbie watched Rack storm out, her thoughts churning. *Was this more of Jezebel's prophecy? And why am I making a fuss, when I know he's right?*

When she got home that night, Shaker was absent, but Myrrh was there with her murder, the flock perched on the kitchen chair backs, as their sorceress read a book, while sipping a steaming mug.

"Is there any more of that?"

"Sure. Pot's on the stove."

Debbie filled a cup with the stew, then sat down. "Thanks for making dinner. I take it Shaker's away for the evening?"

Myrrh nodded, not looking up.

Debbie finished her meal in silence, then went into her bedroom, undressing and taking a shower. When she emerged, she slipped off her jewelry, looking again at her wedding rings. *I really do like them.* She slipped them onto her right hand, surprised that they fit. *But I have lost weight in the last three weeks or so, all those late nights at work.* She looked for her pearl ring, suddenly noticing it was missing.

"Myrrh," she called, going into the kitchen. "Have you seen my pearl ring?"

"In here, and yes," Myrrh called from the living room, where she was just coming in from the deck. One of her crows flew from her shoulder to Debbie, dropping the ring into her hand before returning to his mistress. "Bawdir found it outside, he said."

Debbie frowned. "I didn't have it outside."

"He probably just took it from the bathroom. Crows like jewelry, or anything shiny." Myrrh shrugged. "I've told him to stay away from your things, but they don't go into your bedroom, so I'm not sure what happened. But please tell me if you find anything missing again. I'll either find it or pay to have it replaced."

"It's all right," Debbie said, slipping the ring on her left index finger, now that her ring finger was full. "I need to talk to you about something else." She explained what Rack had said, and Sheila's worry about turning evil, and all of their own fights this year. "Is there anything you can do for her, or that you would recommend?"

"She needs to break with Song," Myrrh said. "I also notice a hint of blackness when I'm in her presence now. I don't like to say it, because they seem very happy. It sounds like the week of prayers didn't do much."

"I will assign Rack then as an assistant," Debbie sighed. "I feel responsible. I got her into this."

"Listen, we're all adults here, and we get ourselves into things," Myrrh stated. "It's up to us to get out of them. Don't blame yourself."

"I'm sorry also, for the death of your husband," Debbie said. "I meant to mention it before now."

"Torren died close to fifty years ago," Myrrh said sadly. "I really did think he and I would be together forever."

"What was it like, being with a vampire?"

"Pretty much like being with a demon except his hard-to-deal-with-issue was sharing him with blood donors instead of sharing him with a human master." Myrrh rubbed her eyes. "But I loved him."

"Why did you ban Shaker from the house?"

"I banned all demons but Titus from the house. Titus himself asked me to."

"How do you really know Titus? You tell me that he's related to you, but you never said how."

"He's talked to you before about blood ties, how they can be used for evil. It's better you don't know."

"Okay, then tell me how you just waltzed past his wards the night you met me and teleported us here. You said that Shaker's wards would have ended, as he'd been sent back to Hell. But Titus made the wards, not Shaker. His wards were *still in place.* How did you get past his level of magic?"

Myrrh just looked at her for long moment, so long Debbie thought she was just going to ignore the question. "Because I have an interesting property," she said finally, and grinned widely. "Most magic doesn't work on me."

"Why not?"

"Natural immunity? I can't say. But that's why they buried me in that rock those ages ago, because there was no magic strong enough to contain me. All their spells failed. It earned me yet another name: Magicbane."

That's probably why she can walk into Hell and out again stealing Hellhounds. "You're pretty amazing."

Myrrh laughed. "Yeah, I have my moments."

~

For the next week, Shaker was oddly absent, as Debbie had Rack work with Sheila, learning her job inconspicuously. Finally on Friday, Titus appeared in her office, as she was packing up to leave.

"Shaker has been injured. I stopped by on the way to see him, as I thought you might like to visit."

"What happened?"

"He tangled with a demon hunter, who came out the loser. But Shaker will be a while recovering. He hasn't contacted you telepathically because he doesn't want you to feel his pain." He held out his hand. "But I know he'd like to see you."

Debbie took it, the two of them appearing in the central room of a small house with simple furnishings, a woodstove burning hot in the corner. Snow was falling fast and furious outside. Shaker was on the couch reading a book, his chest and arms swathed in bandages. The skin nearest them was raw, and oozing.

"Here," Titus said, handing his brother a bag. "Your mistress made you cookies. Chocolate chip."

Debbie shoved down her jealously. *She's just a regular Martha Stewart.* She crossed to Shaker, sitting near him. "What could have hurt you so badly?"

"Blessed weapons. Shotgun shells for bear that have been blessed make hamburger out of us." Shaker put down his book, and patted the couch. "So do assault rifles; that's why demon hunters prefer them. Please sit, I could use a hug."

"I'll be outside," Titus said, disappearing.

"You shouldn't stay long," Shaker said, shifting painfully to a sitting position to embrace her. "He's got to go back, and I'm not strong enough to teleport you home. But thank you for coming. I wanted you to know where I was, why I haven't been around."

"You cut our mind link connection."

He nodded. "The wound was a bad one. My mistress thought she was dying, and it caused a commotion. There's a lot more upheaval going on with her than I planned. I may not be around much this month, until I know that's over. I suspect there was another person working with Cyrus and he's still out there. I'm going to keep my distance from you until I know for sure." He kissed her hand. "But Titus will come each week to visit me. Come with him, if you have time free."

"I will. You always said you were a thousand years old. But then you wouldn't know what Stonehenge looked like, back when it was first built. You're older, aren't you?"

Shaker nodded. "Around four thousand. Original fall from Heaven was about then."

"Why didn't you tell me the truth?"

"Because I sound ancient, being that old," he said, rubbing his eyes. "And much of that time in early history was spent in Hell, where days and years and centuries blended together. Man didn't figure out they could summon us out until Christianity made us famous, and that didn't get going until it became a popular religion, after Rome fell."

"Fair enough. So is the person who hurt you dead?"

"No," Shaker said. "But don't worry. He came close enough to dying that he won't target someone like me again." He kissed her chin, which was closest. "You should leave, I need to sleep again."

"Rest," she said, kissing his lips gently. "And I guess eat your cookies."

"Actually, could you put them in the freezer?" he said, handing them to her. "I don't have the energy to work a spell to consume them right now."

Debbie did as he asked, then came back, but Shaker was already snoring. She covered him up, then went outside. Titus was on the porch, smoking a cigar.

"I didn't know you smoked."

"Only in stressful situations." He took a deep drag, then blew out a ring. "I supposed he told you the hunter's still alive?"

"Yes. Why haven't you gone after him?"

"Because the hunter, Kyle, is a close friend of both Lash and Devlin. Lash is in a killing rage over this, and Devlin is also angry. A spell was done to make Kyle think he killed the demon who hurt him. Shaker needs to heal quietly and quickly, so they never discover it was him. Do you understand?"

Debbie met his eyes, furious. "This is her fault, isn't it? His new mistress?"

"No, it's Shaker's fault, for not covering his tracks better." Titus put out his cigar, then offered his hand. "Come, I'll take you back."

∿

Debbie looked out at her team, happy to see everyone was in attendance, even Sheila. *At least no one has quit in a week.* "Good afternoon, everyone. How are we looking for the release of *Smoke and Ashes II*?"

"All of the social media planned is a go," Adeline stated.

"The editing's all finished, and the final version went over well with the test audience," Bart mentioned. "We even had one guy stand up and clap."

"Ads are all in place, and playing," Rack said. "We've found offering some kind of rewards through various programs online leads to a lot of reposting and sharing. Oh, and the wine's ready to go for the release party tonight."

"The sequel was grittier than the first, but it also had a feel-good ending," Nicole said. "So we're looking at reworking the finale of the third film to match that. But it's going to be more somber with Jett's death. We may need to shoot some scenes of his brother to have Storm's ghost in there, beaming approval at the end or show him passing onto Heaven, instead of Hell, for all that he's done to help people. That's all I've got."

"Good idea, work with that." *Even if it's unrealistic, sigh.* "Great! Like we said earlier this year, we're not going to have a Christmas party, and we will be closed that week between Christmas and New Year this year. But please attend the New Year's Party, if you are able, as well as the release party tonight."

"I have something to say," Sheila said, standing.

Debbie nodded. "Please." *I hope it's not her resignation. She's been avoiding me as much as possible for two weeks now.*

"I just wanted to thank you all for the work you've put in this year," Sheila said, looking at each team member in turn. "Debbie and I asked a lot of you, and you didn't let us down. And new hires Pat and Fredrick, thank you also, you learned fast and deserve kudos for that." She turned to Debbie. "And thank you. You lost your husband this year and still managed to not only keep going, but to hold it together for us, against all that Titan Pictures threw at us. You didn't give in to despair, and we're more profitable now than we've ever been." She began clapping, and the other team members also began clapping, standing up.

Debbie flushed, but also couldn't keep the grin off her face. "Thank you. But we all did this together."

Everyone began filing out, saying they would see her at the party. She looked for Sheila, but her friend had disappeared.

"He's been nominated! He's been nominated!" Sheila said excitedly, to Debbie.

Debbie nodded nonchalantly. "I know, Devlin got nominated for best score, for *Immortal Confessions*."

"No, they just announced Jett's been nominated for best actor!"

Debbie spilled her wine, whipping around to look at the screen. "My God, you're right!"

"Look! It's Jett!" Sheila pointed up, where an interview was now being shown of Jett Black. "It's from right before he died."

It's Shaker, he must have done this interview and not told me! "What are they playing? I never saw this. Hey, stop the music! Turn up the sound!"

"*So you like being Storm?*"

Shaker nodded. "I like being the good guy, he's a hero, even if he's calling on traditionally evil forces to do the right thing. I can identify with that."

"*So what's next?*"

"*We're shooting a third movie in the series. After that, who knows?*"

"We heard you recently married the head of your studio, Debbie Deal."

"Yes, we did commit," Shaker said. "And I've heard the rumors, that it was publicity. But that's not true; we fell in love."

"Tell us about it."

"She's a great woman: strong, fearless, a little ruthless," Shaker laughed. "But she's also a great partner. I wouldn't trade her for anyone."

"So do you have a favorite song?"

"Bryan Adam's Heaven. I like to tease her that since I'm damned, her arms are as close to Heaven as I'm likely to get."

"Sounds like you've been naughty? Are you really worried about your soul?"

"We're all bad sometimes. But like Storm, we often do it to protect the ones we love. If I'm judged for that...so be it."

"So any last words of wisdom for viewers?"

"One of the tools of survival is moving on. Enjoy the moments of happiness you have to the fullest, but don't dwell on them when they're gone. Believe that more moments are coming, if you do what you can to make them happen." He flashed a winning smile. "And don't be afraid to love. It's worth whatever price you have to pay."

Debbie was crying outright at the last, and Sheila handed her some tissues. "You know, I think he's going to win it."

"He'd like that," Debbie sniffled.

~

The next two weeks passed fast, as the Christmas holiday approached.

Debbie was just closing up for the night, when Vassago came to her door. "Hi."

"Hi. What is it?"

"Do you want to go somewhere?"

She turned to look at him. "Excuse me?"

"Shaker asked I look out for you," he said softly, coming into her office and shutting the door. "He said he'd consider it a favor. So I came to see if you wanted to go out to dinner or something."

"That's kind, but not necessary. You're an employee now of the company, it wouldn't be appropriate."

"You married one of your stars. I think a dinner would be tame in comparison."

"But you don't want just dinner, do you?"

"I can be him for you, if you want." Vassago's body shimmered, becoming that of Jett's.

For a moment, Debbie wanted to throw herself into his arms. Instead, she shook her head. "You can look like him, but you aren't him. If you're going to make a play for me, I'd rather you just looked like yourself."

"A woman with integrity, I don't see it often." He laughed, becoming himself again. "Very well. Let me know if you change your mind."

Debbie walked down to her car, her thoughts on Vassago. *He is hot. Maybe I will go to the Black Rose next week and try the Incubus.*

Sheila got out of her car, where she'd been waiting for Debbie. "Just the girl I wanted to see."

Debbie turned to brush her off, then recoiled at Sheila's gun. "What are you doing?"

"We're going for a ride. Someone wants a word with you."

She hasn't recovered, she's turned completely! "Charon! Lazarus!" Debbie shouted.

The two hellhounds launched themselves out of the shadows of the nearby cars, slamming into Sheila, knocking the gun away as they savaged her. Then Charon let out a shriek, falling away, Lazarus rolling after, the both of them smoking and keening in pain.

Shaker! There was no answer. *Damn it, he's still ignoring my telepathy!*

Sheila grinned at Debbie with shark teeth, her eyes red as

blood, her rapidly healing hands clawed. "No one's going to save you now."

"I am," Debbie grunted, ramming the blessed knife into Sheila's shoulder, black smoke issuing forth, as Sheila began screaming. *Titus! Myrrh!*

From the shadows six more figures materialized, all of them demons. To her horror, Debbie recognized one as Nelson, another as Mr. Minor, as well as the new hires Pat and Fredrick. "You're demons? What are you doing?"

"We're sorry, but we can't trust you, now that you're no longer bound," Nelson said. "So you're going to bind one of us now, or we'll kill you. Don't bother calling for anyone, we're blocking you."

"You're all demons?"

"Demons possessing humans. You're ignorant of that, for all Shaker's possessing of Jett. You couldn't even see your own friend wasn't herself anymore." He smiled nastily.

Debbie turned with horror to Sheila. Her friend crumpled, as a female demon stepped out of her body, eyes glinting orange. "Who are you."

"A friend of Azaroth's," she rumbled evilly, reaching for her. "Submit, or we'll make you. Believe me, it's more painful that way."

Debbie brandished her knife, even as she resigned herself. *At least I'm going down with a fight.*

"Get away from her."

Myrrh stepped out of the elevator, fireballs in both hands.

"You're no match for all of us, sorceress, not alone."

"Who said I was alone?" She gestured harshly, bringing her hand into a fist. The murder launched through a new portal behind her, attacking the demons, which laughed at the swooping birds. But their cries turned to screams as the birds targeted one and attacked en masse, ripping the demon's human host into pieces. Black smoke billowed out of the remains, the stink of sulfur noxious.

Another demon threw a fireball at the flock, but Myrrh blocked it. Nelson threw one at her, but she walked through it, as if nothing had happened.

"Magicbane," one of the demons hissed fearfully, and disappeared.

The others renewed their assault, while the last grabbed Debbie, dragging her away from the fighting. Before Debbie could scream it teleported her, arriving in the living room of a large mansion. Mountains were visible outside the floor to ceiling glass panes, snow in heaps against the glass. A stone slab table rested in the sunken living room, with more stone making a bannister leading to the entryway.

Get to the door! Debbie tore herself away from the demon and hurried to the door. Beyond was a lighted walkway that was clear, but beyond that were other buildings similar to this one. *Where the hell am I?*

"You go out, you will freeze, dressed as you are," the demon said, watching her. "But the door's locked anyway. Come back, so I can sacrifice you on this table." He grinned. "That's what it's for."

"What is this place?" Debbie asked, tugging at the door. "Who are you?"

"A hiding place for the one I serve. No one will find you here, even if they could track you, this place is heavily warded." The demon studied her. "You're not that pretty. I thought Shaker would have done better."

"And I thought demons were smarter. Who do you serve?"

The demon smiled, baring his teeth. "You'll meet him. He's tying up a few loose ends in New Orleans with some friends of his."

Another pair arrived, a female demon and a man. The male turned to Debbie, his red eyes and fangs giving him away, as the demons conversed. "You're a vampire?"

"Yes," he said, giving her a slight bow. He sniffed delicately. "You're human."

"Don't talk to her, Michael," the male demon warned.

Michael. Where have I heard that name. Something Shaker said...

304

"I'm a friend of Devlin Dalcon. If you return me to him, I'm sure he'd pay you a ransom."

Michael shook his head, his eyes glinting. "He will kill me as soon as he sees me, for what I did to his Oathed One."

That's it, Michael's the one who held Lash and Devlin's lady hostage. "What's her name?"

"Sarelle. But she prefers her friends to call her Sar."

"He has her back now, and Lash as well," Debbie said quickly. "He'd forgive you, if you helped me escape."

Michael looked at her oddly. "What do you know of this? Devlin is not the kind to share information with a human."

Another two vampires appeared with yet another demon, the female who had been possessing Sheila. These came over quickly, the female's eyes murderous. She backhanded Debbie, the blow knocking her off her feet to crash into a large plant, dazing her. "You bitch," the demon hissed, advancing. "I could have just used that body to run Pandora, and now I'm going to have to wear a glamour or waste energy fixing it."

*God, Sheila...*Debbie closed her eyes, then knelt unsteadily. "Rafael, if you can hear me, please help me."

"She's praying?" one of the vampires cackled in disbelief. "I thought she was a demon's whore?"

"Just leave her to it, it will keep her busy and quiet," the female demon said, moving away with a grimace. "Now get over here, we need to plan our ambush. I've got the leopards ready, they already know where to wait—"

The building shuddered on its foundations. Everyone staggered, holding onto whatever was beside them.

A blast of red-black fire hit the door breaking it down as the glass cracked, but held. Myrrh stepped through, her eyes glowing red. With her came the birds, which dove forward, transforming into black-winged men in loincloths as they landed, swords in their hands. They went for the demons, as the male demon grabbed for Michael and disappeared. The two vampires dove for them as they faded, latching on and also disappearing. But the demons were held fast by the crowmen, who brought them to Myrrh, bleeding freely from multiple stab wounds.

"Hold them fast."

Screaming, the demons were placed on the stone tables. With a flip of her wrist, Myrrh set them both alight, the red-black fire burning into them and consuming them, until a demon-shaped ash block remained. There was a flutter, then the block collapsed, revealing two large crows lying on their sides, panting.

"You will serve," Myrrh intoned, grasping each by their feet, and tossing them into the air. Both birds flapped hard, then flew, their cawing sounding like screaming.

Debbie staggered over to her. "You're hurt."

"We both are," Myrrh said, offering her hand. "Let's go home, shall we?"

EPILOGUE

"So Sheila's going to be okay?" Myrrh said, just before dawn.

"She's back in the hospital," Debbie said. "Song's with her, just for tonight Sheila's in a coma. Turns out, she never came out of one."

"I never thought to check," Myrrh said for the fifth time. "I didn't meet her until she was awake, so I thought she always felt like a demon. But she was possessed."

"Was it Gore who did this?"

"He must have known the demon, at the least. Or how'd it get past Titus's wards?"

"You said that Shaker gave himself up for you and got sent back to Hell. But you never mentioned that Titus also got sent back to Hell this year. His spells done on this plane dissipated, like the Stonehenge spell, so the wards were off. You were unconscious, so you didn't see anything. Sheila's bond with Song was broken, and Song got sent back to Hell. So no one was there protecting Sheila's body, which was ripe for possession, in her state. That explains why she tried to touch the priest; if she'd have known what he was, she'd have stayed back, knowing she'd get burned."

"It also explained why she got burned though her bond with Song was broken. It was the demon inside her then that caused that strong reaction when she touched the priest. Being bound to a demon, you should feel tingling like you described when you entered the church, not anything more than that. The demon vacated her body the day she was in the convent, then repossessed her when she emerged." Myrrh glowered at her. "I told you to tell me everything. I can't protect you if I don't."

"How did you find me?"

"I heard you call for me, and I followed the dogs, the first time. By the way, those demons you used to call employees are all dealt with."

Debbie eyed the flock, which was sporting six new wobbly-perching members. "Where are the dogs?"

"They passed," Myrrh said sadly. "But they went up, not down. They died defending their master, what all dogs consider their true purpose." She took Debbie's hand and squeezed. "They're at peace."

"How did you find me the second time? They said you wouldn't be able to."

"I enchanted your pearl ring with a tracking spell," Myrrh said with a grin. "Just in case."

"I'm glad you did," Debbie said. "But you need to tell me everything, Myrrh. I can't trust you if you don't." She sipped her wine. "Why did they want to bond me or kill me? None of what Nelson said made sense."

"He was told to say that, likely by whomever was working with Michael. It wasn't the truth. Did the demons mention any names?"

"They said that whomever was in charge was in New Orleans, tying up some loose ends with friends. They said the leopards knew where to ambush and were in place. It didn't make any sense to me."

"Hmm," Myrrh said. "I think I know what they meant. And who." She disappeared.

"Nice!" Debbie shouted angrily. "Just fucking go and don't tell me anything again!"

"Shh," a man said in a rusty voice, as he appeared behind her. "She goes to prevent more bloodshed."

"Who are—?"

"Bawdir," the man said, tilting his head, then smiling. It was then Debbie saw the large black wings on his back.

"Are you all demons?"

"We are her souls. She is our Queen of Swords and Ashes."

"That's a name I've not heard before."

"It's from the Tarot deck, the minor arcana. The card of the widow, the warrior woman full of sorrow. The swords is the suit that stands for air: we are her swords. The ashes part of her title is for her Hellfire, a weapon for which there is no defense; it will burn through anything, even a demon."

"The demon that had Sheila, is she dead?"

"She's in a different form, and the Hellfire burned out some of her evil. She'll redeem herself in our queen's service....or Myrrh will cast her out into Hell."

"Do you know why she came to help me?" Debbie whispered.

"Yes."

"Tell me."

"No. She will tell you, when it's time."

The New Year's Eve party was a success, Vassago holding court with a legion of admirers. Brady was attentive, before he headed home to bunk in Debbie's spare room.

"Thank you for staying with me," Debbie said to Myrrh, as they stood on the deck, the crows around them. "And thank you for the hounds."

Three new black hounds were inside near the Christmas tree, eagerly eating from meat-piled bowls, their tales wagging.

"I'm glad you like them," Myrrh said. "But enjoy them, Hell's now empty of hounds."

"How do dogs get there in the first place? Shaker said all animals were good and avoided evil."

"Their masters dabbled in black arts, and they followed their master down into the depths, possibly killed together? I'm not sure. It's a very rare occurrence, whatever it is, which is why they are so expensive to buy."

"I didn't get you anything," Debbie said sadly. "I'm sorry. But nothing seemed like a good present."

"Your friendship is enough present," Myrrh said stiffly. "I'll be out on the lawn for a while." She disappeared.

Debbie turned, knowing who she would see. "Shaker."

"Hi," he said, coming to embrace her. "Happy New Year."

"It's a lot different than last year," Debbie said, biting her lip.

"I know," Shaker said, hugging her tighter. "But we're together, that's what matters."

"We're not, I've barely seen you this month."

"I was arranging the rules that you were so adamant about. I had to get my Mistress to think they were her idea. But it's done now, Debbie. I'm no longer on call, except for emergencies." He smiled.

"Myrrh said that Devlin was attacked in New Orleans. But with the warning we gave him, he prevailed."

Shaker nodded. "He's grateful for that. I'm grateful you're okay, that she kept you safe."

"But Sheila's still in the hospital, and I'm missing half my staff. We still don't know who's behind those odd scripts for our movies for next year, or who was really backing that demon who possessed Sheila, or even if Gore played a part in what happened. How are we going to go forward?"

"Together," Shaker said, slipping her rings onto her finger, as he hugged her again tightly. "Together."

THE END

∾

Don't miss out on your next favorite book!

Join the Satin Romance mailing list
www.satinromance.com/mail.html

AUTHOR ACKNOWLEDGEMENTS

Song referenced (sung by Devlin) in this story is James's Blunt's "Out of My Mind", from the *Back to Bedlam* Album, the same one which contains "You're Beautiful" and "Goodbye My Lover" (the two songs referenced in *The Promise Me Series* previously in Sar/Devlin's relationship.)

THANK YOU FOR READING

Did you enjoy this book?

We invite you to leave a review at the website of your choice, such as Goodreads, Amazon, Barnes & Noble, etc.

DID YOU KNOW THAT LEAVING A REVIEW...

- Helps other readers find books they may enjoy.
- Gives you a chance to let your voice be heard.
- Gives authors recognition for their hard work.
- Doesn't have to be long. A sentence or two about why you liked the book will do.

ABOUT TARA FOX HALL

Tara Fox Hall's writing credits include nonfiction, horror, suspense, action-adventure, erotica, and contemporary and historical paranormal romance. She is the author of the paranormal action-adventure *Lash* series and the vampire romantic suspense *Promise Me* series.

Tara divides her free time unequally between writing novels and short stories, chainsawing firewood, caring for stray animals, sewing cat and dog beds for donation to animal shelters, and target practice.

www.tarafoxhall.com

ALSO BY TARA FOX HALL

With Satin Romance

Novellas
Night Music

Anthologies
Her Frozen Heart in Frozen
One Perfect Moment in Propose To Me
A Love For Michelle in Second Chance for Love

Unhallowed Love Series
A Good Year
Year of the Demon (available 2019)

Promise Me Series
Promise Me
Broken Promise
Taken in the Night
Taken For His Own
Immortal Confessions
Promise Me Anthology
Her Secret
Point of No Return
Lost Paradise
Dark Solace

Eye of the Storm

Tempest of Vengeance

Sundown & Serena

Hope's Return

Fate's Prison

Web of Memory

Forever

Freedom: Elle's Story

Immortal Reckoning

Novellas

Return To Me

Surrender to Me

The Oath

Anthologies

The Origin of Fear in Spellbound 2011 Anthology

Night Music in Midnight Thirsts II Anthology

Partners in Midnight Thirsts II Anthology

Kink in Wicked Christmas Wishes Anthology

The Oath in Wicked Christmas Wishes Anthology

Make Me Behave Anthology

Latham's Landing, An Anthology

www.ingramcontent.com/pod-product-compliance
Lightning Source LLC
Chambersburg PA
CBHW031158020726
47499CB00002B/408